*"Love me, M*

He pulled her over backward in the loose hay, leaning above her with his face close enough so that she felt his breath. "Maggie, I want to marry you so bad I sometimes think I'd kill for you. I love you. We'll get married within the year. You'll be seventeen in April, and if I save all my pay through the summer, it'll be enough to get us started. Love me, Maggie. Love me."

*Married within the year.* The words were balm to her soul, and his touch scorched her skin. Her lips parted beneath his; the miracle of wondrous sensation deprived her of resistance. He cajoled her and won her over in the way of men throughout the centuries, with hands and mouth and body...

Novels by Willo Davis Roberts

*Days of Valor*

Published by
WARNER BOOKS

# Keating's Landing

## Willo Davis Roberts

WARNER BOOKS

A Warner Communications Company

# 1

THE little house where Maggie had been born stood empty, now, on the bluff overlooking the Snohomish River. It was falling into a state of disrepair, so that the rain worked its way through the shingles and the siding. In a few more years, she thought sadly, it would probably collapse, the victim of neglect and the heavy winter rains that kept washing away the earth about its foundation. One day she would come, and the cabin would have slid down the embankment into the river.

Nobody except Maggie cared about it. Her mother, Ann, had always hated the place; it was too small, and too primitive, and she'd loathed living there in the few years before Jake was able to provide her with a "decent" two-bedroom house in the village that had then been called Cadyville. That was long before the Keatings had moved into their present elegant and spacious home overlooking the Pilchuck River. Not even Jake, usually a thrifty man since it was he who earned it all, cared about the little house enough to take the time to make repairs.

Maggie had played in it as a child, and after that it had become a refuge for her when she wanted to be alone, away from her sister Celeste and her mother and Grandma Miles, or from the village children who teased or tormented her.

She was there today, staring out the dirty window over

the marsh beyond the river, trying to gather enough courage to face her father.

Maggie Keating had always thought of herself as skinny and plain, though at seventeen she had finally begun to feel better about her looks. At least, she had until very recently. Her dark-brown hair was done in braids—the easiest thing to do with hair that refused to curl, her mother said—wound around and pinned atop her head in a crown. Celeste had blond curls. Maggie's eyes were a smoky-green and thickly lashed; Celeste's eyes were blue, like Ann's. Maggie's skin was not pale and creamy like her sister's, but tanned from the hours she spent out-of-doors. Like a heathen who worked in the fields, Grandma Miles would say.

At the moment, the gray-green eyes were filled with tears. Maggie did not cry very often, and even now the tears were as much for Jake as for herself.

It was going to hurt him so badly, she thought, when she told him. Yet tell him she must, and here, away from the house and the rest of the family. Jake had never failed her, and she didn't think he'd fail her now, but this time his pain would be as bad as her own.

Her vision blurred, she stared around the single room. Others had lived there since the Keatings had moved on; she didn't really remember living in the cabin so didn't know if anything remained that had belonged to her own family. It was dreary, particularly in the half-light of a rainy afternoon that filtered through the leaves of a stand of alder, and the broken furniture provided not even a safe place to sit. Not that she wanted to sit, anyway; she was too nervous and upset for that.

She had left a message at the mill for Jake to meet her here before he went home, written in her own neat but shaking hand; would he know, from the look of it, how great her agitation had been?

He'd come as soon as he could. In the meantime she

must wait, and think about the events of the recent past, and (with dread) about the future.

Mama would kill her.

No, Maggie thought, I won't think about Mama at all. I'll tell Daddy, and he will handle it after that. Daddy has never let me down, and now that it's something more important than ever before, he'll help me. He'll do whatever can be done.

Yet she felt cold in the dirty little room, and she couldn't stop shaking, waiting for him to come, trying not to think of her mother, or Angus, or anything at all, which was very difficult to do.

One of Maggie's earliest recollections was of hearing her parents quarrel. She grew accustomed to their angry voices, yet never failed to be disturbed by them, for she loved her mother and father both.

From the age of two onward, however, she knew that it was her father she loved the most. Jake Keating returned her affection openly and freely; but Maggie had to struggle to win from her mother what came so readily to her little sister, Celeste.

In later years those around her scoffed at Maggie's claim that she remembered when Celeste was born.

"How could you?" Grandma Miles asked in a tone that brooked no nonsense. "You were no more than two and a half years old."

"I remember," Maggie said stubbornly. And she did.

Jake had awakened her that morning and carried her to her parents' bedroom, the flannel nightgown sliding up above her knees, to kiss Mama and then to peer into the cradle in which Maggie herself had slept when she was an infant.

"See, you have a beautiful new baby sister, Maggie," Jake had said, holding her aloft in his strong arms.

The baby had been red-faced and not, to Maggie's eyes,

beautiful at all. She had turned away, burying her face in Jake's shoulder. "Don't want her," Maggie muttered.

Jake had laughed, while Ann remonstrated. "What a naughty thing to say, Margaret Ellen! You should be ashamed of yourself!"

"No, no, leave her alone," Jake said. "Don't worry, Maggie my love, you'll always be Daddy's sweetheart."

That was all she remembered, yet it was enough. On the very day of Celeste's birth, Maggie knew that she had somehow been relegated to second place.

In 1869, the year in which Maggie was born, there were fewer than six hundred people in all of Snohomish County, a population that grew steadily as newcomers arrived to work in the woods. To begin with, the settlers of Washington Territory were almost entirely men; but as they carved out small homesteads from the great forests, they brought in women to keep their homes.

There were only four other females in the county when Ann Miles arrived with her parents, the Reverend and Mrs. Stokes Miles. There was as yet no church in the town that would eventually be called Snohomish City (the loggers were far more interested in saloons than churches), but the Reverend Mr. Miles organized religious services first in his own modest home, and then, as the size of the congregation grew, in the River Side Hotel.

The real drawing card at the Sunday services was not Mr. Miles's sermons, which tended to be both lengthy and dry, but his daughter. The loggers were primarily men in their twenties and thirties; none of them were married, only partly because of the profound scarcity of single young women, for they were a footloose bunch. No wonder, then, that they elected to endure the sermons in order to gaze, during them, at a beautiful young lady with blond curls and thick-lashed blue eyes, who, while modest, would favor any reasonably civil man with a shy smile.

It was inevitable that Ann should meet Jake Keating. He was only a logger, like virtually every other man in the territory, but Jake was different.

To begin with, it would have been an unusual female indeed who would not have been drawn to a big man with a muscular body, thick black hair, and dark eyes that sparked with either humor or anger at the slightest provocation. It never occurred to Ann that the anger might ever be turned against herself, and she found him intriguing. He could read (something many of the others could not do) and discuss something other than Douglas fir and ox teams and skid roads. Ann had not the slightest interest in those things, though she quickly learned that as a faller Jake earned at the upper edge of the woods' pay scale, at eighty dollars a month.

Jake Keating was handsome and he was entertaining. He was also ambitious.

It was the latter characteristic, even more than the former ones, that Ann found appealing. She had lived a genteel life that sometimes bordered on actual poverty. There was something about this man who talked of owning his own mill and building a great, fine house, that allowed her to overlook the fact that he was rough-hewn and less well educated than Ann herself. Those shortcomings were also true of every other man she'd met since arriving in Washington Territory from the civilization of San Francisco, and Ann could have had her pick of the lot; Jake Keating appeared to be the best.

Jake was not a religious man. He heard, however, along with the other timber fallers, teamsters, sawyers, skidders, swampers, and barkers, about the stunningly pretty daughter of the new parson; he attended services the first time out of curiosity, and was immediately smitten. He was thirty-two years old, more than ready to marry, and he determined to win Ann. From that point on, he was there every Sunday, bathed, clean-shaven, the mud knocked off his boots, and he was neither shy nor inarticulate.

Had Ann known that he'd threatened to knock heads together among any of the other loggers who presumed to make advances to her, she might have taken a different attitude toward him. All she knew, however, was that he was cleaner than most, had a way with words that made her feel feminine and flattered, and that he intended to get ahead.

Ann had always had an instinctive conviction that she was destined for better things than life in a primitive town with an uncouth lot of men who worked long hours in the woods and seldom bathed. The Miles's sojourn in San Francisco had been brief yet stimulating; Ann loved it, admiring the handsome dwellings on the rolling hills overlooking the beautiful bay. Society was elegant there; the ladies were fashionably dressed, the diversions and entertainments far beyond anything Ann had ever known.

Though the San Franciscans had not succumbed to the persuasions of the Reverend Mr. Miles, the gentlemen there had been taken with Ann. Had her father allowed a swift courtship and immediate marriage, she might well have stayed behind them when her parents headed for the Pacific Northwest.

The Reverend Mr. Miles was protective of his daughter, however. She was too young for marriage, too much loved to be handed over to some un-Christian rascal; so she moved with her family to the wilds of wooded Washington.

Jake's courtship was intense though not prolonged. To a man who worked six twelve-hour days every week, time was of the essence. It never entered his head that in his Sabbath attentions he was misleading the young lady about what life would be like if she married him.

\*      \*      \*

Ann made it clear, as soon as disillusionment began to set in, that she had no intention of spending her life in a logging camp. Scrubbing clothes in cold water, on a washboard, ruined the hands, not to mention the disposition. There were no other wives in camp; the idea of being surrounded by hirsute and coarse-speaking males was appalling, and Ann made her feelings known in a softly feminine but firm way.

They spent their first winter in town, which wasn't so bad because the snow was deep enough to shut down the logging operations from November on. Jake was home, and he was happy; he kept the stove well supplied with wood so that the tiny cabin was snug and warm, if somewhat lacking in other amenities. He laughed a lot, and sang at the top of his voice, and it was as if the courting period were extended, except for the nights when they went to bed together.

Ann had been an innocent about the marital relationship when she married, for Millicent Miles did not believe that such matters were appropriately discussed with an unmarried female, not even one about to enter the state of wedded bliss herself. True, Ann had sometimes speculated upon the sounds that issued from her parents' bedroom on occasion; she had not, however, interpreted them in any correct detail. It could not be said that her initiation into the mysteries of marriage was as delightful for her as it was for her new husband.

Still, she was now mistress of her own establishment, which was a heady feeling, and she had a dashingly attractive man of her own, quite different from Papa, who was small and going bald and who could not have lifted her off the floor and swung her around if he'd wanted to. Being kissed and gently caressed was a most pleasurable thing, and being catered to as if she were a princess was precisely what she'd always had in mind.

It would have been far easier if she hadn't gotten

pregnant almost immediately. Being queasy all the time, and violently ill most mornings, did little to smooth the path of this new adventure. If she felt too ill to get up during the day and put more wood in the stove, while Jake was off somewhere talking logging with his friends at the Blue Eagle, the room would become freezing cold; Ann would huddle beneath the quilts until she became sullen or miserably weepy by the time he reappeared.

Jake was always contrite, in those early days; Ann was, after all, a beautiful young woman, his bride, making him the envy of virtually every man in the county.

He would kiss her and hold her and cajole her out of her unhappiness. He could, in those days, make her laugh and bring her back to good humor.

In February, however, when the snows melted, the men were eager to return to the great woods. There were thousands of acres of Douglas fir waiting to be cut down, which drew the men as surely as gold had drawn the forty-niners to California. Ann was left behind with no near neighbors and nothing of interest to fill her days.

Jake had spent plenty of time chopping firewood; it was stacked against the side of the cabin in good supply. He could not haul a week's supply of water for her, however, so Ann suddenly had to wrestle with heavy buckets, make her own fires with wood soaked through from the heavy rains, and spend entire days and nights by herself in the little cabin.

Days were not quite so bad, though with Jake gone there was little to occupy her time. She walked the mile to her parents' home almost every day, visiting with her mother, listening to her advice about how to prepare for the coming infant, stitching small garments and hemming endless squares of outing flannel.

The nights seemed endless. Occasionally she slept in her old bed at the Miles home; most evenings, she went home to a lonely supper (she might have stayed to eat with her parents, except that this would have meant walking home alone in the dark, later) and retired after praying that she'd properly banked the fire so that it could easily be rekindled in the morning, to find that sleep did not come easily.

For the first time in her eighteen years, Ann was totally isolated at night. It was such a small house that there were no dark corners where anyone could be concealed, and she always barred the door as soon as it was dark. Most of the men were in the woods, the same as Jake; those who remained in town went to bed early and did little roaming around. Not even the Blue Eagle was a lively place, except on Saturday nights and Sundays when the loggers returned to town; there was no reason to believe that she was in any danger.

Yet Ann was afraid. She would say her prayers and crawl into the bed warmed at the foot with a hot brick, and lie awake listening to the night sounds of the wind in the tops of the tall cedars; the scrape of a naked alder branch against a window would bring her upright, trembling, trying to convince herself that there was no one there, that she had nothing to fear.

Her belly was swollen, now, so that she was self-conscious about being seen in public; her back frequently ached, and she cried easily. She began to wish she'd stayed a spinster, safe at home with Papa and Mama, forgetting how only months earlier she'd longed to escape their tight controls over her life.

Jake nearly always managed to get home on Saturday night, and of course he had to be back in the woods so early on Monday morning that he had to leave again on Sunday night. As her time approached, Ann's fears mounted.

"What if you're not here when the baby comes?"

"I thought we'd already decided, it's going to happen on a Sunday morning." Jake grinned at her, then bent to kiss her nose.

"It's not funny, Jake. Babies can come anytime. You don't expect me to have it all by myself, do you?"

She was secretly terrified by the entire business; women died in childbirth, sometimes. Discussions with her mother about it had not been reassuring. There was no doctor in town, not even a midwife, meaning she'd have to rely upon the few other women there to help her. It had already been decided that Mrs. McGrew, who had seven of her own, was the one who would be called in at the proper moment, Millicent Miles having declined the entire responsibility of bringing her grandchild into the world.

"It's not even close to your time, yet," Jake reassured her. "When it is, we'll move you over to your folks' until it's over. That way your mother can stay with you while the parson goes for Mrs. McGrew. Honey, don't worry so much. Women have been having babies for centuries."

But not always safely, Ann thought. And usually their husbands were somewhere about, not miles off in the middle of a forest where it was impossible to reach them.

Ann was afraid, and Jake's reassurances did not lessen her apprehensions. When the baby did arrive, on a stormy Tuesday night in late April, Jake was deep in the woods. Though her parents were both in the house, her mother at her side during the ordeal, Ann felt neglected, abandoned.

She had only partially put down her resentment when Jake arrived the following Saturday night. He was delighted with his new daughter, pleased with his wife, and inordinately satisfied with his own part in the entire matter; he was able to tease Ann out of her doldrums and make her laugh, but the handwriting was on the wall, though Jake did not yet recognize it.

"She's such a willful child," Ann would say of Maggie, all her life through. "You spoil her, Jake. Even a two-year-old needs to learn that there are some things she must do, and some things she cannot do."

It was true that Jake indulged his firstborn. By the middle of that first summer, he had thrown up a shack to shelter his family near the job; Ann was torn between gratitude at having Jake around at least at night, and regret at being moved so far from town and her parents, for there were no other wives in the woods at that time.

The cabin was even more primitive than the one in town, and when logging operations shut down in the fall, she was only too glad to return to civilization. He had not, she thought with a twinge of jealousy, thought it necessary to provide living quarters for *her* to be near him; yet once Maggie was born, Jake made arrangements as quickly as he could to bring them all together on more than weekends.

For most of the year Jake saw Maggie primarily on Sundays, for she was usually asleep by the time he came in from the woods, and it was his pleasure to spend the entire Sabbath in entertaining her.

This, in effect, meant that Ann continued to be neglected to some extent, though before Celeste was born they often did things together as a family, picnicking on the banks of either the Snohomish or the Pilchuck, reading or singing together. At first Jake attended church when Ann insisted upon it; later, by the time there were two children to deal with during what Jake considered an incredibly boring service, he began to find excuses for staying away. And as she grew old enough to express her opinions, Maggie tried to find ways to stay home with Jake, though she was not often successful.

Maggie would lean against her father's knee as he sat on the doorstep in the sunshine, sharpening the ax with which he earned their livelihood. It was Jake's boast that he kept an edge on it so that he would have shaved with it, and Ann worried that the child would cut herself on it.

"She's too smart for that," Jake would say, winking at the sober-faced little girl with the gray-green eyes too large for her face. And when he winked, Maggie would smile, and the small, plain features would be transformed.

Only Jake found her beautiful. Ann was secretly disappointed that the child had inherited neither her own blond loveliness nor her own personality. Ann had been a biddable little girl, and she did not always know how to cope with this stubborn, silent child who made up her own mind about things and did not bend before the force of parental authority.

Where Ann had been crushed into submission by the slightest hint of criticism, Maggie stolidly withstood even a passionate tongue-lashing or a spanking; her small mouth went flat and unyielding, her eyes remained dry. She was fearless about climbing anything from buildings to trees; she fell into the swift-flowing Snohomish one spring when it was in flood, sending Ann hysterically screaming for help. Jake came running and plunged into the muddy torrent, grasping the child by one flailing arm to pull her ashore. Maggie gagged and choked until the water was expelled and did not cry a single tear, though she clung to Jake's neck in a manner suggesting that she was very glad he'd rescued her.

Ann, limp with relief, railed at the little girl in a shrill voice. "Margaret Ellen, you simply must learn not to go close to the water! You could have drowned!"

"She'll have to learn to swim," Jake said, precipitating another of the quarrels that marred an increasing number of their days together as a family.

It was true that females did not normally learn to swim. Ann put her foot down and absolutely refused to allow any such thing. It was immodest, it was dangerous, and if the child learned to obey orders, it would not be necessary.

Jake did not make a major issue of the matter. He simply began to take Maggie with him on Sunday afternoon walks beside the water, and he taught her to swim. It was the first of many things of which he would say casually, "Might be better not to mention this to your mama, girl."

Maggie was not deceived by the offhand manner of speaking. She learned at an early age that not mentioning things to Mama eliminated at least part of the disagreements and unpleasantness between her parents, as well as sparing her much personal grief.

And that was why, now that she was in the worst trouble of her entire life, Maggie knew that she could not tell Mama anything; it would be her father, her beloved Daddy—and even that name was an abomination to Ann, who considered the form of address as common—who would save her.

If, indeed, Maggie thought bleakly, anybody *could* save her.

2
===

MAGGIE loved the woods. From the time she could toddle, when Jake took her into his beloved forests, she was totally, blissfully happy.

The smell of fresh-cut fir, the heaps of fragrant sawdust in which she could play (as opposed to a muddy riverbank) without incurring her mother's wrath, the slabs of bark which made satisfying and expendable boats to sail on the river, the resounding crash as a two-hundred-foot fir cut through surrounding foliage on its way to earth, the rasp of the saws as the buckers cut the mighty giants into segments that could be hauled to the water: all these things thrilled her.

It was a world far more to her liking than a small cabin with a mother who fussed over things like clothes and hair and shoes, the cabin where a little sister claimed most of Ann's time, energy, and affection. The forest was a world of danger and excitement, and if it was a world of men, why, that was fine with Maggie. By the age of three she knew that she was more intrigued by the things men did than by those to which women were usually restricted.

At first her excursions into the woods were brief ones, usually on a Sunday afternoon, carried on her father's shoulder. She loved riding on Jake's shoulder; he was strong, and the muscles bunched reassuringly beneath her, to protect her from anything that might possibly be a threat. Maggie felt safe there, and the scents of sweat and tobacco and, occasionally, whiskey, did not put her off. They were a part of Jake, and she adored everything about him.

After Celeste was born, however, Ann found it harder and harder to cope with this peculiar, independent daughter in addition to an infant. When Maggie poked at the baby's eyes in innocent curiosity, her small hands were smacked and Ann's voice rose sharply. When Maggie spilled hot soup over her own feet and cried out in pain, Ann had to stop nursing Celeste and rush to strip off the child's stockings and submerge her feet in cold water. As she smeared unsalted butter over the reddened skin, Ann was frantic, listening to the wailing infant and unable to care for her until she was certain that Maggie's burns were not serious. That episode was followed by Maggie's disappearance ten minutes later, and Ann had to carry the baby outside in a frenzied search. It ended when she found her older daughter sitting, clothes and all, in the edge of the muddy river to cool her still painful feet, and the young mother exploded in mingled rage and relief.

"You naughty, naughty girl! What do you mean running

away like this? I've told you over and over not to come near the river unless your papa is with you!''

Ann, like almost every other woman of her era, did not swim, and the rivers terrified her. Even when the water was low and the current leisurely rather than swift with spring flood, Ann knew that the Snohomish could be lethal.

She would never understand the fascination that the water held for Maggie. It was not normal for a child to have no fear; it wasn't safe.

Juggling the baby in the crook of one arm, Ann used the other to haul the protesting child out of the dirty water. "It feels good," Maggie insisted, and reached to scoop mud over her burns.

She was jerked off her footing by an impatient hand and dragged up the bank toward the cabin. "Now you've washed off all that good butter, and I'll have to waste more of it," Ann said between her teeth. Butter was expensive, and a faller's wages did not always cover all their needs.

"Mud feels better," Maggie insisted, but Ann did not listen. Celeste was squawling because she was wet, the fire needed more wood, and Ann was so tired she thought she'd die if the children didn't sleep soon and let her rest.

Dry garments and warm milk soon lulled Celeste and she was deposited in her cradle. Maggie resisted sleep, as she resisted everything Ann tried to make her do. By the time Maggie was three she had given up on naps, and her mother's efforts to keep her down for the hour when Ann desperately needed her own rest had developed into a daily battle.

Maggie could be put onto her own cot; she could not be made to stay there, nor could she be trusted even if she did. On the afternoon that she'd burned her feet, she sat there after being admonished not to rub the new coating of butter off on the quilt, staring at her mother with a lack of expression that Ann found maddening.

"Now Mama is going to rest, and you are to rest, too, and be quiet," Ann said firmly.

Her mother's eyes had no more than closed than Maggie, looking around for something to keep herself entertained for the coming hour-long ordeal, reached out for the sewing basket on the chair beside her cot. From the basket protruded the handles of Ann's scissors, a forbidden and enticing attraction. Her gaze upon her mother to be sure she actually slept, Maggie eased the scissors from their container.

Ann slept deeply and satisfyingly, until at last, gradually and through the haze of dreams, she became aware of a faint *snick, snick* sound. Reluctant to awaken, she kept her eyes closed for a final few moments of rest, only coming wide-awake and sitting up when she realized what the sound had to be.

Maggie's legs were extended before her, the too pink tops of her bare feet shiny with grease. Her head was tilted forward so that her dark hair swung in a silky curtain over her cheeks, thick lashes hiding the smoky-green eyes, intent on her operation with the marvelous scissors.

Ann gasped and sprang off the bed, stepping on the shoes she had placed there and twisting her ankle. "Margaret Ellen Keating! You nasty little beast, what have you done to Grandma's quilt?"

Startled, Maggie jerked her head, and the scissors, upward. Unfortunately Ann, reaching out to snatch the implement from the small hand, was still groggy with sleep, and there was a throbbing ache in her twisted ankle. When her palm struck the point of the scissors blade, the additional pain sent her rage out of bounds.

Maggie stared in horror at the blood spouting from her mother's hand. She gave up the scissors without a struggle, then waited for the whipping she expected to result from what had been, in her viewpoint, an accident beyond her own control.

Ann, half sobbing, half-enraged, stumbled away from the cot, however, more intent on stopping the bleeding than in inflicting the necessary punishment. It was upon this scene that Jake arrived a few minutes later, to find his wife in near hysterics, the baby screaming, and Maggie sitting on the bed with a small heap of yarn bows in her lap, all neatly trimmed off the quilt that her grandmother had made.

Jake stood just inside the doorway, surveying the scene. "For God's sake, what's going on?"

Ann, her ankle swelling painfully and her hand still bleeding onto the dish towel, turned toward him with a ferocity totally alien to the girl he'd married a few years earlier. "She took the scissors and ruined Mama's quilt! She cut off every single bow of yarn that held it together, every one! And she stabbed me with the scissors when I went to take them away from her!"

Jake glanced at the infant in the cradle, decided that Celeste was crying primarily because her mother was upset, and turned his attention to Maggie. She stared back at him with neither defiance nor guilt; it was not until he'd picked her up that he saw her feet and frowned.

"What happened to her? Did she get burned?"

"Oh, yes, look to her first, the way you always do!" Ann cried, swiping at her own tears with the blood-stained towel. "Don't see if I'm bleeding to death, or if Celeste is hurt! Pick *her* up!"

Maggie leaned into his neck, hiding her face, and Jake hugged her close, being careful not to scrape her pinkened feet against the rough wool of his shirt. "Are you bleeding to death? Is Celeste hurt? Looks to me as if you've scared them both with your caterwauling."

Ann stared at him, incredulous at his lack of fairness. She turned away then, biting her lip against the scream that would have burst forth, the words that no preacher's daughter had any right to know (though married for four years to a logger, how could she not?), let alone say.

When she could bring herself to speak to him in less than a shriek, Ann said through gritted teeth, "There's nothing wrong with Margaret except that she spilled soup on herself hours ago. After that she waded out and sat down in the river, fully clothed, so I had to go after her. Jake, for heaven's sake, pick up the baby before she bursts her lungs! This is still bleeding, and it hurts, and my ankle hurts—"

That was as far as she got before she dissolved in tears.

Jake nuzzled Maggie's neck before he placed her back on the cot on the damaged quilt. It was a gesture that told the child quite clearly how he felt about her. When he lifted Celeste out of the cradle, the infant stopped crying, and he patted her absently against his shoulder as he examined his wife's hand.

"Hurts, but it's not serious," he decided. "Bleeding's about stopped. It'll be all right, Ann."

He put his free arm around her and drew her close, or tried to. She pulled away, still crying though silently now, and sank onto the edge of the bed, turning her face away from him.

Since the baby was calmed, Jake replaced her in the cradle and sat beside his wife, trying once more to take her into his arms. "Honey, Maggie couldn't have done it on purpose. She's only a baby herself. You probably scared her, grabbing for the scissors, and she thought you were going to hit her so she lifted her hands in front of her, so you got stabbed. Here, let me look at it again."

She allowed him to examine her hand more closely; it was throbbing enough to make her almost forget the ache in her twisted ankle. Jake's hands, big and callused, were gentle.

"I'll put a bandage on it, now it's stopped bleeding. It'll

heal all right, and even if it leaves a scar it'll be on the palm where nobody but you and me will see it.''

He bent his head to kiss her cheek. ''Why don't I send Maggie outside to play? The baby's gone back to sleep. We could . . .''

He moved his mouth to her ear, then began to slide it down the creamy skin of her neck as his hand went to her breast.

Ann jerked away from him, suddenly incensed all over again. ''That's all you ever think about, as if *that* could make everything right!''

''It could,'' Jake said softly, ''if you'd let it, Ann.''

She changed course. ''We can't send Maggie outside, even for ten minutes. She's completely untrustworthy. Jake, what am I going to do with her? I can't be with her every minute, not when there's Celeste to care for, and I get so tired I simply want to *die* sometimes! I needed a nap so badly, and Margaret won't take a nap; instead she sat there and cut all the bows off Mama's quilt. . . .''

Remembering was enough to set her off again. This time when Jake pulled her close she sagged into the familiar shoulder, allowing herself the comfort of his strength and his touch. From a few yards away, Maggie stared at them both, small face impassive, and Jake wondered what she was thinking.

''I can't cope with her, Jake!'' Ann said, voice muffled in his shirt. ''She's such a strange child, and I don't know what to do with her!''

''We're working close in for the next couple of weeks,'' Jake said finally, still stroking his wife's arm. ''I'll take her with me.''

Ann reared back, staring at him in astonishment. ''Into the woods?''

''In the woods is where I'll have to be.''

''It's no place for a child! She'll get killed!''

''Do you think I'd let anything happen to her? It'll only

be for a few weeks, give you a chance to rest up, you and
the baby,'' Jake said.

The next morning, when Jake left at dawn, he carried a
drowsy Maggie on his shoulders. She was sound asleep
when he lifted her down and deposited her on his coat on a
pile of sawdust near the corner of the makeshift cookhouse.

"What the hell?" the cook's helper asked, staring.

"Keep an eye on her," Jake said, "and don't feed her
any of that slop you had left over from yesterday, hear?"

"Hey, wait a minute, taking care of a kid ain't part of
my job," the young man protested. Jake paused long
enough to dig a pair of coins out of his pocket, which he
pressed into the youth's hand.

"You take care of her. She's a good kid, she'll do what
you tell her as long as she understands what you want. She
can play here close to the cookhouse. I'll see it's worth
your while."

"I don't know nothing about little girls," the boy
insisted, but Jake was already moving away. The youth
swore, then sighed and reached for his own coat to drop
over the sleeping child, for the sun had not yet climbed far
enough to send its rays between the big trees, and it was
cold in the forest. He swore again, with less force; the
coins were a comfortable weight in his own pocket.

Maggie learned very quickly that if she stayed out of the
way, the men didn't mind having her around after that first
day or two. There were plenty of things to do. She enjoyed
filling a bucket with cones to be used by the cook as
kindling. She liked playing in the drifts of sawdust, and
watching squirrels scamper up the tall, straight tree trunks,
and observing the blue jays and the rarely glimpsed pileat-
ed woodpeckers with the touch of scarlet on their heads.

At noon, when the men put down their axes and saws
and gathered to eat, Maggie sat beside Jake and shared
their stews, biscuits, fried potatoes, and thick slabs of

steak and the apple and berry pies. Before long, she was helping to pick the great black juicy berries, so large that even tiny fingers could garner enough of them for a pie in nothing flat.

The several weeks allotted for Ann's resting-up passed, and nothing was said about leaving Maggie at home again.

Ann managed easily with the baby, who slept most of the time. If she hurried to get out the daily laundry and put on a pot of stew or beans to simmer until suppertime, Ann could easily rest for several hours every afternoon. It made her feel better and improved her disposition so that she complained less about being in a logging camp instead of in town. It made her more responsive to Jake in bed, which in turn convinced him that he had done the right thing, taking Maggie off with him into the woods.

Maggie was so tired that she often fell asleep over her supper. Jake would tuck her gently into her cot under the repaired quilt without waking her, while Ann rocked the baby to sleep, crooning softly. Sometimes Maggie imagined that it was she who was rocked, that the lullaby was for herself rather than for the baby.

The loggers, at first vocally negative about a child in their midst, were soon won over by Maggie's large smoky-green eyes and her smile, which had to be coaxed from her with some effort. She was far more obedient with the men than she was with her mother; if she was told to stay put, she did. They all shared the responsibility for seeing that she was in a safe place when the shout went up—*"Timber-r-r-r-r!"*—and another tree tore its way through surrounding boughs with a crash that made the earth reverberate through the soles of her shoes.

She became the camp pet. The men cosseted her, brought her treats from town: ribbons and sweets and trinkets. They could not, of course, watch her every minute; but the cook's helper found it worth the coins Jake provided to do so, as the little girl obeyed the rules once she understood what they were, and the youth had little to do for his money.

Maggie was wise at a very early age. It was clear to her that if she did not cause any trouble Jake could continue to bring her to the woods rather than leave her at home with Mama and the baby; so she listened carefully to the loggers' instructions and obeyed them to the letter.

She loved listening to the men; when they had time, they talked to her, explaining what they were doing, and why. By the time she was four, she could explain to her grandparents that an apple-knocker was a part-time logger, not very skilled at his job, and that the whistle punk's task was to pass signals from the rigger slinger or choke setter to the men yarding logs, and that a widow-maker was a dangerous limb or treetop or piece of bark that might fall on a man working beneath it, resulting in serious injury or death.

Ann was not much interested in what went on in the woods, and there were times, as when Maggie referred to a cat's ass, that she was stricken with guilt at exposing the child to such language.

When she looked appealing at Jake, he laughed. "A cat's ass is a snarl we get when a choker slips off a log and cinches up tight. It's not swearing, Ann, it's just an expression."

"It *sounds* like swearing. Can you imagine what Mama would say if Margaret said something like that in front of her?"

That only made Jake laugh harder. He considered Millicent Miles a prim and prissy woman, and he spent no more time in her company than was absolutely necessary. His antipathy toward her was surpassed only by what he felt for her husband.

Ann was eventually forced to admit that allowing her daughter to spend so much time with the loggers was not the wisest thing she could have done. The language was bad enough, though the men tried to remember that the child was around and tone down the strongest of their expressions. Ann didn't need her mother's wry observation— "I've never seen such an unladylike little girl!"—to be aware of the truth of the matter. To become a lady, a girl must spend time with women and learn their proper place and function in society. Maggie would never learn about keeping house and cooking and sewing if she spent most of her days with a band of men engaged in cutting down as many trees as possible in the shortest period of time, and cursing when anything went wrong, which it did constantly.

Had Ann herself spent any time in the woods, she would have been far more concerned for Maggie's safety than she was; although she knew there were woods accidents, Jake usually relayed the news about them with a statement like, "The damned fool wouldn't have had to claw bark for his life if he'd rigged it right in the first place." This gave Ann a false sense of security, a belief that the men, if they were careful, were in control of what happened.

She knew in her secret heart that the woods were no place for a child. She also knew that life was so much easier, so much more peaceful and restful, when she had only Celeste to contend with. She delayed, as long as possible, demanding that Jake leave Maggie at home.

Jake, too, knew that it was only a matter of time before Ann would put an end to Maggie's daily excursions to the woods. He got into the habit of saying to the child, "It might be better not to tell Mama how you fell today. She wouldn't understand how you came to be up on the log, and it would frighten her. So we'll keep it a secret, all right?"

Whatever Jake said, Maggie agreed with. She learned to tailor her language to her mother's sensibilities, leaving out expressions that might offend or bring down Mama's justice with a bar of soap to wash out the mouth.

But at last, of course, the time arrived when Maggie had to stay at home and learn to be a lady.

It was the hardest thing anyone had ever asked her to do.

# 3

THE shadows grew long, and Jake had not come to the little cabin where she waited. Tears had dried on Maggie's cheeks, leaving smudges under her eyes where she'd wiped them away with dirty fingers. No one had cleaned the cabin in years, and there was a layer of dust over everything.

Maggie tried to will her mind to become blank, to block off her usually fertile imagination so as not to picture what her mother would say, and her grandmother. Jake would undoubtedly say plenty, or, more likely, bellow profanely, but he'd stand by her. He always had.

Yet the problem was a grave one, and not even Jake could solve this problem as he'd solved those of skinned knees, irate teachers who did not consider daydreaming to be a part of the curriculum, and Maggie's seeming inability to coax bearable sounds from the piano Ann had at last acquired to grace the front parlor.

Maggie had not eaten since breakfast; she felt light-headed and queasy. And tired. Very, very tired. She sank onto her knees, oblivious of soiling her skirts, and stared out the door across the river and the marsh beyond.

Although the scene was one she'd viewed nearly every

day of her life, she had never tired of it. Washington Territory was a land of lush green growth, of sparkling waterways and stately trees. Maggie had never been farther from Snohomish City than Port Gardner, a few miles away on Puget Sound, but she had never had any burning desire to travel to more distant places. Some of her friends liked nothing better than to ride the steamer to Seattle, where they could indulge in grand shopping sprees in the multitude of stores, and eat out at elegant restaurants. Twice Mama and Celeste had gone, returning in a state of exhilarated exhaustion with all the bundles they could carry. Maggie had not even been invited to accompany them.

It hadn't mattered to her overly much, at least not until recently. In the days before she realized that she was in love with Angus McKay, and he with her, she had little interest in picking out pretty gowns and parasols and gloves, and the other accoutrements that turned a young female into a stylish young lady.

Would it have made a difference, Maggie wondered, if she'd had those fancy clothes, the carefully curled hair, the peach-toned skin instead of one that was suntanned?

Or would she still have been betrayed by the man she'd thought would bring her complete happiness and fulfillment?

Angus. Maggie lost her awareness of the surroundings, and her thoughts turned inward, remembering.

Angus McKay had come to the woods the year Maggie was ten. He was only seventeen, but to a little girl he was a full-grown man, one of her beloved loggers.

He was inexperienced, a green hand, and as such he was teased and tormented by the older men. Angus was very tall and not particularly muscular when he first came; he had a thick shock of fair hair, gray eyes so steady they were disconcerting to many, and a Scots burr that was cause for much amusement.

Like nearly all woodsmen, Angus began as a whistle punk and worked his way up. A new man was given much of the dirty work, and Angus did it all. He slaved as a swamper, clearing away brush and undergrowth to make way for the logging operations to come, stripping to the waist to expose a pale-skinned torso that soon took on a rich golden tan with muscles visibly developing beneath it.

Angus wasn't much of a talker, at least at first. He kept still, watched, and listened. It was safer, because the loggers had a bawdy and sometimes cruel humor; the best way to avoid being the butt of their humor was to stay as quiet and invisible as possible.

When he did his stint as a swabber, greasing the skids on which the logs were moved toward the landing on the river, Maggie helped. If she hadn't been allowed to return to the woods during the summers, at least, she would have died, she sometimes thought during the long winters when she was confined to the house and female activities.

Maggie had tried swabbing herself, but had not been allowed to continue for long; the first time she arrived at home smelling of the dogfish oil that was said to be strong enough to skid logs without oxen, Ann had taken one horrified look—and sniff—and sworn that if she came home in that condition once more, she'd never be allowed into the woods again, ever.

"I can't swab anymore," Maggie told Angus after he'd taken on that task. "My mama doesn't like the smell of the oil."

Angus grunted, not turning to look at her as she paced him along the skid road constructed of split tree trunks laid crossways, corduroy fashion, to facilitate movement of the gigantic logs being yarded. "Can't say I blame her. Doesn't make me very popular when I get to town Saturday night, either. Damned stuff doesn't wash off." He *did* look at her, then. "Sorry. I forget I'm talking to a young lady."

"I don't mind swearing," Maggie said. "I'm used to it."

Angus scrutinized her more closely, then. All he really knew about her was that her father was Jake Keating, a top faller and a genuine bull of the woods, not a man to be crossed. "How come a little girl like you is out here with a bunch of loggers?" he wanted to know.

Maggie was fascinated by his accent. She'd never heard anyone who spoke quite the way Angus did, in excellent and grammatical English yet with that touch of a Scots burr. She would talk about anything to keep him replying, so that she could listen to him.

"I like it here," Maggie said. "If I were you, I'd put on more grease than that, or Old Saul will holler at you."

"That right? All right, more grease." Angus slathered the smelly oil, no longer trying to keep it off his person. "How long you think I'll have to do this job before they'll give me something better to do?"

"Until somebody else comes along to grease the skids. Are you going to be a faller, like my daddy?"

Angus paused, straightening to push back his hair and brush the sweat from his forehead with a rag carried in his hip pocket. He stared across the clearing at the crew rigging a tree to be brought down, and in particular at the man over two hundred feet in the air near the top of a Douglas fir so straight it could have been used as a ruler. "I don't know yet. I never climbed a tree that far off the ground."

"It's dangerous," Maggie said seriously. "Last month, before you came, Sol Engstrom got caught by a fool killer and knocked out of a tree. He broke both legs."

Angus was swabbing grease again, swallowing against the stench that rose from the oil in the summer heat. "What's a fool killer?"

Maggie knew the men would have derided the youth's lack of knowledge, knowledge she had been garnering since she was a toddler. "It was a branch that was bent—caught, you know—and when it came loose, it hit Sol and knocked him off the spar tree."

Angus grunted in reply, and for a few minutes said nothing more. His back was already aching, though it was not yet noon, and he was determined to reveal no weakness, no softness, before the other men.

"Hey, Maggie! Fetch me that toe splitter, will you?"

She turned toward Joe French, broke away from Angus McKay's side to take the logger the adz he had requested, then returned to walk along the skid road beside the blond young man.

"Have you got a wife?" Maggie asked.

The gray eyes rested briefly on her. "No. No wife."

Few of the men had wives, for there was a profound scarcity of females in Washington Territory in that year of 1879, though enough had come in so that a few of the men besides her father had married. Maggie knew that it was important to her mother that there be more women in Snohomish City; respectable women meant schools and churches, more culture and refinements. They had long since moved from the tiny cabin on the riverbank into a respectable two-bedroom house on Cedar Street, where Ann was much happier with other women for neighbors.

"I don't think *I'll* ever get married," Maggie said.

"Oh? Why's that? I thought all females hankered after a man of their own." Angus moved along the skid road, resisting the urge to ease his back by standing upright for a few minutes, hoping the cook would ring the dinner bell before the discomfort became agony. "Out here in the woods all the time, looks as if you like men all right."

"Of course. Only Grandma Miles says it isn't likely that any man will have me."

His eyes narrowed. "Why would she say a thing like that?"

"Because I'm not ladylike, like Celeste. Nor pretty, the way she is."

At that he did straighten, not even thinking about his aching muscles. "Your grandma said that? That you're not pretty?"

He stared at her, this skinny little girl with gray-green eyes too big for the small face, dark hair drawn back severely into braids that hung halfway down her back, and a mouth a trifle too broad, though finely shaped, for the size of her. When she grew up to match the size of her eyes and her mouth, Angus thought, it was quite possible that she was going to be a raving beauty. He thought of his own young sisters back home in Boston, and anger stirred beneath the outwardly calm exterior.

"People who are beautiful early on, when they're very young, fade early, you know," he told the child. "By the time this Celeste gets all grown-up, chances are she'll get fat and lose her prettiness, when you're just getting yours."

Maggie looked into his face and saw nothing to indicate he was making fun of her. "I'm plain," she said. "Mama despairs of my ever being a lady. She says I ruin all my clothes so she won't make me pretty ones like Celeste's."

"You're not plain," Angus informed her. "You have good bones." He lifted a finger to his own cheekbone, tapping it. "Here, and in the shape of your face. I know a man who's an artist, and he told me how important a person's facial bones are. They'll determine what you look like when you're grown-up, and I can tell. You're going to be very pretty."

She searched his eyes for some sign of levity. "Are you sure?"

"Positive." Angus realized that he'd forgotten what he was supposed to be doing, and went back to work, feeling moisture running down his flanks and soaking his head and neck so that the smell of the dogfish oil mingled with that of his own sweat. "Who's this Celeste?"

"My sister. She's eight. She has blond curly hair and blue eyes."

"I have two sisters who are blond, but their hair doesn't curl. Their names are Rosa and Carolyn. Carolyn's about your age, I think. Eleven."

"I'm ten," Maggie told him. "Are they pretty, Rosa and Carolyn?"

He considered. "It's hard to tell about your sisters. Yes, I think they're pretty. More important than that, though, they're nice. They're fun to be with."

"Hey! You, McKay!"

They both turned to see the boss approaching. Ed Newsome was not a tall man, though he gave the impression of size because he was bulky. He stalked toward them in his plaid flannel shirt with the red suspenders holding up his pants, a man of middle years who looked as tough as the trees he'd been cutting down for much of his life.

Angus stepped toward him with alacrity, hoping to hell he hadn't somehow misunderstood how he was supposed to be doing this business of slopping fish oil on the skids. He needed a job, any job, and the best-paying ones were in the woods.

"We got a man down, and we gotta get the job finished. You ever handle a misery harp?"

Angus had no idea what a misery harp was, but he responded without hesitation. "No, sir, but I'm a quick learner."

"Good. Give Risku a hand over there. Maggie, fetch your pa. We got a broken arm needs settin'." Newsome turned and strode away, taking it for granted that they'd obey orders.

"Which one's Risku?" Angus asked, setting down his bucket and swab. "And what is it they want me to do?"

"Risku's over there," Maggie said, pointing. "The big redheaded one in the red shirt. They want you to man one end of the crosscut saw."

Angus brightened. "A bucker? They want me to buck logs?"

The work would be harder than greasing skids, but it paid more and was far more prestigious; he knew that much.

"Yes!" Maggie said, and ran along the path to find Jake.

Maggie had seen her share in injured men. After the time she'd nearly sent her mother into a swoon describing what a logger looked like who'd taken a sixty-foot fall, she'd had sense enough to keep such things to herself. Like the men, she always felt a freezing sensation when the call went out—"Man down!"—but today there had been no commotion, no shout of warning or for help. It wasn't her father, she knew that, for Ed had sent her to get Jake, so she didn't have to nurse *that* fear. Yet most of the men were her friends, and until she knew who it was—and maybe afterward—the constriction would be there in her chest, and the ice in her blood.

Jake was the best faller in Newsome's operation. He could put a two-hundred-and-fifty-foot tree down precisely where he wanted it, and he often wagered with a new hand (an old hand didn't care to lose his money by gambling on such a fool thing) that he would bring it down in such a way as to drive into the ground a wooden stake placed for the purpose. Jake almost never missed the stake, and usually hit it dead center.

Today he was preparing to adminster the "coop dee grace," as he referred to it in front of his better-educated father-in-law for the purpose of annoying the Reverend Mr. Miles, to the first in a stand of cedars. He shouted a warning to the men when he saw Maggie's blue-and-white-checked gingham through the trees.

"What're you doing out here?" Jake demanded when he was certain the procedure had come to a halt.

"Ed sent me to get you. Somebody's got a broken arm,

and he wants you to set it,'' Maggie gasped, pushing at the
pain that had begun in her side from running.

They moved quickly, Maggie trailing because she was
already tired and Jake's legs were longer. The injured man
was propped against the base of a fir stump with a six-foot
circumference, white-faced, but conscious and talking.

Jake looked at the exposed arm from which the shirt had
been cut away, then barked orders about splints and dish
towels to secure them. Two loggers stationed themselves to
pull, one at the wrist and one at the shoulder, to allow the
ends of the fractured bone to be maneuvered into place,
the traction held by a hastily removed belt, and Maggie
watched from a safe distance as Tom Berquist's brawny
arm was set.

Angus watched, too, wondering what it would be like to
have this done without even a slug of whiskey to take the
edge off the pain.

Tom gave one uncontrollable yelp, then sagged against
the rough bark of the stump, breathing heavily.

"Get him over to the bunkhouse,'' Ed Newsome or-
dered, gesturing at the whistle punk and the cook. "The
rest of you, get back to work."

Maggie retired to the cook shack to help with the
preparations for the noon meal. For some reason, this was
more acceptable than performing similar tasks at home.
For one thing, the cook, Mr. Murphy (nobody knew what
his first name was, though he'd been in the crew for longer
than Maggie had lived) was not nearly as particular as Ann
was about how things were done. If the plates were on the
table and there were utensils to eat with, they could be
placed any old way without exciting comment. Ed Newsome
was smart enough to know that good grub kept a crew on,
while poor grub ran them off. Cakes and pies were made
in enormous quantities for healthy appetites, and although
the men grumbled about the food in all logging camps, this
was one of the better ones in that regard.

This noon there was a huge iron pot of beans with salt pork, and the cornbread the men referred to as Arkansas wedding cake, as well as fresh-baked blackberry pies with the sweet purple juice oozing onto their tin plates.

Maggie ate with the men. She didn't remember the time when Ed Newsome had objected to her presence there; he'd long since admitted that the little girl earned her keep by running errands and doing various small chores, and he'd stopped worrying about something happening to her. She wasn't accident-prone, she was as agile as one of the squirrels that chattered from the trees, and she reminded him of the small daughter of his own who had been lost to smallpox twenty years earlier.

Today she slid onto one of the benches at the table where Angus McKay sat and allowed him to pile her plate high. It occurred to him that this child could be of considerable help; she knew as much as many of the men, yet made no fun of his ignorance. Even learning the terminology peculiar to the woods was of value, since a logger was likely to yell for a peavey (which he knew to be the heavy-handled tool with both a spike point and a free-swinging hook for rolling logs) or a shim hoe (which was obviously a tool, but Angus had not yet learned which one) and expect to get it immediately without having to explain what it was.

He was amazed that the child's mother allowed her into the logging camp this way, though after talking to Maggie he decided that she was a very self-reliant little girl and that she had a will of her own, a will to be here partly because she adored her father and partly because she was enchanted with the forest itself.

Maggie was quite willing to feed him information freely. She considered no question to be foolish—she had asked them all herself at one time or another—and Angus found that she never gave him misinformation or deliberately misled him as some of the men, with the perverted sense of humor common to the loggers, tended to do.

Besides that, Angus liked her. She reminded him of his little sisters and home. She was bright and amusing, and he was a long way from his family and friends in a strange new country; Maggie eased his loneliness. He decided to cultivate her and encourage her company; as he went back to his first day of bucking timber, her earnest advice rang in his memory.

"You have to be careful to do your share of the work. If you ride the saw and let the man on the other end do most of the work, he won't work with you. He might even," Maggie warned with an endearing earnestness, "beat you up."

Angus remembered the wisdom of that as fiery pain seared his back, shoulder, and leg muscles throughout the rest of that day. He didn't slack off, even though the strain took a tremendous toll; he no longer thought about what he was doing, manning one end of a crosscut saw to cut through an eight-foot butt, pushing the blade forward, drawing it back, until he thought his lungs would burst, his arms fall off, his shaking legs betray him by collapsing.

As it turned out, his stint on one end of the saw was temporary. An experienced bucker applied for a job the day after Tom Berquist broke his arm, and Angus was pulled off the saw. His regret was mingled with relief; he would adjust to the work eventually, as the others adjusted, and being a bucker was more to his liking than swabbing smelly fish oil on the skids.

He didn't go back to that job, either, though.

"Hired a new swabber," Ed Newsome informed him. "You go with Charlie Lindquist. He'll teach you what a choke setter does."

Angus agreed with alacrity. Choke setting couldn't be any more physically demanding than bucking logs, or more unpleasant than greasing skids, or any more poorly paid than being a whistle punk. Maybe, by next summer, he'd have built up his muscles and his endurance so that bucking wouldn't kill him, he thought.

Maggie sat beside him at the table all that season. At first the men teased them both—Maggie had her first fella, and McKay was robbing the cradle, trying to win points with Jake Keating—but the subject grew old fairly quickly and was dropped. Angus knew the things Maggie read about in her books; he treated her as an equal and a friend. The summer she was ten was the happiest she could remember.

That fall was the one when she remembered knowing that she was growing up, and realizing how painful it was going to be.

# 4

FEW of the citizens of Snohomish City were much aware of what took place beyond the reaches of their own community. There was a local newspaper, which dealt primarily with matters of interest to those engaged in the logging industry, with a sprinkling of local politics, and society items for the benefit of the ladies; almost no one subscribed to papers from outside. They relied largely on word of mouth for information about most things and did not unduly trouble themselves in regard to what happened far from their own homes and businesses.

One publication that found its way into town during

Maggie's tenth year was the Montgomery Ward catalog, owned by Millicent Miles and commonly referred to as the "wish book." She lent it throughout the settlement, and Ann and her daughters pored over it as avidly as everyone else. Maggie and Celeste were each allowed to choose a doll for Christmas; they waited anxiously, not at all certain that it was actually possible to order from a book something that would then come from several thousand miles away, though Grandma assured them that this was the case.

Anticipating the arrival of the doll, which was described as being dressed in pink gingham and having a china bisque face of exquisite loveliness, was the only bright spot in Maggie's life that winter.

She knew from autumn on that her mother was not feeling well, and that her parents quarreled more often than usual. More than once she was awakened late at night to hear their voices, heavy with suppressed emotion, in the next room.

The walls of the small house were thin enough so that unless one's words were whispered they carried from one bedroom to the other. Beside her Celeste slept, while Maggie listened, not wanting to hear, unable to avoid it.

"Damn you, Jake Keating!" Ann said one night, and Maggie stiffened. She was used to swearing, but not from her mother. "All you care about is yourself!"

"That's not true, and you know it." Jake's voice was low, yet it had considerable carrying power. "It's been over a month, Ann. How the hell long do you expect a man to wait?"

"Until I'm feeling halfway decent; is that so much to ask?"

"You expect me to believe you haven't had half an hour of feeling halfway decent in a month?"

"If I haven't, it's hardly my fault, is it?" Ann sounded bitter, helpless, resigned. "I didn't want another child,

BOARDING PASS

| Flight | Date | Gate |
|---|---|---|
| PA 268 | 3 AUG | 1 |

✈ No Smoking Seat

🚬 Smoking Seat

Class Inf.

11A

V

MCO/NEWARK EWR

From/To

VORA          M

Passenger Name

🌐 PAN AM

**BOARDING PASS**

PAN AM

| Flight | Date | Gate |
|--------|------|------|
| PA 28  | 3 AUG | 1 |

Ⓢ No Smoking Seat

Ⓢ Smoking Seat

| | Class Inf. |
|-----|-----|
| 11E | Y |

From / To

MOONPARK FWB

NORA S

Passenger Name

you *knew* I didn't want another child, I've lost two already, and that's enough. It isn't my fault that having a baby is so difficult for me, is it?''

Through the wall, Maggie heard her mother begin to cry. Her heart twisted. She didn't know why Daddy so often made Mama cry, but he did. She'd asked him, once, and he'd given her a level response. "It's something you're too young to understand, sweetheart. Something between grown-up people."

For once he hadn't tried to explain fully, as he usually did. He'd changed the subject and left Maggie unsatisfied and vaguely frightened.

She heard his words now, soft and compassionate, the way he was with *her* when her need was great and he could not give her what she begged for.

"Ann, I know you feel sick a lot of the time. I'm sorry it affects you that way, but I don't know anything to do about it. I try not to upset you, and God knows I don't want to force myself on any woman, let alone the wife I love. But I'm a man, with the needs God built into me, and I can't spend the rest of my life this way. Please, Ann, for my sake, will you try? You're not sick right now, are you? You don't feel like throwing up? You were laughing and singing when you put the girls to bed, and I thought maybe, tonight . . ."

The words became muffled then. Maggie couldn't make them out, though the sounds of movement and soft voices continued for some time. After a while she heard Jake's feet hit the floor and move around out in the main room, pacing from one end of it to the other, while closer to Maggie, beyond the wall, Ann wept quietly.

Maggie, falling asleep again at last, cried, too, though she did not know exactly why except that her parents were unhappy.

The following day, a Sunday, the family prepared to go to church together. Ann had trouble fastening her dress at the waist, and Celeste fell down and dirtied her frock so that it had to be changed at the last minute. Why that should have sent tears spilling over from Ann's eyes was beyond Maggie. Ann's customary reaction to such things was mild annoyance and an equally mild scolding for the culprit. While she waited for her mother and little sister to reemerge from the house, Maggie leaned against Jake's side.

"Daddy," she asked hesitantly, "is something wrong with Mama?"

He hugged her automatically. "She thinks you're too young to know yet, but if you're old enough to notice that . . ." He sighed. "Mama's going to have a baby. That makes females weepy, sometimes. She'll be better when the baby comes."

Maggie perked up. "A baby? Will it be a boy or a girl?"

"No way of telling until it gets here. Anyway, be a good girl and don't upset your mama, will you? She needs extra rest these days, and extra help."

"Where will the baby come from?" Maggie asked, wide-eyed with growing excitement.

His hesitation was brief. "It's growing inside her belly. When it's big enough, it will come out. Maggie, having babies is something people don't talk about to just anyone, you understand? Not outside the family. Not to the men in the woods, and I think maybe not even to Grandma Miles, not unless Mama says you can."

"Why? Is there something wrong with having a baby?"

"No, no. It's what all women do after they're married. But it's like not showing your underwear, or relieving yourself in public. Some things are private, within the family. It's like the things the men say in the woods, you don't tell those to Mama because it upsets her, see? Well, she'd be upset if you talked about having the baby to anyone else."

"Oh," Maggie said without comprehension. "Will the baby come out soon?"

"Not for quite a while yet. A little bit after Christmas. Here come Mama and Celeste; we'd better get going or we'll be late, and you know how your grandparents like *that*."

Grandma Miles was good to them, except for an occasional remark on the differences between her granddaughters, which always left Maggie feeling that she would forever come out second best. Millicent made them thick, chewy cookies, and thin crisp ones, and sewed dresses for them, though every time she presented a gown to Maggie she remonstrated over Maggie's tendency to tear and rip her garments. Grandma Miles would let them squeeze into her rocker beside her, or sit upon her lap, and sing them hymns in a fine, clear voice.

Grandpa Miles, whom Daddy referred to in an odd tone as "the Reverend," was not one of Maggie's favorite people. Celeste didn't care for him much, either, though Mama explained how he was the best-educated man in the community and was to be respected for his knowledge of the Bible.

Neither of his granddaughters would have dreamed of crawling up into Stokes Miles's lap, the way they did with Jake. He would have considered it undignified and it would have put unwanted creases into his trousers. He was not a good singer, though for such a diminutive man he had a powerful speaking voice; those in the back row at church had no excuse for falling asleep because they couldn't hear the sermon. He didn't need to look at the Book so often open before him in order to quote Scripture; sometimes Maggie thought he knew every bit of the Holy Book by heart. And though he was always pleased when they had learned new verses, he did not believe in lavishing praise on children for doing what they ought to do.

Their walk to services this morning was not as leisurely

as usual because of the delay caused by changing Celeste's clothes. There were still people standing outside in the crisp October sunshine, however, reluctant to go in until the final bell pealed.

Few of the churchgoing men were loggers. Most were business people in town, along with the teacher, Mr. Hogan, and the undertaker, Mr. Shadpole. Jake spoke to them easily enough, though Maggie knew he wasn't especially friendly with any of them. Once Mama had urged him to be more gracious, adding that he did not need to feel inferior to any of them because he was a woodsman.

Jake had been astonished. "Inferior? My God, it's *them* who ought to feel inferior, if anybody does! The lumber industry supports the whole territory! Without me, and the others like me, there wouldn't be any town, or any need for any of them."

This morning, however, he was on his best behavior. He had a new pair of red suspenders over his plaid flannel shirt, which was open at the throat to reveal the crisp mat of dark hair on his chest. It had long been a bone of contention between her parents, that open-throated shirt at church, but Jake was adamant.

"Nobody wears a tie with a flannel shirt, Ann, and I don't see any reason to waste money on any other kind, just to have it to wear on Sunday for an hour. Besides, my neck's too thick to button any shirt all the way up. I'd choke to death."

Maggie thought he looked splendid, no matter what he wore. If she were ever to marry (and she harbored a small, secret hope that it might come to pass, in spite of what Grandma Miles had said about her looks), it would have to be to someone exactly like Jake.

The women smiled and nodded and greeted the Keatings. *They* thought her daddy was handsome, Maggie knew by the expressions on their faces that they did.

Maggie paused when her sister lagged behind. "What's

the matter?'' she wanted to know when Celeste tugged free of her restraining hand.

"I've got a stone in my shoe. Wait, while I get it out."

Thus it was, bent over to help the younger girl get her shoe off and then back on, that Maggie overheard two women who were looking after the Keatings.

"There, now, I told you she looked like she was in the family way, didn't I? Look at her now, Alice. She's either expecting or she's getting fat."

Getting fat? Mama? Maggie straightened, staring at the women indignantly, though with an underlying concern. What had Angus McKay said about pretty women? That when they got older they tended to get fat?

It wasn't fat, though, not with Mama.

Mrs. Nilsen, whose husband owned the bakery, addressed her with a sly smile. "You having a baby brother pretty soon, are you?"

The other woman gave her friend a slightly scandalized glance, yet listened with interest to Maggie's reply.

"We won't know if it's a boy or a girl until it comes out," Maggie said with dignity, and reached for Celeste's hand to jerk her along after their parents. Behind them, Mrs. Nilsen cried, "What did I tell you?"

If the baker's wife could tell that Mama was going to have a baby, Maggie supposed that everybody else could tell, also. So why had Daddy said she mustn't talk about it? The whole thing was most peculiar.

They sat in the second row, as they usually did. The girls slid onto the bench beside their father, and Celeste leaned against Maggie to whisper into her ear. "Is it true? Is Mama going to have a baby?"

"Shhhh!" Mama said, and Maggie whispered back, "Yes, Daddy said after Christmas."

"Oh, good," Celeste murmured. "If there's a new baby, maybe they'll stop fussing over me so much."

Grandpa Miles took his place behind the pulpit and

announced the first hymn. When they had been sung and everyone had resumed their seats, he announced in a voice less firm than usual, "The Gospel today is from the Book of John, in the . . ."

He paused and stared out over his small flock, a strange expression upon his face. Was it possible that Grandpa Miles had forgotten the text?

Maggie fixed her gaze upon her grandfather, aware that her mother stirred uneasily on the hard bench. The Reverend Mr. Miles wiped at his face with a handkerchief and his mouth worked for several seconds before he produced any words. "The Book of John, chapter . . . chapter . . ."

Maggie heard Ann's low "Papa!" and then saw Grandpa Miles's hands grip the edges of the lectern until his knuckles turned white. A moment later, he gave a gargling sort of sound and pitched forward over the open Bible before him. As Maggie watched in horrified fascination, his hands released their grasp, and he slid downward, out of sight.

Ann, Jake, and Millicent all sprang to their feet, as did several others. In the confusion, Celeste was knocked off the bench and began to cry.

Maggie pushed against the crush of bodies and drew her sister under the bench to comparative safety. "My dress is torn," Celeste said. "I couldn't help it, someone stepped on the hem!"

"It doesn't matter," Maggie said. She turned as her grandmother gave a low, keening cry. "I think Grandpa Miles is dead. They won't care about the dress."

Behind them the shocked congregation was murmuring, then rising to their feet. Jake and the undertaker had carried the minister to the side of the church where he could be stretched out flat; from the back, old Doc Proctor moved forward, and the people parted for him to pass through.

"Maggie?" Celeste clutched her sister's hand, small face uplifted. "Is Grandpa dead? Really?"

Maggie climbed on the bench to see over the heads to where her mother stood, pale and stricken. "I think so," she said.


There was no one in town to preach the funeral sermon, so they sent for a minister from Port Gardner, at the mouth of the Snohomish on the Sound.

Grandma and Mama cried until their faces were swollen and red. Everyone else spoke in hushed voices, and the neighbors brought in food to eat after they'd all come back from the cemetery. Even Jake was quiet and respectful. He went back to the woods as soon as he'd eaten, though Ann protested.

"Ann, it's not only my job. If I don't work, I throw the others out of work, too. I have to go. I'll be back Saturday night, as usual." He kissed her on the forehead and stroked her back, right in front of everybody, when she clung to him and wept. "Be strong, sweetheart, for your mother's sake. And for the girls."

Ann swallowed hard. "Yes. I'll have to take care of Mother, won't I?"

Maggie was sorry that Daddy had gone back to the woods, mostly because she hadn't been allowed to go with him. She didn't feel much of anything about her grandfather, but it was profoundly disturbing to see her grandmother and mother in such distress.

"Come on," she said to Celeste, "let's go outside. Nobody will miss us, with all these people here."

Celeste came readily. They passed two women on the front steps and overheard their words. "Well, if it's true that death comes in threes, that's the second one."

"Mrs. Worthy was nearly eighty," the other woman said. "But Mr. Miles went before his time, sure enough."

"I wonder who the third one will be. Nobody else sick,

is there? Probably be an accident, next time. Hasn't been an accident in the woods for nearly two months.''

The words sent a chill through the listening child. Not Daddy, Maggie thought prayerfully. Please, God, not Daddy. Not ever Daddy.

And, for a moment, she had a flickering understanding of what her mother must be feeling now. Poor, poor Mama, Maggie thought.

Maggie was in the woods the following Saturday when the dreaded accident happened.

Normally she did not go to the logging camp unless she accompanied her father. Because school had started, however, she could no longer go for the entire week, and Jake was unable to make the long trip to get her.

This week, however, the camp cook, Mr. Murphy, had come to Snohomish with the wagon for supplies on Friday. As he was heading back, he stopped by the Keating house in town to see if Maggie would be allowed to go with him.

He enjoyed the child's company, and she was a fairly good hand in the cookhouse, too. There was no need to ask if she wanted to go; the only question was whether or not she would be allowed to.

He was a rotund, bald man who had been a choke setter before an injury with a snapped chain had made him decide to cook instead. He stood on the doorstep, waiting for Ann's decision.

Millicent Miles was there, rocking before the fire. She looked at the intruder with pinched lips.

"Be just tonight," Mr. Murphy said. "Jake'll bring her home tomorrow night. Thought with all your troubles, ma'am, it might help to be rid of one of the younguns."

Ann's pregnancy was not going well, though it was long past the time when she ought to have been over things like morning sickness. Even Celeste was getting on her nerves; and though Ann had not yet admitted it, she found it increasingly difficult to deal with her mother. Millicent was devastated by her husband's death, and in addition to her sense of personal loss she was terrified about what would become of her if her daughter and son-in-law did not take her in. Ann knew this, and recognized the necessity for some arrangement to provide for her mother, while knowing that Jake would go mad with Millicent a permanent part of his household.

Neither Millicent's own home nor the Keatings' was large enough to contain both households. And without her husband, Millicent had no means of support whatever. It was a matter that would have to be discussed—fought about? Ann wondered—when Jake was at home, and talked about endlessly until then.

"May I go, Mama?" Maggie asked, trying to conceal her eagerness to be away. Sometimes it didn't pay to appear too eager.

"Well, all right. Get your things," Ann told her.

"Couldn't I go, too?" Celeste asked. She had never been included in the excursions to the woods, and while she was not as enthralled with them as her sister, she thought anything would be better than staying here at home with Mama and Grandma, with both of them breaking into tears every few minutes.

Maggie stared at her sister. Celeste had never asked such a thing before, but she was, after all, eight years old. Maggie had been in the woods long before that age. "I'll take her, Mama, if you like."

Ann hesitated. The temptation was strong—with the girls gone, she'd have only her mother to deal with, which would certainly be easier. Yet Celeste had never been away from home overnight except to stay with her grandparents occasionally.

"She's too young to go," Millicent stated, dabbing at her nose with a sodden handkerchief. "And a logging camp is no place for a girl, anyway. God only knows it's already affected Margaret Ellen, being in the company of those roughnecks so much.''

Something inside Ann snapped. "Her father is one of them, if you'll remember, Mama. He's always seen to it that she's well taken care of. All right, then, Celeste, get your nightgown and a blanket. They'll be right with you, Mr. Murphy.''

He nodded and replaced his hat. "I'll wait in the wagon. Thank you, ma'am.''

The door had no more than closed after him than Millicent spoke. "I'm surprised you trust the girls to that man.''

"Mr. Murphy? Why? He's worked with Jake for years, and Margaret's known him since she was an infant, practically. He's the camp cook, and he's been good to her. He would no more harm her than Jake would.''

"How can you be sure of that? He's a man, isn't he?''

"Mama, for the love of heaven, half the population of the world consists of men! More than that, here in Washington Territory!''

"That's what I mean. How can you be sure that a man so long without a woman is trustworthy with little girls?''

"Because Jake trusts him," Ann said quietly. "And while Jake has his shortcomings, lack of concern for his children isn't one of them. It'll be good for all of us to have a change of pace for a day or so. You can sleep in the girls' bed tonight, with them gone. Maybe we'll both rest better that way.''

Maggie heard this and speculated, briefly, on what Grandma thought Mr. Murphy could possibly do to harm them. It was not something *she* worried about. Her spirits soaring, she supervised Celeste's packing, and they hurried out to Mr. Murphy's wagon.

# 5

It was dark by the time Mr. Murphy's wagon reached the logging camp. He had entertained the girls during the journey with tales Maggie had heard many times; she never tired of them, however, and they were new to Celeste. The child listened wide-eyed, occasionally turning to her sister for confirmation of the astonishing revelations about the fillyloo bird, which ate red pepper and flew backward for cooling purposes, and the whingety-whong-whang-whoo bird, whose story must never be repeated in front of Mama or Grandma.

"Why not?" Celeste demanded.

"Because they'd be shocked," said Maggie, who was seldom shocked about anything. "Tell her, Mr. Murphy."

The old man was dubious. "It ain't exactly the kind of story for a little girl."

"I've known it for years," Maggie said. "And it's funny, Mr. Murphy! You can tell it better than I can. Please?"

So Celeste heard about the creature that slept with its head in a very peculiar place, and how impolite it had to be to get it out again in the morning. At first her blue eyes were wide with disbelief, and then she saw Maggie's amusement, and she burst into laughter, too. "It's not really so," she accused the old man, who only kept a sober face and insisted that any logger knew the truth of the matter.

"I don't reckon you ever heard about the side hill gouger, neither, then," he told her, winking over her head at Maggie.

"No. Tell me," Celeste begged, getting into the spirit of things.

"Well, there's lots of stories about the gouger. You ask your pa, he'll tell you he's seen the marks of the critter on the steep hills. The gouger has two long legs, on the downhill side of hisself, and two short legs on the uphill side, so he can stand upright and not tip over when he's running across a hillside. He always goes around the hill in the same direction, you see; he can't turn around, because then his short legs wouldn't reach the ground on the *downhill* side, and his long legs would be so high on the *uphill* side that he'd fall over and roll downhill into the river. I don't think side hill gougers can swim, you see."

Celeste's eyes danced, imagining this creature. "What does he do?"

"Do? Why, he creates predicaments for loggers. Makes things fall the wrong way, you know, makes accidents happen, though they ain't usually *fatal*." He had to pause to explain the meaning of fatal. "He lays square eggs. Otherwise, if they was regular round ones, they'd roll downhill, but the square ones don't get away. On the downhill side, he's woolly as a buffalo hide, to keep him warm. On the uphill side, though, the wool is wore off from rubbing against the brush; he's smooth like alligator hide, and tough, too. And he's got mean little eyes; they say if you make a mistake and look him straight in the eyes, you can't move. You just hafta stand there until he looks away, and sometimes a logger gets mighty cold and wet, waiting for that doggoned critter to look away."

"Did you ever see one?" Celeste wanted to know, forgetting that she didn't believe in the mythical creature.

"No, but I seen their tracks more'n once. You got to watch out for 'em."

Gradually the younger child grew sleepy, and when she dozed off and nearly pitched forward off the seat Mr. Murphy reined in the horses. He hollowed out a place between a crate of tinned milk and two hundred-pound sacks of flour so that Celeste could curl up on a blanket with Mr. Murphy's coat over her.

Maggie didn't feel sleepy. She didn't mind when Mr. Murphy finally ran out of stories and fell silent; she listened to the sounds of the woods, the gurgle of small streams, the rustle of rabbits or other wild creatures in the ferns along the way, and exclaimed in delight when a grouse flew up, spooking the horses so that Mr. Murphy had to pull back sharply on the reins.

Even after it grew dark, Maggie sat upright, eager to reach their destination, to see her father. She always felt happy and secure when she was with Jake.

The men were gathered around a dying fire when the wagon rattled to a stop before the cookhouse. Mr. Murphy's shout brought them to assist in unloading the supplies, and he had special orders for Jake Keating.

"Brought you a present," Mr. Murphy said. "Two of 'em, as a matter of fact. T'other one's sleeping; you'll have to lift her out."

Jake reached for Maggie, swinging her down and pausing long enough for a hug before he peered over the sideboards. "Celeste, too? What's wrong? Something happen to Mama?"

"No, she's all right. We just both wanted to come," Maggie assured him. "It's all right, isn't it, Daddy?"

"Sure, why not? I'm just surprised your ma let you both loose in the woods. I'll bring your sister; you get the door, Maggie."

Jake did not sleep in the bunkhouse with the other men. Because he had been bringing Maggie with him for so long, he had for years thrown up his own shack at each camp. A bonus, he laughingly told Ann, that kept him away from everybody else's fleas, bedbugs, and odors.

The shacks were never very large, only big enough for a set of bunks. There was no stove, no windows, only a door that could be left open to let in the fresh air for anyone who didn't get enough through the cracks.

Ann would have been appalled. Maggie was used to it, and she ran ahead, flinging open the door and turning back the covers on her own bunk. Jake followed, ducking his head to get through the doorway, depositing the sleeping child on the coarse wool blankets. ''Take her shoes off, and cover her up. I'll be back when we get the wagon unloaded. You'd better crawl into bed yourself, honey; it's late.''

Late, in the woods, meant dark. The men would be up at dawn; there was seldom any lingering around the fire for more than an hour, at most, after the evening meal. For one thing, there wasn't much to do; Ed Newsome, like most sensible bosses, forbade any drinking in camp. A man who wanted alcohol had to indulge himself in town on Saturday night; he'd be fired if Newsome caught him with a bottle on the job or even in the bunkhouse. Drunkenness and logging didn't go together; a man needed all his wits and his skills at a peak to operate safely when trees were being felled or yarded, and the loggers in general were a tough, aggressive bunch. A few drinks inevitably led to an ax-handle party, as they called the fights that broke out spontaneously when a man was criticized or insulted.

Maggie had seen a few fights, several of them involving her father, which she found rather frightening. For the most part, however, the men were too tired after a twelve-hour day to have the energy to batter each other, which was a good thing. An injured man was of no use to his employer, and a battle between loggers tended to be brutal.

She covered Celeste now, then took off her own dress and

shoes and stockings, and crawled into the bunk beside her sister.

A few minutes later Jake came in and undressed in the dark. Maggie spoke to him softly. "Daddy, is Grandma going to come and live with us, now that Grandpa's dead?"

"Christ, I hope not," Jake muttered. Then he bent over her, smelling of chewing tobacco and honest sweat and wool underwear. "Don't worry about it, sweetheart. We'll figure out some way to take care of Grandma."

"Mama says if we had a bigger house it would be easier."

He made a sound she couldn't interpret, somewhere between a groan and a laugh. "Yeah, and if I was a millionaire, that would make it easier, too. Good night, honey."

She lay awake after he'd begun to snore, reveling in her presence here in the woods in the little shack, knowing that her father was only an arm's-length away. Jake would make everything all right, as he always did, she thought; and then, curled around Celeste's small, warm body, she slept, too.


Like most accidents, it should never have happened. It wouldn't have if the new man, Hank Pallison, had known what he was doing.

Maggie was at the cookhouse with Celeste, helping to stir up the dough that would eventually become gigantic oatmeal cookies, rich with brown sugar, for the supper table.

In the distant, sun-drenched woods, a man shouted.

There was nothing unusual about that, and at first the cookhouse crew paid no attention. Mr. Murphy poked more wood into the iron stove, and held his hand briefly inside the oven. "It's about ready. You got a pan for me, Maggie?"

She dropped the last generous spoonful of dough onto the cookie sheet and was swinging it toward him when they heard the whistle punk's signal: a four-four. Four longs, four shorts.

Mr. Murphy swore. He took the unbaked cookies from Maggie and put them on the big, scrubbed table, then headed for the door.

"What's the matter?" Celeste asked, her blue eyes widening.

"An accident," Maggie said. There was a tight, painful constriction in her chest; she remembered what those women had said about deaths coming in threes, and their speculation that the next one might be in the woods.

"It's not Papa, is it?" Celeste demanded, but Maggie scarcely heard her. She was out of the doorway, running after Mr. Murphy, hearing more shouting now. She had listened to the men enough to interpret the tone of their voices before she could make out the words; the accident was a bad one.

"Margaret, wait for me!" Celeste cried, and Maggie slowed, looking around for her sister. Suddenly, feeling sick and weak, she didn't want to know who had been hurt.

"Margaret, it's not Papa, is it?"

"I don't know. How can I know, until we get there?" She took Celeste's hand and walked now, rather than ran, toward the place where men were shouting orders, though the shouts had ceased by the time the girls reached the scene.

It was not Jake on the ground; she saw his red plaid shirt at once and felt something break within her, allowing her painful breath to escape. Nor was it Angus McKay, though his face was very pale beneath the growth of blond beard.

"Angus, what is it?"

The man on the ground, with Jake and several others kneeling beside him, was the owner of the logging outfit,

Ed Newsome. The girls were close enough to see the blood—so much blood—and Celeste suddenly blanched and clutched convulsively at her sister.

Angus looked down at them, putting out a hand to Maggie's shoulder to hold her back. "Stay here, out of the way. Your pa will handle it."

"What happened?" Maggie demanded.

The woods had fallen silent, the men standing in a ragged circle around the victim; not even the raucous call of a jay disturbed the quiet. All Maggie heard was Angus's breathing, and her own.

"Ed got caught in the bight. Pallison went to pull the wire tight, and it lashed out and caught him in the head."

From his position on his knees, Jake turned and shouted. "McKay, I need some towels!"

Angus spun and took off on the run. Jake gestured to several of the watching men. "We gotta have a stretcher. Murphy, he looks bad. We better get the wagon out, get him to town and a doctor, if he lasts that long."

Mr. Murphy nodded and moved past the children as fast as his bulk and his years would allow. Celeste shrank away from him, trembling.

"What is it, Margaret?"

Maggie's mouth was dry, though her relief that it was not Jake made liquid of her bowels. "Mr. Newsome got hit in the head with the end of the wire rope. There was a kink in it, and Pallison must have jerked on it to straighten it out, and it flipped around. It happened to Red Risku once, and knocked out two of his teeth."

Clearly, this time it had done more damage than to teeth. Ed Newsome was carried on the door hastily removed from the cookhouse to where Mr. Murphy had harnessed the horses to the wagon. Bedrolls were brought from the bunkhouse to pad the wagon bed; the girls watched as Ed Newsome was lifted into it.

"Is he dead?" Celeste whispered.

"I don't think so," Maggie murmured back, though she wasn't sure. The man's face was unrecognizable, a bloody pulp, and his right arm and shoulder hung at an angle suggesting a broken collarbone.

Beside her, Maggie heard Jim Ballantine mutter, "Jesus, looks like it took one ear right off."

His companion cursed in agreement. "Poor bastard's got a tit in the wringer, for sure. He don't look to me like he'll make it to town, not long enough for the sawbones to do him no good."

The language, familiar to Maggie's ears, was not of the sort that would bear repeating in Ann's presence. Maggie looked at her little sister to warn her of this, only to remain silent. Celeste had not heard; she was watching the grisly drama in horrified petrification.

Maggie was acutely aware of all activity, too, but her eyes had gone beyond the battered body of the boss. Hank Pallison stood alone, opening and closing his fists, his eyes red-rimmed.

Pallison had been on the job only a few weeks, and Maggie didn't know him except by name. He was a big man, heavy through the chest and shoulders; he'd had a bit of a paunch when he'd arrived, which told even Maggie that he was not a logger by trade. Men who worked as hard as loggers seldom had an ounce of superfluous flesh.

She'd heard him referred to as a shagpoke-gut, the woodsmen's term for a voracious eater; in the company of many hearty eaters, it usually meant the others considered the new man to be something of a pig.

Pallison was a good-looking man in his late thirties, easygoing, and given to story-telling. To hear him tell it, Jake had remarked, you'd think he'd been around the world twice and tried everything at least once. The others had enjoyed his tales, though; entertainment was hard to come by in their lives, and they'd listened with only minimal ridicule to the implausible epics Pallison related.

Now, as Ed Newsome was made as comfortable as possible for the long trip to town—though what difference it made to a man who was unconscious was a question—the muttering grew louder. Maggie felt the hostility as well as heard it in the familiar voices.

"I told Ed last week that Pallison was throwing the rope over the top. He's careless, he don't think what he's doing."

"Ed warned him about being in the bight; I heard him. Pallison said he'd watch it, and now he's gone and done exactly what he was warned against, the damn fool."

"It's too bad that Pallison don't have two heads," Risku remarked, almost loud enough for the words to carry to the subject of them, "so we could knock them together."

It was a common expression, usually offered with wry humor; today, there was an underlying animosity in the remark that made Maggie apprehensive. She glanced at Pallison, but the man gave no indication that he'd heard. As she watched, Pallison stepped to the wagon, looking downward at his victim, and spoke hoarsely to Jake Keating.

"He's gonna make it, ain't he? He ain't gonna die?"

Jake gave him a level look as he leaped down from the wagon bed. "Nobody but the good Lord can tell you that one. If he lasts 'til the boys get him to town where the doc can work on him, he might pull through."

Beads of perspiration stood on Hank Pallison's brow. "You think I ought to go along with him? See what I can do?"

Beside Maggie, Jim Ballantine swore. "Done plenty already, and all of it bad, you ask me."

"Yeah. Damned if I want him working alongside o'

me," Risku agreed. "Get him the hell out o' the woods and we'll all live longer."

Pallison went red as he waited for Jake's decision. As usual, Jake wasted little time in making up his mind. "All right. You drive the wagon—careful, mind you, don't dump him over—and McKay, you ride in the back with Ed. After you deliver him to the doc's place, you better go fetch his wife. And hope to God," Jake concluded, "that by that time she's not a widow."

He turned from the wagon, leaving Newsome now to the appointed men. "Come on, let's get moving some timber."

It was taken for granted that Jake would give orders in Ed Newsome's absence. Subdued, they picked up their tools and went back to work.

The third death? Maggie wondered. Or would Newsome live? And in that case, whose would be the third death the gossiping women had predicted?

# 6

ED Newsome did not die. Angus McKay brought the wagon back alone, leaving it to Mr. Murphy to unhitch the horses while he reported to Jake.

"Doc says he's in bad shape, but he wasn't dead yet when I left. His wife was there with him. The side of his head is stove in." Angus cleared his throat. "Might be better if he never wakes up, considering how bad he's hurt. Doc says the bone splinters are bound to be sticking into his brain.''

Jake swore in grief and futile frustration. "Where's Hank Pallison?''

"Getting drunk.''

"First sensible thing I've seen the man do,'' Red Risku snorted. "And as useful as anything else at this stage of things. What's going to happen now, Jake?''

Jake's whiskered jaw firmed. "We're going back to work. We're supposed to have another two thousand feet of prime Douglas fir on the landing when Horsman is ready for it, and it's going to be there. Let's go.''

They were a subdued crew who gathered for supper that night. There was no laughing or teasing, and though the biscuits were burned on the bottom because Mr. Murphy had been preoccupied and hadn't watched them close enough, nobody even commented.

Ann met them at the door when they returned home, her face revealing her concern.

"Mama and I talked to Mrs. Newsome. It looks very bad for Ed.'' Her lip quivered; any such accident struck close to home, because every wife knew that next time it might be her own husband who was the victim.

Jake slung his jacket over the back of a chair and moved toward the fireplace to warm his hands. "I know. I saw how his head was caved in.''

"What will it mean to the operation? They're saying in town that Ed won't live, and that his logging show will shut down. That'll put everybody out of work.''

"If somebody doesn't run it, it'll be so dead the buzzards wouldn't touch it,'' Jake admitted. "I thought about it all the way home. Ann, I'm going to talk to his wife, see if she'll sell me the operation, guts, feathers, and all.''

She stared at him, an arm unconsciously circling each of her daughters as she drew them close against her bulging belly. "How? With what? How could you buy it? Jake, we don't have any money. Do we?"

"Not a hell of a lot, but maybe I can scrape up enough. Look at it this way. If she leaves it alone, it'll just die. She won't have anything but that cabin they live in. If I can keep it going, split the profits between her and us, why, we'll all be better off. I've been waiting for a chance for a show of my own for years, and maybe this is it. I hate to see it come at Ed's expense; and if he gets better, why, nobody will be gladder than I will. But it's not too likely to happen, and certainly not in time to salvage the present operation. The timber we're falling right now is already sold. Ed had an order for it, and if I keep everybody moving, we'll deliver it on time. I'm the only one out there able to do it, keep them all working, get the timber to the landing. I'll go talk to Sarah Newsome tomorrow."

His talk was delayed, however, because that night Ann went into labor, nearly a month early.

Maggie woke up and knew at once what the sounds were in the next room, though she did not remember them from when Celeste was born. She slid out of bed and walked quietly out into the main room.

"Daddy? Is Mama having the baby?"

Jake turned from the bedroom door. "Yes, honey, she is. You go on back to bed. I'm going to go for Grandma and the doctor."

"Shouldn't I stay with Mama, then?" Maggie asked seriously.

He hesitated, then spoke to his wife. "Ann, would you like Maggie to sit with you?"

"I won't sleep, anyway" Maggie asserted. "And maybe I can help."

"Having a baby can be a messy business," Jake said uncertainly. "I wouldn't want you to upset your mama by getting upset yourself."

"Having a baby isn't any worse than being caught in the bight, is it? Or falling off the top of a tree?"

Ann's voice came on a soft gasp. "Let her stay, Jake. Fetch Mama, and hurry, please!"

Maggie stayed quite calm after her father had gone. She built up the fire in the stove and put on another kettle to heat water to bathe the baby when it came. Then she sat beside her mother's bed, waiting.

Charlie was born only moments after Millicent and Jake arrived, much to Maggie's disappointment. She felt she could have done the whole thing herself, had not Grandma shooed her out of the room at the last minute. When the baby cried, however, Millicent called out to her. "Margaret Ellen! Come and take the baby and keep him warm while I attend your mama."

The infant was put into her arms, tiny, frail, yet exquisitely beautiful, so different from the way she remembered Celeste. Maggie cradled him against her breast, touching one of the little hands with a forefinger, crooning instinctively to him. When Millicent came to take him away, she was reluctant to let her grandmother have him.

"Came too soon," Millicent muttered. "He's awfully small, Jake."

"The Keatings are a sturdy lot," Jake said. "He'll grow."

Maggie watched their faces, trying to read the slightest nuance of vocal inflection, the attempt to keep their concerns from showing.

Neither of the adults suggested that Charlie might be too small to survive, but Maggie felt uneasiness swell within her, and she prayed for the new little brother.

Ann recovered slowly from the ordeal of childbirth, though since Charlie was premature and very small, the birth had not been a difficult one. The weather turned bad, with rain drenching the landscape; it sluiced the last of the gold and brown leaves from the alders and maples, leaving a landscape cold and dreary without sunshine.

Ed Newsome's wife had agreed readily to Jake's proposal; it was obvious that her husband was not going to return to his own logging operation for months, if indeed he ever returned at all. Jake begged and borrowed what money he could to pay for equipment; the house that Ann had been hoping for must wait a little longer, Jake said, and to her credit Ann didn't protest. Tired as she was of the small house, and concerned about a place for her mother, she recognized that Newsome's tragedy could be Jake's golden opportunity. If the logging operation thrived, the Keatings would thrive with it.

Millicent walked over some days, but she found it difficult to battle wind and rain and cold; with her husband's passing, something had gone permanently out of her makeup. She no longer had any taste for struggle against nature. Had there been a place for her to sleep she might have moved in with her daughter; but after Jake had returned home once after Millicent and Ann had gone to bed together, forcing him to make an uncomfortable pallet before the kitchen fire, the widow dared not assume that she was welcome in his home.

And so, on the days that Millicent did not come, and Ann lay wearily in bed or dragged herself around to care for the new infant, more and more of the daily chores fell upon Maggie.

At ten, she was quite capable of learning to knead the bread dough and form it into loaves, and to fix stews and soups and beans of which their winter diet consisted. Celeste was eager to help, too, at least at first, and in relief Ann gave them full rein.

Maggie's favorite "chore" was caring for Charlie. He was so tiny, yet so perfect. She learned to bathe him and change him, and when she did not have other things that must be done, she would hold the baby and rock him and sing to him.

The dolls came for Christmas, and they were as lovely as promised, but no doll could compare with a living, breathing child. While Celeste played with her doll, Maggie played with Charlie.

Shortly after Christmas, the woods were shut down by deep snows.

Maggie loved snow. She wanted to bundle Charlie up and take him for a ride on the sled through the miraculously beautiful wonderland, but Ann said no. Charlie was too small, too frail. He was growing, but not as fast as he should have. Charlie must stay inside by the fire.

So Maggie and Celeste romped outside with the other village children, and walked over to visit their grandmother and eat her freshly baked cookies, and, for the time the snow lasted, to be children again.

At first Maggie was glad to have Jake at home every day. But Jake was a man uncomfortable in a confined area, a man used to considerably physical exercise, and there was only so much need for chopping wood and repairing the small house. He began to join his comrades during the afternoons and evenings, occasionally neglecting to come home even for supper; when he did return, after the children had gone to bed, Maggie would hear her parents' voices, her mother's angry, her father's ranging from pacifying to irritated, and she would pray that they would not quarrel anymore.

As the winter wore on, Jake's restlessness infected them all. "If the damned snow would melt, we could get back to work," he'd say, gazing out at the blanket of white over the surrounding fields and houses. "I think I'll go over and see how Ed is."

Ed Newsome was recovering very slowly. He could sit up now, and he knew who his visitors were, but his speech was labored and difficult to understand, and he had no use of his right arm, though the doctor did not exactly know why. When pressed on the issue, he remarked with some justification, "The man's lucky to be alive at all. Don't expect miracles, Mrs. Newsome; just count your blessings."

After the duty call on Ed Newsome, Jake had no inclination to return to the small house filled with drying diapers and noisy children and a wife who found him nearly as annoying when he was underfoot as when he stayed away altogether. It was easier to drop in at the Logger's Saloon, where there were always men to talk and drink with, to pass what remained of the afternoon.

On one such day, the weather turned so bad that Ann kept the children inside after a session when they'd built a pair of snowmen and soaked their garments so that the odor of drying wool was added to that of Charlie's diapers and the stew that simmered for the evening meal. The snow came down in great flakes, wiping out Jake's tracks and those of the children, clinging to the cedars so that the boughs bent beneath the weight of it. Charlie wailed thinly and incessantly, and no amount of rocking by either Ann or Maggie could console him.

"Mama, he's hot," Maggie said, resting a palm on the tiny forehead.

"I know. If only your father would come home, I could send him for the doctor." She scooped up the baby and held him against her shoulder, pressing her cheek against the velvety softness of Charlie's head. "I don't know if he could do anything, but I'd feel better about it. Charlie, darling, don't cry, don't cry!"

"I could go for the doctor," Maggie offered.

For a matter of seconds, Ann considered the proposal. Then, "No, dear, I don't think so. It's going to be dark very shortly, and the snow is getting so deep. Surely Papa will come soon, and then he'll fetch the doctor."

But Jake did not come. Beyond the windows the snow continued to fall; twilight turned to full darkness, and Ann and the children ate their supper alone and left the kettle on the back of the stove for Jake.

It was increasingly obvious that Charlie was very ill. His cries subsided into whimpers, and then to no protest at all; he lay passively on his mother's breast, limp, dangerously hot.

"Maybe I should go for the doctor," Ann speculated, "though I daren't take Charlie with me. Maybe you could hold him, Margaret, until I get back."

"I'll hold him," Maggie agreed at once.

"You'd better go to bed, Celeste. It's late. And you, Margaret, don't fall asleep and drop him. I'll be back as fast as I can."

Ann bundled herself as warmly as possible, wrapping a scarf around her face so as not to chill her lungs by breathing the icy air before it was warmed a little. There was a terrible blast of arctic air when she opened the door, and then she vanished into the night.

"I don't want to go to bed," Celeste said.

"You'd better get your nightdress on, anyway. Maybe Daddy will meet her, and she'll be back right away. Go on, Celeste, and then you can sit before the fire until you're sleepy."

The child stared at her little brother, sagging against Maggie's chest as if he'd given up. "Margaret, he isn't going to die, is he? Charlie isn't going to die like Grandpa?"

Maggie's throat felt sore. "I don't know. Maybe if we prayed about it, God would make him better," she suggested.

God did not make him better. And a quarter of an hour after Ann had left, the door suddenly burst open, bringing both girls to their feet as their mother stumbled into the room.

There was a great bloody gash on her forehead; the blood had not run down into her eyes because it had frozen there. Her lashes were encrusted with snow, as well, and tears sparkled in icy droplets.

Ann stared at them with bleak blue eyes. "I couldn't make it," she said, exhausted. "I fell and hurt myself, and I couldn't see. I got turned around, and I couldn't find the road at all, the snow is so deep. . . ." Her breath caught on a sob. "It's so cold, and I kept falling. . . ."

She put a hand to her head and brought away a mitten smeared with red, at which she stared blankly. "How's Charlie?"

"The same," Maggie said. "Very hot." She felt terrified. She had counted so heavily on the doctor being able to do something for Charlie, and her mother hadn't even reached him. The baby felt as if he were burning a hole through the front of her dress.

Tears spilled over and ran freely down Ann's face, though she didn't seem to notice them. With stiff fingers she peeled off her outer layers of clothing, then reached for the baby, sucking in a shocked breath when she touched his fevered body.

"His breathing sounds strange. How long has he been sounding this way?"

"I don't know. Maybe, maybe I could find my way. I've walked it so many times—"

"No. No," Ann said decisively, "it's terrible out there. I would be frantic about you. You wouldn't find the road, not in the dark, and it's still snowing so heavily. Surely your father will be home soon!"

Jake did not come, however, and nobody went to bed. Maggie kept putting wood on the fire, yet the room seemed colder and colder. Except for Charlie, the heat was not enough to warm them.

Ed Newsome hadn't died, Maggie thought. Did that mean the third death would be Charlie's? Was it true that death came in threes? She wanted to ask her mother, but she didn't dare.

Celeste fell asleep on the hearth at last, and Maggie was very tired, too, yet she had the dreadful feeling that if she closed her eyes, something awful would happen to Charlie. It had been distressing when he cried; it was worse now that he did not.

Maggie sprang up to unlatch the door when Jake finally called out. He kicked snow off his boots, swept off his knitted cap and slapped it against his knee to dislodge the worst of the lacy flakes, and stepped over the threshold.

"Daddy, Charlie's awful sick," Maggie told him. "He needs a doctor."

There was the smell of whiskey on him, though Jake was not drunk. Immediate concern swept over his face as he strode toward his wife in the rocking chair. "How bad is he? Jesus!" He had touched the tiny cheek with one finger. "How long's he been like this?"

"All afternoon," Ann said, holding her voice level with an effort, unable to completely conceal her frustration and fury. "If you'd come home, I'd have sent you for the doctor hours ago, before it was dark."

He stared at the wound on her head; she had attempted to do nothing with it, and the dried blood was a dark, jagged slash against her white skin. "What happened?"

"I fell. I left the baby here with Margaret and tried to go for the doctor myself, and I fell and cut my head." Her voice rose, wavering out of control. "I couldn't see the road, and I was bleeding, and I had to come back. Jake, why didn't you come home?"

He moistened his lips and brushed at his beard with the back of one hand. "I was just talking to the men, planning for spring. I didn't know there was anything wrong, honey."

"But you didn't care enough to come home and see, did you? The house could have burned down, the baby could have died. . . ."

The terrible word had been said. Maggie swallowed and saw the fear in her parents' faces, and her hands curled into painful fists against her thighs.

"I'll go get him now," Jake said quietly, and pulled the cap back over his dark hair. "I'm sorry, Ann, I didn't know, but I'll get the doctor now."

After he had gone, Ann sat in the rocking chair, crying silently, and there was nothing Maggie could say or do to comfort her.

Jake returned with the doctor three-quarters of an hour later, but it was too late. Charlie died within minutes of the time they got there.

"He wasn't strong enough," the doctor said sadly. "He came too early in the first place, and he just wasn't strong enough."

Ann seemed not to have heard his words. Clasping the infant to her breast, eyes streaming, she stared at her husband and said the awful words, words Maggie could not forget as long as she lived.

"I'll never forgive you, Jake. I'll never forgive you for this."

Jake took a step toward her, putting out a hand, and she moved away, out of his reach.

"It would have made a difference if you'd been here when you should have been," Ann said, too engulfed in her own anguish to consider his.

The doctor, a middle-aged man already worn out from the duties of the day, remonstrated mildly. "Mrs. Keating, it's doubtful I could have done anything for the child even if I'd been here. He's been ailing since birth, and the winter's a severe one. Several infants have died, through no fault of anyone's. He simply wasn't strong enough. With your history of miscarriages . . ."

Ann didn't hear. She rocked the baby as if this still mattered, and Maggie moved against her father's side until he drew her into his arms and held her, their tears mingling. Tears for Charlie, and tears for themselves, and Maggie wondered in despair if their lives would ever be happy again.

# 7

MISCARRIAGES were one thing, and they'd been bad enough. The death of a child she had held and nursed and loved, even for only three months, was another. Ann was inconsolable. While she did collapse into Jake's arms and seemingly accept what he was able to offer in the way of solace, her grief was terrible to see.

The day after Charlie's death, the atmosphere in the Keating house was so thick with pain that Maggie escaped from it into the outdoors.

The snow had stopped falling and left a soft cover over her world. She stared across the fields where the sun glinted from every surface, struck by the incongruous beauty of the landscape on such a sad day. How could it all be so beautiful, when Charlie would never see it?

Maggie wandered toward the woods, breaking a trail through the virgin whiteness, unable to stanch the tears.

She had been touched by her mother's sorrow when Grandpa Miles had died, though remaining relatively unaffected by his death herself. This time, the anguish threatened to tear her apart. She moved blindly, occasionally wiping at her face with a mittened hand, until she stumbled over a hidden root and fell. The snow was cold on her face, and she'd scraped her wrist where the mitten had slid down; Maggie got up as far as her knees and then folded forward, wracked with sobs.

She didn't know how long she knelt there, but it must have been for some time, because the cold had seeped through her garments and her legs ached with cramps when she heard the voice.

"Maggie? Maggie, you all right?"

She lifted a swollen, reddened face to see Angus McKay standing over her, tall and with a countenance reflecting her own sorrow.

"They're worried about you," Angus said, reaching out a hand to pull her to her feet. "You've been gone for hours."

Maggie had thought herself drained of tears, yet now a few more squeezed between the puffy eyelids. She leaned into him and cried, "Charlie died, Angus! He was so little and so helpless, and he died, and Mama thinks it was Daddy's fault because he didn't come home in time to fetch the doctor!"

Angus brought his arms around her, hugging her close to him. "Babies die, Maggie. Everybody dies, sooner or later. Your mama's very upset, and she said things she didn't really mean. Your pa wasn't to blame, the doctor said so. Nobody's necessarily to blame when someone dies. Come on, you're half-frozen. Come home and get warmed up and have something to eat. The neighbors have brought in food."

"I'm not hungry," Maggie said, her voice muffled in his midsection. "I don't care if I never eat anything again."

Angus continued to hug her, the warmth of his body gradually coming through their heavy clothing to her. "I felt that way, too, when *my* little brother died."

Maggie lifted her head to look at him. "I didn't know you had a little brother who died."

"Actually, I had a little brother and an older sister who died. Elizabeth was a lot older, and I didn't feel so fond of her, but Andrew—Andrew was a lot like Charlie. Very small, and we didn't have him long before he died. I expect he and Charlie are together now."

"In heaven, you mean. Grandma says Charlie's in heaven." Her voice was thick; she had cried so much that her head and nose were all stopped up. "I guess that's supposed to make us feel better, but I don't. What good's heaven? Oh, Angus, I didn't want him to die!"

Angus hugged her to his side and began to walk her back across the frozen expanse, between the dark firs and cedars of the woods. "Nobody ever wants anyone else to die. Well, mostly they don't. Didn't you listen to any of those sermons your grandpa preached? Heaven is where we'll all get together again someday. It means Charlie isn't missing forever. He'll be waiting when the rest of us get there. When *you* get there. Right now you're missing him, but eventually you'll see him again, and after a while thinking about that will make you feel better."

Maggie sniffed. She didn't know if she believed that or not. All she knew was that never again, in this life—the only life that mattered at present—would she hold her little brother and feel the warmth of his body against her, or see his toothless smile.

"I don't want to go home, Angus. I can't bear to see Mama."

"Your mama needs you, Maggie. So does your pa. Your whole family needs to stick together now."

She could see the logic of that, but she wasn't sure how well her parents were going to stick together, not with Mama blaming Daddy for not getting the doctor in time. She reached out, from habit, and tugged at the end of a snow-laden cedar bough; when she released it, it sprang upward, sending a shower of wet snow over them.

The two of them left the woods and headed out across the open field, crossing her tracks, and then those that Angus had made, and for once there was no joy in tramping through the fresh snow. Maggie's eyes ached, squinting into the glare of it, and she closed them and allowed Angus to steer her with an arm around her shoulders.

That was all that happened with Angus that day. Maggie was not immediately aware of any change in their relationship. It was not until days later when she rose from bed at night to ask for another blanket against the freezing cold that she became more aware.

The house was silent, and she thought her parents had gone to bed. There was no lighted lamp, only the glow from the dying fire in the fireplace to light the main room of the house when Maggie emerged on silent bare feet.

She had turned toward the door of her parents' bedroom and opened her mouth to speak when she saw them, standing in silhouette before the hearth.

Ann and Jake stood wrapped in each other's arms, pressed tightly together; Ann's head was uplifted and they were kissing each other.

Maggie had seldom seen anything of a demonstrative nature beyond an occasional touching of hands. Once in a while her father would pat her mother on the backside as he passed, grinning when Ann protested that such behavior was unseemly before the children.

She did not ever remember seeing them kiss in this way before. It was not a gentle soothing kiss such as either of them bestowed upon their daughters. There was an urgency in their stance, a fervor, that Maggie recognized as being different; it was disturbing in its intensity, though she did not know why.

Maggie stood there, forgetting to breathe, and wondered that her mother did not cry out in pain, so tightly was she crushed against her husband's body. Yet her arms were around his neck and it seemed that she, too, was a part of the force, the violence that Maggie sensed between them.

Hesitating, the child stood there unseen as her mother groaned and then was swept off her feet and carried into the bedroom.

Was Mama sick? Maggie wondered, yet something made her think not, and prevented her from calling out. She stood in the darkness, her feet growing icy. She wondered what it was like to be a grownup, and suddenly in her mind's eye Maggie imagined herself straining in such a compelling embrace as she had just witnessed, and the man in her vision was Angus McKay.

It made her feel strange and dizzy and vaguely sick, yet the fascination of it persisted after she'd returned to her bed and curled against her sister to get warm. Was it wrong to think of herself hugging a man, kissing him? Probably Grandpa Miles would have said so, yet she could not believe that her mother would do anything wrong, and she had been hugging Daddy. Of course, they were married, and she knew that somehow that made a difference, though she did not quite understand why.

In the morning she watched her parents for some indication of how they felt about the events of the past night. They were the same as always, however; Jake was jovial and ate heartily of the thick sourdough pancakes, Ann cooked and served and spoke softly, and rested a hand on each of her daughters' shoulders in a gesture of affection before they went off to the village school.

After that, for a time, whenever Maggie thought of Angus, her mind shied away, though he crept insidiously into her thoughts more often, and she could not always control her imagination.

The snow lasted another week, and then one morning they awoke to the sound of dripping eaves; on the way to school that day the children all played at sword-fighting with two- and three-foot icicles, and threw snowballs that packed readily from the slush. In the afternoon, they all returned home with their coats unbuttoned and scarves undone. By the following day, the snow remained only in the sheltered places untouched by the sun, beneath heavy trees and in deep gullies.

"Spring," Jake said with satisfaction. "Thank God. We'll be back in the woods before long."

Spring. Charlie was gone, and though Mama sometimes looked sad, she no longer cried all the time. Maggie felt the first faint lifting of her heart and prayed that Mama would allow her, too, to return to the healing serenity of the woods.

Being boss of an outfit was different from being head faller.

"I need to be out there all the time," Jake said. "Come with me, Ann. For the summer, anyway. Bring the girls and stay with me. We'll put up a cabin, something small and easy to take care of. You won't even have to cook; we can eat at the camp cookhouse. I just want my family together. We'll be working close enough to the landing, on both sides of the river, so that we could live there all summer, probably."

"Farther upstream than where you were last year," Ann said faintly.

"A few miles farther," Jake admitted. "What do you think, girls? You want to live in a cabin in the woods?"

Ann spoke over their enthusiastic chorus. "That's not fair! You knew what *they'd* want!" She didn't sound angry or petulant, though, Maggie noted hopefully.

"Well, doesn't it matter, what they think? They like it in the woods, honey. You would, too, if you'd let yourself enjoy it."

"We wouldn't get into town all summer, probably. Mr. Cathcart is going to fix up the Athenaeum Building into an opera house and a meeting place. I told Elsie I'd help when they were ready to put on musicals and plays, and there will be dances and plays. . . ."

Her wistfulness did not escape her older daughter. Maggie stifled an indrawn breath, sure that her newfound enthusiasm was about to be doused in cold water.

Jake, however, had thought this out carefully. "The Athenaeum will still be there in the fall. In fact, they aren't likely to be ready to go with it before then, anyway. There's still a lot to do. Listen, Ann. This first year is going to be difficult. But if all goes well, next year will be a lot better. Maybe I can buy the Newsomes out completely by then. But even if I can't, I'll have paid back what I borrowed to pay for the equipment, and more of what the timber brings will be mine. Spend a summer with me at the landing, Ann, and next year I'll start building your house. The *real* house you've been wanting."

Maggie watched her mother's face, the play of emotion across it that was almost as poignant as it had been when Charlie died. She had heard her mother "talk new house," as Jake called it, many times. Not until now had she realized the depth of this yearning, and Maggie's own burning desire dimmed somewhat before her mother's need.

"Jake, do you promise? Do you promise we'll build the house?"

Victory within sight, Jake would have promised anything. "By next summer," he said, and swept his wife into his arms for an exuberant kiss that made Celeste laugh.

Maggie didn't laugh. She knew that her father meant the promise at the moment he made it, but she was not certain that he felt as strongly about promises as Mama did. And she felt a deep-seated conviction that this promise was extremely important to her mother.

She was happy, though, that they were going to the woods for the whole summer. In fact, the more Maggie thought about it, the more the swelling gladness inside her dominated every thought, every action.

As soon as the summer cabin was built, they would go, and her world would begin to settle back into one of contentment.

*      *      *

The summer of 1880 was a milestone in Maggie's life. It was the year she watched her mother struggle to make do in a primitive one-room cabin with a lean-to added where the little girls slept. Ann was introduced to the woods at first hand, and she found them alarming and, at times, terrifying.

The first—and last—time she saw Jake top a tree, she went so deathly white that Maggie feared she would faint. The actual operation of removing the top of a tree took no more than five or ten minutes; to Ann they seemed an eternity.

Jake climbed the cedar as easily as he walked across a road. This one was well over two hundred feet in height; he stopped a dozen feet short of its top and proceeded to use first an ax, and then a small saw, to undercut the upper section of the tree.

Ann watched with apprehension at the height of the climber, and then clasped both hands over her mouth to stifle the scream when Jake suddenly kicked the top loose.

The remaining section of the tree whipped wildly as its top crashed away through surrounding boughs; it seemed to Ann that her husband would surely be thrown to the ground and killed.

The backlash was brief, and ceased before Ann could draw a much needed breath; then Jake was moving down the straight, tall trunk with the agility of years of practice.

"It's all right, Mama," Maggie said, pressing close to Ann's side. "He did it just right, the way he always does."

Ann was in a moderate state of shock. "You mean that's the way it's done? All the time?"

"He likes it, kicking out the top. They all do," Maggie said earnestly. "It's fun to sway back and forth that way."

Simply imagining it made Ann dizzy and sick. "My God. Oh, Margaret, I'm so glad you and Celeste are girls! I couldn't bear to think of one of my children up there! . . ."

She swallowed and turned away; she was still chalky when Jake came over to exchange his small saw for a larger one ten minutes later.

He didn't even notice her perturbation. "Maggie, honey, run and tell Mr. Murphy to put back dinner an hour. We want to get this job finished before we break for noon. Celeste, get Daddy a dipper of water, will you?"

To her credit, Ann did not spill out her fears to Jake. If she continued to quake inwardly, she did it in silence; though when there was an unexpected shout she held her breath until it was clear that there was no emergency, no accident, only the routine of bringing down the gigantic trees.

The cabin Jake and the others had thrown up near the river was crude indeed compared to their snug little house in Snohomish. The fact that there was no need for her to cook, and that cleaning responsibilities were lessened, because there was no need to sweep a dirt floor and it was pointless to dust, did not really provide Ann with a life of ease. The laundry must, as always, be done on a washboard in water hauled laboriously from the Pilchuck River. There were beds to be made, garments to be sewed, knitted, or mended, and little diversion to be had when she was not busy with those tasks.

The hardest thing for Ann was the lack of female companionship. She had mixed feelings about her mother, for whom she felt profound sorrow. Millicent had been emotionally as well as physically and financially dependent upon her husband. Besides being lost with no one to cook and clean and care for, she was inept at chopping her own wood and hauling her own water and doing those things that made a cabin secure for winter. She was nervous being alone, yet unable to control her grief and anxiety when in the company of others, so that she was not exactly a sought-after companion.

Still, though she got on Ann's nerves, too, to some

extent, Millicent was company. She had reared Ann, had instilled in her daughter her own ideas and ideals, and in many ways they thought alike. Ann missed her when they were apart for more than a day or two.

Having her in the makeshift home on the river would have been impossible even had Millicent cared to travel that far from friends and village. There was simply no room and no privacy. Indeed, the girls were getting to an age where Ann felt strongly that a real house was becoming a necessity; Jake's lovemaking tended toward the robust side, and Ann was constantly admonishing him to remember that his daughters might hear if he did not take care to be quiet. Ann knew that if her mother had been there, on a pallet before the stove which was the only conceivable place for her to sleep, Ann would have been too inhibited to indulge Jake's sexual appetites at all.

The image of the promised house hung ever in Ann's mind, and she talked about it constantly. There would be a first parlor, for visitors, as well as a family parlor for everyday use, a pantry large enough to hold a winter's supplies, and a kitchen with both a fireplace and a modern iron stove for cooking. There would be water piped inside so that no longer would they have to carry it for bathing and laundering. There would be a bedroom for each of them, and one for Millicent, too, where she could live out her old age in security and comfort.

The Montgomery Ward catalog grew tattered as Ann pored over it, weighing the advantages of various fabrics for window hangings and carpets and wall lamps. She would, eventually, have a complete set of fancy painted china for entertaining. The possibilities took her mind off the dangerous work that Jake did to earn their living.

Ann was an accomplished seamstress and enjoyed the hours she spent stitching for her family; had there been another female to share those hours, she might have been quite content. As it was, there was only Celeste, who at eight could not be trusted to complete a garment without frequent inspection and continual supervision, and who wanted to be entertained by stories rather than contributing to Ann's own entertainment.

Maggie was made to spend a part of each day sewing, too, but the results were so poor that Ann despaired of ever seeing a project of wearable quality. Maggie chafed under the restrictions of spending time indoors, let alone sitting still in a chair, and her stitches were too large and of uneven size. Had it not been that Ann believed every woman must master the art of sewing, she would have given up on her older daughter sooner than she did. Maggie seemed to have no housewifely virtues at all except for cooking, and then she followed the lead of Mr. Murphy toward hearty, filling meals with no attempt to set a gracious table.

To Maggie, the summer was sheer delight. She was back in her beloved woods, mingling with the men who didn't worry about such things as neat stitches or tidy cabins, free to roam on her own for a good part of each day.

Sometimes Celeste came with her; more often Maggie went alone. And increasingly Maggie ventured to whatever part of the job was currently occupying Angus McKay.

It made her feel peculiar now when she was with him, because it was impossible not to remember her thoughts after she'd seen her parents in a passionate embrace. Once Angus looked over and said, "Your face is red, Maggie. Maybe you'd ought to be wearing a hat."

She didn't need a hat, she knew. It was only that the blood rushed to her face when she thought about being close in that same way to Angus, someday, when she was older.

It was clear that he thought of her as a little girl,

perhaps like one of his younger sisters. He teased her and
told her stories about the rest of the world and answered
freely when she asked questions. (Like Jake, Angus
could and did read, anything he could put his hands on.)
Above all, Angus listened when she talked. He was the
only person she knew with whom her speech was unre-
strained on the subject of herself, her sister, and the
death of her little brother. If she spoke of Charlie at
home, tears would come to her mother's eyes, and
Maggie did not want to inflict more wounds on one
already so wounded. Yet the need to speak of Charlie
was strong, and Angus listened.

By her eleventh birthday, Maggie knew she was hopelessly
in love with Angus.

## 8

HER love had grown through that eleventh summer, and
the years that followed. Angus, like everybody else, seemed
unaware of her devotion to him.

It had been a busy time for the adults around her. Jake
worked hard, determined to deck enough logs to pay off
his debts; he hired more men and drove the crews to their
limits, felling timber, hauling it to the landing, impatient
for the rise in the river in December when the logs could
be floated downstream to a mill in Snohomish or to Port
Gardner on the Sound.

When Ann thought they could sigh in relief and wait out
the winter, Jake quickly disabused her of this notion. As

long as the woods were not too wet to work, or too covered in snow, the operation would continue, so that by the spring freshet there would be another valuable log jam ready to release on the river.

In December, Angus brought Maggie the dog.

He was a stray, a half-grown mongrel who cowered and shook from the cold. When Maggie dropped to her knees beside him, hand extended to touch his ribs through the ratty hair, he licked at her, and the bonding was instantaneous.

"Is he mine?" she asked, incredulous.

The Keatings had never had dogs. Ann had been raised to believe that animals were unclean, and she had neither tolerated them in her house nor wanted them outside.

"If you want him," Angus said. He had filled out after a few years in the woods; he was still tall and slim, but his chest and shoulders had broadened, and the muscles in his arms were the equal of anyone's, even Jake's. He grinned down at her. "He's been starving for so long he may eat you."

"Oh!" Maggie sprang to her feet and ran for the house, returning with the remains of a roast and scraps of bread and gravy. "Oh, the poor thing! What's his name, Angus?"

"Whatever you want to call him, I guess. I've been calling him Dog."

She gave him a look of disgust. "I thought you had more imagination than that."

"Well, I do, but if he's going to be your dog, why should I give him a name he'll have to unlearn? How about Pal? Or Rover?"

"Why not Spot?" Maggie countered, laughing. Then her laughter faded. "First, I'd better see if Mama will let me keep him."

"Get your pa on your side first, and you'll have a better

chance,'' Angus predicted. ''Just don't get too attached to him until you know if he can stay.''

That was easier said than done. Maggie looked into the soft brown eyes, eyes that said he adored her on the basis of one meal and a lick on the hand, and knew that she was already lost.

Jake took her side. ''I always had a dog when I was growing up,'' he said. ''And the way that girl wanders around, he'll be protection for her. If she falls and breaks an ankle, he'll go for help. If anybody tries to harm her, they'll be torn apart.''

Ann couldn't help laughing. ''By that poor unfortunate creature? He doesn't look able to catch a rabbit, let alone run off an attacker. Besides, everybody in the county knows Margaret, and knows she's your daughter. It's not likely that she'll be needing any protection.''

''Please, Mama,'' Maggie begged. ''Please, let me keep him.''

''I'll think about it,'' Ann said, amusement subsiding.

Maggie heard them later, when they didn't know she was listening.

''Let her have the dog,'' Jake said. ''She needs it, honey. She's missed Charlie real bad.''

''Charlie?'' There was a shrill note to Ann's voice. ''How can you think having a dog will make up for Charlie? For heaven's sake, Jake!''

''I'm not saying the dog will make up for Charlie. I'm saying she loved the baby, and she needs something to love now. Something to love her back, give her affection.''

''*We* love her! You and I and Celeste, and Mama!''

''It's not the same, Ann. She needs that warm body to snuggle up to, to pet, to hug. To talk to.''

''Talk to a dog?'' She made a strangled sound. ''Jake, have you lost your mind?''

''Honey, just because you never had a dog to talk to doesn't mean it doesn't do a lot to ease the loneliness. It does. I remember. Whenever I had a falling out with my old man—which was at least once a week, as I recall it—I'd take a walk with old Joe and tell him all my troubles, and he'd lick my hand, or my face if he could get at it, and I'd feel better. I loved that dog better'n I loved anybody in my whole family.''

"That's crazy," Ann said, but her words were soft.

"No, ma'am, it ain't crazy," Jake told her, and then Maggie heard the sound of a kiss, and a giggle. "Let her have the dog, honey."

Ann never did actually give Maggie permission to keep the dog. She just didn't say he had to go. She would set aside a bowl of scraps for him, and when, during a blizzard, Maggie dared to bring the animal inside to a place near the hearth, Ann ignored him.

Jake's beloved dog had been called Joe. Maggie said the name under her breath, looking down at the skinny hound with his floppy ears pricked up at the sound of her voice. "Joe. You want to be called Joe?"

The dog wagged his tail.

Angus pretended to exaggerated astonishment when he heard it. "Joe? And you said *I* didn't have any imagination!"

"It suits him," Maggie said, and Joe it was.

It seemed to her that Ann was in better spirits than Maggie could ever remember, those two years it took to build their house, except for the period when she and Jake fought about where it would be located.

Ann had assumed that Jake was talking about a fine house in Snohomish, perhaps on Avenue B, at the top of the hill, so that the windows would overlook both the main part of town and the river, where she would be within walking distance of church and the Athenaeum Building where so many entertainments and recitals would be held.

Jake had taken it for granted that the house would be constructed where it was handy for him.

"If we build it at the landing, I can live at home instead

of at some damned logging camp. I can see all my family every day instead of one day a week."

"But we'll be miles from town! I won't be any better off than I am now when it comes to visiting or going anywhere!"

"I'll get you a horse and a buggy," Jake offered. "You can go to town whenever you want. Better you taking a buggy once or twice than me going every day from town to the woods. Well, no, I couldn't do that, I couldn't spare the time. I'd have to live in the woods with the men and leave you and the girls by yourselves, and I don't want to. Besides, you want your ma to live with us, so you won't have to travel to town to see *her*. It'll be better for all of us, Ann. No question but what I can run the operation better if I'm closer to it."

Jake played his trump card. "We'll get it built a hell of a lot quicker—maybe by a full year—if we do it at the landing. I can put my own men to work on it during the winter when the logging shuts down; they can stay on in the bunkhouse, and Mr. Murphy can keep on cooking for them instead of warming his butt in Port Gardner for the winter."

"Quicker by a year?" Ann asked uncertainly, and Jake knew he'd won.

Once she'd given in on location, she watched in mounting enthusiasm as the edifice rose from its foundations. It was placed well above the reach of the river when it was in flood, for in December and again in early spring the Pilchuck was transformed from a trickle to a torrent capable of sweeping away anything in its path.

To his credit, Jake let her have her way about almost everything in connection with the house. She wanted half a dozen bedrooms, why in hell not? She wanted two parlors; well, it meant there'd be one in which he could sit with his feet up if he chose.

Stones were hauled from the river bottoms, from the Pilchuck and the Snohomish and as far away as the

Stilliguamish for the fireplaces. There would be a fine iron stove in the kitchen for the actual cooking, but Ann liked an open fire for heat and the illusion of it, impossible to achieve when the wood burned out of sight behind black iron doors.

There would even be a music room, for the piano Jake had been induced to order sent from the East at mind-boggling expense. There was only one other such instrument in Snohomish, owned by the Athenaeum Society; Ann was already, a year before she had a house to put it in, gloating over future possession of the second, and only privately owned, one.

"I learned to play when I was younger than Celeste, on my grandmother's piano in Ohio," she said. "You can't imagine how I've longed to play again! I'll be terribly rusty, of course, but after I've practiced a bit, I'll teach both of you girls!"

Maggie put down her misgivings about that; the piano and lessons could not come in less than a year's time, if Jake's estimate of the building schedule was accurate. The house came second to the logging operations, and there would be workers for it only when nothing could be done in the woods.

Jake's loans were paid off. Ed Newsome had recovered to a greater extent than anyone but his wife had thought possible, but he would never again work in the timber. He was happy to sell out to Jake Keating, and though this second transaction left Jake once more in debt, Jake was optimistic about it. The whole country was moving west; there were houses to build, and houses took lumber. Jake envisoned himself, in the near future, as a wealthy man.

The house, when it was completed, was unquestionably one of the finest in the territory.

It was of two stories, with a wide verandah circling it on three sides, and of an elegance that even Ann found totally satisfying. The Keatings held an open house that brought out virtually the entire population of Snohomish and others from as far away as Machias and Monroe.

There were new dresses for everyone. Maggie thought her mother looked absolutely stunning in blue silk; Grandma Miles was stylishly garbed in her black taffeta.

Celeste wore green, a simple frock with a crocheted lace collar and cuffs, her blond curls caught back in a green ribbon. Maggie's dress was a deep winey-red worsted, and she stared at her image in the mirror in astonishment.

Was it true, what Angus had told her so long ago, that with her bone structure she would someday be beautiful?

She wasn't beautiful yet, exactly, especially when she compared herself to Celeste, but she wasn't ugly anymore, either. She pinched her cheeks to bring a touch of color to them, though as she still had the summer's tan it took a rather painful pinch to make the color show through. If only her hair would curl, she wouldn't mind it being dark instead of fair, she thought. Only nothing could induce it to do anything but hang straight down, except putting it in braids. Tonight it was hanging straight, because everybody had been so busy with other heads of hair more easily coaxed into fancier coiffures that there had been no time to do anything with Maggie's. If she didn't stand close to her sister, she thought, perhaps no one would be so aware of the contrast between them. The dark-red dress definitely did something for her that she'd never noticed before.

Maggie felt an unexpected inner flicker of excitement, for Angus would be here tonight. She was nearly thirteen and tall for her age; perhaps Angus would finally see that she was female, and growing up, she thought.

One of the first things Ann had realized when they moved into the new house was that it was far too large for her to run it alone; and after only a token protest, Jake had agreed to hire a housekeeper. Mrs. Totting was only a little older than Ann, though she looked fifty. She'd had a hard life, Jake said, having been widowed when her husband was crushed by an inexpertly felled tree after a nine-year marriage during which she'd lost four children to smallpox. Her brown hair held as much gray as Millicent Miles's did, and her hands were chapped and work-worn; but Mrs. Totting was industrious and eager to please. She promised earnestly to keep the big house spotless.

Her only surviving child, Nancy, was a year younger than Maggie. Maggie felt comfortable with her, because Nancy was plain and ordinary, as Maggie saw herself.

"You don't put on airs," Maggie once said, and Nancy laughed.

"What would I have to put on airs about?"

Nancy was at the housewarming party, though not as a guest. She wore a white apron over her dark calico dress; she was to help her mother serve.

"I'll die if I spill anything," she confided to Maggie.

"No, you won't. People don't die of embarrassment. You might get a nasty look from Mama if you pour wine down the front of the mayor's good suit, or trip over Mrs. Bascomb's big feet, but you won't *die* from it."

Nancy's giggle held a nervous note. "Not unless your mama kills me, I guess." She studied Maggie's new dress. "It's lovely, Maggie. It suits you. You look . . . *pretty*."

"Do you think so?" Suddenly self-conscious, Maggie changed the subject. "Have you seen the piano, yet? Come and see it."

The instrument was a magnificent one; Ann and Celeste had fallen upon it with cries of delight. Maggie was more cautious. Mama expected her to learn to play it, and her first stumbling efforts had been discordant and far from promising.

"Margaret has no talent for that kind of thing," Millicent had said, and Maggie caught the flash of echoing doubt on her mother's face before Ann replied firmly, "Mama, it's too early to know. She's never seen a piano before. When she's had a few lessons, she may do very well."

"Celeste has a natural instinct for music," Millicent observed. "She has a lovely singing voice, too."

"So does Margaret," Ann defended her older daughter. "Let's wait and see, shall we?"

The lessons had not yet begun. Maggie lifted the cover to display the keys, and poked a tentative finger at one of them to produce a chiming note. She was uneasily certain that her grandmother was right.

"It's beautiful," Nancy said, admiring. "Oh, my, isn't that a buggy arriving? The party's beginning, Maggie!"

It was a festive affair. All the guests wore their Sunday best, and they all admired the house excessively. Ann spent most of her time taking each newcomer on a tour of the ground floor, adding casually that the upstairs bedrooms were not yet completely furnished, but they numbered six. There was no other house in the whole of Snohomish County that was larger or more grand.

Maggie had never seen so many people in one place at one time, but she wasn't interested in the townspeople. It was Angus she looked for, Angus who must see her in the new dark-red dress.

Jake, looking strangely stiff in the new suit, white shirt, and unfamiliar cravat, hugged her when he saw her. "Why, honey, you're the best-looking female here!"

She knew it was an outright lie, but it made her feel a glow of happiness. The one constant thing in her life was Jake's love; she was only lately realizing that love from one's father, however, comforting though it was, was not the only or even the most important love in one's life.

Maggie made her way through the rooms thrown open for inspection, speaking politely to women she knew from church, to the schoolteacher, the mayor, the loggers so slicked up that she almost didn't recognize them. (There had been some discussion about who should be invited to the open house, Ann contending that the loggers might be more comfortable if they were invited separately from the

townspeople, Jake adamant that they all be invited at once.
Jake had won after his declaration, "Ann, if the loggers
don't come, too, there isn't going to be any goddamned
housewarming." It had put some restraint on the plans for
a few hours, but Ann was too excited about showing off
her new treasure to let the presence of a few loggers spoil
it for her.)

Angus, where was Angus?

Maggie stood on tiptoe to see over the heads, craned her
neck to see around them, and finally spotted him, standing
just inside the door of the music room.

Eagerly Maggie made her way toward him, then stopped,
disappointment swelling painfully in her chest.

Angus was not alone. He was talking to Deborah McVea,
laughing at something she had said.

Maggie stood still, watching them. Deborah was seventeen, and very pretty. Her chestnut hair was becomingly
curled and caught up with tiny combs, and her blue
sicilienne frock molded a perfectly curved body.
Unconsciously, Maggie put her hands to her own still
nearly undetectable bosom.

Angus said something Maggie couldn't make out over
the chatter of the visitors, and Deborah laughed again and
touched Angus lightly on the arm.

A searing pain cut through Maggie, as sharp as a knife,
stopping her breath. To touch Angus that way, to have him
smiling down on her, to turn with her arm entwined with
his . . . She longed for it with a passion until now undreamed
of.

They didn't even see her. They were heading for one of
the long tables set out with a variety of delicious foods—
cold salmon and venison and a variety of sweets and
salads—talking with animation, absorbed in each other.

Jealousy, wild, hot, surged in Maggie's chest. Somehow
she had assumed that Angus was staked out, in some way,
for *her*, when she was old enough. She'd never seen Angus

do more than speak to a girl, casually, at Sabbath services, and now he was acting as if Deborah were an old friend.

Maggie' eyes stung, and she turned away. The party was spoiled. She wished she could go upstairs and escape from them all, but she knew that Ann would miss her and send Celeste to seek her out, to feel her forehead and ask if she'd eaten too many of the sweets.

Was that an escape? Could she pretend to be sick?

No, Maggie decided at once. That would only disturb her mother, spoil the good time she was having; she couldn't do that to her. She would have to keep a stiff upper lip and wait it out.

In the kitchen, she approached Mrs. Totting. "Is there anything I can do to help?" she asked.

Mrs. Totting gave her a grateful smile. "Why, you could take that tray out to the table. They've nearly finished off that salmon aspic, so you'd better put the second one out. It's a lovely party, isn't it? Your ma looks so happy."

Maggie carried the molded aspic to the table, unable to refrain from glancing around to search out Angus and Deborah. They had carried plates to a row of chairs along the front parlor wall and were eating, still laughing and obviously enjoying themselves immensely.

"Maggie! I'll be damned, I didn't know you!" The voice was familiar, big Red Risku, smiling down on her. "You look all grown-up in that pretty dress."

She tried to smile back at him, feeling oddly uncomfortable; she wasn't used to compliments from the loggers. "You're looking pretty fancy yourself," she managed, and heard his guffaw.

"You're right there. So fancy I feel like I been starched and ironed and can't bend enough to sit down. What's that stuff you just brought out? Is it good?"

"Everything's good," Maggie assured him, and escaped as he began to fill a plate.

The party went on and on, until Maggie wanted to

scream at them all to go home. It was torture when she watched Angus and Deborah from across the room; it was worse when they disappeared.

Where had they gone? It was too cold to venture outside, at least without wraps. Where, then? What were they doing?

Nancy emerged from the kitchen bearing a platter of sliced turkey. "It's a wonderful party, isn't it, Maggie?"

"Wonderful," Maggie echoed.

Nancy didn't notice the strain in her voice. She said in a half whisper, "Romantic, for some. I can't wait until I'm old enough to have a young man. Can you?"

"Romantic?" Maggie echoed, insides suddenly churning. "Who?"

"Deborah McVea, and that Mr. McKay. I suppose it's natural they'd like each other, both of them being from Scotland."

Maggie fought rising nausea. "The McVeas didn't come from Scotland."

"Well, Deborah's grandfather did. They're both Scottish, I meant."

"That doesn't mean anything, necessarily." And then, because she couldn't *not* ask, "What did you see?"

Nancy's small, plain face was split in a grin. "They're in the back vestibule. Go out and get the cider Ma wants put out, and you'll see them."

She moved on, so enchanted with the house and the gathered company that she failed to detect Maggie's misery.

She didn't want to see them, Maggie thought. To hell with Angus McKay. (Though she knew better than to get into the habit of swearing—she remembered from early childhood what it was like to have her mouth washed out with soap—Maggie often thought in the vocabulary she heard in the woods.) She dodged around two enormous, tightly corseted ladies engrossed in an avid discussion of the chandeliers in the two parlors and the dining room, and retreated once more to the kitchen.

"Oh, Maggie," Mrs. Totting called out, "would you mind bringing in that other jug of cider? It's chilling out back, and the bowl is empty."

She could have refused. For a moment the words trembled on her lips, because she did not want to see whatever it was that Nancy had seen.

And yet, in a strange, perverted way, she did. She had to know.

She pushed open the door on the far side of the kitchen. There was a lamp left in the pantry because they were making one trip after another out there to fetch things left chilling. Maggie saw the cider, then glanced beyond to the vestibule in spite of herself.

The cubicle was dark except for what illumination seeped from the pantry. Maggie's slippers were soundless as she stood, watching.

Angus was there all right. She recognized the glint of the lamplight on his fair hair. No one else was as tall as Angus, so even though she could not really see his face she knew who it was.

There was a low laugh, and Angus bent his head. Maggie saw their shadowy bodies come together, heard a soft, murmuring feminine voice, and then silence as the pair strained against each other in an embrace that sent Maggie spinning on her heel. She grabbed the cider jug, pushed through the doorway back into the kitchen, and handed it over without a word. She didn't even hear Mrs. Totting speak to her. She only knew that she was going to cry, and she had to be alone to do it.

The party was still in full swing. Nobody saw her run up the stairs, nobody cared when she entered the new bedroom— where for the first time in her life she slept alone in a big bed—nobody came looking for her when she did not rejoin the festivities.

Maggie lay in the dark, eyelids swollen and aching, and wondered why she'd ever been such a fool as to think that she had a chance with Angus.

She hated him; she hated Deborah McVea; she hated Nancy for having told her the couple was on the back porch. And most of all she hated herself, for being stupid and plain and unworthy.

When her parents came, hours later, to check on her, Maggie pretended to be asleep.

# 9

"MARGARET Ellen," Celeste said in excellent imitation of her mother, "If you don't get out of that bed this minute, you'll make us all late for church."

Maggie burrowed more deeply into the covers. "Go away. I'm not going to church."

Shock made Celeste's voice squeak. "You are, too! Margaret, please get up."

"No. Leave me alone," Maggie said, and pulled the quilt completely over her head.

She heard her sister leave the room and wished that for once in her life someone would take her at her word, let her make her own decision. She was not surprised, however, when the click of her mother's heels sounded only moments later.

The quilt was pulled away, leaving her exposed and vulnerable. Ann's voice was crisp. "Margaret, are you ill?"

"No. Mama, can't I stay home this once?"

"Please don't be difficult. We will be eating immediately, and we expect you to join us."

Ann's heels clicked away, and Maggie reluctantly opened her eyes and sat up.

Mrs. Totting had not yet cleared away all the mess from the party, and they were not using the dining room. The family was gathered around the kitchen table, where there were platters of ham and eggs and Ann's sourdough pancakes.

Maggie slid into her chair and filled her plate; her misery had not ruined her appetite. The others were nearly finished, so she ate quickly, knowing her mother would be extremely annoyed if they were late to church.

Everyone else talked about the housewarming all the way there in the new buggy that was almost as much a source of pride as the house. Ann was learning to drive it, under Jake's supervision, though it looked perfectly simple to Maggie. All you had to do was hold the reins and the horse did the rest.

It was a fine day and virtually everyone was attending services. The ladies smiled and told Ann what a marvelous party it had been, and how much they admired the new house. "No doubt you'll be having entertainments from time to time," Mrs. Bascomb said, and Ann smiled and nodded.

"I certainly hope to," she agreed.

Maggie sneaked a glance at her father and found his face impassive. Or was it resigned? Why build a big fancy expensive house if you didn't invite people in to enjoy it? Privately, Maggie felt it was all unnecessary. She herself had been perfectly happy in the little house in town or the cabin in the woods.

Her stomach muscles tightened. There were the McVeas, all eight of them. Mrs. McVea was a dumpling of a woman with faded blond hair and a merry smile, which today did not seem as jolly to Maggie as it always had in the past. Mr. McVea ran the hardware store; he was as tall and thin as his wife was short and round, and all five of his sons were built the same as their father.

It was at Deborah that Maggie looked, however. Deborah was smiling, radiant, happy. Happy because Angus had kissed her last night?

Deborah turned, laughing, to greet a friend, and Maggie was free to stare at her openly. She had a tiny waist, and a pretty high bosom molded now by a deep rose-colored gown of foulard that was most becoming. It was no wonder, Maggie thought in dull despair, that Angus thought her lovely enough to kiss.

The bell tolled and those standing about in the churchyard began to file inside. Maggie moved with her family, eyes searching for Angus. She didn't see him. Maybe, she hoped, he realized that he'd made a fool of himself last night with Deborah, and he was too embarrassed to show up today.

The preacher who had replaced her grandpa was younger and livelier, yet just as concerned with hellfire and damnation. Maggie didn't listen to the sermon; instead she allowed her gaze to drift around from pew to pew, entertaining herself by speculating about each of the parishioners.

Mr. Hulburt, the blacksmith, had a boil on the back of his neck. Once Red Risku had had such a boil, only on his backside. Maggie had not seen it, of course, but she'd heard him yell when her father had applied the mouth of a heated bottle to it. She wondered if Mrs. Hulburt didn't know about heating bottles to draw out infection.

Beyond him, his old father was nodding, jerking upright when the minister pounded on the lectern to emphasize a point. One of these days old man Hulburt was going to fall into the aisle as he slept. She wondered if the minister would be annoyed, as Grandpa Miles would have been.

She wished Mama didn't always insist on sitting so close to the front of the church. Daddy always said it was from being the parson's daughter, that she'd got used to sitting in the front row where no one else wanted to sit; *she* said there were fewer distractions if the rest of the congregation were behind her, so that she could more easily concentrate on the sermon.

Maggie welcomed the distractions, if they were where she could see what was going on. Only her mother would pinch her if she swiveled around to look when a hymnal was dropped or somebody's baby cried too long. If she turned to search for Angus, she'd probably not only be pinched, she'd be scolded once the service was over.

Well, at least Angus wasn't sitting with Deborah McVea. Out of the corner of her eye, across the aisle, Maggie could see the older girl, sitting demurely with her hands folded in her lap.

In profile, Deborah's nose was shown to be less perfect than it appeared when one looked directly at her from the front. Still, it didn't detract much from her looks. Maggie wondered dismally if Deborah had always been attractive, or if she'd had to grow up to her own bone structure.

Beside her on the hard pew, Celeste squirmed until Mama reached out and put a restraining hand on her knee. Maggie shifted her gaze from Deborah to her little sister.

Why, she wondered, had God seen fit to make Celeste so perfect when He'd allowed Maggie to be so plain?

Celeste's blond curls cascaded from a green ribbon onto her shoulders. Her skin was creamy and clear, and there was nothing wrong with *her* nose as seen in profile, or from any other direction. Blue eyes thickly lashed, a mouth that looked as pink as if she'd colored it, quirking into a grin when she realized Maggie was looking at her (a surreptitious grin, so that Mama wouldn't reprimand her for *that*, too) and those dimples that Maggie would have given her eyeteeth for.

Yet for all that Celeste was an exquisitely beautiful rival for the admiration and affection of nearly everyone but Jake, Maggie could not resent her too much. Celeste was a sunny, good-natured child, and she deferred to Maggie as an expert on almost everything.

She was, Maggie grudgingly supposed, a good influence, though sometimes she was tiresome in her refusal to get involved in anything interesting. She wouldn't climb trees or wade in the river, and more than once she'd run for help when Maggie had taken on some hazardous enterprise from which she'd been unable to extricate herself unaided. Now that she had Joe in case she got into real trouble, Maggie found him in some ways a better companion than Celeste for her adventures. He wasn't afraid of the water, and he never told tales.

Maggie's musings came to an end as the congregation suddenly surged to its collective feet to sing. "Praise God from whom all blessings flow, Praise Him all creatures here below; Praise Him above, ye heavenly host, Praise Father, Son, and Holy Ghost."

Beside her, Celeste's voice rose clear and true. Across the aisle, Deborah McVea's rich contralto overpowered the other, more hesitant, voices. Beside either of them, Maggie thought, *she* sounded like a frog.

Praise God from whom all blessings flow, Maggie mused as the assembled company began to file from the pews into the center aisle. Yet not all that happened was a blessing. God allowed innocent babies like Charlie to die. He allowed bad feelings between married people sometimes. And He made unbeautiful creatures who must live in loneliness and struggle against their lack of beauty in a world that seemed impressed with little else.

"Hey, what are you looking so doleful about?"

Maggie's heart twisted painfully in her chest. He was here, he'd been here all the time, behind her and out of sight. She paused, then moved on as her sister nudged her

from behind. Angus fell into step beside her, looking his
normal ordinary self except that his fair hair was unruffled
and his boots had been cleaned.

"What's the matter? You eat too much last night and get
sick?"

Reference to the housewarming party brought back,
vividly, all the things she hadn't wanted to think about.
She groped for a reply that wouldn't give away how hurt
she was, and found that her throat closed against any
words at all.

Angus didn't seem to notice. "I could have foundered,
myself. That was some food! Who cooked it, you?"

For once she failed to note that he was teasing. "Mrs.
Totting and Mama cooked it. I only helped serve some of
it."

"That's a really fancy house you live in now." They
stepped out into the sunshine and halted in the churchyard
while foot traffic flowed around them. Somehow she'd
gotten separated from the rest of the family; no doubt
Mama had stopped to accept yet another compliment on
the house or the party. "Must be nice, having a room all to
yourself."

"I guess," Maggie said. Actually, she hadn't enjoyed it
all that much as yet. She rather missed Celeste's warm
body in the bed on a cold night, and her chatter. Celeste
talked a lot.

Angus was looking straight at her now. "Say, that's a
really pretty dress. Makes you look quite grown-up."

She stared at him. "I wore it last night."

"Did you? I guess I didn't notice. I didn't get a chance
to talk to you."

She couldn't say the words, not in front of all these
people. *You were too busy looking at Deborah McVea and
kissing her in the back vestibule.*

Angus grinned. "You're getting to be very pretty, Maggie

Keating." She was so astonished at that that words again failed her. And then *she* had to spoil everything.

"Why, Angus, good morning."

Maggie didn't have to turn to learn who was speaking. She recognized the sugary tones.

"Good morning, Deborah."

Now the warmth of Angus's grin was turned away from Maggie; he'd already forgotten her, she thought bitterly. Her father was bringing up the buggy, and Maggie moved toward it blindly, restraining the urge to run.

That afternoon Mama began the piano lessons.

"Let Celeste go first," Maggie said uneasily when the subject came up.

"Nonsense. You're the oldest, we'll take you first. Then you won't have to sit around waiting for Celeste, and you'll be free the rest of the afternoon. Come and sit beside me," Ann directed.

It was such an ordeal that Maggie forgot all about Angus and Deborah. The instrument that tinkled so prettily under Mama's fingers sounded flat and heavy under Maggie's. By the time the allotted half hour was over, she was drenched in perspiration; her hands were cramped and icy, and she was convinced that she would never be able to wring a melodious note from the piano she'd already come to hate.

Millicent Miles, who had listened while she rocked and knitted on a sock, said nothing. Her silence, however, was as eloquent as words would have been.

Ann's sigh was nearly inaudible. "Well, it's only the first lesson. It will be easier next time, Margaret."

Maggie knew that it wouldn't. She resolved to ask Jake's intercession in the matter of lessons. They would be a complete waste of everyone's time, and would serve only to heighten the contrast between Celeste and herself, with Maggie on the losing end, as she so often was.

Celeste was there to slip eagerly onto the bench as soon as Maggie had vacated it. Maggie fled, wishing she could shut out the first tentative notes that floated after her. Yes, floated. Celeste had, as expected, a lighter touch.

Maggie went through the kitchen, scooping up a few leftovers as she passed, which she fed to Joe when she met him on the back steps. So far, Joe hadn't been inside the new house, though Maggie had assured him that by the time it got cold again, next winter, he would surely be allowed in by a fire, even if she had to hide him under her bed.

Joe had grown larger and his ribs no longer showed. His spotted hide was sleek from regular feedings, and his tail was quick to wag whenever Maggie showed up. He gulped her offerings and took off beside her along the riverbank.

The Pilchuck was running full in the way that Ann considered dangerous, but Maggie gave it no thought. She'd fallen in more times than she could remember, and she swam well enough to have gotten herself safely out each time, though she fully realized that in flood the river really *was* hazardous.

Joe was good company. She could tell him anything, and he never contradicted or scolded her. If she sat down on a fallen log or a big rock, he would press close to her side, and when she spoke to him he would reply in the only way he knew, with a comforting lick on her hand or cheek.

Today she didn't feel like sitting down. She walked briskly, making up a story about Angus and herself, imagining being kissed by him as she'd seen him kissing the other girl. It made her have strange and disturbing sensations, yet it was not as satisfying as previous imaginings. Because it was all make-believe. It would never happen, Maggie thought.

She walked until she was tired, then still had the walk back. Mama was in the kitchen fixing supper of the party leftovers, no doubt; Maggie saw her through the window and so continued on around the house to the front door. She had no wish to encounter Ann before she'd cleaned off her shoes. "Stay," she said to a disappointed Joe, who sank obediently onto his rump.

She found a stick to scrape off as much of the mud as she could, then paused on the verandah to remove the shoes before she entered the house in her stocking feet.

That, like everything else that she'd done lately, was a mistake. No one heard her.

Maggie moved through the hallway toward the stairs, intending to ignore the voices she heard from the back parlor, the one Ann had decreed to be for the informal use of the family.

It was impossible to ignore the words she heard.

Celeste's voice, happy, carrying. "Papa, I played the piano! Mama said I was very good!"

Jake's voice, deeper, good-humored. "I knew you would be, honey."

"Celeste has definite musical ability," Millicent asserted. "She's so much like Ann. Such a fine woman, a fine housekeeper. Celeste is learning to keep a house, too. She can already sew quite well for eleven years old, and she's learning to cook."

"Good," Jake said, sounding as enthusiastic as he ever did in response to anything his mother-in-law said. "I'm proud of you, Celeste. You can play a tune for me as soon as you have it mastered."

Millicent's next words were more crisp. "When are you going to do something about Margaret?"

Maggie stood still, muddy shoes in hand, unable to avoid eavesdropping.

"What do you think I ought to be doing about Maggie?" Jake asked, a warning coolness in his words now. "I'm happy with her just the way she is."

"She isn't learning to be a *woman*. She can't sew a

straight seam, her cooking ability is limited to slicing a loaf of bread and buttering it, and when she sweeps she doesn't bother with the corners. What sort of housewife is she going to be?''

''How many housewives does one house need? Seems to me that you and Ann and Celeste should be able to manage this one between you, especially with Mrs. Totting coming in regularly.''

''*This* house is not the point, though the fact that there are others to attend to necessary matters shouldn't mean that Margaret's development and training can be neglected. It's going to be a terrible handicap to her to grow up untutored in the things every woman should know.''

''Maggie's only a child,'' Jake stated. ''I'm not worried about what she'll be like as a woman; she'll be a fine one.''

''That's what I'm trying to tell you, that she *won't* be unless she has some training soon. She's not a child, she's nearly fourteen! At that age her mother was an accomplished cook and seamstress!''

Maggie was frozen, so absorbed in their words that had any of them emerged from the parlor they would have caught her there, listening. Was Grandma Miles going to make her stay at home from now on, *this summer,* which she'd looked forward to with such pleasure, in order to learn cooking and sewing and cleaning? Not to mention being tortured by having to learn to play the piano?

''I'm proud of Celeste,'' Jake said evenly. ''But I'm just as proud of Maggie, and she doesn't have to be a copy of Ann or Celeste to suit me. Leave her alone.''

Maggie heard her heart thumping in her chest, even over the reply from her grandmother.

''Do you think it's going to be all right to let her run loose in the woods when she's a grown woman? To associate with all those rough men? Who's going to want to marry a female who doesn't know the first thing about a woman's work?''

''I'm one of those 'rough men' and she's survived contact with me pretty well,'' Jake said, sounding flatter and flatter as his exasperation rose. ''The men like her, they admire her. There isn't a one of 'em would harm a hair on her head.''

Millicent, too, was becoming frustrated with the conversation. ''None of them is going to marry her, either.''

''That's something neither you nor I know anything about, but I refuse to push her into being something she's not in order to prove anything to anybody. Celeste, are you going to show me what you learned on the piano today?''

Maggie ran up the stairs only moments before they crossed the hall to the music room. She closed her bedroom door behind her and leaned against it, feeling as if she'd been running a long way, pursued by unseen monsters.

She was grateful to her father for his defense of her. Yet, somehow, she felt like crying, too, for she was afraid that there was a lot of truth in what her grandmother had said.

She did not actively seek Angus out the following day, though she was at all times aware of watching for him. Mr. Murphy's rheumatism was bothering him and he was rather crotchety; after he'd growled at her for the second time because she wasn't peeling potatoes to his satisfaction, Maggie decided to let him peel them himself and walked away from the cookhouse. She didn't like peeling potatoes, anyway.

It wasn't fair, what Grandma Miles had said about her lack of ability in the kitchen. She could not only slice bread and butter it, she could make it, and often had, under Mr. Murphy's watchful eyes. She enjoyed kneading it, punching and pummeling the dough that felt like a creature alive under her hands, warm and growing. She had a lighter hand with biscuits than her tutor, even he admitted, and though her pie crust wasn't *quite* as good as his, it was passable. Certainly none of the loggers had ever refused a piece of her pie, or thrown it at her as she'd once seen them do with a helper who had not lasted out his first week on the job.

Life wasn't fair, Maggie reflected. If beauty was the only thing other people thought about, then why weren't all people beautiful? The women at least, she amended. It didn't seem to matter so much about men.

She knew enough not to walk aimlessly through the woods in an area where trees were being felled. She kept to the skid road, which meant watching her footing because it was possible to step between the corduroy logs and twist an ankle.

The skid dauber was an old man with a crippled foot, by the name of Harry Jarvis. He had once been a faller, but he'd thrown the rope over the top too many times, as the loggers put it; he was a careless workman, and he was lucky his carelessness hadn't cost him his life. As it was, he could no longer climb, and his final fall had affected his mind somewhat, too, though there were those unkind enough to suggest he hadn't had all his fittings to begin with.

Maggie suspected that he kept a bottle hidden away somewhere, for there was usually the odor of spirits on him. He explained this away to the boss by stating that somebody had spilled whiskey on him the previous Saturday night in town, and the smell hadn't gone away yet. Since he almost never changed his clothes, it could have happened weeks earlier than last Saturday, though she didn't know if the odor would have held on for that long. His own personal smell was almost enough to overpower that of the whiskey.

He looked up at her with rheumy old eyes, so faded it was impossible to say what color they had been, and stepped aside, tugging perfunctorily at the cap he wore. "Mornin', missy."

"Good morning," Maggie said, maneuvering upwind of him to avoid breathing in his fumes. He was one of the few men on the crew she never visited with, and she was nearly past him when his raspy old voice stopped her.

"That McKay feller was askin' after ya," he said.

She was unable to control the sudden lurch of her heart. "Angus? When? What did he want?"

"He come by here hell for leather, little bit ago. Ast if I seen ya."

"What did he want?" Maggie repeated.

"Didn't say. He's up thataway." The old man gestured with a thumb that was not well acquainted with soap and water.

"Thank you. I'll find him," Maggie said, and walked briskly on. She had written Angus off on Saturday night, despised him on Sunday, and now couldn't wait to see him again. What was the matter with her?

The woods were still cool and damp in early spring, and she inhaled deeply of their fragrance. The men were into a stand of cedar today, gigantic trees in their prime, and she loved the pungent smell as the saws bit through them and the sawdust piled up around their massive bases.

She found Angus standing beside a magnificent specimen— Maggie had learned to estimate height nearly as well as a timber cruiser, and judged it to be close to two hundred feet tall—bent over a crosscut saw laid over a stump. He glanced up when he heard her coming, looking the same as he'd always looked, a navy knitted cap keeping his fair hair out of his eyes, the sleeves of his plaid flannel shirt rolled up to expose muscular bronzed forearms.

"Harry Jarvis said you were looking for me," Maggie said, and hoped that her breathlessness would be assumed to result from her running.

"Yeah." The familiar word always sounded odd when

touched with his Scots burr. "I dropped my oil bottle and broke it. I hoped you'd fetch me another one. Your old man's going to kick my butt if I take time to walk back to camp for it, he's in such an all-fired hurry to get this stand out of here. Would you?"

Maggie stared at him, disappointment sharpening her tone a trifle, though in all fairness there was no reason she should have thought he'd wanted her for anything personal. She was always running errands for Angus, as well as for the others.

"I think I'm getting too old for you to use that kind of language in front of me."

He straightened and stared at her, trying to think what he'd said that called for the rebuke. "What, about kicking my butt? Would you prefer I said—"

"Never mind," Maggie said hastily, realizing what his alternative would probably be. "I'll get you another bottle."

She turned and trotted back the way she'd come before he could say anything else. Not that he'd intended to, anyway; when she looked back from the edge of the road, he was intent on sharpening the saw.

The oil bottle had originally been a whiskey bottle, enthusiastically emptied by some willing logger; when filled with oil and then sealed with a notched cork, its contents could be sprinkled on a saw to cut the pitch that gummed up the blade. Maggie had no difficulty in finding a bottle, and she'd notched corks and poured in oil many times before. When she took it back to Angus, he would fit it with an iron hook affair which would enable him to hang it on a stump to prevent it from leaking.

There was a saying among the loggers that an empty whiskey bottle was no good, because a man couldn't tell if it would leak. The only sure way to know was to buy a quart of whiskey and drink it, then pour a gallon of oil into the four bottles he would now appear to have in his four hands. It was the kind of tale that had amused Maggie, and that she'd learned early on did *not* amuse her mother or grandmother.

Angus was still working on the saw when she got back. He accepted the bottle with a grunted "Thanks" and kept on with what he was doing, barely looking in her direction as he took it.

She had considered Angus her friend for such a long time, long before she decided she'd fallen in love with him. They had talked of so many things she discussed with no one else, and he'd never ridiculed anything she said. Although he teased her, as all the men did, it was never in a cruel way, and he'd often come to her defense when someone else forgot himself with a thoughtlessly hurtful remark.

He looked the same now as he always had. Her friend, Angus. Maggie watched his hands, the brown, sturdy hands that could be so gentle with a stray dog or a scraped hand, so strong with a saw or an ax, and could bunch into a large pair of fists if the need arose.

He had put those hands onto Deborah McVea's arms, then drawn the girl even closer, when he'd kissed her.

Heat swept through her, tormenting, confusing, and Maggie blurted out the question that had plagued her over the past two days.

"Are you going to marry Deborah McVea?"

That brought his head up with a snap that made him put one hand on the back of his neck, leaving an oil smear. "What in hell gave you that idea?"

Her mouth felt as if it had been filled with cotton. "I saw you . . . Saturday night. Kissing her." Her ears were so warm that she knew they must be red, and she hoped her hair covered them. "And then . . . you walked her home from church yesterday."

"Kissing a girl doesn't mean you're going to marry her," Angus told her, reapplying elbow grease to the saw blade. "And walking her home doesn't, either. She's a pretty girl. I enjoy her company. But no, my friend, I am *not* going to marry her, or anybody else.''

He stopped what he was doing and looked directly into her face. ''I'm waiting for you to grow up, didn't you know that?''

She felt dizzy, unbalanced. ''I'm . . . almost fourteen,'' she said, swallowing hard.

Angus grinned. ''That's not quite grown-up enough, I'm afraid. Your old man would skin me alive and nail my pelt on the cookhouse door. Listen, Maggie, why don't you find out how they made that chocolate cake your ma served the other night, and see if you can get Mr. Murphy to make one? That was the best damned cake I ever ate.''

She didn't remember what she said to him after that, or how she got away. She remembered looking back through the trees from the skid road and seeing him at work with the saw; Hank Pallison had come from somewhere—dear God, he hadn't been listening to their conversation, had he?—to man the other end of it. Neither of them acted as if she were within miles of them.

She walked back to camp in a daze. Had he meant it? Had he really meant that he was waiting for her to grow up, and that he would then marry *her*?

She didn't know for sure, but even the possibility of such a prospect made her euphoric.

How old, she wondered, would she have to be, to be grown-up enough for Angus?

# 10

To the astonishment of everyone, Maggie invaded the kitchen.

"I don't want to peel potatoes, I want to make a cake," she said. "A chocolate cake, like the one we had at the party."

"Of course," Ann said. "I'll teach you myself."

The first effort was, for some reason, a poor one. Even Ann agreed that it would not do to put it on the table, for it had a hollow in its top and leaned drunkenly to one side.

Maggie was disappointed, but not discouraged. "I'll feed this one to Joe. Show me again," she requested.

This time the results were excellent. Maggie was not sure enough of this to take it to the loggers; it was served to the Keatings that evening, and all pronounced it to be nearly as good as Ann's.

The third cake was put on the table two days later at the cookhouse.

Maggie watched anxiously as Angus took his first bite, and saw the smile come over his face. "Ummmmm," he approved and devoured the slice that was his share without further comment.

She would have given him the entire cake if she'd dared, but it would have caused speculation and teasing from the other men. Their entertainments were few; ribald or cutting remarks placed high on the list. She couldn't bear it, Maggie thought, if anyone made fun of her for loving Angus, or of him for being her friend. The only safe thing to do was to keep her feelings a secret.

This was not easy when she overheard Red Risku say jokingly on a Monday following the weekend in town, "How far did you get with that little redhead at the Watering Hole Saturday night, McKay?"

Angus stuck half a biscuit in his mouth and chewed. "None of your damned business," he said, which made all the men around the table laugh. Only Maggie did not join in.

Indeed, it was impossible for her to fail to be aware that Angus sought out female company. In this respect he was no different from any of the others, except that she didn't care about *them*.

Though the men tried to temper the ribaldry when she was within hearing, they were so used to having her around that they sometimes forgot. At times they were careless, assuming they were speaking in purely masculine company; her ears would burn when she understood the significance of their references to various females.

She mentioned it to Nancy Totting, without being specific about her concerns over Angus.

"It seems to be mostly what they think about, except for their work and how much they drink on Saturday night. I think . . ." She hesitated, uncertain of how to word this. "I think they do things they shouldn't, with women they're not married to."

"Oh, Ma says they're a scandal," Nancy agreed. "There was a fight in the Riverbank Saloon a week or so ago, over a woman, and Mr. Henning said it was the worst case of logger's smallpox he ever saw. The fellow was bleeding all over."

Logger's smallpox, Maggie knew, was a reference to injuries inflicted by one logger upon another by stomping upon him with the calked, or spiked, shoes that enabled a man to climb trees more easily and safely. The only case she'd seen at close hand was when Tom Dunnigan had been so unfortunate as to have his arm in a position for another logger to walk on it rather forcefully. The closely patterned puncture wounds had made her cringe, though Tom had simply poured raw whiskey over them and gone on with his work.

"I guess they all have to do it," Nancy observed philosophically. "I mean, God made men, and He made women, and they . . . go to bed together."

It made Maggie feel easier that the other girl had put her own thoughts into words. "Mama says they aren't supposed to do it, though, unless they're married to each other."

"Oh, yes, Ma says the same thing, but that don't mean they all bother to get married first. My aunt *had* to get married."

Maggie's attention was arrested by that statement. "What do you mean? How could she *have* to do it?"

"Well, they talked about it mostly when I wasn't around, or they *thought* I wasn't. So I don't know *everything*. But I know whatever she did with Karl made her have a baby. She was crying, and Karl was swearing, and my grandpa said he'd marry her, by God, or Grandpa would take the shotgun to him."

Maggie's brow furrowed. "You mean, really? Shoot him?"

"That's what it sounded like. And so they got married, though Grandma and Ma cried all through the ceremony— my aunt didn't cry, so I don't know why *they* did—and when the baby was born I heard Ma talking about how it was a shotgun wedding, and they couldn't expect people to believe such a big baby was early."

Maggie digested that for a moment, then returned to what was bothering her. "Do you think all men do things like that? Go to bed with girls they don't intend to marry?"

Nancy shrugged. "Most of 'em, I reckon, if they get the chance. Of course, Ma says a decent girl won't do nothing wrong, and I guess it's wrong to do that with a man before you're married to him."

Nothing about the conversation made Maggie feel any better. Was Deborah McVea a decent girl? Did she let Angus do anything more than kiss her and hug her?

And if it wasn't right for the girl, how could it be right for the man? Would Angus do something really bad, *knowing* it was sinful?

Kissing a girl didn't mean a man was going to marry her, he'd said. That sounded wrong to Maggie, and she didn't want to believe that Angus would do anything wrong. Besides, all the other men did the same things, didn't they? It was confusing and disturbing.

That summer after she turned fourteen was one of the best, and the worst, that she could remember.

Most of the time she was very happy. She spent hours in the kitchen learning how to cook things, which she always tried out on the family before carrying her knowledge off to the cook shack to show off to the men. They were appreciative, and it was good for her ego to know that she had at least one of the attributes that Grandma Miles felt was necessary for a female.

On the days when Angus found a few minutes to talk to her, even if it was only to ask her to fetch a log stamper to brand a log, or a can of beaver oil to grease his boots, Maggie glowed with happiness.

On the days when she didn't get to speak to him at all, she wallowed in despair, especially if she heard references to Angus and some female in town; if he really cared about her, he'd make a point of seeking her out and speaking to her, wouldn't he?

Once she had to comment on the fact that he hadn't spoken to her in three days.

Angus gave her a keen-eyed stare. "Maggie, your old man was around the whole time, and I don't think it would be smart to let him know I've got my eye on you. He gets a bee in his bonnet, he's apt to give me my walking papers, and I need this job. Besides that"—the gray eyes narrowed—"it would be a good idea if you didn't hang around me, girl. It won't matter who pays too much attention to who. If Jake sees it, we're both goners."

Was it true? Would her father be perturbed if she appeared to be interested in Angus? If so, what would he do about it?

Angus had the answer to that. "If he thinks you're interested in anyone on the crew, or anyone is looking at you as more than a little girl, he'll keep you home. No more woods. No more logging camp."

The idea was horrifying.

She often helped Mr. Murphy around the cookhouse, even to washing dishes, though that was only when his helper was sick; there was neither pleasure nor glory in washing dishes, and it was hard on the hands. He was perfectly willing to allow her to cook, though.

That fall Maggie found a way to make herself valuable to Jake in the logging operation, and she latched onto it at once. If she had a real *job*, her father would be more likely to encourage, rather than discourage, the things she wanted to do.

She had taken piano lessons in the evenings all summer, along with Celeste, but where her sister had a natural aptitude for music, Maggie had none whatever. Her fingers felt wooden on the keys and the sounds she produced had none of what came so easily to Celeste—rhythm and melody and joyfulness.

Nobody criticized her efforts. They didn't have to. Maggie knew she was impossible at the keyboard. Ann tried to be optimistic. "Some people take longer than others to learn things. You're very good with cakes," she said.

"I'll never be any good with the piano," Maggie replied. "Mama, why can't I give up the lessons?"

"Playing the piano is such a marvelous accomplishment. Let's stick with it a little longer, Margaret. Please," Ann said, and Maggie bit her tongue and continued to try.

One evening in the fall, when Celeste was at the piano and Maggie sat dreading her own turn, trying to darn a sock that was going to be totally unwearable when she finished, Jake turned from the table where he was working on his accounts.

"Maggie, love, take this list and read it back to me, will you? There's a mistake here somewhere, and I can't find the damned thing."

Maggie dropped the lumpy sock into the mending basket and moved to his side, taking the proffered list. She read from it while Jake checked the figures against those in his ledger. Standing beside him this way, where the lamplight shone upon his head as well as upon the open account book, Maggie saw that there were silvery hairs mingling with the dark ones at his temples.

She felt a pang of dismay that caused her to stumble in her reading. Was he growing old? Everybody did, of course, yet Mama, across the room, was as blond and young-looking as ever. How could she bear it, to see her beloved daddy getting old?

He gave a muffled grunt of satisfaction. "There it is, right there. Here, Maggie, add up that column and see if you get the same thing I did, will you?"

She did, and he hugged her before he closed the book. "You were a big help. Maybe I'll let you help me all the time."

"All right," Maggie said. "I like adding up numbers."

Jake laughed. "So do I, especially if they're showing a profit, and the profit is mine." He raised his voice to carry across the room to his wife at the piano. "If nothing goes wrong, we'll be out of debt by the time we get paid for this last cutting. We can begin to think about things like schooling for the girls, something more than they can get in Snohomish. Maybe a good school in the East, what do you think?"

Maggie, still encircled by his arm, dug her fingernails into his shoulder. A school in the East? In a city, leaving Angus and Joe behind? A tremor ran through her, and Jake lifted his gaze to hers.

"What's the matter? You don't want to go to a fine school and learn to be a lady?"

"No," Maggie said, the intensity of her feeling making her voice husky. "No, please, Daddy. I can learn what I need to learn right here at home."

Ann had swiveled on the piano bench, looking very pretty in a soft blue gown, her fair hair gently waving around her face. "It might be something to think about, if we can afford it."

"Can I go away to school?" Celeste demanded.

"We'll see," Ann temporized. "We have a year or two to think about it before *you'll* be ready. You like reading, Margaret, and at one of those schools there would be all sorts of books you don't have here."

"I don't want to go," Maggie said, feeling an iciness in her bones that made her clutch at Jake with an arm around his neck. "I like it here. I want to help Daddy with the bookkeeping."

He regarded her thoughtfully. "You know, I've been thinking about hiring someone to do the books."

"Not Margaret!" Ann protested quickly. "I won't have it, Jake. It's bad enough that she's out there so much of the time, but to actually hold a job there . . . no. It's not the place for a well brought up young lady."

"I do the books here, mostly," Jake pointed out. "Well,

anyway, honey, you can give me a hand until I find someone who really knows accounting."

It was at best a compromise, and it didn't guarantee that she would never be sent away to school, but it was better than nothing. Maggie resolved to do such a good job, to make herself so indispensable, that Jake would not only need her on the operation but get her out of the hated piano lessons as well.

At first Nancy didn't understand Maggie's loathing of the lessons. "It's such a beautiful piano! Nicer than the one the Athenaeum Society has, actually. And when your mama plays it, it's so lovely!"

"Of course it's lovely," Maggie conceded. "Mama knows how to play. Even Celeste can make it sound good. But I have no ear for the music and I'll *never* play well if I practice for a hundred years." She looked at her friend morosely. "It's no fun to do something you can't do well, when you know you'll never get much better. It's like sewing; I just *can't* get tiny, neat stitches like Mama does."

"I don't sew very well, either," Nancy admitted. "Even Ma doesn't sew the way *your* mama does."

"No, but your ma can cook better than almost anybody. Grandma Miles says each of us has some talent we should be grateful for, and your ma's is cooking. I'm not sure what my talent is; maybe I don't have one."

Ann laughed when Maggie repeated that forlorn statement. "Oh, I'm sure you do, dear. You simply haven't discovered yet what it is. You're becoming quite good as a cook. That last cake was marvelous. It might be wise to do something other than cakes, though. How about trying a good stew?"

Angus didn't laugh when Maggie told him her concern that she might be without talent.

"I know one special talent you have right now," he said quietly.

"What?" Maggie demanded, torn between hope and suspicion that he was pulling her leg, as the men put it.

"You're a warm-hearted, kind person who makes everyone around you feel better, about the world and about himself," Angus said, and there was nothing to indicate he was not perfectly serious. "It's a pleasure to watch you walk, or run, or talk. Whatever you do. You're graceful and healthy and we are all very fond of you."

She'd have liked it better if he'd said *he* was very fond of her, instead of including the entire crew, but it made her feel *a little* better. Not a great deal, though. It didn't seem much of a talent. Certainly not on a par with the talents other girls had.

Throughout that summer, Maggie was aware of a growing dissatisfaction on her father's part with Hank Pallison. More and more often she heard him bawl the man out or criticize his work. Twice spontaneous ax-handle parties broke out because Pallison did something to which his fellow crew members objected.

"Damned fool nearly got me killed," Rich Salter exploded when Jake had broken up a mixup from which Salter emerged with a split lip and a black eye, and Pallison spat out a tooth. "I ain't gonna work with nobody that's gonna knock me out of a hundred-foot tree because he's stupid! He's crazier than an outhouse rat!"

There was a lot of shouting and swearing before everybody simmered down.

A few weeks later, there was another incident in which Hank Pallison did a poor job of securing a rigging. It resulted in a narrow escape for Red Risku when a chain broke, wrapping an end around the latter's body in a blow that knocked him momentarily senseless.

Maggie didn't see that happen, though she heard the shouting and later saw the great purple welts across Red's torso.

"It wasn't my fault," Pallison protested when Red

Risku called him a name that made Maggie's mouth drop open. "The damned hook broke."

"You fastened the hook, didn't you?" Red demanded. "Did you look at it ahead of time? Was it all right then? A hook don't just suddenly crack open—not like that, it don't."

"He knew we had a deadfall," Rich Salter spoke up, animosity clearly written across his countenance. "When you know it's extra dangerous, you check everything twice. *Every*thing."

Pallison threw a glance at Jake, coming out of the cook shack. "It's ain't my fault if the equipment's falling apart. It *looked* all right."

For a moment he and Red Risku glared at each other and Maggie wondered if they were going to fight; the thought of anyone landing a blow on that discolored flesh was enough to make her shudder.

Then Risku turned and walked away, and the moment was over.

The situation was not resolved, however.

The men began to mutter among themselves, usually at a time and place where either Jake or Pallison could hear them.

"If I was Keating, I'd tell the bastard to get the book, or take his bedroll and walk."

(There was no book of correct procedures, but everyone understood the inference: Pallison was too ignorant to do the job right.)

"He gets my tit in the wringer the way he did with Risku, I'll kill him."

"I learnt my loggin' by hand, and I don't want to work with no damned fool that won't bother to do the same."

"He's goin' to be lookin' at the daisies from the wrong end, he has about one more o' his accidents when I'm around. He come within a frog's hair o' droppin' his damn oil bottle on my head. Spilt it all over my good shirt."

The complaints were endless.

Walking home with Jake a few weeks after the incident when Risku had been injured, Maggie broached the subject in a subdued way.

"Is it true the men are in danger because the equipment isn't safe, Daddy?"

Jake looked at her sharply, not breaking stride; she almost had to run to keep up with his long steps. "They saying that? I'm not keeping the equipment up right?"

"Well, there was a chain snapped again this afternoon. Nobody was hurt, but they could have been. They didn't blame this one on Hank Pallison, but when they talk about him they sound so . . . ugly."

Jake sighed. "Yeah. I'm going to have to do something about Pallison. I hate to fire a man's got a family to support, but if I don't get rid of him, I'm going to lose the whole crew. I guess we need to check over all our equipment, make double sure it's not too old and wore out to be safe. I haven't bought much new since I took over the outfit from Newsome."

"Don't we have the money to get new equipment?" Maggie thought of the piano in the new music room, and what it had cost.

"Well, the price of lumber is good, and we're cutting it as fast as we can, but the money won't be in for a few months yet. The stuff we got will be fine, if everybody's careful," Jake said, leaving Maggie with an uneasy feeling.

Two days later, it happened.

Maggie had made half a dozen blackberry pies with fruit she'd gathered that morning; she had just taken them out of the oven and was admiring the tender, flaky crust with dark-purple juice oozing through the vent holes cut into it, when she heard the signal.

Four longs, four shorts.

The whistle had no more than died away when the signal was repeated. After that there was only ominous silence.

The crew was not so far away that those in camp would have failed to hear shouting from the nearer workers, had there been any.

Maggie's mouth went dry. She put up a hand to brush back a strand of dark hair, moist with perspiration from the heat of the big iron stove.

Mr. Murphy, in the act of pouring himself a cup of coffee, met her eyes in shared alarm.

Very carefully, Maggie put down the last of the pies and untied her apron. Not Daddy. Please, God, not Daddy, she begged silently. She placed the neatly folded apron—for some reason it seemed important that she do it properly—on the edge of the table, and stepped out into the late-summer sunshine.

There was a breeze that touched the tops of the firs around the clearing; a jay screeched from the top of one of them. The mingled scents of the trees and woodsmoke and the warm aroma of the pies were familiar and pleasant, as they always were, yet there was a prickle of gooseflesh on Maggie's bare arms.

Mr. Murphy joined her, silent, apprehensive, and they stared off through the woods to the place where the men were working.

"They're two miles out," Mr. Murphy muttered at last. "Too far for an old man to run."

Maggie's tongue touched her lips. Her silent prayer was constant, almost mindless. Not Daddy. Not Angus. Please, please.

They stood listening, waiting, for what seemed a very long time.

A sound behind them brought the old man and the girl around, startled, but it was not loggers. It was Ann and Celeste, in the buggy, Ann leaning forward urgently even before she brought the horse to a stop.

"We heard the signal. What is it, Margaret?"

Maggie made her lips move, putting down the fear. "We don't know. They're working a long way out today."

"They signaled twice. Does that mean it's worse than if it was only once?"

Maggie didn't answer. Mr. Murphy sighed. "Could be," he said.

Ann made no move to get out of the conveyance. "Can we get through to where they are in the buggy?" She was pale yet controlled, knowing what she might find at the end of her brief journey, knowing as well that if the grief were not to be hers, it would belong to someone else. At worst someone was dead; at best, only injured. The whistle punk would never have signaled twice for anything less than a genuine disaster.

Maggie swung up onto the seat, squeezing Celeste against her mother. "Maybe. I know where they are. Let's take the skid road and find out."

Ann spoke to the cook with apparent calm. "Do you want to come with us, Mr. Murphy?"

"Got stuff cooking will scorch for sure if I leave it," the old man decided after a brief hesitation. "Even if somebody's killed, the rest of 'em'll still have to eat."

The skid road was easy to follow, though not very smooth. The buggy jarred and jolted. The girls hung on to the edge of the seat to keep from being thrown to the ground; it was almost a relief to Maggie to have something to take her mind off speculations about what had happened this time, to fight instead to stay on the seat.

*Please God, don't let it be an accident because the equipment failed because it was too old.*

The thought hit her with the force of a blow. Did she think Jake would have allowed the men to use unsafe gear in order to save a few dollars? No, no, of course not. Yet the idea, once implanted, refused to go away.

The silence was oppressive, except for the clop-clop of

the horse's feet on the corduroy road and the faint squeaking of the buggy wheels. Not even a bird sang.

There were no normal sounds of a logging operation, no saws, no axes, no voices.

Maggie didn't remember it ever being so still in the woods before.

They reached the end of the skid road; and then, before anyone but Maggie had jumped down, they saw the men coming through the trees.

It was impossible to tell who they carried on the splatter sheet, as the men referred to a stretcher. He wore a red plaid shirt, as did half the men in the crew; his arms dangled over the sides, fingertips at times brushing the ferns as the men stumbled over rough ground. Maggie hadn't seen Angus that morning, she didn't know what he was wearing, but Jake had worn red. The cramp in her chest was so painful that she pressed the heel of her hand against her breastbone. She was past the point, now, of being able to formulate a prayer.

She didn't see either Angus or Jake. Maggie stepped off the grade, skidding a little in loose earth, and made her way toward the silent, approaching men.

The two on the front end of the stretcher came to a halt. "Don't look at him, Maggie," Rich Salter warned her. "He ain't a pretty sight. He fell a good two hundred feet."

"His soul was in hell before he ever hit the ground," Red Risku said, but there was no satisfaction in his voice. "Least it was himself he killed, not anybody else."

Maggie examined their faces and knew they would be registering different emotions if the victim had been her father. Whoever he was, the victim was a big man. As big as Jake, but the boots were not Jake's. She made a guess. "Hank Pallison?"

The men began to move again, and after a quick glance that brought bile up into her throat, Maggie looked away, striding beside the leaders toward the road. "What happened?"

"It was like tryin' to butter up a wildcat with a hot awl to get him to check equipment or pay attention to what he was told," Salter said, and spat into the brush beside the trail. "We had a hung tree, and McKay told him to stay out of the way until Risku got there to help, only he knew it all. Always thought he knew it all, Pallison did. Well, this time he got hisself killed. Lucky it wasn't McKay."

Terror coursed through her anew. "Is he hurt? Angus?"

"Nah, just scraped up a little. Jake's with him, he's all right. Trunk didn't get him, just the branches."

Maggie had come to a stop, feeling too weak to move for a moment, and the men went on past her. She heard Red call out, "Can we use the buggy to get him back to the landing, Mrs. Keating?"

Ann was already sliding down from the seat. "Yes, of course. Only it's a terribly rough ride...."

"Won't matter to him," Salter said flatly, and spat again. "He's deader than a wedge."

Maggie glanced back at them, then began to walk, and then to run, through the woods, to make sure that Angus was really all right.

# 11

THE men stood around, avoiding looking at the body that had been hastily draped with a blanket in the back of Mr. Murphy's supply wagon.

"Who's gonna tell his missus?" somebody asked.

There was considerable shuffling of feet, a slapping of a cap against a thigh, cleared throats.

Maggie heard them and pressed her hands against her own chest as if by so doing she could calm the tumult there. She had been sick with relief that it wasn't Jake or Angus, though the latter looked rather battered after having the branches of a two-hundred-and-twenty-foot fir knock him down. He'd been pinned there until the others came with saws and axes to free him.

Angus had never been one for profanity, at least not to the degree that most of the others were; to hear him swearing as she approached the site of the accident had been profoundly reassuring, and she'd nearly cried with the release of tension. Anyone who could curse that fluently was certainly going to live.

She hadn't cried, of course. She would have felt a disgrace to them all, to have done that. Ann hadn't cried, either, though she had been very pale and had been reassured only when she'd actually put a hand on Jake's shoulder to see that the blood on him was not his own.

"You and Celeste go back to the house. I'll take care of everything," Jake told his wife.

"Margaret—" Ann began, only to have Jake interrupt her.

"I need Maggie here. Celeste, go with Mama and the men will clean out the buggy so you can go on home."

Ann had not protested, as Maggie half expected she might, but had bravely driven back to camp with the buggy and its terribly burden while the others walked behind it.

Maggie didn't even remember the walk, only that she'd been between Angus, who though bleeding and in obvious pain was not in serious condition, and her father. Jake's hands were bloody and there were stains on his clothes, as well.

"I should have fired the poor bastard," Jake said once, and Angus agreed with more vehemence than was customary with him.

"At least he'd still be alive, if I had," Jake said, and Maggie reached out to put her hand in his before she remembered that the hand was covered in Pallison's dried blood.

Now the men stood around, ignoring Mr. Murphy's question about dinner. Nobody was hungry.

Tom Dunnigan cleared his throat and voiced, again, the question on everybody's mind.

"Who's goin' to tell his old lady?"

This time Jake heard it. Perceptibly, he drew himself together, inhaling and squaring his shoulders. "I'm the boss. I'll tell her. Anybody willing to volunteer to take the body in to the undertaker's?"

There was a small silence before several men stepped forward, their tones subdued. "I'll go." "I'll drive the wagon."

Maggie touched her father's sleeve. "Do you want me to go with you to Mrs. Pallison's, Daddy?"

"I'd be pleased to have you, honey. The rest of you might as well eat. Murphy's got it all cooked."

"You want us to go back to work?" Red Risku asked, twisting his cap between his large hands.

"Maybe you better spend the rest of the day checking equipment," Jake said heavily, after a moment's hesitation. "Go over every damned rope, every chain, every hook, every saw. Anything looks like it's too worn, set it aside. We got trees to get down, and we can't afford any more accidents like today's. We'll cut timber again in the morning."

Slowly, the men dispersed. Rich Salter was driving the wagon, and he would give Jake and Maggie a ride to the landing, where they'd get the buggy for their own journey to Snohomish.

Maggie had seen Hank Pallison's wife at the housewarming, though she'd paid little attention to her. Older than Mama, probably thirty-five or-six, Maggie guessed.

She met them at the door of the shack in which the Pallisons had lived on the north edge of town, near Blackman Lake. It wasn't much of a house, Maggie thought as they rolled into the yard.

She glanced at Jake, whose whiskery jaws were locked and jutting. How did you tell someone her husband had died? Maggie slid a hand onto his knee, and he covered it with one of his own.

He gave her a bitter grin. "One of the privileges of being the boss, getting to convey the bad news. I never envied Ed that job."

"She has children, doesn't she?"

He sighed again, as he'd been doing ever since it happened. "Three of them. You want to wait in the buggy, Maggie?"

She would have liked nothing better, but it wouldn't be right. She'd come to try to provide some small measure of comfort to him, and maybe she ought to do something for Mrs. Pallison, too. She mentally braced herself as Jake brought the horse and buggy to a stop in front of the unpainted wooden cabin.

Jaisy Pallison stood in the doorway, a child on each side of her, clinging to her skirts. She was what Millicent Miles would have described as "blowsy" or "overblown" and it was true that she was too well rounded to fit the classic mold of beauty. Yet there was something about her that was attractive; even Maggie saw it, in the carelessly dressed auburn hair and the clear skin. Full breasts strained at the fabric of the faded calico gown, and the waistline was too tight, so that a button or two had been left open. Yet the wide mouth looked kind, the hazel eyes compassionate.

Jaisy smiled uncertainly. "Mr. Keating. Nothing wrong, is there?"

Jake had forgotten to lift Maggie down from the buggy; she scrambled after him as he approached the doorstep, cap in hand. "I'm afraid so, ma'am. We had a bad accident in the woods this morning."

The smile wavered, then vanished. Involuntarily, her arms tightened around the children's shoulders. "Hank? He's hurt?"

Jake inhaled deeply, and Maggie reached him in time to see the way that he groped for the right words. And then he didn't have to say them, after all, the phrases he'd been rehearsing all the way from the landing.

Maggie watched comprehension creep over Jaisy Pallison's face. Tiny lines appeared around her full-lipped mouth and around her eyes. She looked suddenly years older.

"He's dead? Hank's dead?" It was little more than a whisper.

"I'm sorry," Jake said inadequately. "The men are bringing him in the wagon. They'll take him to the undertaker's." He hesitated, then added quietly, "It might be better if you didn't go see him, ma'am. He fell a long way."

Jaisy visibly pulled herself together, drawing strength from some unseen source. "No. I'll have to go." She turned to speak to someone behind her. "Ned, you'll have to watch the younguns. Fetch my shawl."

Unable to look at the naked grief in the woman's eyes, Maggie studied the children instead. A boy of about six, a girl of perhaps eight. The boy who appeared with the shawl was probably Maggie's own age, thirteen or fourteen. His hair was carroty-red; the younger children's heads were capped in a pale red-gold. Beautiful hair, Maggie thought, but all three of them had something else in common. They were too white, the look of the undernourishment emphasized by the natural pallor of their skin. The older boy had a wild crop of freckles. She'd seen him at school, though he didn't come very often and she hadn't known his name.

"Mrs. Pallison, you have any money to live on?" Jake asked.

She stared at him in a state of shock, as if she didn't understand.

"Hank had a paycheck coming. I'll see you get it."

She moistened the full, red lips. "Thank you, Mr. Keating." She wrapped the worn shawl around her shoulders and stepped outside, disentangling herself from the children. The boy clung to her, beginning to whimper, until the one called Ned took him inside and closed the door.

"If you insist on going, ma'am, let us give you a ride," Jake offered, and Jaisy Pallison made no protest.

She sat beside Maggie; the warmth of her came through their clothes as thigh pressed against thigh. Hank Pallison was probably already cold, Maggie thought, and guessed at the agony this woman must be feeling, the agony that would one day be her own when she lost Jake, or her mother.

Maggie's throat ached, but she couldn't think of anything to say. She was glad when Mrs. Pallison got down at the undertaker's, and Jake headed the horse for home.

By suppertime Ann had recovered her composure, and she did not add to Jake's burden by telling him how frightened she had been, how convinced that *he* was the victim this time. She had made chicken and dumplings, which Jake loved, and he ate heartily while ruminating on the situation. "He had about fifty dollars coming in wages. She's got a garden and a few chickens, but the lazy bastard hadn't put in the winter's wood. On payday we'll take up a collection for her, which'll probably give her another ten, fifteen dollars. That's not going to get her and those kids through the winter."

"Does she have any family?" Ann asked, face troubled.

Jake shook his head. "Nobody nearer than Illinois, from what Hank said." He swore softly. "I'm going to have to pay to bury him. She can't afford a pine box, from the look of that place. I'll bet the damned roof leaks, from what I saw. It's going to make me feel guilty if I don't see that's fixed, too."

Ann touched his sleeve. "It wasn't your fault he was killed, Jake. You've said for months that he was a careless worker. He caused the accident himself."

"That's just it. I *knew* he wasn't safe in the woods. I should have fired him.

"He'd only have gone to work for some other outfit."

"Then he'd have broken himself all to hell falling out of somebody else's tree, not mine. *I* wouldn't be the one feeling guilty about him."

"I'll talk to Mrs. Totting," Ann said, withdrawing her hand and taking up her fork. "We'll put together a basket of things to send over. Margaret, maybe you could make one of your cakes, and there's a haunch of that venison left. What do you think, Jake?''

"Go ahead. She's going to need all the help she can get."

"She doesn't go to church anywhere, does she?"

"Not that I know of. Hank sure as hell didn't. That shouldn't stop the church ladies from lending a helping hand, though. Didn't Christ tell his followers to help the sinners as well as the saints?''

It always seemed to make Ann mildly uncomfortable when Jake spoke of matters religious. It was as if she suspected him of sardonic irony, because though he made no profession of faith for himself, he had an annoying knack for throwing biblical quotations back at her at the most inopportune moments.

This time, however, she didn't bother to think about it. She felt genuinely sorry for the woman who had been widowed, and not entirely without guilt herself; she was so grateful that it was not *she* who must cope on her own with raising a family.

"I'll talk to the church women," she said, "and see if they can help, too."

The following day, the work went on as usual in the woods. Angus McKay exhibited various abraded and scabbed-over areas, but no more than many of the men acquired on a normal Saturday night in Snohomish.

Two weeks after Hank Pallison died, Ann learned that she was pregnant.

"I can't be!" she protested to her mother. "I'm thirty-three years old, and I don't want another child!"

"Wanting or not wanting hasn't much to do with it," Millicent said. "If your husband were more considerate, you wouldn't have to worry about such things. Your father—" She colored slightly, for she almost never spoke of such matters, even though her daughter had been a married woman for nearly fifteen years. "After you were born, and he knew that all that business was . . . distasteful to me . . . he never forced himself on me." The color deepened. "At least, not very often."

Much as she had cared for her father, Ann was under no illusions about his masculinity. Stokes Miles and Jake Keating had been completely different species. Jake, Ann suspected, would not give up his physical pleasures until they nailed down the top of the pine box in which he would be buried, though he had reduced the frequency of the demands he made upon her.

She made no response now to her mother's observation. Sex was not something Ann strongly craved, though she delighted in the flirtation of the drawing room and would have enjoyed the preliminary sexual maneuverings if they had not inevitably led to the messy act itself. Even if it had not skirted the dangers of pregnancy, however, Ann would have been far less interested in lovemaking than her husband was.

That evening, in the privacy of their bedroom, Jake undressed and then looked at his wife, sensing something out of kilter. There was an expression on her face that made him pad across the flowered rug to where she sat before her dressing table, looking into the mirror.

"What's the matter, love? You feeling peaked? It's not the wrong time of the month, is it?"

Ann met his eyes in the mirror without looking around. He was forty-seven years old, yet his body, white where it was protected from the sun that had so deeply tanned his face and arms, was as firm and muscular as it had been when they married. Aside from the fact that there were a few strands of gray in the mat of hair on his chest and at his temples, there was little sign of aging.

"It should be," she said with a wry twist of her mouth. "Only it's not."

For a moment he looked blank, and then a grin widened

his mouth. "You mean you're going to have another baby?"

"So it seems. Jake, I don't *want* another baby."

"Why not? Maybe it'll be a boy this time."

"It was a boy last time." Her eyes were suddenly brimming. "I can't go through that again, Jake. I can't!"

His hands came down on her shoulders, and she felt the warmth of his body pressed against her back. "Honey, there's no reason to think you'll lose this one."

"I'll be lucky to carry it full term," Ann said, in an odd juggling of logic that Jake wisely chose to ignore. "It'll die before it's time for it to be born. Or afterward, like Charlie."

She began to cry, and Jake turned her around and took her in his arms. "Don't, Ann. It'll be all right. I promise you. Come on to bed, you're worn out."

She allowed herself to be drawn to bed, and after the light was blown out, into his arms. "No, Jake," she began, but this time he didn't simply kiss her and roll over and go to sleep.

"Honey," he said, "why not? If you're already expecting, it can't do any harm, and we need each other. You need me as much as I need you."

Memory tore at her, the memory of the way she'd felt when she'd thought it might be Jake dead in that terrible accident, and for once she knew he was right. She *did* need him. She opened her lips to his.

## 12

It was a difficult pregnancy.

Ann was queasy not only when she arose in the morning, but most of the day. Only in the evening did the nausea subside so that she could eat with any expectation of keeping the food down.

Even in their enlarged household, with more privacy than they'd ever known before, it was impossible to keep the matter a secret from the girls.

"Why is Mama throwing up all the time?" Celeste wanted to know.

Maggie had figured it out, after a consultation with Nancy Totting. "She's going to have another baby."

It made her feel very strange, to know that. She'd been so young when Charlie was born that she'd been unaware of the significance of his conception and birth; this time she was grown-up enough to realize what it all meant. First, that her parents had been doing something in bed that was humiliating to think about—and the proof of it would soon be evident in a swollen belly, so everyone in town would know—and second, she thought about the infant developing inside of Ann, a child like Charlie, who might be luckier than poor Charlie had been. Maggie was torn between joyful anticipation and embarrassment on behalf of her parents.

It wasn't long before she was made aware of other sources of discomfort.

When Ann didn't feel well, she was waspy and unreasonable; for a time she insisted on continuing the piano lessons in the evening, when she felt her best, but she became more sharply impatient with Maggie's ineptitude.

"No, *no*, Margaret, like *this*! Can't you remember anything from last time?"

After one particularly frustrating session, Maggie was rendered into a shaking state which could not, she thought, continue. She slid off the bench and stood up, not looking at her father or grandmother on the far side of the room.

"Mama, I know you don't feel well, and that's making it difficult for you. But I can't help not having any musical ability. I can't be like Celeste, I can't do it. I'm not going to play well if I practice for a hundred years, so I'm not going to practice anymore at all. I never want to touch a piano again."

Ann swiveled on the bench to stare at her in astonishment. "What do you mean, telling me what you're going to do and not do?"

Behind her, Jake's newspaper crackled as he lowered it onto his knees.

"I'm sorry, Mama, but I mean it. I won't play the piano anymore." The stubbornness that had driven Ann wild through Maggie's childhood surfaced again; there was a jut to her jaw (much like the one Jake sometimes displayed) and a spark in her eyes that bespoke determination. "I'm nearly fifteen years old. I'm old enough to decide a few things for myself, and that's one of them."

Ann had gone pale. Now she flushed hotly, and rose to her feet. "I will not have you speaking to me in that manner, Margaret Ellen."

At that point Jake took his cigar out of his mouth, tossed it into the open fire, and folded his newspaper. "I've been meaning to talk to you about that, Ann. I agree with

Maggie; she's never going to be a piano player, so why torture her and the rest of us listening to those damned scales and exercises? Especially when there's something she *is* good at, and I need some of her time to help me. She's got a head for figures, she's quicker than I am, and it would help like hell if she'd take over the accounts so I didn't have to do them at night when I'm too tired to think straight.''

It didn't end that simply, of course. Maggie heard them arguing long after they'd gone to their room that night; though she couldn't make out the words, the tones were plain enough.

She felt bad about causing a quarrel, because the disagreements between them had not been so noticeable for a time, but she was undeniably pleased that Jake had taken her side in the matter of the hopeless piano lessons. She had no doubt about having won that battle, even though the end of it went on behind her parents' closed bedroom door.

Had her own words tipped the balance? she wondered later. Or had it been going on all along, and she'd been so busy with her own concerns that she'd failed to notice?

Now that she *had* noticed, the friction was obvious. And one of the causes of the friction was Jaisy Pallison.

Until the logging operations shut down for the winter, Jake had only Sundays to relax with the family. Gradually, it seemed that he spent no time at home at all.

"You're not going to church with us?" Ann asked, at first mildly annoyed, then growing more angry about it as the weeks passed and Jake refused to clean up and join them at services.

"Risku and Dunnigan took a load of wood over to Pallisons' last week, but it needs to be split. I thought I'd take my ax over and do it."

Ann's lips compressed. "Doesn't she have a son big enough to do that?"

Jake grunted. "Kid's working his butt off as it is. He's a puny little thing, skinny as a rail. Looks to me like he's been underfed and overworked most of his life. He can't begin to do everything needs doing over there."

At first it was the firewood. Then it was fixing the roof, which took four successive Sundays even though some of the other men managed to ignore their customary Sabbath hangovers and help for a few hours each time.

Ann drove the buggy past the place on the way home from services, not stopping, but addressing her husband with asperity when he finally came home half an hour after the others had sat down to supper.

"I suppose you paid for the shingles," she pressed, as Jake dug into the roast and potatoes and vegetables she had not bothered to reheat for him.

He gave her a tolerant look. "Yes, I paid for them. Who else you think could? The damned roof was so full of holes it soaked their beds the last time it rained. Maggie, get me some more butter, will you?"

It was one of his frequent tactics, to change subjects rather than openly argue with her, but it didn't always work. Ann was as aware of his purpose as he was. "How much longer are you going to be spending time over there?"

"Until the roof's done. Probably take us another two Sundays, if we're lucky and it doesn't rain on one of them. Maggie, sweetheart, did you have a chance to add up those figures?"

This time Ann allowed the switch of subjects, but no one thought she had dropped it permanently. Not unless Jake stopped going over to Pallisons' on his free time.

No one could doubt that Jaisy Pallison needed a man's help around her place. Hank hadn't done much to keep up any part of it, and while the boy, Ned, did his best, he was neither strong enough nor knowledgeable enough to handle everything that needed doing.

Besides that, Jake liked working there.

He was sympathetic toward his wife, and had there been any way he could have undone the pregnancy, or helped her through the physical discomfort of it, he would have done so.

However, he was helpless in both regards, and Ann did not welcome his affectionate overtures even when they did not lead to the bedroom. The sharpness of her tongue grew in direct proportion to her own discomfort or unhappiness, and he found it increasingly difficult to stay in the same room with her without coming to verbal blows.

Jaisy, on the other hand, was pleasant and grateful for every chore he performed.

Jaisy was very different from Ann. Uneducated, she had little coquetry about her, little pretense that things were other than they were. Her voice was perhaps louder than those of the ladies who belonged to the church, and she spoke quite naturally about matters that any of them would have sidestepped as being inappropriate for females to discuss.

There was a lack of artifice about her that Jake found appealing. She was hospitable insofar as it was possible for her to be; she offered him coffee when he paused in his labors, with only a mild apology.

"I've used the grounds a couple of times already, so I hope it's got some taste."

It didn't have much, and there was no sugar to put in it, but it was hot. Jake sat at her table and drank it, watching her sip at her own.

Her brown dress was open at the throat, providing a tantalizing glimpse of the full breasts that strained against the material. Her skin was lovely, pale and creamy, except for the hands that were constantly in water as she scrubbed clothes and washed dishes. She'd have beautiful hands if they weren't so chapped, Jake thought. They were nicely shaped, and strong.

Everything about her was strong, he decided. Living

with Hank Pallison, no doubt she'd had to be. He was too shiftless to tend to things, and she'd taken on what she had to.

The first time he caught her chopping wood, he'd dressed down the boy. "That's too much of a job for her, Ned. You ought to be able to keep enough chopped for the stove, so she doesn't have to do it."

The boy gave him a sullen look. "Yessir," he muttered.

Still, when Jake watched him later, Ned seemed too frail to accomplish much. Jake took to chopping a stack of wood and carrying it inside to drop beside the stove whenever he finished whatever else he was working on.

He sipped at the nearly tasteless brew and admired the way her eyebrows grew in thick auburn arches above the hazel eyes, the well-modeled nose, and the wide, full-lipped mouth that could turn up in a smile at the slightest provocation.

He suspected she hadn't had much provocation, living with Pallison.

Jaisy didn't often talk about her husband. The first week or two after Hank was killed, her eyes were red-rimmed most of the time, and there were no smiles. After that, she seemed to accept her fate and try to make the best of it.

"I appreciate what you've done for us, Mr. Keating," she said now, draining her own mug. "I don't reckon that roof would have held up through another winter. First good snow and we'd have had roof, snow, and all right in our laps." She smiled a little, as if the idea were amusing rather than appalling.

"My name's Jake," he said, his gaze on the spot where her blood pulsed visibly at the base of her throat.

"All right. Jake," Jaisy said, and the hint of a smile remained around the corners of her mouth.

He didn't know another woman who would have accepted that, called him by his first name, on such a limited acquaintance. He liked it that Jaisy did.

By the time the operation shut down in the woods because of the cold, heavy rains, everything was in fairly good shape at Pallisons'. The cabin was snug, there were six cords of wood stacked under the eaves and in the lean-to, and strings of onions hung drying from the rafters while potatoes, carrots, and cabbages were preserved in layers of sawdust in the shed.

That should have ended it. It didn't.

Sitting around the parlor on Sunday afternoons, listening to his mother-in-law read from the Scriptures, watching Ann stitch on baby garments or mend socks, was impossible. He had to have fresh air, exercise, friendly conversation, not pious platitudes.

He began to join his crew over their ale and their whiskeys in town, and though he never appeared drunk when he returned home, Ann would turn away from the smell.

Jake knew he was asking for trouble, but he couldn't help it, he told himself. He needed a friend, a pretty face, a sympathetic voice. He fell into the habit of stopping off at Jaisy's for a cup of coffee or tea—he brought her some of each, so that she didn't have to reuse them until all the flavor was gone, though he suspected she saved them mostly for his visits, instead of enjoying them when she was alone—and letting Ann, of course, think he'd been at a tavern.

Jaisy never seemed to care if he dropped in unannounced. If she was kneading bread, sleeves rolled to the elbows revealing fully fleshed arms with a spattering of freckles on them, she would go on with her task after offering him a chair and a steaming mug.

If he wanted to talk, she listened. If he encouraged her to talk, she did. Jaisy, he decided, was the most comfortable female to be around that he'd ever encountered.

It didn't escape his notice that the boy, Ned, viewed him with hostility.

Well, why shouldn't he? Jake thought wryly. He'd lost his own father, and this stranger was taking up more of his mother's time than he had any right to. Especially considering the fact that the stranger had a wife and a home of his own a few miles out of town.

Thereafter, however, Jake tried to be more circumspect. The Pallison cabin was fairly isolated, and if he went only when the children were in school, no one would be aware of his visits except Jaisy herself. Jaisy never went anywhere, never visited any other women, and he knew instinctively that she wouldn't mention him to anyone anyway.

He didn't try to justify, even to himself, these clearly illicit visits.

He only knew that he wanted to go to Jaisy's.

At first Maggie wasn't concerned about the time her father spent at Jaisy Pallison's. The woman had recently been widowed, she needed help, and Jake felt guilty about her husband's death. Jake had often taken the responsibilities for many things beyond those of his immediate family, so helping Mrs. Pallison was not out of the ordinary. He had helped Mrs. Newsome after her husband was injured, too, and occasionally still did. When she thought about it at all, Maggie decided that her mother was overly touchy because of the pregnancy, that she was making the proverbial mountain out of a molehill, as she'd been known to do in the past.

Maggie was so happy dreaming about Angus McKay that she was less perceptive than usual about what went on around her. On a day that Angus talked to her, even for a few minutes, she could spend the rest of the day in fantasy that made her oblivious to everything else. She could pretend that Angus didn't talk to Deborah McVea at church, or dance with her at the Athenaeum when there was a community dance, or do anything that made his fellow loggers taunt him about the girls who worked in the saloons.

Maggie longed to go to the dances herself; Ann and Jake went sporadically, or at least they had until Ann got pregnant. If she went, surely Angus would dance with her, at least once. She was a far better dancer than she was a pianist; she didn't think she'd disgrace herself and Angus if she had a chance to try out the steps with someone other than Celeste and Nancy Totting. .

"Next year," Ann said firmly, and Jake backed her up. "Grow up a little more, sweetheart," he added, smiling.

She suspected that Angus was right, that Jake didn't really want her to grow up too fast, and that he'd be very particular about who her friends were. Her suitors.

She only wanted one suitor. Angus. When she was sixteen, Maggie thought, that would surely be old enough to be allowed to attend dances and plays, and to invite Angus to come calling upon her.

When school started in the fall, she saw Ned Pallison. She smiled and said hello, and was taken aback when his manner was less than cordial. He turned and walked away, leaving her embarrassed and uncomfortable, without knowing why.

By early December, she knew why.

The boy was waiting for her as she walked home from school through the slush remaining from the first snowfall. It was half-melted, quite slippery in spots, and the trees along the road dripped wetly, so that she'd moved out into the center to get out from under them.

He stepped into her path, and Maggie came to a stop, clutching her books against her chest.

"Hello," she said uncertainly, for it seemed that there was something threatening in his stance.

She wasn't physically afraid of him. He was no taller than she, and nearly as slender. Yet there was something in his face that put her on the defensive.

"You tell your old man to stay away from our place," Ned Pallison said.

"What?" She couldn't believe she'd heard him correctly. "I don't know what you're talking about."

"I'm talking about him stopping off to visit my ma when there ain't nobody else there." The boy's face was very white, so that the freckles stood out on it with vivid clarity. His hands formed impotent fists. "My ma don't need any trouble, and your old man's trouble. You tell him."

"I don't know what you're talking about," Maggie said again, although it was becoming sickeningly clear. "He was there to put on a new roof, and build a shed or something. . . ."

"The roof's done, and so's the shed. There ain't no reason why he needs to come back. We don't need him. Just because Pa died, don't mean we need *him*."

Maggie carefully moistened her lips. They were cold to her tongue. "If your ma doesn't want him, I guess she'd tell him, wouldn't she?"

Were there tears in the blue eyes? Certainly there was no mistaking the ferocity and frustration in Ned's face. "She ain't got no sense. She don't know what to do, with Pa gone. But she's got no business having Jake Keating in to sit and drink coffee with her every afternoon."

That was a shock. Every afternoon? Even allowing for some exaggeration, this was a matter for concern.

"I can't help what my father does," Maggie pointed out, "any more than you can help what your ma does. I'm sure he doesn't mean her any harm, he only wants to help because he feels sorry that your pa was killed."

Ned's mouth twisted. "You're such a baby, you don't know nothing. A man don't come every day and sit and drink coffee with a woman he ain't married to, and split kindling for her, just because he's sorry her husband died."

She recognized the truth of that, yet knew nothing to say to ease the burden he carried. The burden he had now transferred, at least in part, to her. For a moment she hated him for having told her.

Maggie stood there in the middle of the muddy road, her feet growing cold, her chest feeling as if it contained a lump of lead. Daddy and Mrs. Pallison? She wanted to deny it, yet she could not. She said nothing, and after a time Ned Pallison said, though with less heat, "You just tell 'im," and turned and walked away.

Maggie wanted to throw up. It couldn't be true, what he'd insinuated. Yet all the little things she'd managed to ignore up to now came flooding back to her.

The cross way Mama spoke these days when Jaisy Pallison's name came up. The way she protested that Jake had done his duty by the woman, that he wasn't responsible for her. The increasing number of quarrels that took place, mostly behind their closed bedroom door but sometimes over the supper table. Only a few days ago Jake had risen, leaving a half-eaten meal, to walk out of the house because Ann had questioned where he'd been all afternoon again.

Again, and again, and again, Maggie thought. It was true. He was almost never there when she came home from school, and occasionally he was late for supper. He often left home after supper, too, saying he was joining the loggers for a drink and some talk, leaving Ann with a pinched mouth and an inability to finish her own meal.

Did her mother know where he really was? How it must hurt her, if she did! And her not feeling well, either, and worried about the coming baby.

Maggie's anger turned from the tale-bearing boy to her father. How could he do it? How could he hurt his wife and his family this way?

And then, of course, came deeper consideration. Ned had said Jake went and drank coffee with Jaisy every day.

Was that all they did? Or were there worse things, the things that Granpa Miles had said were so wicked that they would lead to eternal hellfire and damnation?

She felt as if the word were branded in her brain.

*Adultery.*

Was her father guilty of that, of doing things with Mrs. Pallison that he had no right to do with anyone but his wife?

Maggie trudged on toward home, her throat and chest aching, tears blurring her eyes.

# 13

THE winter was a miserable one. It was not the weather so much, although heavy snows alternating with near freezing rains made it difficult to spend as much time out-of-doors as Maggie would have liked. Indeed, the weather would not have kept her inside had not Ann insisted that she would be sick if she got cold and wet and must therefore stay by the fire. Maggie almost never got sick, and she couldn't remember a single instance in which she'd had a cold or a fever after getting drenched or half-frozen.

The misery emanated from within the house at Keating's Landing, as their place had become known.

Most pregnancies, Nancy Totting confided from her fund of superior knowledge about such things (learned from a large and prolific clan of uncles and aunts and cousins), were only wretched through the first three or four months. After that, the morning sickness had subsided and, except for the swelling belly that gave away the secret to one and all, the discomforts were relatively minor until the final weeks and the actual delivery of the baby.

This was not the case with Ann's present pregnancy.

She continued to feel queasy enough so that it interfered with eating and retaining enough food to be healthy. She had no energy and took long naps every afternoon, periods that were a blessing to her family, though none of them spoke of it. Even Millicent found her daughter difficult to understand or handle; speaking to Ann on the most innocuous of matters might suddenly make the speaker feel she'd grasped a handful of nettles.

Jake spent as little time inside the house as he could manage. In truth he did not feel at ease in this big, expensive, elaborate house. He had no need for high-ceilinged, spacious rooms; he liked his space under a blue sky, with the wind stirring the cedar and fir boughs at the tops of the trees several hundred feet overhead. A house, to Jake's mind, should be warm and cozy, with small rooms and roaring open fires where one could warm a backside or wet feet. A simple main room was to his liking, a room where there was a comfortable chair and the aromas of baking bread and the soup kettle.

A place, in short, like Jaisy's.

There was, for most of that winter, nothing romantic about his relationship with Jaisy Pallison. She grieved for the husband she had lost, and she did nothing to entice Jake into a forbidden situation.

Unless, Jake thought wryly, simply being the woman Jaisy was was enticement enough.

She moved about the cabin with graceful steps, and when she worked close to the fire—which failed to heat the far corners but warmed the area directly in front of the fireplace or the iron stove well beyond the comfort level—she would loosen the top buttons of her dress, and push up the sleeves, revealing the creamy skin and lush lines of her breasts. There would be moisture on

her forehead, which Jaisy would occasionally wipe away
on the corner of her apron; Jake found this unaccountably
sensual.

He never touched her, though he thought about it. It was
impossible not to, especially after Ann informed him
that the doctor had said it was best that they not engage
in marital relations before the birth of the baby. He was
frustrated and humiliated that he, a man married nearly
sixteen years, should be having wet dreams like a young
boy. And he was too proud to seek relief with a whore.

There was no physical release with Jaisy, but there was
something almost as important. Her presence, her calm
acceptance of whatever he offered in the way of conversation or chores, and her complete lack of demands upon
him were a healing balm.

Maggie, of course, did not know that her father was, as
yet, still innocent of breaking the seventh commandment.
She was tormented by imaginings about her father and
Jaisy Pallison and avoided the Pallison children as if they
had smallpox. She felt guilty if she even thought of them,
and was afraid the guilt was written on her face for anyone
to see.

Nancy was her frequent companion that winter; she
came with her mother and helped with the cleaning and the
kitchen work, but since Ann insisted that Maggie and
Celeste also take on responsibilities, there were many
opportunities for Maggie and Nancy to work together on
some chore or other. While they worked, they talked.

Nancy had her eye on one of the village boys, an Adam
Welker, who had as yet paid her little attention beyond
pulling her hair from time to time. The girls talked about
boys, and men, and growing up, and marriage. Nancy was
the only one who knew how Maggie felt about Angus
McKay.

Angus, of course, was the root of most of Maggie's
suffering. In the summer, she saw him in the woods. Now,

with the logging operations shut down until spring, there were few opportunities to see him at all. If he came to church he sat behind the Keatings, so that she could not watch him; a few exchanged words on the doorstep on Sunday morning were hardly enough to suffice for the full week, so that Maggie longed for spring and the reopening of the woods. And her fifteenth birthday, as well, at which time Mama had promised her that she might attend a dance at the Athenaeum.

In January Ann commenced spotting.

This sent ripples of alarm throughout the household, although the girls did not at first realize exactly what was happening, only that Ann was confined to bed and felt so poorly that she did not even welcome their visits or Jake's.

It did not escape Maggie that her father then spent less time at home than ever. She wanted desperately to talk to him about Jaisy, yet she, who had always been so outspoken that her mother continually chastised her for her bluntness, could not bring herself to put her feelings into words. Not on this matter.

How many people were aware of her father's transgressions? Maggie wondered desperately. Did everyone in Snohomish look at her with condemnation or pity as she passed by, because her father was calling on Jaisy Pattison?

Nancy might have known—her mother lived in town most of the time, though she and Nancy shared a small room at the back of the house at Keating's Landing some nights when there was no ride for them back to Snohomish— but Nancy said nothing, and Maggie dared not ask.

Some things it was better not to be sure about.

This situation would have been enough to depress her. In addition to it, the separation from Angus was nearly unbearable.

He came to the house one Saturday afternoon, warmly bundled against the freezing temperature, his nose red and steamy vapors issuing from his cold lips as he breathed.

It was Millicent who answered the door and invited him in. "I think my son-in-law is out back somewhere," she said. "Would you like to step into the back parlor and warm yourself, while I see if I can find him?"

Angus accepted the invitation to stand before the open fire, and the cup of tea as well, but it wasn't Jake he'd come for.

"There's to be a skating party this evening on Blackman Lake. It's frozen over three feet thick, near as we can figure. Everybody in town's going to be there with skates, and then they'll go over to the Beckers' for hot cocoa and cookies afterward. I thought Celeste and Maggie might want to go."

"Oh." She sounded dubious. "Well, perhaps so. Let me consult with my daughter, and then the girls," Millicent said, and left him sipping tea so hot it burned his mouth.

Angus glanced around the room which he had previously seen only on the night of the housewarming. Charming, he thought, with its antimacassars on all the chair backs and arms, handworked needlepoint covers on the straight chairs, the elegant striped wallpaper and the floral-patterned rug so soft under his feet. The chairs looked comfortable, and there were knitting and mending baskets beside two of them, a folded newspaper in the seat of a third. He wondered if he'd ever be able to afford a place like this.

"Angus?" Maggie's dark head showed around the door-frame, surprise written on her face, to be quickly followed by delight. "What are you doing here?"

He grinned. "Inviting you to a skating party. You and Celeste," he added quickly.

"When? Oh, I do hope Mama will let us go!" She came toward him, laughing. "Does Mama know you're here?"

"Your grandmother let me in, and she's gone to speak to her. Oh, hello, Jake. We're getting up a skating party on Blackman Lake for this evening. Whole town will be there. Want to put on your skates and join us?"

Jake, too, had a ruddy complexion from the cold; he'd been chopping wood, a constant chore during much of the year. He rubbed his hands together and held them out toward the flames as Angus moved to one side of the fireplace.

"Haven't been on skates in years. I'd probably break my neck. You sure the ice is thick enough?"

"Tom Dunnigan chopped a hole in it to make sure. Three feet through," Angus assured him.

"Well, we'll see what Ann says," Jake said, and Maggie reached out to tug at his arm.

"Please, Daddy! We haven't skated since last year, and we haven't gone anywhere but to church in ever so long!"

She would, she thought, positively expire if she were not allowed to go. Surely Angus would skate with her, at least once; who knew what would happen, out there on the dark ice, beyond the light from the bonfire that would be built on the shore?

Ann was not feeling well, and would not have joined them in any case, but upon Jake's assurance that he would go along to keep an eye on them, the girls were given permission to attend.

"See you all tonight, then," Angus said, and took his leave for the long walk back to town.

Maggie and Celeste were both wild with excitement. Living at Keating's Landing was fine except for the fact that it was so far out of town. Ann didn't mind their walking back and forth to school, but an evening event was out of the question unless someone took them in the buggy.

They planned and prepared all afternoon.

There were long woolen drawers laid out to be worn under several warm petticoats, and dresses with the fullest skirts of the heaviest material they owned. There were caps and mittens to be rounded up, with bright-colored scarves to be wrapped over the lower part of their faces, so that the air would be a little less frigid when inhaled into their lungs.

"Take extra mittens," Ann cautioned. "So if the first ones get wet, you can change. And don't keep them out too late, Jake. Tomorrow's Sabbath."

Angus had not exaggerated by very much when he'd said the entire town would be there.

When the Keatings arrived after dark there was a leaping bonfire; each family had contributed an armload of wood to feed it. Nancy was there with her cousins, on the tail end of a crack-the-whip; when her attention was distracted by the new arrivals, she was snapped loose and slid to a laughing stop a few yards from them.

"Come on, Maggie! They'll be around again in a minute!"

Maggie joined her, looking around for Angus. The fire cast great flickering lights and shadows over the swirling figures on the lake, and with everybody bundled to the eyebrows it was hard to tell who was who.

She saw a face she recognized. Jaisy Pallison, buttoned into a coat that surely must have belonged to her husband, judging by its size, a bright-blue scarf around her head and neck, face flushed from the cold, or perhaps from her proximity to the fire.

Or maybe, Maggie thought in a gush of dismay, proximity to Jake Keating. They stood talking, plainly illuminated in the soaring flames. Oh, Daddy, please, no, Maggie begged silently. Not in front of everybody.

They were both laughing, seemingly unaware that they were being observed, and then little Lucy Pallison ran up to them for help with her skates, and to Maggie's relief her father went to bring more wood, leaving Jaisy to deal with her daughter.

Where was Angus? There was a tall figure far out on the ice, beyond the reach of the bonfire's glow. Was that Angus?

Maggie had put on her skates before she got out of the buggy, for there was enough snow on the ground to protect the blades. She felt awkward at first, as she always did when she hadn't skated for a time; it wasn't every winter that the lake froze over thick enough to be safe for skating.

Nancy grabbed for her hand and tugged her along, attaching them to the end of the passing line of skaters; a moment later, they were both sprawled, laughing, while Maggie rubbed an elbow that had connected, hard, with the ice.

Unlike many of the town girls, Maggie was used to lots of walking; her leg muscles were strong, and her confidence returned quickly. Skating was fun, only where was Angus?

And then she saw him. With Deborah McVea.

The couple glided toward her, clasping hands, his arm around her, their steps perfectly matching. Maggie stumbled, and again went down. Embarrassment warmed her cheeks, but when she regained her footing, she saw that Angus had paid no attention, he hadn't even noticed that she'd fallen.

Well, she certainly wasn't going to let him know that the evening would be spoiled for her if he ignored her. Maggie sprinted toward the end of another of the whips, then dropped back as she saw whom she'd have had to hold hands with. Ned Pallison's white, freckled face stared at her for a moment, then was gone.

"Margaret, skate with me until I get my balance," Celeste said behind her, and Maggie complied, trying not to watch Angus and Deborah as they glided out of sight into the darkness.

From time to time she glanced back at the shore; Mrs. Pallison was staying by the fire, not skating. Jake had donned his own skates and suddenly swooped on them, putting an arm around each of his daughters.

"Care to skate with your old man?" he asked and,

taking their consent for granted, swept them along at high speed.

Jake was an excellent skater, as he was good at everything. Maggie felt the strength in his strides, the muscles in the arm that encircled her. He was laughing down at her and Maggie felt a surge of affection—no, of love—for this man who had championed her in almost everything from the day she was born. Would he continue to do so if he knew how much she wanted Angus McKay? Or was Angus right, that Jake wouldn't think anyone was good enough for her?

Red Risku called out from the shore. "Hey! Anybody want to get up a race? From here across the lake and back!"

Jake cut his speed and brought them effortlessly to a stop. "I'll see you later," he told the girls, and joined the men around Red, where Maggie caught the glint of light off a pocket flask.

A moment later, an arm came around her waist, and the voice she'd been waiting for spoke in her ear. "Skate with me, little girl?"

"I'm not a little girl," Maggie said automatically. "I'm nearly fifteen."

"Not quite grown-up yet," Angus said, sounding cheerful. "Excuse us, Celeste."

He skated almost as well as Jake. It seemed to Maggie that her own skating was better, smoother, stronger, with Angus's arm around her, her mittened hand held in his. She could have spent the entire night that way, gliding around the other skaters, far out onto the lake, flying along with the wind in their faces, then back to the bonfire to get warm.

He left her there while he took Celeste for a whirl around the inner group of skaters. Maggie had not realized she was cold until she approached the fire, peeling off her mittens to extend her hands as close to the blaze as was possible.

Mrs. Pallison was still there, across the fire. Except for her own youngsters, Maggie had seen no one approach her or speak to her. Jaisy bent to pick up another length of wood, then came toward Maggie after she'd added it to the conflagration.

"Good evening," Jaisy said.

Maggie's face felt stiff. "Good evening," she responded. She concentrated on rubbing her hands together, then putting her mittens back on.

"It looks like great fun," Jaisy said.

Maggie looked directly at her then. "Don't you like to skate?"

"I don't have any skates," Jaisy said matter-of-factly. "I used to skate a lot, when I was a girl. My grandpa had a pond that stayed frozen most of the winter. Not as big as this, but we skated every winter."

"It would be nice," Maggie conceded, "to have ice all winter. Excuse me, I'm going back out now."

Why had Jaisy sought her out to speak to? Had the others noticed? Would they attach any significance to it? *Was* there any significance to it?

She skated alone for a time, then with Nancy and her cousins, and then with Celeste again. And the whole time she was aware of Angus.

He was certainly spreading himself around, she decided. If there was any female under forty that he hadn't skated with, she couldn't imagine who it was. At least he wasn't monopolizing Deborah.

Someone fired a gun, and the across-the-lake racers were off. Angus finished the circle he was making with Andrea Clark and sprayed ice over Maggie's feet when he stopped in front of her. "One more go-round?" he asked, and Maggie held out her hand to be clasped once more.

They floated over the ice, seldom speaking, touching

only through thick mittens and layers of garments; yet to Maggie the contact was as intimate as any she'd ever known. She longed to tell Angus that she loved him, yet she was held back by the thought that he might be amused by such a declaration.

This time he skated with her for a longer time; indeed, it was not until they heard the racers returning that Angus freed her and took another turn with Deborah. This time it didn't matter quite so much. While Jake was off racing, Angus had spent almost all his time with *her*.

The racers were cold and tired, and the supply of firewood was nearly exhausted. It was decided that the men would retire to the nearest tavern for a shot of something more warming than the cocoa that would be offered at the Beckers'.

"I'll pick you up there later," Jake told Maggie, and left her standing uneasily, hoping that he would not forget Ann's admonition about getting them home early.

The Becker house was full of red-cheeked skaters padding around in their stocking feet, sipping cups of sweet cocoa and munching on sugar cookies. Celeste huddled with a group of her friends, who were in that silly stage of girlhood where they watched the boys and giggled without addressing them directly.

Maggie drifted into the parlor where some of the older young men and women were gathered. (The truly older people had all gone home to their own firesides, rather than extending the party away from the lake.) Angus and Tom Dunnigan sat on the hearth, telling stories that had everyone laughing, including Deborah McVea and Andrea Clark. Maggie sank onto the floor between Nancy and her cousin Alice, warming her hands on the mug, and listened. She felt not quite part of the group, but almost. The warmth spread over her, and she was content, the evening a success.

The evening, however, was not yet over. Gradually the

other guests found their coats in the pile on Mrs. Becker's bed, and wound scarves around their faces and pulled on their boots to depart for home.

There was no sign of Jake, and finally there was almost no one left except Maggie and Celeste and Angus and a family who were still looking for someone's boots.

Angus shrugged into his own outer garments and then paused to look at the two remaining waifs. "What's happened to Jake, I wonder?"

"He went with Red and the others to the tavern," Maggie said, hoping that that's where he still was, that he hadn't decided to take Mrs. Pallison home. There was certainly no need for it, since she lived no more than half a mile from where they'd had the bonfire on the shore of the lake.

Angus glanced at their hostess, who was showing signs of wanting to go to bed. "Maybe I'd better take you girls home. I'll see if I can borrow Steadman's sleigh; it's snowing again, so that would be better than looking for Jake with the buggy."

"Our sleigh is out," Mrs. Becker offered. "And I'll tell Jake when he comes along. Just put old Dobby in the barn when you get him home."

It was, indeed, snowing again: great lacy flakes that landed on coats, mittens, and eyelashes. Celeste stuck out her tongue to catch some of them as they were bundled into the confined space with a robe over their knees.

Maggie didn't know if it was deliberate or not, but Angus handed her up first, then Celeste, so that Maggie was squeezed between them. Celeste was soft and yielding; Angus was hard and emanated strength along with body heat, so that Maggie was perfectly comfortable in spite of the cold, and totally elated. Angus hadn't walked anyone else home tonight.

It was a beautiful night, Maggie decided. There was no problem for the horse in staying on the road, because the firs on either side showed up black against the snow; they had only to stay between the trees.

Celeste sighed and snuggled more deeply under the robe. "It was fun, tonight. I hope we can skate again this winter. Thank you for coming out to invite us, Angus."

"If it stays cold, maybe we can do it again next weekend," Angus said. It was a tight squeeze, and after a few minutes he worked his right arm loose and rested it along the back of the seat, pressing against Maggie's shoulders. "Gives us a little more room. That's not uncomfortable for you, is it?"

"Not at all," Maggie assured him, and allowed herself to relax into his side. She hoped the horse would go very slowly; she didn't care if it took all night to get home, even if Mama was annoyed. It would be worth it.

On her other side, Celeste fell asleep, head flopping against Maggie. Maggie felt warm and snug and happy.

That was only until they reached Keating's Landing.

The bells on the sleigh brought someone to the door; Maggie caught a glimpse of a woman's figure in silhouette in the lighted doorway as Angus brought the sleigh to a stop. "Now we're in for it, I suppose," she murmured.

It was not Ann who stood there, however, but Millicent Miles. She stepped forward onto the verandah, arms crossed on her chest as she huddled against the cold, peering forward.

"Jake? Come quickly, it's Ann, she's fallen!"

Angus had just lifted her down and Maggie turned away from him, looking up at her grandmother. "Daddy's not here, Angus brought us home. Is Mama badly hurt?"

Millicent retreated into the warmth of the front hallway, the others following. "Your father didn't come with you? Where is he?" Her face was pinched in the lamplight, anxiety deepening the lines around her mouth and eyes.

"He's . . . with the other men," Maggie said. "Where's Mama? How is she?"

"She's in bed, and she needs the doctor, but there was no one to go. I didn't dare leave her alone even if I'd had the buggy."

"I'm going straight back to Snohomish, ma'am," Angus offered. "I'll find Jake and have him bring the doctor right away."

On impulse, Maggie put a hand on his arm. "I'll go with you."

"You'll do no such thing, I need you here!" Millicent said at once. "Please, Mr. McKay, fetch my son-in-law, and the doctor, and tell them to hurry."

Celeste was peeling off her outer garments, dropping them carelessly over the small lamp table in the entry hall. She was halfway up the stairs, running, when they heard the scream.

It was a sound of unmistakable anguish. Celeste paused, looking upward, then continued, two steps at a time.

They heard her open the bedroom door, heard Ann's sobbing cry. "Oh, God, somebody, help me!"

Millicent turned away from the frozen pair at the foot of the stairs. "Take off your coat and come upstairs, Margaret. I'm going to need all the help I can get," Millicent said, and hurried after her granddaughter.

Angus pulled his cap back on, well down over his ears. "I'd better get going."

Maggie still clutched his arm. "Angus, if Daddy isn't with the others at the tavern . . ."

She stopped, not wanting to say the words, yet knowing that getting Jake here quickly with the doctor was more important than revealing scandalous secrets.

"I'll probably meet him on the road," Angus said, moving toward the door. "Don't worry, I'll find him."

She had to tell him. "If he's not with the others, go to Mrs. Pallison's house."

He stared at her for several long seconds, then nodded. "All right." And then he was gone. After she'd closed the door, Maggie heard the faint tinkle of the bells as the sleigh moved off.

She turned from the door, throwing her coat and mittens and knitted hat onto the table atop Celeste's, and ran up the stairs.

Millicent stood over the bed, helplessly holding her daughter's hand. Ann lay in the bed in a pool of yellow light, and when Maggie drew closer she saw that there was red in the pool, too.

Blood.

"Is she having the baby?" Maggie asked, hushed.

Ann's eyes flickered open, searching out Maggie's face. "Where's your father? Isn't he with you?"

Maggie stood beside the bed, her heart beating so hard that it was uncomfortable. "Angus brought us home; he's gone back to fetch Daddy. What happened, Mama?"

Ann drew up her knees with the sheet over them, the sheet showing blood soaked up from the one beneath her. There was a sheen of perspiration on her face, though the room was cold.

"I fell. I tripped on the hem of my gown at the top of the stairs, and I fell." She twisted to stare up into Millicent's face. "The baby's coming, and it's too early. Just like Charlie."

Ann closed her eyes and tears squeezed from between her lids.

Maggie's chest constricted. She looked around the room, at the clothes dropped where they had been hastily removed, at the unlit fireplace, both visible signs of her grandmother's agitation.

"Celeste," she told her sister, "get that fire going and get it warm in here. Grandma, do we need hot water? To bathe the baby when it comes?"

Millicent relinquished Ann's hand. "Yes, yes, I suppose we do. If only Mrs. Totting were here tonight! She knows more about birthing babies than I do. I'll put on the water, you stay here with your mother, and if she needs me . . ." Millicent paused, her distress and uncertainty evident. "I'll be back in a few minutes."

Maggie knew nothing to do for her mother other than to bathe her forehead and hold her hand. Ann clung to her through the spasms that contorted her body, then fell limp when each one had subsided.

"Too early," she murmured. "I told him, I *told* him, that I couldn't stand another dead baby. . . ." The tears began again, sliding down waxy cheeks.

It was too early, and the baby was surely small, yet it did not get itself born. An hour passed, an hour of hard labor, and during each convulsive contraction Ann crushed their hands in hers and cried out while bloody fluids continued to soak the bedding under her.

During one of the periods between contractions, when Ann sank into a sort of stupor, Maggie whispered to her grandmother, "Why doesn't it come? Why isn't it being born?"

Millicent looked gray and drawn. She didn't reply to Maggie's questions, but returned to the bedside and reached for the lamp. "Here, hold this up so I can see."

She drew back the sheet, exposing her daughter, who seemed not to notice, as the next contraction began.

Maggie held the lamp and her breath.

Millicent sighed and replaced the sheet. "Something's wrong. I suspect it's turned wrong end to; she's been this way for hours, and she doesn't seem to be making any headway. Ordinarily, the baby is head down, and the head acts as sort of a battering ram. Hard, you know. But if it comes feet first, or buttocks . . . there's nothing firm that way to push through."

Her eyes were red-rimmed, her mouth twisted in misery for both Ann and herself. "I don't know anything about this. I don't know what to do for her." She sounded exhausted and near tears. The fact that she was discussing such matters with Maggie at all was a measure of her emotional state.

Maggie looked at her grandmother with compassion. "Why don't you rest for a while? Celeste and I will stay with her, and probably Daddy and the doctor will be here any time now."

Millicent's uncertainty increased. "You won't know what to do, if anything happens."

"I'll send Celeste for you if we need you," Maggie said. "I was there when Charlie was born, remember? And besides, I guess whatever is going to happen will just happen, won't it? No matter who's here?"

The room was silent after Millicent had gone down the hall to her own room. Celeste had fallen asleep in a chair, looking a perfect blond angel in her blue dress with her curls falling forward across the heightened color in her cheeks. Ann lay breathing through her mouth, hands resting on the swollen mound of her abdomen, eyes closed. In the fireplace, a log fell, sending a shower of sparks out toward the carpet, so that Maggie moved quickly to extinguish them.

Tears prickled in her eyes. Please, God, she prayed, let them come soon.

And don't let Daddy have been at Mrs. Pallison's.

# 14

To his credit, Jake had had no intention of going anywhere near Pallison's that night. He had enjoyed the skating, been tired and cold after the race, and had looked forward to a warming drink or two with his men.

Keating's own men were not the only logging crew in town that Saturday night. Several other outfits were on hand, as well, and the talk was such that Jake was immediately drawn into it.

When the Keating crew walked into the warm room from the freezing temperatures outside, heads turned and hands were lifted in greeting; the newcomers pulled off knitted caps and unbuttoned heavy coats. They stamped off as much of the snow from their boots as they could, not so much out of concern for the floor of the tavern as because melting snow chilled the feet even more than they already were.

"You mark my words," one old-timer said, shaking a grizzled head as he quaffed his ale. "It's gonna bust."

A murmur of derision ran around the room as Jake and the other racers moved toward the tables, but there was an undercurrent of uneasiness. Kurt Jorgeson, who had his own small outfit, tossed a shot of whiskey down his throat and waved a beckoning arm toward the newcomers.

"Hey, Jake, what do you think?"

Jake swung a chair out from a table and straddled it,

waving a hand at the barkeep for his usual drink. "What do I think about what?"

"We gonna have a bust? Hell, the railroads go all the way across the country now! We gotta way to get our lumber clear to my granny in Boston in only a week, and they ain't nobody east of the Rockies ever seen trees like these!"

"These Douglas firs don't match the redwoods they got in northern California," a serious-faced young man asserted. Jake didn't know him, which meant that he was new to Snohomish. "You take those trees down there around Crescent City, Eureka, in there, my God, they're giants compared to these."

Jorgeson drained his glass and lifted it aloft to signal for a refill. "Once it's cut up into lumber, what the hell difference does it make what size it was to begin with? A board foot is a board foot. Don't matter if you can make a couple of houses out of one tree, instead of taking a tree or two for one house, if that was the case. Hell, these firs are superior trees, and they're a hell of a lot easier to bring down than some monster twenty or thirty feet at the butt."

There was a murmur of agreement around the room. They would concede nothing to the redwoods.

"Maybe so," the old man said. "But you see if I ain't right. There's signs already, things are slowing down. We gonna get us a bust. Good times can't last forever, and with that damned Chester Arthur in the White House, they comin' to an end."

Jorgeson looked at Jake. "What do you think?"

The barkeep brought Jake's whiskey, and beer for the others. Jake took a swig before he answered. "I don't give a damn who's in the White House, long as he minds his own business. And I hope to hell you're wrong, old man, about a bust, because I'm just getting out of debt, and I want to stay that way."

There was a ripple of approval, but there were those

who believed that whoever was president had an effect on the economy even as far away from Washington, D.C., as Snohomish, Washington Territory.

Whenever the men drank and talked politics and business, they forgot the time. It was something their wives never seemed to understand, yet they could talk endlessly, well past suppertime or bedtime.

When at last they bundled up and braced themselves against the cold, it was later than Jake had thought. "Got' to go get my girls and get them home, or my old lady will be up in arms," he said.

It was the sort of statement a man dared to make when he knew that every hearer knew he wore the pants in his own family. Nobody doubted that about Jake Keating.

A pedestrian, a youth who had been at the gathering at Becker's after the skating party, kicked through the snow which by this time was several inches deep. "Your girls already gone home," he announced, pausing. "Angus McKay was takin' 'em in Becker's sleigh."

"You sure?" Jake demanded.

"I seen 'em, half an hour ago. You can go look, if you want, but it's half a mile out of your way, I reckon. I saw 'em, Jake. They done gone home."

Jake grunted. "All right. Thanks, Jimmy. No use to go out of my way, then, even with the buggy."

There was a chorus of good nights, muffled behind woolen scarves and turned-up collars, as the men went their separate ways. Jake turned into the alley where he'd left the buggy and heard the horse whinny a welcome, then paused as another sound came from a dark shape in the snow near his feet.

"What the— Who's that?"

There was no reply, only a faint retching sound. And then, as he bent over the figure, he smelled the stench of vomitus.

It was too dark to identify the individual, though Jake's

impression was that he was not very big. Jake reached to grab the boy under the arms and hauled him out onto the street where he could get a look at him in the dim glow from the windows of the Gem Saloon.

There was only one kid in town with hair that color, and that pale freckled skin.

Jake swore. Kid was too young to be drinking, but he'd tried it anyway, and now he was too drunk—or too sick— to get home. Damned fool would freeze to death if Jake left him here, and he couldn't count on anybody else coming along and finding him. Not with most of the revelers already having gone home.

Jake swore again and hoisted the boy over a shoulder, plodding back into the alley. He'd have to take him home.

It was snowing heavily and the cold was getting to him by the time he got to Jaisy's. His feet never had warmed up while he was in the saloon, in spite of the whiskey. There was a robe in the buggy, but he'd put that over the boy. No telling how long he'd been sprawled in the alley in his own stink; he felt icy to Jake's touch.

Jaisy opened the door to his knock, took a startled look at his burden, and stepped backward, allowing him to enter.

"What's happened to him?"

"Too much to drink. First time, maybe? I found him in the alley beside the Gem. We better get him warmed up right away."

Ned Pallison was in a stupor from which he did not fully awaken as they pulled off his clothes; they rubbed briskly at the pale skin with towels heated before the fire. This brought a slight pinkness but no reaction other than a muttering under the boy's breath.

"He couldn't of bought liquor himself," Jaisy said, bending over the bed and rubbing more vigorously. "He didn't have any money, and besides, they oughtn't to sell spirits to a boy."

"Somebody else supplied it for him," Jake affirmed. "You got a brick heating, anything to get more warmth to him?"

Jaisy nodded. "I got two bricks in the oven. I'll get them."

She was back in a moment, carrying the heated bricks wrapped in old towels. They placed those at Ned's feet, then piled all the covers over him that were to be had without stripping them off the other two sleeping children. Jake noticed that she took the top quilt off her own bed.

"You're going to have to keep the fire up in here tonight. I'll bring in another load of wood," he said, and did so.

He was not there long, only until he was assured that they'd done all they could for the boy. He didn't think there was any frostbite, though the kid would be damned lucky if he suffered no more than the nausea that had already passed. He might well have frozen to death if he'd lain in the alley all night.

And he won't thank me for rescuing him, Jake thought as he said good night to Jaisy and got back into the buggy. Little bastard doesn't like me. Can see it in his eyes whenever he meets me.

Well, Jake didn't especially like Ned, either; though his coloring was his mother's rather than his father's, Ned reminded him of Hank Pallison. But he was Jaisy's first-born, and no doubt she loved him the way Jake loved his children.

He flapped the reins over the rump of his horse, stepping up the pace through the wintery night. God, to think of Maggie or Celeste freezing in an alley . . . It made his blood run cold.

He met Angus halfway to the landing.

He heard the faint tinkle of the bells, at first wondering if he imagined it, and then the dark shape of horse and sleigh loomed against the snow. Jake reined in his own horse and waited.

"That you, McKay?"

"Jake? You're wanted at home, and they want you to fetch the doctor. Mrs. Keating's had a fall."

Jake swallowed hard. "How bad is she? Baby coming? She hurt?"

Angus drew alongside and halted. "Mrs. Miles didn't say much, too delicate a subject for me, I reckon, so I'd guess the baby's coming, but I don't know for sure. You want I should go for Doc when I get back to town, and you go on now? I could bring him back in the sleigh if he doesn't want to ride out by himself. The Beckers were all going to bed; they won't know whether I bring the rig back right away or not."

Jake's decision was instantaneous. "I'd appreciate it. I'll get on home and see what I can do."

"I'll hurry," Angus promised, and was on his way.

When he came up the slope toward the house, Jake found it ablaze with lights. Ground floor, top floor.

Jake urged the horse on to the foot of the steps, then ran across the porch and into the house without unhitching the buggy or putting the horse away.

"Ann? Ann? Anybody down here?"

His long legs took him up the steps two at a time, and into the bedroom.

He saw it in every face except Celeste's; she was asleep in a chair near the fire. Reproach, indignation, even from Maggie.

Jake went to the bed and reached for Ann's hand, though she did not respond to his touch.

Her fair hair was wet with sweat, plastered to her skull. Her eyes were sunken, her face clearly showing her exhaustion and pain.

"Honey," Jake said, stroking the flaccid hand. "I'm here."

She gazed at him with glazed eyes, eyes that filled with tears as he watched.

"You're never here when I need you," she said, then suddenly convulsed into another contraction that made speech, even thought, impossible.

Millicent spoke from her position beyond the bend. "It's turned wrong," she said. "It just can't get itself born."

Fear twisted in his gut, fear and guilt. "Angus has gone for the doctor. In the meantime, maybe I better see what I can do. I helped my old man pull a calf once was turned wrong."

He didn't see the spasm of distaste that crossed his mother-in-law's face at the comparison between her daughter and a cow. Ann cried out, and Celeste stirred, coming erect.

"Mama? Dear heaven, hasn't anything happened yet?"

Jake spoke over his shoulder to Millicent. "Would you get her to bed, please, ma'am? She can't do any good here. Maggie, come hold the light for me, please."

The baby was born a few minutes before the doctor arrived. It was a girl, and the cord was twisted around her neck so that her entire body had a bluish cast that was most alarming to everyone in the room except Ann, who was unaware of anything more than the end of her ordeal.

Jake hurriedly cut the cord and tied it off, then handed over the infant to Maggie. "Get her warm, see if you can get her breathing all right. Mama's bleeding pretty bad. Have we got any towels?" This last was addressed to Millicent, who hurried forward with them.

Maggie cradled the tiny body, feeling the same exultation and magic that she'd felt when she'd first held Charlie. Only this time there was an overpowering fear, as well, that this little sister would be no luckier than Charlie had been.

She wrapped the baby warmly and held her, sitting in the rocker before the fire. When the baby emitted a tiny cry, like a newborn kitten, Maggie hugged her fiercely, and prayed.

They named the baby Sarah Ann.

She was so tiny that she had to be fed every hour or so, and they had difficulty in getting her to suck.

Ann nursed the child. She did nothing else. She made no attempt to rise from the bed, and her only words to Jake were, "We'll have to have help. Ask Mrs. Totting to live in."

Jake was hardly in a position to argue the matter. Millicent had never had the responsibility for such a large house; she tired easily, and could not be up around the clock to attend to Sarah. Maggie and Celeste helped all they could, but it wasn't fair to them, either, to be asked to take on all the burdens of the household.

Mrs. Totting and Nancy, who could not be left behind, were installed permanently in the downstairs back bedroom. The baby had to be kept close to her mother, for the sake of convenience.

"It would be better," Ann told Jake distantly, "if you slept somewhere else for now."

It hurt him, to hear the words and recognize that there was no concern in them for himself, no forgiveness for not being there when she fell. Yet he admitted the validity of her reasoning; he'd get no sleep in a room where lamps must be left on, an infant cared for constantly. And there was no question of inflicting his own needs on his wife. She continued to bleed, though less copiously after the first few days, and she sought no comfort in his presence or in his arms.

"She's so sweet," Maggie said, cradling the baby against her own breast, feeling the deep maternal stirrings within herself. "So tiny, but now that she's eating, she'll surely be all right. Won't she?"

She looked to her grandmother for confirmation and saw a shadow pass over Millicent's face. "I certainly pray so," Millicent said. "Rock her to sleep, Margaret, then put her in the cradle. I'm going to bathe your mama, and then she'll sleep, too, I hope."

And so, again, Maggie took on responsibility for an infant. Sarah was carried to Ann for feeding; after that, Maggie bathed and dressed and changed the baby, and often rocked her when she was awake.

Having Sarah to tend to helped fill the hours of winter days when there was nowhere to go and little in the way of entertainment. It was so cold and the snow was so deep that the children who lived beyond the town limits didn't go to school for several weeks, and after the school stove overheated and caused a small fire, not even the town children went until the weather eased a bit.

Maggie missed Angus fiercely. He did not come back to the house; there were no more skating invitations, though the ice held for some time. Maggie hugged to herself the happiness she'd felt at the skating party. Angus had singled her out for attention, and it would soon be spring—time to return to the woods, where she would see him every day. And she was nearly fifteen years old.

Jake was right about Ned Pallison's feelings for him. Ned had no appreciation at all for having been brought home, sick and drunken from his first experience with hard liquor.

It seemed to the boy that his mother had already forgotten his father. She was beginning to smile again, to hum as she moved about her tasks. When she made a dried-apple pie, she set aside a slice, without comment, that Ned knew was being saved for Jake Keating.

And so, on a fine sunny afternoon when Ned was

heading home from school and glimpsed Jake plodding along the road ahead of him, the boy stopped in his tracks.

There was no way he was going to walk with Jake Keating. The man carried a gunnysack slung over one shoulder, and the road he took was the one to Pallisons', not to Keating's Landing.

"If he's going to be there, I'll be damned if I will," Ned said aloud.

Still, he was hungry. Usually when he got home from school he would cut thick slices of his mother's delicious bread, and spread it with jam from the blackberries he and the younger children had picked last summer. Sometimes it took three or four slices to fill his belly so that he could last until the evening's soup or stew was done.

The more he thought about it, the hungrier he grew. And it was only by going home that he could alleviate the hunger.

Maybe, Ned speculated, he could beat Jake to the cabin. His mother had warned him about crossing the lake anymore this year; the temperatures were going too high during the day, she'd cautioned, and the ice would be softening. But she was always warning him about something, especially since his pa had died.

Ned stepped out upon the edge of the ice, testing it with his weight. It seemed as solid as when they'd all skated on it a few weeks earlier. In fact, he and some of the other kids had skated on it less than a week ago.

Jake had to walk the long way around. Ned's gaze followed the solitary figure, black against the snow, then saw that Jake had paused to speak to someone who emerged from the nearest house.

Angus McKay, Ned thought, recognizing a red knitted cap on the taller man's head. Good. Let 'em talk, and in the meantime Ned would cut across the lake and get there ahead of Jake; he'd have his bread and jam and disappear into the woods behind the cabin before Keating showed up. He'd stay out there, even if it was only twenty above zero, until the bastard left.

Ned had no doubt at all that his own home was Jake's ultimate destination. He'd seen him before, from a careful distance, carrying that gunnysack. And later that night, there would be sugar in the bowl again, and fat pork in the next day's beans, and the aroma of bacon frying when he woke up early in the mornings.

Damn Keating and his charities, Ned thought angrily. He took another step or two out onto the ice, which was as solid as the earth around the shore, beneath the frozen snow.

He set off with confidence, moving at a half trot, glancing back from time to time to see that the men on shore were still talking. Good. The longer they talked, the better.

He was more than halfway across when he heard it.

The first ominous cracking sound.

Startled, Ned stopped, listening. There was nothing. On the far shore he saw his younger sister and brother playing around the igloo they'd built of blocks cut from the snow weeks ago. He glanced in the other direction and saw the figure he knew to be Jake Keating, though he couldn't have recognized him at this distance. There was no one else in sight.

None of the people on shore seemed to be aware of him. Ned took a tentative step forward. This time there was no mistaking it.

Not only was there a sound like that of a rifle shot, but he could see it, the crack in the ice that ran too swiftly to follow it with the eye, under his feet, around him, spreading, splintering off into other cracks.

This time standing still didn't help a thing. The cracks multiplied, the snapping sounds continued, and he didn't know what to do.

There were as many cracks behind as before him, and he was closer to his home shore.

His heart thudded in the thin chest, and his mouth was dry. Maybe, Ned thought desperately, if he ran, as hard as he could, he could make it before the ice gave way.

He had taken four strides when he saw the water oozing through the largest of the cracks, making a shallow lake before him that rapidly melted the snow covering the ice.

Ned hesitated, skidding, then turned and plunged backward toward firmer, thicker ice.

He was too late.

From the shore, Jake had noted the boy's progress and cursed under his breath, hoping the damn fool kid knew what he was doing.

He, too, heard the ice break.

Jake swore again, and looked around desperately for something to use to attempt a rescue: a long branch, anything that would extend far enough over the solid ice to reach the boy.

Snow covered everything, a crusty snow that was not easily clawed aside, and there was no telling what lay beneath it. The trees around him were fir and cedar; they offered nothing in the way of long, strong branches that could be torn off easily, and he had no saw or ax.

He heard the boy's cry, a cry he would never forget: the same sound that a man makes when he falls from a two-hundred-foot tree and has time to scream on his way down. Not in pain, but in mortal fear.

It was too late. Jake knew it. The boy was too far out on the ice, and there was nothing to throw out to him across the surface that was breaking into hundreds of segments, none of them capable of bearing a man's weight.

Yet he tried. He dropped the gunnysack on the shore and moved toward the boy carrying the only branch that came to hand. It was too short, too slender, and probably too brittle, an alder bough that had come down during a recent windstorm.

He had not gone a dozen yards when he saw that Ned was gone. The ice was empty. No head bobbed in the small patch of open water, no hands clawed for a grip on the edge of the broken ice.

Jesus, the kid was trapped under the ice, and there wasn't even any way to tell where, which direction he'd gone!

The scream brought his head around. His stomach knotted as he saw her there, the auburn-haired woman with a child at each side, starting out across the lake from their shore.

Jake yelled a warning, and they heard him, because they paused and looked toward him.

"Go back! Get off the goddamned ice, you'll all go through!" He waved his arms violently, motioning them away.

Even as he spoke, he heard the sounds again, beneath his own feet. Jake turned and ran for shore, on an angle he hoped would keep him from going through yet get him to Jaisy and the children more quickly than going back to the road.

They'd halted, anyway, though Jaisy cried out, "Ned went through! He's under the ice!"

"We can't get to him," Jake yelled back. "Not without going in ourselves. Go back to shore, Jaisy! For God's sake, go back!"

He knew, in that moment while she hesitated, what it would mean to him if Jaisy drowned, too.

Sweet Jesus, he thought, and for once he did not mean it in a blasphemous way. How had he let this happen? And what in hell was he going to do about it?

He didn't mean the boy. It was too late for the boy.

He meant Jaisy Pallison.

He had no right to feel the way he did about Jaisy. He could offer her nothing.

His steps slowed, because his wind was giving out; Jaisy waited for him there on the edge of the thawing lake, and when he reached her, he gathered her into his arms.

# 15

IT was eight days before Ned's body was found.

No one else in Snohomish ventured onto the ice after the boy fell through. Though it was considerably out of her way, Maggie walked home from school past Blackman Lake, as did many of the other children. Even Celeste, who did not always walk with her sister, joined Maggie.

Their eyes scanned the expanse of softening ice. Ordinarily there would have been boys fooling around near shore, deliberately cracking the ice by stomping up and down on it, or cutting holes in it with picks or axes. If they fell through into a few feet of water, it was an adventure, something to be laughed about, a mild feat of daring not revealed to their elders.

Now, however, there was no fun in the ice. Somewhere beneath it in the frigid water was Ned Pallison's body.

Maggie could see it in her mind, floating, eyes wide in his final terror, hands outstretched as he groped for the opening somewhere above him, and seeing overhead only the never-ending ice.

"I dreamed about him last night," Celeste said soberly as they plodded through slush, coats open to the first tentative warmth of the approaching spring. "It's so sad. I didn't really know Ned very well, but I felt sort of sorry for him.''

Maggie didn't answer. She was thinking about what the entire town knew, now, that her father had been there when it happened. If there was any malicious gossip, she hadn't heard it, but then maybe she wouldn't have. A couple of years ago when Tim Rittman had made a scathing remark about her father, Maggie had knocked him down and scratched his face. While she was too grown-up to do that sort of thing anymore, she knew she *did* have a reputation for a temper.

Jake had come home late to dinner with the news about Ned, making no bones about the fact of his presence when it happened, though he admitted only to being on the road around the lake, not at Pallison's.

Maggie's heart had lurched in her chest, and she hadn't missed the tightening of her mother's mouth.

"What were you doing over by the lake?" Ann asked. It was only her second trip downstairs to eat with the others, and she looked tired and wan. For a few seconds her knuckles showed white as she clenched her hand where it rested on the table, and then she dropped it into her lap, out of sight.

Jake didn't seem to notice. "I stopped by the Mercantile for some tobacco, and Deevers mentioned that Mrs. Pallison had bought some groceries and had to leave part of them. The boy usually helped her carry them home, but he wasn't around. So I thought, what the hell, I wanted to talk to Angus McKay, anyway, about getting ready to get back into the woods. He's boarding with the McAllmers, you know. So I'd be halfway to Pallison's by the time I got that far. I figured I might as well carry her stuff on out there. I saw the boy on the ice, and heard him yell, but there wasn't a goddamned thing I could do for him."

There were deep lines forming around his mouth that Maggie had never seen before, lines of age and pain. He was getting old, she thought in an anguish of her own. Her beloved Daddy was edging toward the half-century mark, and many people didn't live much longer than that.

Ann said no more, but Maggie was not reassured, for her mother's carefully controlled face, the visible tremor in her hand, and her lack of appetite were all cause for concern.

Another reason why Maggie chose to walk along the lake, aside from what she knew to be morbid curiosity about Ned Pallison, was that she hoped to encounter Angus McKay. Except for Sunday services, when he had merely said "Good morning" to her and then gone off with Norman McAllmer, she hadn't spoken to him since the skating party, and there had been nothing in his manner then to indicate whether or not he felt the same way about that night as she did.

They were approaching the McAllmer house now, where there was no sign of life except the curl of smoke from the chimney.

"Margaret," Celeste said, drawing her out of her own thoughts, "do you think there's something very bad wrong with Sarah?"

Startled, Maggie stopped in the middle of the road. "Bad wrong with her? What do you mean?"

"I don't know." Celeste stopped, too, and Maggie really looked at her for the first time in ages. Celeste was incredibly lovely. Her blue knitted cap was pushed back so that the fringe of blond bangs showed, and curls tumbled about her shoulders. Her skin was clear and fair, cheeks tinged pink by the cold, and her blue eyes were shaded by unexpectedly dark lashes which she was already, at the age of twelve, learning to use to advantage with the opposite sex. Maggie stifled a pang of envy at the thought of how easily Celeste enchanted everyone around her.

"What are you talking about? What's wrong with Sarah? I didn't think she was sick." A cold dread formed at the pit of Maggie's stomach.

Celeste bit her lower lip with perfect white teeth. "I don't think she's sick, exactly. But Grandma said..."

Maggie fought down the compulsion to take her sister by the shoulders and shake her. "Celeste, for heaven's sake! Grandma said *what*?"

"Well, Mama was bending over the cradle, looking at Sarah. She didn't know I'd come to the doorway, and I couldn't see her face, but her voice sounded peculiar. Sort of as if she were going to cry, you know?"

"Mama sounds like that a lot these days. She has for months," Maggie said, though the dread was growing.

"I know. Only this was different. It was as if she were *afraid*."

"Afraid of what?" Two small boys were approaching pulling a sled, and Maggie fixed her gaze upon them without really seeing them.

"That something's wrong with Sarah," Celeste said. "Mama said, 'Mother, do you think she's all right? Lately I've had the strongest feeling that there's something wrong with her.' And Grandma didn't say anything for a minute, and then when she did she sounded peculiar, too. She said, 'I thought maybe it was only my imagination.' And for a minute they looked at each other, and then Mama began to cry. Grandma hugged her, and they stood there and didn't even know I was there, crying, with their arms around each other, and finally I went away."

The dread had become a sickness, spreading through her system. Maggie swallowed past a painful lump. "When was this?"

"This morning, before school. I kept thinking about it all day, so that Mr. Kennedy spoke to me very sharply when I couldn't answer the question he asked. I didn't even hear what it was. Margaret, Sarah isn't going to die, is she? Like Charlie?"

Her lower lip trembled before she brought it under control.

Maggie couldn't reply. Not Sarah, too, not after Charlie had been taken from them! Not when her parents were not really getting along very well, when everybody was already miserable. She blinked away the sudden tears, and forced words from an aching throat. "There's Angus. Come on, Celeste, let's keep walking. He's coming this way."

Celeste inhaled deeply, then exhaled, willing to be diverted from the subject that had bothered her so much. Obviously Maggie didn't know any more than she did about it. They began to walk again, past the boys with the sled, to where Angus was coming down the path from the McAllmer house where he boarded when he wasn't working in the woods.

He saw them coming and lifted a hand in greeting, but the familiar friendly smile was missing. "What are you two doing way out here?"

"Walking along the lake," Maggie said. "They haven't found him yet, have they?" She knew they hadn't; the news would have been all over Snohomish within half an hour. She didn't have to say *who* she meant.

"No," Angus confirmed. "Stay off the ice, for God's sake."

They both looked at him indignantly. "We're not that stupid," Maggie said, finding her voice first. It was a relief to feel a stirring of anger, however mild, to wipe out the emotion she felt about her baby sister.

Angus immediately sighed in contrition. "No, of course you aren't. I'm sorry. It's only that it makes me so sick to think of that boy out there, and I wouldn't want it to happen to anybody else. Especially you." He looked directly into Maggie's face when he spoke, causing the warmth to rise into her cheeks. She hoped Celeste didn't notice. Celeste meant well, but she was likely to say anything to Mama or Grandma, without thinking what trouble it might cause.

"Are you going in our direction?" Maggie asked, hoping he'd walk along with them.

"No. Well, actually, I'm going to walk around the lake, and I guess there's no reason I couldn't walk with you partway and circle the lake in the opposite direction from the way I usually go."

"Do you walk all the way around the lake every day?" Celeste asked.

Maggie spoke at the same time. "Are you looking for Ned?"

He nodded and reached up to put his cap on. It was one Maggie had knitted for him; if one didn't look closely enough to see a few dropped stitches, it was a handsome hat. In order to give Angus a Christmas present without eliciting any suspicion or teasing comments, Maggie had had to make hats for the entire logging crew, and since she was not much more expert at knitting than she was at sewing, this had taken a great deal of time and effort. It was a bright-red hat, one that she could recognize from a considerable distance if the wearer was tall and broad-shouldered. She hadn't seen him without it since she'd given it to him, which ordinarily gave her a welcome inner glow.

It would have taken a lot to make her feel anything like an inner glow at the moment.

"Better I should find his body than his mother," Angus said, as the trio fell into step and moved along the road beside the lake. "It's going to be hard enough when someone else does it and takes him home."

"Will he be . . . I mean, he's been in the water so long," Celeste said. "Will he look . . . awful?"

"Probably not. The water's just above freezing, so a body wouldn't deteriorate much." Angus swung the subject away from Ned Pallison's body. "How are things at home?"

He meant well, Maggie knew, but what could she say

that would be cheerful? "The same as usual," she said, before Celeste could reply. "Do you think it will be an early spring, Angus? Will we be back in the woods soon?"

"I hope so." Angus's tone didn't lighten. "If there's any demand for lumber, that is. From what we hear, prices are dropping. If people don't want lumber, or won't pay a fair price for it, they may not need any loggers this summer."

Alarm flared anew. Was there no end to the things that tore a person apart? "People will always buy *some* lumber, won't they? I mean, everybody needs houses and other buildings. . . ."

Angus shrugged. "I don't understand it any better than anybody else. All I know is that we hear there's going to be a big bust, and the price of lumber is dropping."

Celeste leaned out around her sister so that she could see his face. "What's a bust?"

"It means the economy—the whole financial structure of the country—goes bad. People are out of work, can't buy things, the prices of everything go way down."

Angus's long strides had been difficult for them to keep up with, but now he came to an abrupt halt, staring out across the lake.

"What is it?" Maggie demanded, breath catching in her chest. She followed his gaze, seeing nothing out of the ordinary, yet apprehensive all the same.

"Nothing, I guess. I thought for a minute—" Angus began to walk again, and they hurried to keep up with him. "The ice will be gone in a week or two, more than likely. Then we'll get back in the woods, soon as they dry out a bit."

It wasn't only getting back to the woods that he was thinking of, and they knew it. When they reached the point where the path led away from the lake, toward home, the girls parted from Angus. Maggie looked back to see him plodding along the lake road, attention on the shoreline, and she shivered.

It was Angus who eventually found him.

Celeste was staying the night with a friend so Maggie walked home alone that day. She didn't go by the lake road, because it was so much farther, but the boys of the town ran all over with the news, and two of them intercepted Maggie's path and told her.

"We saw him," Willie Fisher said, out of breath from running, his eyes huge. "Angus McKay found him, not more'n half an hour ago, washed up onshore. He looks like he's made out of wax, only with freckles."

"Angus is goin' to get a cart to take him home," the other boy said. "You goin' over and see him, Maggie?"

The spasm that ran through her was a combination of revulsion and pity. "No," she said, and walked away from them.

She walked so fast, the rest of the way home, that her chest ached by the time she got there. The sun was shining, and the snow was melted from all but the most deeply shaded places, yet she felt cold and upset.

Her parents were in the family sitting room, her mother rocking Sarah and her father greasing a pair of boots to set before the open fire. They looked up when she appeared in the open doorway.

"Well, sweetheart, you're home early. What'd you do, run all the way?" Jake asked, smiling.

She didn't bother to answer that in so many words. "Angus McKay found Ned Pallison's body," she blurted, and saw both of her parents change expression.

Jake swore softly and stood up, reaching for the jacket he'd dropped over the back of a chair. "About time it turned up, instead of hanging over the whole town like a nightmare about to happen. Now maybe everybody'll talk about something else for a change."

Ann had stopped rocking, holding the baby against her shoulder. "Where are you going?"

"To town," Jake said, thrusting an arm into a sleeve. "You want me to bring back anything?"

"To town?" There was a shrillness in Ann's voice that she made no attempt to control. "What for?"

Jake buttoned the jacket. "To see if there's anything I can do to help."

"Snohomish is full of people who can help. If Angus found the boy, he can take care of whatever needs to be done, can't he?" Ann asked.

Maggie stood in the doorway, beginning to be too warm inside her winter coat but not thinking to remove it while her parents stared at each other this way, while the hostility was so palpable in her mother's voice.

For several silent moments Jake looked at his wife, looked as if for the first time, at a stranger. When he finally spoke, it was softly. "What's happened to you, Ann? You used to be a warm, compassionate woman who cared about what was happening to other people."

She went as white as if he'd struck her. Maggie wanted to go away, to stop watching and listening to them hurt each other, yet she could not move.

Ann's words trembled with emotion. "How dare you speak to me of compassion! Where is your compassion for *me*, and for this poor helpless child?" Tears glistened in her blue eyes and spilled over, leaving forlorn tracks over her pale cheeks. "Why is it you're so readily available to anyone else, Jake, and never here to help *me* when I need you?"

He seemed not to breathe, for his chest stopped rising and falling beneath the heavy jacket. "Do you need me, Ann? I'd never know it from what you say or do. You haven't let me touch you in so long I don't even remember when the last time was. You never say anything to me in such a way that I can respond with affection or kindness.

You've put up a wall between us that I can't get over, or around. And you know the really sad thing?" He hesitated, and then finished in a tone so quiet that it added emphasis and validity to his words. "I'm not sure I care anymore, Ann."

With that he picked up his cap—the one Maggie had knitted for Christmas—and walked out of the room.

If Maggie hadn't stepped aside, she thought he'd have run right into her. It was as if he didn't even see her there. She wanted to run after him, to grasp his arm and make him talk to her, but the sight of her mother, the small gasping sound that escaped Ann's lips, held Maggie where she was.

The front door slammed. Jake was gone. The infant in Ann's arms whimpered slightly, and she patted the tiny back and set the chair to rocking again, while another pair of tears escaped down her cheeks.

"Mama," Maggie said. She took a few steps into the room. She couldn't speak about where Jake was going, couldn't risk Ann's questions about how much she knew of his relationship with Jaisy Pallison, couldn't bear to hear what Ann knew or guessed of it. Yet she must say something, must break Ann's glacial façade before it was ruptured from within, horribly, irrevocably. "Mama, what did you mean about Sarah? Is there something wrong with Sarah?"

Ann stared at her blankly; for a moment it was almost as if she didn't know who Maggie was. And then, instead of replying, Ann began to cry. Not single tears, but great wracking sobs, doubling over in misery, so that the baby was nearly crushed.

Maggie didn't remember crossing the room or kneeling at her mother's side. She put a hand on Ann's arm, feeling through the material of her sleeve how thin her mother had become.

"Mama, tell me. About Sarah. Is there something wrong with her?"

Ann drew a ragged breath and tried to regain control of herself. "I'm afraid so, Margaret. She's so little it's hard to tell for certain, but she . . . she doesn't respond the way you and Celeste did. She's not like any infant I've ever seen. She just . . . lies there, all the time, doesn't even cry like a normal child. I don't know what's wrong, and I don't know anything to do."

Again she cried, though with less violence this time. Maggie knelt beside her, holding her and little Sarah, and wondered if anything would ever again be right in their lives.

# 16

THE rift between Jake and Ann was an open one now. There was no pretense that theirs was a contented marriage; they scarcely spoke, communicating, when necessary, through the girls. It was not as blatant as "Please tell your father to pass the sugar," when they were all at the table, but everyone in the household was aware of it, including the servants.

Mrs. Totting and Nancy had been established in the small bedroom at the back of the ground floor. It wasn't long before the housekeeper took full charge of cleaning and meals, as Ann spent more and more of her time with Sarah, trying to coax the child into smiling and moving about, with a discouraging lack of success.

Millicent had neither the experience nor the desire to be mistress of such a large household, yet when the responsibility fell upon her simply because Ann no longer seemed to care, she did her best. Fortunately, Mrs. Totting was able to cope with a minimum of supervision, and Millicent filled her own hours with heaps of mending and darning and knitting for the family, as well as sewing new garments for them all.

It was a relief to everybody when Jake returned from an all-day excursion into the woods to announce that another sunny day or two should dry up the mud enough so that they could get back to work.

Maggie loved spring. The air became balmy, the skies were mostly blue except for occasionally fluffy clouds, and everything turned a rich, vivid green. When the snow melted on the mountains, the rivers rose in a surge that was exciting. Quite apart from the fact that a flooding waterway made it possible to move felled timber, it was fascinating to see the muddy water bubble and boil around the rocks that failed to impede its progress, to be aware of its power beyond that of man to control it.

The village boys sometimes built rafts or rode logs through the torrent, though this was extremely hazardous and made them subject to severe punishment if they were caught at it. Maggie had persuaded Celeste to try riding a log once when they were ten and seven and a half; the resulting near-drowning of her little sister (which neither had ever revealed to anyone else) put an end to that sort of adventure, though Maggie continued to be enthralled by the surging water.

The demand for lumber diminished in that spring of 1884, but though prices were lower than they had been, there was still enough of a market to keep them going. The crew returned to the bunkhouse. Mr. Murphy, groaning about his rheumatism, fired up the big cookstove, and saws and axes were sharpened and made ready.

Maggie, determined to be in the woods as much as

possible because Angus was there, braced herself for opposition at home. There was none.

Ann was too busy caring for an infant who did not thrive, and she had yet to recover fully her own strength after a difficult delivery. Millicent, not strongly backed even by her daughter in anything that did not bear directly on herself or her baby, found it more of a struggle than it was worth to protest at the way that Maggie was allowed to run free. There was, after all, a more amenable and conventional Celeste to form into the kind of granddaughter Millicent had always wanted.

Maggie was both relieved and troubled by this prevailing attitude. Not even Jake seemed to notice or care how much time she spent away from home. Jake was busy (she noted that he made more frequent excursions to town than usual, as well as expending the customary effort on reopening the logging operations); but though he was affectionate when she was with him, he didn't seem to miss her when he didn't see her all day long. She enjoyed the freedom while feeling saddened over the loss of his companionship.

Still, there was Angus, and she turned fifteen years old on the twenty-third of April.

Mr. Murphy baked her a huge cake, and the entire crew had chipped in to buy her a tiny, elegant gold watch that hung upon a chain around her neck. Maggie exclaimed over it in genuine delight as she put it on.

"That's so you'll be on time, doin' the books for your pa," Red Risku told her. "Set up regular hours, just like it was a job same's a choke setter."

"Pretty as a picture, you're getting to be," Mr. Murphy said, beaming as she cut the cake and handed out generous slices to each of them. Maggie blushed, though she knew it wasn't true. Pretty was what Celeste was, and there was no comparison between the two of them.

Angus took his slice of cake, not commenting on the extra gob of icing that she scraped from the knife onto the edge of his plate. "And grown-up," he commented. "We're going to have to be careful around Maggie, from now on. She's a young lady, not a little girl anymore. You know, when my sister turned fifteen, everybody at her birthday party gave her a kiss."

Maggie felt suddenly light-headed. She couldn't believe he'd actually said that, and again the hot color swept into her face.

The men were standing around eating their cake, grinning. Tom Dunnigan was the first to put down his plate, lick off his fingers, and step toward her. "Sounds like a good idea. Don't get many chances to kiss a pretty girl."

"Not without getting your face slapped," somebody agreed, and there was boisterous laughter.

"Don't be silly," Maggie said, cutting her own, the final slice of cake. She had always felt comfortable, companionable, with these men, most of whom she'd known for as long as she could remember. Suddenly, she was embarrassed and ill at ease.

Angus was chewing, laughing, watching her. She determined to give him no reason to think her immature, though in truth she didn't know what she ought to have done to handle the matter he'd set off. Probably Mama would have said they were all acting improperly, and she'd have known a dignified way to put them in their place; Maggie couldn't think of a thing to do except go along with them and get it over with.

Tom held her face between big callused hands and planted a kiss on her forehead. His bushy mustache tickled and was withdrawn, and Rich Salter stepped forward to repeat the performance.

Maggie knew she was bright-red, and that the men were enjoying her discomfiture. Her father was nowhere in sight, though he couldn't be far away; what would *he* think about his entire crew kissing his daughter this way?

Well, she hadn't gotten through years in their midst by

being overly sensitive to teasing and displays of masculine humor. She'd survive this, too, she told herself, and allowed Jim Humphries to plant a moist buss on one cheek.

Angus was going to kiss her, too, she thought, and hoped that she would show no more reaction to his kiss than to the others. For a moment she felt a wave of panic; she wished he had not instigated this.

She had dreamed for years of being kissed by Angus McKay, but not this way. Not in broad daylight, in front of all these men.

He didn't wait for the end of the line, but came in the middle of it, right ahead of Red Risku.

"Oh, McKay's had lots of practice kissing the girls," Red said. "More'n likely, he'll be the best of the lot of us."

Maggie felt her legs go wobbly, and she raised a silent, urgent prayer: Please, don't let anyone see what I feel about Angus.

He didn't hold her face as most of the others had done; instead, he put his hands on her shoulders, and for a terrible moment she feared he would kiss her on the mouth and so set himself apart from everyone else, so that there would be more ribald remarks and teasing speculation.

Angus was laughing, but then, as he looked down into her face, the laughter was suddenly gone, unnoted by any except herself. She had never looked into his face this way, from only inches away, and she knew that it was indelibly imprinted on her mind: the strong, tanned features; the wide, sensitive mouth; the steady gray eyes under thick, fair brows.

"Happy birthday, Maggie," he said softly, and placed a gentle, chaste kiss upon her forehead, as the others had done.

She endured the rest of the birthday kisses, even managing to laugh when they'd done and she could eat her own cake, though it stuck in her throat.

Nobody had noticed anything. She was sure they hadn't, or someone would have commented on it. She knew them well enough to be sure of that. They had no mercy on each other, and would have none for her, either.

When she and Mr. Murphy had finished cleaning up, and she'd wrapped the remaining wedge of cake in a dish towel to take home with her—"Better that than having them fighting about it," Murphy said—Maggie looked around for Jake, to tell him she was going home.

He was nowhere in sight, so she left the message with the cook and started along the skid road. Now that it was over, she felt a happy tingle at having been kissed, and she gave her imagination free rein. One of these days—no, nights—she was going to have a real kiss, Maggie vowed.

At home that evening they had a proper family celebration, with another cake. This one was much fancier, with pink and white icing and candles. There were smiles around the table when she blew them all out, and even Ann looked at her with an affection that she had lately reserved almost entirely for Sarah.

Maggie had no way of knowing that her mother would have forgotten the date entirely had not Millicent reminded her; she only knew that, at least briefly, they were a normal, happy family again.

"What did you wish for, Margaret?" Celeste demanded.

"If I tell, it won't come true," Maggie reminded her.

"So I won't tell. Mama, may we have Nancy and Mrs. Totting in to share the cake with us?"

"Yes, of course," Ann agreed, and for the second time that day Maggie sliced cake and shared it.

There were brightly colored packages to be opened and admired; from Ann, a brooch for her shirtwaist that Ann had been given by her grandmother, many years before; a longed-for dictionary of her own from Jake; a trio of soft linen handkerchiefs embroidered with her initial by Celeste; and a crocheted lace collar and cuffs from Millicent.

Maggie thanked them all sincerely, including the Tottings who had brought her a spray of dogwood blossoms gathered in the woods behind the house. She put the flowers into a vase and looked expectantly at her father as the family pushed back their chairs from the table.

She'd hoped that Jake would remain at home with them, that the pretense would last for a while longer, but he rose and looked down at her with a smile that held a hint of regret. "I can't believe that my Maggie is all grown-up already," he said. "It was such a short time ago that I carried you around on my shoulder, and now look at you. Happy birthday, honey."

He was going out. Until recently, after a twelve-hour day in the woods he stayed home, read the paper and smoked a cigar after supper, and went to bed early. Why couldn't he have done that tonight?

Maggie glanced at her mother, expecting a reaction, but Ann was paying no attention to him. "It was an excellent supper, Mrs. Totting. I think there's enough of the roast for hash, perhaps, for breakfast in the morning. What do you think?"

Mrs. Totting concealed her surprise at this interest in any mundane household matter. "Yes, ma'am, I'd certainly think so."

Ann turned then to Maggie. "Happy birthday, dear. You might put your hair up now, if you like. I did, when I was fifteen." Her soft smile faded perceptibly. "My, what a long time ago that was. Well, excuse me now, everyone. I've left Sarah long enough, and I'm sure she's hungry."

Celeste and Millicent drifted off toward the music room, for it was now Millicent's privilege to listen to the girl practice on the piano. Maggie followed Jake to the front door, where he paused to put on a jacket.

"Daddy? Do you have to go to town tonight?"

He paused with one hand on the doorknob. "I'm afraid so, honey. I'll see you in the morning."

She didn't know where the courage came from, to say the words she'd been putting together in her mind for weeks. "Are you going to see . . . her?"

He didn't pretend to misunderstand her. The sorrow was still there in his eyes, in the slight twist of his mouth under the dark mustache. "It was a nice birthday, wasn't it, Maggie?"

"As nice as it could be," she conceded, "when everything's so . . . so wrong. Daddy, don't see her. Stay here with us. We need you."

The twist deepened into what was meant to be a smile. "I've promised, Maggie."

"What about us?" she asked desperately. "What about Mama, and the promise you made to her when you were married? It's not right, Daddy, you know it isn't, and—"

He stopped her with a finger laid across her lips. "You're too young to understand. When you're older you'll see—"

Maggie twisted her head to one side to escape the silencing finger. She didn't know how she'd dared to bring up the forbidden subject with him, except that it was so important to her, and now she couldn't stop. Not if there was any chance at all that she could make him see what he was doing to them as a family.

"It's hurting Mama, and all of us! Please, please, stop seeing that dreadful woman!"

He might have been angry. She really expected that he would be. Yet the only thing she saw on his face was sadness. "You don't even know her, Maggie. It's not like you to revile a person unfairly."

She felt cold and shaky and as if she were about to cry. "She can't be a good person, or she wouldn't encourage you to go there. Not when she knows you're married to someone else. Daddy, think about it! Think what it's doing to us all!''

For long seconds he stared down into her face, and she dared to hope that he was seriously considering what she said. Then he sighed deeply and opened the door.

"You don't know what you're asking, honey," he said, very gently, and went out into the night.

She stood there after his footfalls had died away, muffled by soft earth and fir needles. Below the house, the Pilchuck made its noisy way through the darkness. Everything was familiar and beloved, the sounds, the surroundings, but Maggie felt as if her heart were literally breaking. There was no comfort anywhere.

Behind her the piano tinkled in some tune Celeste had been practicing for weeks and had almost perfected. Upstairs, light from the open doorway revealed Ann's presence in the room she now shared only with Sarah. In the back of the house, the Tottings washed up with a murmur of conversation and a clatter of china.

Maggie couldn't bear to join any of them, and she didn't want to be alone, either. At least not in the house.

She snatched a shawl off the hook beside the door and wrapped it around her against the spring chill, letting herself out onto the porch, feeling her way down the broad steps.

What good was it to be grown-up when your family was disintegrating around you? When your little sister had something so wrong with her that nobody was willing to discuss it, and your mother and father weren't speaking to each other, and your father was committing adultery with a woman who ought to have died in her son's stead, if there were any fairness in the world?

Her eyes stung as she moved through the darkness, knowing the way to the path along the river, wishing the blackness would somehow swallow her up.

It didn't, of course. Nothing happened to her at all,

except that Joe came from behind the house and accompanied her on her walk, pushing his cold nose into her hand from time to time. There were some things even Joe couldn't make seem better.

It might have been some consolation to Maggie if she'd known how guilty Jake felt, striding through the spring night toward the Pallison cabin on the shore of Blackman Lake.

He didn't feel guilty as far as his wife was concerned, at least not very much. Ann hadn't slept with him for months, not since long before the baby was born.

The trouble was, nobody else had slept with him, either, and the tensions were building up, tensions he was unable to ease by working himself into a state of exhaustion in the woods. He knew he was irritable and at times unreasonable. Who the hell wouldn't be, under these conditions?

The only thing that helped, short of drinking himself insensible (which he'd tried a few times, only to decide that the morning-after hangover made it less than worthwhile) was visiting Jaisy.

He assumed from what Maggie had said that though he'd been circumspect, he hadn't been circumspect enough. Was it true that there was gossip in town about him and Jaisy?

If so, it was unfair to everybody. Nothing had happened between them, nothing important. He hadn't been, technically, unfaithful to Ann. Yet.

He knew it was only a matter of time. At first he'd held back because he knew Jaisy genuinely grieved for her dead husband. And now there was the boy. Jake hadn't especially liked the kid, and he knew the feeling had been mutual, but what the hell? He was her son, her firstborn, and he knew what a parent felt about a child, particularly the first one.

No, he hadn't touched Jaisy. The urge was growing in

him, though, and was reaching the point tonight where it was going out of control, Jake thought. There was no real satisfaction in the realization. Given a choice, he would not have picked an illicit liaison over a lawful marriage, but what could he do?

There were no indications that Ann ever intended to return to his bed, or, rather, let him return to hers. The room he'd shared with her had been turned into a god-damned nursery, with everything arranged for Sarah's welfare.

His heart ached when he thought of Sarah. He'd talked to the doctor about her, and he supposed that the man was right when he said that having the cord wrapped around her neck during the difficult delivery might have damaged her, somehow. She was too young for them to know for sure how bad it was, but it was obvious to everyone that Sarah was not normal. She was pretty, nearly as pretty as her sister Celeste, but though she could sometimes be coaxed into a smile, it was an empty one. Jake had stood over the cradle, looking down at the child, and wondered if there would ever be a flicker of intelligence in those blue eyes, or if they would remain the way they were now. Blank, vacant.

He swore aloud. He'd thought that when he got his own logging operation he'd have just about anything a man could want. Pretty wife—well, she was pretty, but what was the use of a pretty wife if she didn't allow you in her bed?—big house, though he'd never felt comfortable there, and his two daughters. Nothing wrong with Maggie and Celeste. They were beautiful, intelligent girls. Maggie didn't realize it yet, but she was growing out of her ugly duckling stage into what he thought might be true beauty. She probably wouldn't believe she was beautiful until some man came along and told her so—certainly she only laughed when *he* mentioned her looks—and that gave him another pang. The thought of handing Maggie over to some lout who wouldn't be worthy of wiping her shoes was painful, though he knew it would have to come.

His long strides carried him through the evening darkness, his feet sure on the familiar road. He felt in his pocket for the bag of sweets he'd picked up for Jaisy's kids. Lucy and Will Pallison weren't as handsome as his own daughters, Jake thought; a pity they took after Hank rather than Jaisy, except for that red hair. Lucy was only eight, so maybe she had time to grow into some of her mother's looks, eventually. They were good kids, though, and they weren't hostile to him. He hoped they'd be asleep in the lean-to before he got there tonight, though. It wasn't kids he wanted, or he'd have stayed home with Maggie and Celeste.

It was a woman he needed, and he'd been making up his mind for days now, as to what he was going to do. Enough time had passed so Jaisy ought to have eased her grieving over Hank—indeed, he thought the way she laughed and talked pretty well showed that this was the case—and it was clear that she needed a man around. Ned hadn't been quite that but better than nothing. The closest she had to a man now, to do the chores and earn a living, was Will, and he was only six.

Hell, he told himself, approaching the cabin where candlelight streamed out in a welcome banner from the kitchen window, the whole family would have starved this winter if he hadn't brought them groceries and a young buck he'd shot last fall. It was for their good as well as his own, if he solidified the relationship.

He called out before he knocked on the door, so that it wouldn't startle her. He listened to the wooden bolt being slid back, and then looked into her welcoming face.

Jaisy had just taken a bath. The tin washtub was still sitting before the fire, and intimate apparel was draped over a nearby chair. Jaisy's skin was moist and pink, and she'd pulled on an old green wrapper that set off her auburn hair and heightened the color of her eyes.

"I thought maybe you wouldn't come tonight," she said, "seeing as it's Maggie's birthday."

For a moment he almost told her, how Maggie had begged him not to come, had pleaded with him to give up this other woman.

And then he stepped inside and closed the door behind him and looked down at the face that had become increasingly precious to him.

"My God, you're beautiful," he told her, and watched the smile light her eyes and turn up the corners of the wide, full mouth.

There was something there—not an invitation, exactly, but a receptiveness—that gave him the courage to do what he wanted to do.

With one hand he slid the bolt into place, and then he reached for her. Jaisy came willingly into his arms, face lifted for his kiss, which was almost brutal in its urgency.

His voice was hoarse. "Why don't we put out those damned candles?" he asked. Even before she could murmur agreement, he reached out and snuffed them with thumb and forefinger, leaving only the glow from the fire to illuminate the main room of the cabin.

The bed she had shared with Pallison stood in one corner, covered with a colorful quilt. Jaisy offered no objection when he lifted her—God, she was a lot heavier than Ann, he thought fleetingly—and carried her there.

There was no coquetry in Jaisy. With Ann, he'd felt he had to woo her all over again, from the beginning, as if she were still a virgin, every time he'd made love to her. Not so with Jaisy.

She was soft and firm at the same time, fresh-smelling from the soap and with her own natural fragrance, yielding, yet not passive. Her arms came around his neck, her lips parted beneath his, and when his fingers tugged at the sash of the wrapper, Jaisy's agile fingers worked at his own fastenings. Ann had never done that in the entire sixteen years of their marriage.

Firelight flickered over exposed skin, breast and belly and thighs; blood thundered in his ears and he sank into the warmth, the sweetness, the sheer joy of her.

For a space of seconds Jake held a rational thought: There would be no turning back after this. And then he gave himself up to animal pleasure, thinking of nothing, only enjoying the sensations of which he had been so long deprived, sensations he wanted to go on for as long as they could be sustained, knowing he was giving Jaisy as much pleasure as she gave him.

It was the first night that he didn't bother to go home at all.

## 17

MAGGIE tapped lightly on the bedroom door, then opened it a crack, expecting that her father would emerge still buttoning his plaid shirt, with his customary remark about how hungry he was. For as long as she could remember, he had greeted every day with a statement that he was starving, or could eat a horse, a bundle of shingles, or some other unlikely object. It had made her laugh when she was a little girl.

Though she remained troubled about his trips to Jaisy Pallison's house, she had forgiven him for leaving her on her birthday to go there. She always forgave him anything, as he did her.

She was feeling moderately uncomfortable about facing him, however; she had spoken so frankly to him last night about something that was, perhaps, none of her business. It had hurt him, she'd seen that plainly enough on his face, but it hadn't changed anything. He was infatuated with that Pallison woman, and not even for Maggie did he intend to give her up.

It made her face burn to think of what the two of them did when they were alone together. Well, not alone, for there were two small children at the cabin, and she couldn't believe her father would do anything improper in front of *them*. Except that simply being there was improper in the first place.

Her imagination caused other things than burning cheeks, too. There was much that she and Nancy Totting had not learned in eavesdropping on their elders, but they'd admitted to each other that under some circumstances they had each experienced oddly disturbing physical sensations. Nancy noted this when she was in close proximity to Adam Welker, particularly on an occasion or two when he'd actually touched her hand. Maggie had felt this way, both excited and frightened/repulsed (though the excitement was the overwhelming emotion) when she was with Angus.

She did not understand why, then, she should have similar stirrings when she thought about her father and Jaisy Pallison.

"Daddy? You're late for breakfast, and there's hash and eggs and . . ." Her voice trailed off as the door swung fully open.

The room was empty.

Besides that, the bed was neatly made up. As if nobody had slept in it.

Shock washed through her. He couldn't have stayed the

whole night with Jaisy, could he? No matter how infatuated he was with that woman, he wouldn't deliberately create a scandal, would he? Making the entire family subject to ridicule and contempt, and perhaps pity?

Her eyes felt hot and stung as if she'd gotten soap into them. Oh, Daddy, how could you? she thought.

Jake never made up his own bed. There was no question about it; he simply had not come home last night. Maggie moved across the room with sudden purpose, jerking back the covers, punching a fist into the pillow to make it seem that a head had lain there, mussing up the sheets a little.

That didn't solve the problem of the garments he would ordinarily have left there, the socks and underwear he'd worn yesterday and which Mrs. Totting would collect for Monday's wash. She looked wildly around for something to use to deceive the housekeeper, seeing nothing that would serve. Maybe if she crumpled up a few clean things, and carried them downstairs herself to be put in with the other dirty laundry, Mrs. Totting wouldn't notice the difference.

She had to prevent everyone from knowing that Jake had stayed away all night.

She opened several dresser drawers and grabbed out various items, wadding them against her chest as she ran back down the stairs.

"Daddy's already gone," she announced to the room at large, pushing past them without looking anyone in the eye. "I brought down his laundry, but I didn't have time to make up his bed, Mrs. Totting."

"Gone?" Millicent echoed, looking up from the table where she was enjoying tea and toast.

"Without breakfast?" Mrs. Totting asked, astonished, holding a spatula in midair with a pancake on it. Jake's early-morning hunger was legendary.

"He had a lot to do today. I suppose he woke up early

and decided to get a head start. Hurry up, Celeste, or we'll be late for the last day of school.''

Maggie slid into her own chair and tried to eat, though the food scratched her throat going down and formed a heavy lump in her stomach. She knew they'd wonder if she didn't eat, though, so she tried.

She was grateful that her mother had not yet come down—she often didn't, these days, preferring to have a tray sent up after the others had eaten, so that she could stay with Sarah—for Ann might have asked the questions that nobody else voiced. Maggie was by no means sure of that, since Ann paid less attention to the other members of the family than she used to, but she was sure she couldn't lie convincingly to Ann.

All day she thought about Jake and that woman, smoldering inwardly until she couldn't concentrate on what the teacher said or what she was supposed to be doing. Once he reprimanded her sharply, and Maggie tried to pull herself together. If she attracted attention, people would wonder, and there must be enough speculation about the Keatings already without that.

She saw the two young Pallison children after school, easily recognizable by their red hair, and noted that both wore new boots. How had their mother paid for them? Maggie wondered. Or had her father bought them?

Bitterness twisted inside of her, hard, painful. It wasn't that they lacked anything at home, buying for *them* didn't deprive Jake's own family, and he knew it; and Mr. Deevers at the Mercantile probably either knew or guessed where the funds had come from to buy new boots. What one person knew, others might well know, in a town the size of Snohomish. It made her feel as if everyone watched her, snickering behind her back.

For once the beauty of the day was lost upon her. There was almost a summertime warmth in the air as she headed toward home, and then she remembered that Mama had asked her to pick up some embroidery floss several days ago, and she hadn't yet done it.

Reluctantly, Maggie retraced her footsteps. She didn't want to go into the Mercantile at all, didn't want to see Mr. Deevers peering at her through his little round glasses and have to wonder if his smile meant anything more than it usually did. Still, she wouldn't be coming to town to school anymore—ever, probably, since hardly anybody went to school past the age of fifteen—and if she didn't get the floss today Mama would have to depend on Daddy to get it. Jake was not much use at things like that. He didn't even know what cerulean was, and wasn't likely to get the right color unless he had a sample to match.

The store had several customers, which was fine with Maggie. It meant that the proprietor had other things to do than pay attention to her.

Maggie went to the back of the establishment and selected the embroidery floss (Ann spent hours making and embroidering little dresses for Sarah) and looked at the new shipment of yard goods that Mr. Deevers had piled on a counter. There was a pink mousseline de soie, very fine, that took her fancy, and on impulse Maggie picked up the bolt of silk to carry with her. Maybe she'd try to make herself a dress; if she had trouble, her grandmother would help her out, and it would be nice to have a new dress . . . just in case she needed one for anything special, she thought.

Hugging the bolt of material against her, Maggie turned to go to the front of the store where the cash register was, and ran smack into Jaisy Pallison.

Maggie stopped, heart suddenly hammering. It was a big store, and there was nobody near them. Mr. Deevers, at the front of the counter, was talking to Mrs. McAllmer. It was impossible to make out their words, so nobody heard the inward breath—almost a hiss—except for Jaisy.

Jaisy nodded, and would have moved on if Maggie hadn't spoken in a tight, hard voice. Words she never

intended to speak, words forced out of her by the knowledge of this woman's guilt, and her father's.

"Why don't you leave him alone?" Maggie demanded
in a ragged whisper. "He's got no right being with you, no
right at all."

Jaisy stared at her, green eyes wide and thickly lashed,
the rich auburn hair carelessly escaping its pins to frame
her face. Maggie did not see its beauty, or its kindness, or
even note the obvious happiness that dimmed, a little, at
Maggie's words.

At a loss, Jaisy said nothing, and Maggie didn't wait for
her to come up with anything. She swept past the woman,
knocking something off a shelf with the end of the bolt of
silk, not bothering to stop and pick it up, shaking so that
she thought Mr. Deevers would notice and realize, when
he saw who his remaining customer was, that Maggie
knew about the woman and her own father.

Mr. Deevers ploddingly measured out the amount of
material she asked for and figured the cost. "Let's see,
seven yards, that'll be . . ."

"Put it on our bill," Maggie managed to say, and
waited, gritting her teeth and trying not to let him see the
tears in her eyes as he wrapped her parcel.

"There you are," Mr. Deevers said, noticing nothing,
and she emerged a moment later into the sunlit street,
clutching the package so tightly that her fingernails went
through the wrapping.

The tears stung and she determined not to let them spill
over, not to let anyone know what had caused them. Damn
the woman, anyway, the brazen hussy! No doubt Jake
Keating was paying for whatever the bitch was buying,
right this minute. Did Mr. Deevers put it on a bill for her,
too, for Jake to pay at the end of the month? Or did Jake
give her cash?

Her anger was almost more than she could contain, and

she didn't know whom she was more angry at, her father or Jaisy Pallison.

Jaisy stared after the girl, feeling pity and regret. She knew Jake was crazy about the child, though the way she'd looked today, maybe she wasn't a child anymore. Jaisy would have liked being friends with her, had that been possible.

She turned back to the bolts of fabric, fingering a lovely green silk mull, knowing it would be stunning on her, knowing as well that she'd never have a dress of it. She wouldn't have anywhere to wear it, even if she owned it; yet she was a woman, with a woman's craving for beautiful things. Jaisy sighed and reached instead for the bolt of plain blue chambray that would do for both the children's shirts and frocks.

Someday maybe Jake's daughter would understand how it was, to be a widow with children to raise and no means to do it. She wasn't qualified to teach school or work in a store where she'd have to keep accounts or make change. She had no schooling to speak of; Lucy could read and write better than she could.

If it hadn't been for Jake Keating, Jaisy didn't know what she'd have done since Hank Pallison's death.

At first she'd been numb, though not so numb that she didn't feel gratitude when he'd given her Hank's pay and some extra besides. When he'd fixed the roof and repaired the steps and put in a new window, after Will and Ned broke it wrestling around, and saw to it that she had a supply of winter firewood, why, she'd just thought he was a kind man, doing what he could for an employee's surviving family.

It wasn't until she began to come out of her own pit of despair that it gradually dawned on Jaisy that Jake came for his own sake, as well as for hers.

The day she'd seen him watching her and recognized the

look—a man admiring a desirable woman—she'd felt a tremor that ran all the way through her and left her shaken yet not apprehensive or insulted in any way.

She knew Jake Keating was married and had a family. She'd seen Ann Keating, skinny little thing in clothes that were stylish compared to those Jaisy herself wore. Pretty, Jaisy admitted, and rather elegant. She didn't look the type Jaisy would have felt comfortable with as a friend, to sit across the table and exchange confidences with.

She hadn't been comfortable with Jake at first, either, in one sense. From the day that she realized how he was looking at her—before he even knew it himself—she knew that sooner or later Jake Keating was going to try to take her to bed. And for almost that long she'd known that when he did, she wasn't going to resist him.

She'd married Hank Pallison at fifteen, knowing nothing, expecting what all young girls expect—romance, living happily ever after. Well, Hank had been an affectionate husband, good to her in his own way, though he'd never earned enough to provide much more than a roof over their heads and a couple of meals a day. He'd been good in bed, she had to say that, and she'd enjoyed that part of their marriage and learned to live with the rest of it.

Jaisy, though not a churchgoing Bible thumper, as she thought of the more righteous ladies of Snohomish City, considered herself a reasonably moral person. Hank was the only man she'd ever slept with, until Jake. She wasn't promiscuous.

Yet she knew she had to have a man. She needed one in bed, and she needed one to take care of her and the kids. The fact that Jake Keating was married was unfortunate, but a female had to be practical. Maybe she'd have found someone else—after all, Snohomish boasted some seven hundred citizens now, and there were plenty of single men, though none of them she knew of was as well situated as

Jake Keating—but she needed help immediately, when Hank was killed, and Jake was there.

Besides that, he was the most attractive man she'd ever met. Better looking than Hank had been, owner of his own logging show, better educated than most men of his day. From the first time she really looked at those brawny arms, bronzed by the sun and covered with fine dark hair, Jaisy imagined them around her, and found the image both comforting and exciting.

And he wasn't satisfied at home.

It didn't take her long to figure that out. A man in love with his wife, and she in love with him, would have settled for the basic things of seeing that his employee's widow was taken care of with a snug cabin and food for the winter, then left her on her own. He wouldn't have kept finding excuses to return again and again and spend hours sitting at her kitchen table drinking watery coffee and talking if he'd been happy at home.

He never mentioned Ann to her. He did talk about his children, particularly Maggie. He was proud of his daughters, and he obviously loved them very much. He talked about problems in the woods, and the dropping price of timber, and things he read about in the newspaper. He told her about things that had happened when he was a boy, and when he was growing up, and his dreams for the future, of expanding his logging operation and hiring more men.

And he listened to her. More than that, he drew her out. Asked her questions. Smiled, listening to her answers. Smiled like a man content. It was only when he rose to go, saying "Well, I better get on home," that the smile slid away. She didn't think he realized that either.

She was ready for him considerably before he made that final move. The ache had built up in her loins, and she spent hours alone in the darkness wondering how much longer it would take him and if she ought to take some step to hurry him along.

Jaisy decided against the latter course. Waiting was better. Let him come when he was ready, let it be his decision, so that no one could say she'd seduced him away from his lady wife.

There was the practical part of the arrangement, knowing that as long as Jake Keating was interested in her he'd see that she and the kids didn't go hungry, and there was the physical part of it, having a vigorous, virile man in her bed again. Jaisy couldn't have said which of these factors was more important to her.

All she knew was that she cared about Jake Keating, and she needed him, and not even for that big-eyed little girl or her skinny lady mother was she going to give him up, not as long as he wanted to keep coming around.

# 18

MAGGIE arrived at camp the following morning to find affairs in a state of confusion.

She had dreaded seeing her father, and had begun to worry that Jaisy would tell him what Maggie had said to her. If that happened, Jake might be very, very angry, and while Maggie had often seen that anger directed at someone else, it had never yet been turned on her.

What she had done was stupid. She knew that as soon as she'd walked out of the Mercantile, and now she might have to pay too large a price. If she lost her father's love and affection . . . But she couldn't allow herself to think that way.

She had waited in an agony of suspense for him to come home for supper, had not dared to walk out to meet him as she might ordinarily have done. She'd longed for this day, of finishing school and at last being able to really help with the books and in camp, assisting Mr. Murphy; and now she felt no elation at all. Only fear that speaking before she thought might have spoiled the special relationship she'd always had with her father.

Suppertime arrived, and there was no sign of Jake.

Nancy, wearing an apron that dwarfed her slight figure, appeared in the doorway of the family sitting room, clearing her throat nervously.

"Ma says, ma'am, should she set things back until Mr. Jake gets here?"

It wasn't clear which of them she was addressing, for she stared between Millicent and Ann, twisting the apron so that she put wrinkles into it.

Millicent glanced at her daughter, absorbed as usual in rocking small Sarah, and replied when it appeared that Ann would not. "Perhaps we'd better wait a few minutes more."

At that, Ann turned her head toward the doorway. "It's half-past six, isn't it?"

"Yes, ma'am," Nancy acknowledged.

"Then we'll eat. We *always* eat at half-past six. No doubt Mr. Keating has been delayed and will be along shortly."

"Yes, ma'am," Nancy repeated, and scurried away. The family set aside their various activities and rose as one, heading toward the dining room.

No one, with the exception of Maggie, seemed alarmed that Jake had not shown up, though it didn't happen very often. They were close enough to the operation so that they'd have heard the whistle punk's disaster signal, had there been one. There was no reason to think that anything had happened to him.

Except, Maggie thought, taking her chair, that he had not come home the previous night. There hadn't been any big fight between her parents, at least not that she knew of, so he wouldn't have simply moved out, would he? No, no, of course not. And even if such a thing happened, he wouldn't leave all his clothes behind.

The Tottings served the roast and potatoes and vegetables, and the family ate mostly in silence, though Celeste and Millicent tried to carry on a conversation about music.

Maggie forced herself to eat, listening tensely for the sound of a door closing, of Jake's footsteps in the hall. What if he never came home again? She felt sick with the fear of it, a fear heavy with guilt for her own part in driving him away.

When the word came, however, it was not Jake himself who brought it. Angus McKay, on his way to town, stood just inside the door to deliver the message.

"Jake said to tell you it'll be late. He's got some problems."

For once Maggie was more interested in the news than in the one who carried it. "Is he all right?"

"Oh, sure. There was a little trouble among the men. A fight. Nobody's seriously hurt. He fired those two dead-heads he hired on last month."

Still, Jake didn't come home until after Maggie had gone to bed. She lay rigid, listening to his feet in the hall outside her room, slow, heavy footsteps that hesitated before Ann's doorway and ceased when he'd entered his own room.

He sounded so tired, she thought. Usually he walked with energetic steps that had been known to make Millicent mutter (under her breath) about a bull in a china shop, though he'd never knocked anything over that Maggie could remember.

She thought about him, over there alone in the room that had taken on none of his personality, where he simply slept. For a moment she considered slipping out of bed and crossing the hall, reestablishing touch with him; but something held her back. If he rebuffed her overture she could not bear it, so she continued to suffer from her own loneliness and guilt, until she finally fell asleep.

In the morning she overslept. Everyone else had eaten by the time she came down, and Jake was gone.

Nancy brought her oatmeal and toast and blackberry jam, and then at Maggie's invitation sat down to share the toast, although she'd eaten earlier, too.

"Did Daddy eat with everybody else?" Maggie asked, spooning brown sugar over her oatmeal and lacing it with thick cream.

"Yes." Since there was no one else in the room, Nancy helped herself to a liberal blob of jam and carefully spread it over the toast. "He asked where you were, and was going to send Celeste to wake you, but your ma said no. Let you sleep in today."

"I wish she hadn't." In spite of her concern, Maggie had a healthy appetite, especially after only picking at her food the night before. "Did he say what happened yesterday that kept him so late?"

"No. Nobody asked, and he didn't say. You going out to camp today?"

"Yes. As soon as I make up my bed, I guess."

"I'll do it," Nancy offered. "If you want to go right away. We're going to town this afternoon." A touch of color showed in her normally sallow face, and Maggie knew at once the reason for it.

"You going to see Adam Welker?"

"Well, maybe. Ma said we'd stop at Welker's and see about getting some potatoes, if they've any good ones left."

"I wish you'd get brave enough to talk to him," Maggie told her. "Instead of just looking at him. I can tell, the way he looks back, he likes you. He's just shy."

Nancy nodded. "I know. If Ma gets to talking to Mrs. Welker, though, maybe there'll be time enough to get around to something. Did you know there's a dance at the Athenaeum next Saturday night?"

Maggie's interest quickened. "Will your ma let you go?"

"Well, she hasn't said yet, so maybe." Nancy, too, had turned fifteen a few weeks earlier. "Wish me luck, Maggie."

Maggie did, and sincerely, hoping that she, too, would now be allowed to attend. Although it was unlikely that her parents would go, she supposed. They hadn't been anywhere together since before Sarah was born. The only place Ann went these days was to church, and Jake no longer accompanied her.

It seemed to her, as she walked down the stairs and out of the house half an hour later, that the place was too big, too silent, too empty. It was a house intended for a large family, for parties and entertainments, and without those things, it was oppressive.

She was glad to escape to sunshine and woodsy smells; she loved the fragrance of the fallen cedar boughs crushed underfoot, the lush growth of ferns beside the road that could be used to ease the itching bumps caused by nettles, should one be unwary enough to touch them, and the fluttering yellow-and-white butterflies that drifted around her. It was familiar and beloved.

She could pretend, at least until she reached camp, that all was well in her world.

Logs were cold-decked on the riverside, but there were no men working there. Maggie went on along the skid road, realizing only when she could smell the smoke from Mr. Murphy's cookstove that there were no sounds of saws or chains.

She hurried the last hundred yards, coming into the clearing to find not working men but a crew standing around in several small groups, talking.

Jake was there, in earnest conversation with Red Risku and several of the other older men. Angus stood alone, leaning against one corner of the bunkhouse, chewing on a toothpick, and Maggie approached him and stopped.

"What's going on?"

Angus pushed himself away from the wall. "Sudds and Harley cleared out all right. Only it seems they took a bunch of equipment with them. Four saws included. Jake's furious."

That was obvious even from this distance. Jake was gesticulating with both hands, his movements powerful, angry.

"They just stole our tools?" Maggie asked, incredulous. She'd never heard of such a thing. "Did anybody go after them?"

"Jake tried, but they were seen in town after dark last night, so they had a long head start. Listen, Mr. Murphy's rheumatism is bad today. He'd probably appreciate your help. Especially since his helper didn't show up, either. We don't know if he ran with Sudds and Harley or what, but the old man's working alone."

Maggie would have liked to stay with Angus—it wasn't often that he was on the ground long enough to talk to, except at mealtimes—but she knew how miserable Mr. Murphy could be when his joints ached. She walked across the clearing, not sure whether Jake would acknowledge her presence or not, longing desperately to know that she was forgiven and that they were friends again.

He didn't even see her. She heard a stream of profanity and the names of the absconding men and decided this was no time to draw attention to herself.

The cookhouse was built in such a way that on warm days, when the stove was going hot enough to cook the cook, as Mr. Murphy put it, the upper part of the walls at the front and sections of the sides could be opened out and up, held in place by sturdy sticks, to allow for ventilation.

This also enabled the cook to see what was going on in camp.

The old man looked up from his chopping board, resting the cleaver amidst a bunch of carrots. "Well, I thought you weren't coming today."

"Sorry. I overslept. Daddy's pretty upset, I guess."

Mr. Murphy shook his head. "Bad business, stealing a man's equipment that way. Them saws are expensive, and nobody in Snohomish's even got any more, leastways not four of 'em. Maybe have to shut down while Jake goes into Port Gardner, or maybe even Seattle, for new ones."

It wasn't only losing a day or two of work, or having to travel so far to obtain saws, that was the worst of it, Maggie knew. It was the price of the saws, at a time when income was down and Jake was watching the pennies more closely than ever, that was putting pressure on the situation.

There was nothing she could do about any of that, and she brought her mind back to more ordinary matters. "What do you want me to do, Mr. Murphy? Do you want pies? There's still plenty of dried apples."

"Pies, yes. You have a good hand with the crust. Make one with less cinnamon—that Humphries, he don't like so much spices. Stir that pot, will you, while I get my honey and vinegar. You can't believe how my knees are aching, and no sign of rain, either."

He firmly believed that the honey-and-vinegar concoction he drank daily eased his pain, though Maggie didn't know how he could tell that it would be worse if he didn't take it. At least he felt as if he were doing something about the problem.

She reached for the apron hanging on a nail on one of the supporting posts and stopped, startled.

A young man sat at the nearest of the tables, in shadow so that she hadn't noticed him when she'd come in out of the bright sun, drinking a mug of coffee.

Maggie stared at him openly.

He wasn't a logger, that was for certain. Not with those store-bought clothes, a dark suit and a white shirt and a tie. Most of these men didn't even own a suit or tie, and not even Jake would wear the latter to dress up.

Since he was seated, it was hard to gauge his height; she had the impression that he was tall. One leg, elegantly clad in black broadcloth and with well-polished boots showing, was extended into the aisle between the tables. He couldn't have walked here without getting dust on his boots, so he must have wiped them off after he arrived, she thought irrelevantly.

The stranger bestowed on her a tentative smile and sipped from the steaming cup. "Hello! I didn't expect to find a young lady out here in a logging camp. I'm Wilkie Andreason."

Maggie was suddenly, acutely, conscious of her old dress, the sort of thing she normally wore in the woods, a brown gingham that had been mended around the pockets, though that didn't actually show. Her shoes were scuffed (she never attempted to keep them polished when she knew she'd be walking through mud and wet underbrush), and her hair . . .

Dear heaven, what must he think of her hair?

Mama had said she could put it up, now that she was fifteen, but so far she hadn't bothered to try to do anything with it. Maggie had no knack for fixing hair and she knew it. Her dark tresses were almost perfectly straight, and though her hair didn't curl like Celeste's it *was* pretty hair, soft and shiny, so she let it hang loose down her back. When she was smaller, Mama had often braided it because it stayed neater that way, but Maggie hadn't even wanted to bother with braids; when she did them herself they came out uneven and messy looking, not tight and tidy. It was easier simply to brush it out and let it hang.

Only now she knew it needed brushing again, and he

probably thought she was only a little girl, except for her height, because of her stupid hair.

Maggie swallowed. Wilkie Andreason, she thought, tucking the name away in her memory. Nobody would call him Willie, she knew that instinctively, too. He was too elegant to be a Willie.

"I'm Maggie—Margaret—Keating," she said. She'd forgotten the apron; now she put it on and tied it behind her neck, remembering too late that this action pushed her bosom into prominence. The bosom that was regrettably small, though she hadn't given up hope that it would grow larger.

Wilkie Andreason's smile widened. "Hello, Maggie-Margaret."

"I'm not—I mean, my name is Margaret Ellen, but I'm mostly called Maggie."

He considered that while she tied the apron strings at the small of her back. "Probably I should call you Miss Keating, if we're to do this properly. Have you a mother who's concerned with proprieties?"

She felt heat climb into her face. The way she looked, like some half-wild thing, he probably had reason to think she was motherless, unsupervised. "Yes," she admitted. "A mother, and a grandmother."

Wilkie Andreason rose to his feet, as if suddenly remembering his own manners. He *was* tall, though not quite as tall as Angus, and slimmer, less muscular. That didn't detract from his attractiveness, though. He had black hair and dark eyes, and was clean-shaven; that alone would set him apart in this group of bearded and mustachioed men.

"I'm happy to meet you, Miss Keating."

She wasn't quite sure how to respond to that; she felt flustered and foolishly young and gauche. "Thank you. What are you . . ." She stopped, wondering if that was going to sound rude. "Are you here to see my father?"

"If your father's Jake Keating, yes. I guess I picked a bad day. It seems there's been trouble."

"Yes, some men walked off with some of our equipment, and it'll have to be replaced before the whole crew can go back to work." It struck her, then, that he must have a reason for being here. "Are you . . . are you looking for a job?"

He gestured with the cup. "Do you mind if I sit down? It was a longer walk out here from town than I expected, and in new boots." He grinned. "I have sore feet."

"By all means, make yourself comfortable. Would you like more coffee?"

He extended the mug for a refill and stirred sugar into it. "To answer your question, yes. I'm looking for a job. I hope you don't mind if I sit here until your father has time to talk to me."

"No, of course not." Maggie got out the large dishpan she used to mix pie crust, and took the top off the flour barrel. "Excuse me if I do the pies, will you?"

She felt rather sorry for him, if he'd walked all the way from Snohomish in the hope of joining the operation, because she couldn't imagine Jake hiring anyone who looked and dressed like this. Not that he seemed a sissy, not at all, but he certainly didn't look like a man who knew his way around the woods, either.

She was aware of his gaze upon her, and she didn't know if she liked it or not. If only she'd done something with her hair, if she only knew *how* to do something with it. And almost any dress would have been better than this ratty old thing.

"Maggie." Jake's voice brought her sharply around. There were worry lines in his face, but he sounded the same as ever. "I'm going to have to go and see if I can get some saws to replace the ones those bastards took. And hope I can talk somebody into credit if I have to go all the way to Seattle. I'll stop at the house first; I've already missed today's boat, but if I ride on over to Port Gardner I'll get the next one that comes along. I may have to be gone for a few days. Risku will be in charge here, they'll have to work with a reduced crew until I get back.''

The newcomer had risen to his feet. Maggie felt compelled to introduce him. "Daddy, this is Mr. Andreason, he wants to talk to you.''

Jake's gaze slid over the young man, dismissed him. "Sorry. Not today. With any luck, I'll be back on Monday, Tuesday at the latest. You might bring the ledger up-to-date before then, honey.''

"Yes, all right,'' Maggie said. Relief filtered through her. He wasn't angry at her.

Jake strode away, and Wilkie Andreason gave her a rueful look. "My timing wasn't very good, was it? Monday or Tuesday.''

"I'm sorry,'' Maggie said, feeling inadequate.

"Not your fault.'' He put down the mug on the plain board table. "Well, I guess I'll be back next week,'' he said, and moved toward the open doorway.

"Would you like something to eat before you start back to town?'' Maggie asked quickly. "There isn't much cooked yet today, but there's bread and cheese and meat from yesterday.''

He hesitated, then grinned again. It made him look younger. Twenty-two or-three, she guessed. "That would be great, if you don't mind,'' he accepted.

Maggie saw Mr. Murphy watching her, but she didn't care. It was only hospitable to offer a man food when he was hungry, and her father paid for the food. It didn't belong to Mr. Murphy.

She reached for the bread and a knife and began to slice, oddly excited by this stranger who was so different from any of the other men she knew.

# 19

JAKE returned on Monday evening, tired and out of sorts. Though he'd brought back replacement saws, he'd had to pay more than he'd hoped for them; and it hadn't been easy to get them on credit, which was the only way he could afford to get them at all. There was cut timber at the landing; but until it had been moved downstream to the mill at Snohomish, and he'd been paid for it, he had a limited amount of cash for new purchases.

He'd have liked nothing better than to go directly to Jaisy's; he knew that would be a mistake, but he savored the knowledge that she would be there, warm and sympathetic to his needs, when he could manage it. Jaisy wasn't a woman who made demands on a man. She didn't insist on knowing where he was, or what he was doing, or when he'd be back. She was simply there, waiting, when he chose to show up.

His family was waiting, too, yet except for Celeste, nobody threw her arms around his neck and kissed him. Maggie looked up from something she was stitching and asked, "Did you get the saws, Daddy?"

Ann put out a hand to rock the cradle beside her where Sarah slept, looked at him without speaking, and went back to her needlework, while Millicent murmured a greeting as she turned the heel of a sock she was knitting.

"I got them, but they aren't paid for, so you'd all better

pray that the price of lumber doesn't drop any further. Is there anything to eat?''

Millicent always hesitated, waiting for her daughter to take her rightful responsibility on such matters; when Ann made no response, Millicent rose from her chair. "I'll ask Mrs. Totting to fix you something."

"Cold meat and bread will be fine," Jake said. "I might as well say this now, while you're all here together. We may be in serious financial trouble if things don't take a turn for the better within a few months."

That did catch Ann's attention. "Are we going to lose this house?" she asked, and Maggie could not tell from her voice whether that prospect was devastating or whether Ann could take it in stride.

Jake made an impatient gesture. "No, no. The house is ours, and it's paid for. But there won't be as much cash as usual. Anything you can save on, do it. We'll keep eating, but there won't be money for fripperies for a while. No pianos or organs or fancy clothes.''

Maggie felt a twinge of guilt. She'd charged the pink silk muslin for a new dress, which she didn't really need. She had enough clothes, and besides, they didn't entertain these days, or go anywhere except to church. She wouldn't even be going to school anymore.

Ann returned to the pillow cover she was embroidering, apparently satisfied, though for a moment it seemed she might ask something, a question she decided to swallow.

How much was Ann aware of, Maggie wondered, in regard to the Pallisons? Did she know that Jake took them groceries and bought boots for the children? She could hardly be blamed for the resentment she would naturally feel when told to curtail her own spending, if part of the family income was going to support the widow and her children.

Only Maggie, of them all, really looked into Jake's face. She saw fatigue there, and frustration, and wished there were something she could do to alleviate his problems instead of adding to them.

She followed him into the dining room, where Nancy served him a cold supper, and sat across from him at the table which was absurdly large for the two of them.

Jake seemed to have the same thought. "Silly," he said, "sitting here with hand-painted china and a lace tablecloth, instead of at a kitchen table. You know something, Maggie? I liked the old house better. The little one, where we did everything together in the same room."

"I did, too," Maggie agreed, subdued. "This was what Mama wanted, but I don't think even she's enjoying it very much now."

Jake buttered slabs of bread and layered them with slices of beef, forming a sandwich almost too thick to bite. "If she enjoys anything, I don't know what it is. Is Sarah all right?"

"The same as always." Maggie spoke around the lump in her throat. "She just lies there. She doesn't do anything. She's never going to be normal, is she?"

Jake swallowed half a glass of milk before replying. "Maybe she'll be better when she's older, honey. I don't know. How did things go while I was gone?"

He meant in the woods; she knew that without his being specific. Maggie sighed, leaning on her elbows.

"Tom Dunnigan cut his foot with an ax," she said.

Jake forgot the bite of sandwich he was about to take. "How'd that happen? How bad is it?"

"He just slipped. His footing, I mean, right when he brought the ax down. It cut through his boot and bled an awful lot. The doctor said he probably couldn't walk on it for a few weeks, anyway."

Jake swore and resumed eating. "What else?"

"Everybody's tempers are sort of short. I suppose it's because they're worried and frustrated, because there isn't a full crew and they needed the saws, and they're worried about their jobs."

"Fighting?"

The way he was talking to her, as if she were an equal, an intelligent *male* equal, suddenly filled her with gratitude and love. She wanted to reach out and touch him, but she didn't know how to do that anymore. When had it happened, that she'd outgrown being able to climb into his lap and lean against his shoulder, to have his arms around her and his whiskery chin against her cheek? The time was gone, and she hadn't even noticed, and now it was too late for that.

"Yes, a couple of squabbles. Even Angus."

Jake raised his eyebrows, waiting for details.

"Everybody's in a bad humor. They say nasty things to one another, then take offense, and somebody takes a poke at somebody else. Not just fooling around the way they usually do, but as if they want to hurt each other."

"Who's hurt?" Jake asked.

"From fighting, Red Risku has a split lip and a big bruise on his cheek, and Rich Salter's right hand is swelled up so bad he couldn't hold his end of the saw today."

Jake swore again. "Just what I need. Two men missing from my crew and half the rest of them laid up with injuries. Damn it to hell, I told them I wouldn't lay anybody off if I could help it; but if they can't cut trees, how am I supposed to keep on paying them?"

Since there was no answer to that, Maggie went on to the next subject. "That man was back today. Mr. Andreason."

Jake looked blank.

"Remember, the man who came the day you left? I think he wants a job."

"Oh, yeah. The dude in the suit. What the hell kind of job is he qualified to do? I'll have to replace Sudds and Harley, but I don't need any more greenhorns. That fellow never worked in the woods in his life, by the look of him."

"He said he'd come back tomorrow."

"Well, I feel sorry for anybody needs a job, but I can't

hire anybody who's no use to me. God, I'm tired. I think I'll go on up to bed. You going to go out with me in the morning?''

"Yes, I think so. I did the ledger. It's on your desk in the sitting room."

Jake rose, then bent to kiss her cheek. "Thanks, honey. I always know I can depend on you. See you in the morning."

"I think I'll go up, too," Maggie said, and they went up the stairs together, shoulders occasionally touching. She wished he'd put his arm around her and hug her, the way he'd so often done in the past, but he didn't.

She felt sorry for Wilkie Andreason, she thought as she entered her own room and lighted the lamp. She stared past it into the mirror at her own reflection. Her eyes were good, her lashes as thick as Celeste's, and darker, her skin was perhaps too tanned to be truly feminine but at least it was free of blemishes. It was her hair that kept her from looking her best.

On impulse, she grabbed the locks on either side of her face and pulled them back, twisting them into an untidy knot at her nape, then lifting them atop her head. Other people put their hair up and looked marvelous, but how did they do it?

Maggie sank onto the bench and reached for her hairbrush. She tried sweeping her hair first one way, then another, only when she tried to secure it in any position, there were straggling hairs that escaped her pins, and the overall effect was one of lopsided messiness.

She was staring at herself in despair when there was a light tap on the door and Celeste put her head in. "Margaret? Are you going to bed already? It's only a quarter of nine."

"I thought I would, so I can leave with Daddy in the morning. Celeste, what can I do with my hair?"

The younger girl came into the room and stood appraisingly over Maggie. "You have lovely hair, Margaret."

"Except that it won't curl, and it doesn't seem to stay in pins. I look as if I'm twelve years old."

Celeste took the brush from her hand. "I think maybe curls are wrong for you, anyway. You have a sort of . . . elegance . . . that doesn't call for curls," she said.

Maggie heard her in amazement. "Elegance? *Me*?"

"Yes. I heard Grandma tell Mama that your bone structure was quite striking." That wasn't as good as being called beautiful, Maggie thought dazedly, but it was better than nothing. "I wonder if we couldn't roll it back, like this, and up. . . ."

Celeste moved at first experimentally, then more surely, brushing, smoothing, combing, and pinning. She left once to fetch several small tortoiseshell combs to hold Maggie's hair in place, and Maggie stared at herself in disbelief.

It was incredible how much difference the new hairstyle made. She looked years older, and perhaps Celeste was right: there *was* a sort of elegance about her, particularly when she held her head just so.

Maggie suddenly made a moaning sound, and Celeste picked up the comb she had just put down. "What's the matter, don't you like it? Maybe we could part it this way and—"

"No, no, it isn't that I don't like it! But I'll never be able to do it myself so what good is it? Everything I tried was so *messy*!"

"I'll do it for you," Celeste offered generously.

"Early in the morning? Before dawn? I'm going to the woods with Daddy."

Celeste reconsidered. She would rise before dawn only if the house were on fire. "I know. I'll get one of Mama's nets, and if you sleep carefully, you won't muss it much."

"How do I sleep carefully?" Maggie asked, trying to keep the edge of irritation and hopelessness from her tone.

"Mama has a satin pillow that helps. I'll get that, too.

It's slippery, so it doesn't pull your hair loose. Let's try it, Margaret.''

And so she went to bed with a net securing her new coiffure, lying stiffly on the satin pillow, wondering how she'd manage to stay in this rigid position all night.

Maybe Angus would take her seriously, as an adult, when he saw her now. And at the back of her mind was the thought that Wilkie Andreason might find her attractive, too, when he realized she wasn't a child after all.

Choosing the right clothes the following morning wasn't easy. Maggie discarded the first few garments that came to hand as being dowdy and schoolgirlish. After a few frantic moments, she came to a depressing conclusion: although there were plenty of garments in her wardrobe, she didn't own anything except the dresses she wore to church (which were totally unsuitable for walking through wet ferns or stirring stews in Mr. Murphy's cookhouse) that looked any better than what she'd already thrown across the foot of her bed.

The hairdo had survived surprisingly well. When she carefully peeled off the net, the combs and pins were revealed to have done their job, holding her dark hair smoothly in place.

How much good would it do, though, if she had to wear the same shoddy, ugly old dresses?

Celeste had nice things, she wore them every day because she had few activities that would damage her clothes, but Celeste was shorter and slightly smaller through the waist. Nothing of her sister's would fit Maggie.

Maggie bit her lip. She had to make up her mind or she wouldn't have time to eat before Jake left the house, which meant a brisk forty-five-minute walk before she got to camp where she could forage among Mr. Murphy's leftovers.

She settled on a school dress that, unfortunately, *looked* like a school dress, but it was not as old as most of the other things, and it was a rather nice shade of medium-blue. Of course, if she tore the hem, walking along the skid road, Mama would kill her. Or maybe, Maggie amended sadly, she wouldn't. Mama didn't even notice such things these days.

Jake was finishing a stack of pancakes drenched in butter and syrup, with sausages and a side dish of fried eggs. He looked up at her with a smile.

"Well, I thought you'd overslept. Say, what have you done to yourself?"

Maggie self-consciously took her place at his elbow. "Celeste fixed it for me."

He nodded approval. "You're lovely, Maggie. I suppose you're going to be thinking about finding a young man one of these days. You haven't picked one out yet, have you?"

It was a relief to her that he hadn't noticed her feelings for Angus, yet at the same time a disappointment, too. If he knew and didn't disapprove, it would be a help. She remembered what Angus had once said to her about Jake not encouraging any man to look at her.

She shook her head. "No, not yet. Daddy, there's a dance at the Athenaeum next Saturday. Do you suppose I could go? I think Nancy's going."

"A dance?" He looked at her more closely. "My God, are you really old enough for that?"

"Some of the girls go when they're only fifteen. Mama said when I was sixteen, but everybody else . . ."

"Well, we'll see," Jake said, which was about the best she'd hoped for. He probably wouldn't give permission unless he was sure Ann would agree with him. They weren't fighting so much anymore, and it was probably mostly because they had to talk to each other to fight, but she hoped they'd communicate enough to agree on letting her go to the dances.

"Come on, eat up, girl, it's time to be on the way. On the job at sunup, remember?"

Maggie rolled up several sausages inside each of a pair of pancakes, complete with butter and brown sugar, and stood up. "I'm ready," she said. "I can eat these on the way."

It had rained during the night, not an unusual occurrence, and the footing was treacherous. Mud was slippery, and it was barely light enough to see where to put one foot in front of the other. She'd considered carrying a better pair of shoes to change into in camp, rejecting the idea only because the more changes that were wrought at once, the more likelihood there was that the men would comment in their customary teasing way.

She licked the brown sugar off her fingers, then finished the cleaning job with her handkerchief. Jake pulled the small cart used for moving supplies from one place to another, its wheels rattling over the corduroy surface of the road, the saws adding their own small sounds to break the morning quiet.

They didn't talk much. Maggie was content in her father's company, thankful that he didn't hold it against her that she'd thrown up to him the matter of Jaisy Pallison.

A few men were still at breakfast when the Keatings arrived. The mingled aromas of coffee and bacon and woodsmoke hung on the air, momentarily overpowering the natural fragrance of fir and cedar. Jake poured out his usual cup of black coffee from the great pot that stood all day on the back of the stove, sipping from the tin cup with caution, surveying his crew.

"The saws are here; McKay and Humphries, you see to it they're good and sharp. The rest of you, let's get moving. We got timber to bring down."

"Who's going to take Sudds's place?" Rich Salter asked. He was nursing a badly swollen hand, and there were bruises on his face. "He wasn't worth a hell of a lot, but I can't do his job and mine, too."

Jake looked pointedly at the hand. "Looks to me like

you aren't in any shape to do your own, even. You all listen to me. I won't stand for anymore fighting, you hear? You want to fight, go work for somebody else. I can't afford to have my crew out of commission because they've been splitting each other's heads. Come on, let's get organized." Maggie was glad they were so busy with their own concerns that they didn't pay much attention to her. Maybe if they noticed sort of gradually, not all of them at once, that she looked different, they wouldn't make a fuss over it.

Mr. Murphy was already starting on his preparations for the dinner he would serve at noon. The day's bread was out of the oven, golden-brown loaves cooling on one of the tables, wafting an inviting scent to mingle with those of the coffee and the bacon. He stopped in midstride to look at her.

"Well, is it my own little Maggie? Or some town lady?"

"Does it look all right?"

He scrutinized her critically, then pronounced, "Very nice. Makes you all grown-up. You ain't going to quit helping out an old man because you're too grown-up, are you?"

Maggie smiled. "I don't think so. Shall I make cookies today? Or should I start peeling potatoes?"

It wasn't until two hours later that anyone else noticed her altered appearance. By that time the morning sun was high enough to be filtering down through the tops of the tall trees, though the cookhouse was still in deep shadow. The men had dispersed to their jobs; from a distance she could hear the rasp of a saw, and closer by the sound of the files as Angus and Humphries put the sharpest possible edge on the new blades.

They were working out of her sight, but sooner or later they'd be over for a cup of coffee and a few of the cookies that were just coming out of the oven. The men always smelled cookies long before they reached the cookhouse.

She had, almost, forgotten Wilkie Andreason. Until she turned around to lower another pan of cookies onto the table and saw him standing there.

"Oh! Mr. Andreason! Good morning." She hoped she didn't sound as flustered as she felt.

"Good morning." There was instant recognition of her new status—could it really make so much difference, to change the style of one's hair?—in his eyes, his smile. "Is it too much to hope that your father made it back?"

"No. I mean, yes, he's back. He's out with the crew, though. He's had a difficult day so far; I don't know if it's a good time to talk to him. I wouldn't advise it," she added candidly, "if he's in the middle of anything important. Like climbing or setting chokers or anything."

Andreason grinned. "No sense in making him mad before I ask him, eh? Is there any chance I could get another cup of that good coffee?"

"Yes, of course." Maggie brought it for him, adding a few of the fresh cookies on a plate. "Maybe when he comes in for dinner," she suggested. "Just let him eat a little bit, first, so he's not starving."

The grin widened. "I appreciate the advice, Miss Maggie." His gaze grew bolder. "You're looking very fetching today."

She hadn't had enough honest compliments to know how to handle them. She was accustomed to teasing. She was glad that Mr. Murphy called out to her then, so that she didn't have to make a reply.

It made her feel peculiar to go about her usual tasks with Wilkie Andreason sitting there watching her. She knew that his dark gaze followed her, and twice when she looked directly at him she found him openly staring. It was disturbing, yet gratifying, too.

She waited, in mixed anticipation and apprehension, for

the men to show up for the noon meal. They came straggling in, hungry, warm from their exertions, arguing, talking. The same as always.

They'd seen Andreason before, of course, since he'd been there earlier on two occasions. She saw their attention slide over him, dismiss him, go on to more important things. Nobody spoke to him.

Maggie carried platters of bread and meat, bowls of potatoes and beans and stew, to each of the tables where the men took their places. Several of them finally noticed her.

"Hey, Maggie, what we got here? A lady, by God! Put her hair up!"

It didn't get any worse than that. They noted the difference, approved it, the teasing mild by their ordinary standards. Nobody really made fun of her. Angus hadn't come yet, though. It was Angus who mattered.

He was among the last to take his place, when she was already refilling the bowls and serving more bread. The latter was cut in great heavy slices, to be thickly spread with butter or honey, and there were few who didn't eat four or five slices per meal. Maggie put down a platter of cold venison as Angus folded his long legs under the table, glancing at her as he did so.

"Well, aren't you pretty today," he said, and speared a slice of meat. "Have they eaten all the potatoes already?"

She was disappointed that she'd held his interest no longer than that. Still, he'd said she was pretty. She didn't believe it was true; she thought he'd only intended to be kind.

Kindness was't what she wanted from Angus, though. He hadn't been stunned by her new look. Not smitten. Maggie dished up more boiled potatoes to take to the table, wryly amused at herself. What had she expected? That he'd be so taken with her without her schoolgirl look that he'd propose?

Jake sat at the end of one of the tables, eating from a mounded plate. He ignored the banter around him, lost in his own thoughts. Maggie hoped the problems weren't more than he could deal with. She'd never seriously considered, before, that there might be problems too large for Jake. There was more to growing up than putting up one's hair; there was an increased perceptiveness that made her uneasily aware that her father was not the near-god she'd always thought him, but a man with flaws and weaknesses like her own, a man limited in his power to control things around him. It was all she could do not to hug him, the way he'd done with her when she was little and had skinned her knees.

Andreason had taken her advice, waiting until Jake had emptied his plate and was working on a cup of coffee and a plate of cookies, before he made his approach. She heard his opening words, in an educated voice and manner.

"Mr. Keating, I'm Wilkie Andreason. I've been waiting to talk to you."

Jake looked him in the eye and spoke bluntly. "You don't look like a man belongs in the woods."

"I belong anywhere there's a business being conducted," Andreason said with a quiet confidence. "I'm a bookkeeper, sir."

A bookkeeper! Maggie forgot what she was doing and burned a finger on a hot pan. She sucked at the small injury, straining to follow the rest of the conversation. It wasn't easy, because there was a burst of hilarity from the next table over; the men were laughing and banging on the table, for all the world like four-year-olds, covering some of what she wanted to hear.

"I keep my own books," Jake said, dunking an oatmeal cookie in his cup.

"Can you afford to, Mr. Keating?"

Jake gave a bark of laughter that held little amusement. "I can't afford *not* to," he said.

"Will you listen to what I have to say? While I try to persuade you that you're mistaken about that? That what you can't afford to do is waste your time doing book-work when you could more profitably be working with your crews? You're an experienced faller, and as such are worth more—to yourself or anyone else—than a bookkeeper."

The idiots at the next table roared again, wiping out a few more of Andreason's words. Maggie wanted to yell at them to shut up. She moved a little closer to her father's table.

"You're wasting your time," Jake said clearly. "There may be some truth in what you say, but I can't pay a bookkeeper, and I don't even need one full-time. I've only got a small business."

"Hey, Maggie, more coffee!" someone shouted, and she had to pick up the pot and carry it around, refilling cups. A glance in their direction revealed her father and Andreason in earnest conversation; she moved back to their table as quickly as she could.

Wilkie Andreason thanked her with a smile when she refilled his cup, while continuing to address Jake. "That's the beauty of what I'm offering you, Mr. Keating. Most of the logging operations around Snohomish are relatively small. Nobody needs a full-time bookkeeper. But they all need someone to keep their books, and I have the answer to that. I've already lined up jobs with three outfits, doing their books one day a week. I've arranged to do two others twice a month, because even a day a week is more than they need. Nobody is going broke paying me for part-time, professional bookkeeping, yet they all have first-class service."

Jake opened his mouth to speak but Andreason cut him off. "It isn't only a matter of adding up your figures, sir. I can show you ways to cut costs, to make your money go as far as possible. I suggest that you take me on, on a trial basis, and let me show you how much difference it will make in your net income. I've made an arrangement like this with Mr. Kurt Jorgeson, I think you know him, and I'm sure he'll vouch for my work and tell you how much improvement we've been able to make in his operation.''

Maggie was torn between wanting her father to give Wilkie Andreason a job, and distress at the thought that the bookkeeping chores wouldn't be handed over to *her*. She put the coffeepot back on the stove and could no longer think of an excuse for further eavesdropping, for now the men were getting up and there were the tables to clear.

It wasn't until midafternoon that she had a chance to ask her father how the matter had turned out.

"What did you tell him?" she asked when Jake had paused for another cookie before returning to the woods after a consultation with Angus.

"I told him I'd think about it," Jake said, and bit off half the cookie.

Maggie didn't know whether she was pleased or not. She wanted the bookkeeping job herself, not because she especially wanted to do that instead of helping Mr. Murphy, but because it was a way to help Jake, to be close to him.

On the other hand, Wilkie Andreason was a very attractive young man. Very different from any of the others in camp.

She was still musing over it when she headed for home, uncertain of what she'd say if Jake asked her how she felt about it.

# 20

For a few weeks, Celeste helped with her hair. Eventually Maggie got the hang of it, after hours of practice before a mirror, which left her arms aching with the effort of holding them up for so long.

Maggie hauled out and examined her wardrobe. She had asked for Millicent's help with the mousseline de soie, having decided it was too fine a piece of goods to risk ruining it with her own inept stitching. There were two dresses she'd been wearing for church that could be demoted to everyday status, and a few others could be brightened up with new collars and cuffs, so that she would look a little less like an orphan when she went to work in the woods.

The family discussion about attending dances at the Athenaeum took place at the supper table, tentatively introduced by Maggie on an evening when there was at least no perceptible hostility between her parents.

Ann's initial reaction was a wrinkling of her brow in instinctive rejection, but for once Jake spoke directly to her.

"Maggie's old enough to start doing things like that once in a while, don't you think?"

"Please, Mama. Nancy's going," Maggie urged, her mouth dry, heart beating more quickly with hope. "You *said* someday I could go."

"But not unchaperoned," Ann said slowly. "And I can't possibly go to supervise, Margaret. I can't leave Sarah that long."

Millicent cleared her throat. "Perhaps I could do it in your place, dear. She won't have to stay past ten, will she?"

Ten, Maggie thought, only until ten? The dances lasted at least until midnight. Still, it would be better than nothing.

Millicent's voice sounded brittle, as if she feared to enter dangerous waters and churn up an unwanted storm. "Perhaps if Jake is going to town as usual on Saturday night, he could drive the buggy,and pick us up at ten."

Jake spoke into the small silence of Ann's consideration. "I suppose I could do that. Though I don't see any reason to cut things off at ten. Everybody's bedtime could be put off an hour more than that, couldn't it?"

And wonder of wonders, Ann agreed.

Celeste was almost as thrilled as Maggie. "I wish I could go, too. When you come home, wake me up, Margaret, and tell me everything about it, will you?"

Celeste helped with her hair, and also with her dress. The pink silk was cut out and basted together, not yet ready to be worn. Maggie settled for a dress of her mother's, taken in a bit through the bosom, delighted that she didn't have to wear one of the gowns she had worn so many times to church.

Ann had had to take in most of her garments since Sarah's birth, as she was very thin. She hadn't done anything with the dress Celeste chose for her sister from those frocks hanging in Ann's wardrobe. The gown was a stylish one of deep-green mozambique, and though it did not have the bustle that was returning to fashion, there was a deep flounce in the back, edged in narrowly pleated matching lawn; when she was finally dressed in it, dark hair swept smoothly back and upward, Maggie was astonished and delighted at her own appearance.

"Is it really me?" she asked, surveying herself full-length in the standing mirror.

"You look beautiful, Margaret," Celeste told her. "You need only one more thing. Let me run and ask Mama if you may borrow her seed-pearl brooch to have at your throat."

She felt so elegant, heading off for the Athenaeum half an hour later. Everyone in the household had admired her, and Maggie began to feel that she really *was* attractive. For the moment it didn't matter that she would never be beautiful, as Celeste was beautiful. She was, as Millicent put it, *striking,* and that was not at all a bad thing to be.

Jake left them at the door of the Athenaeum, grinning his pride in her, with the admonition to have fun. How could she not, when she felt the best she'd ever felt in her life?

There was little worry for any female about a lack of partners, since in spite of the number of families that had moved into the county there were still far more men than women. There was already a good crowd, including a row of men along one wall, smoking and inspecting the newcomers, while the musicians were tuning up at the far end of the hall.

A thrill of excitement ran through her. Maggie glanced at her grandmother, staid as always in her widow's black. "Do I need to do anything to my hair, Grandma? Or did the scarf hold it in place?"

Millicent smiled. "You look lovely, Margaret. Your hair is fine. I'm going to sit over there with Mrs. Windsor. Enjoy yourself, dear."

Maggie felt as if she were floating. She saw Nancy, who had come into town earlier in the afternoon and would be spending the night with her aunt and uncle rather than make the long walk back to the landing. Maggie worked her way in Nancy's direction, needing the moral support of a friend, although she knew virtually everybody here.

Nancy's usually sallow face was flushed with excitement; her brown hair was frizzed from a session with a curling iron, and she, too, had a new dress. "My aunt took it in for me," Nancy said, tugging at one of the pale-blue sleeves. "Does it look all right?"

"You look wonderful. Who's here, Nancy? Have you seen Adam Welker yet?"

Nancy giggled. "He's over there, by the punch bowl. I think he and Willie Fisher are planning to spike the punch when no one is looking."

Maggie turned so that she could survey the room. "Have you seen Angus?"

"No, but I think he comes to almost all the dances. There's Deborah." Her expression changed. "I didn't mean he comes just because of *her*."

"No, of course not," Maggie agreed, although Nancy's observation cast a faint shadow over the promising evening. She knew, from the remarks the men always made on Mondays, that Angus sought entertainments and diversions in town the same as all the other bachelors. Still, she hoped he wouldn't devote himself entirely to Deborah.

The fiddlers and the piano player were ready. They struck up a lively tune, and partners were chosen for the first dance.

Maggie had a moment of panic as she stood alone at the edge of the floor, until George Becker said her name. "You want to dance, Maggie?"

It was as easy as that. She was whirled around the floor, tapping and stomping to the energetic rhythm; she had time to note that even though all the girls were dancing, there was a row of men, unpartnered, along the wall. Then the music ended and Roger Stone, who'd been a year ahead of her in school, claimed her; the evening melted into a blur of music and voices and rushing blood that made her dizzy with the sheer joy of it.

Through it all, however, she watched for Angus. He didn't arrive until nearly nine, and it was at once obvious that she hadn't been the only one watching. He came in the front door just as a tune ended, and Deborah McVea, delectable in cream-colored faille with crimson cord trim, swung away from her dancing partner and moved to his side, even stretching out a hand to touch his arm.

A sensation moved through Maggie with the cutting edge of a razor; she turned her face away and smiled brightly at the young man approaching her, even before she realized who he was.

"Miss Maggie-Margaret," Wilkie Andreason said. "May I have the next dance?"

It was crucial to her that when Angus glimpsed her she have a partner, that she appear to be having a good time. She laughed up at Wilkie and moved into his arms, very carefully pretending to be unaware of anyone else at all.

Wilkie danced well, and he was probably the handsomest, most elegantly dressed man in the room. Maggie caught a few feminine glances turned in his direction, and experienced a small surge of elation that he had sought her out. It helped to make up for the fact that Angus had *not*, although of course he might have done so had not Deborah greeted him in that brazen way.

It was at least half an hour later, after he'd spun around the floor with Deborah and three or four other girls, that Angus finally turned up at her elbow.

He grinned as if they were old and good friends who had no need of ceremony, which of course they were. "Maggie, you're beautiful! I can't believe you're the same little skinny, big-eyed brat who used to follow me along when I was a skid dauber, talking my ear off!"

"I wasn't a brat," Maggie objected. Wilkie, who had just danced with her for the third time, still stood beside her, and she moved an inch closer to him. "You two have met, haven't you? Angus McKay, Wilkie Andreason."

The men regarded each other without enthusiasm. "Sure. The bookkeeper," Angus said flatly, making it sound somehow inferior.

Wilkie maintained a façade of restrained cordiality. "Mr. McKay."

"I think this is our dance," Angus said, dismissing Wilkie. "Excuse us."

The fiddles struck up a new tune, and Maggie allowed herself to be drawn with him back onto the floor. She'd never danced with Angus before, yet it was as if they'd always danced. The prickle of excitement was something she wanted to go on and on, singing through her veins.

It was a marvelous evening. Every male there asked her to dance at least once. Angus and Wilkie both danced with other girls, but it was obvious even to Nancy, herself thrilled by the attentions of young Adam Welker, that the two men vied for Maggie's company.

"Mr. Andreason's so good-looking," Nancy confided during one of their brief moments together while they waited in the line for punch. "You didn't tell me that."

Everybody else apparently thought so, too. The girls watched him, the men studiously ignored him. "They're jealous, I think," Maggie said, and hoped that that accounted for Angus's coolness, as well.

They rode home through the warm night, Maggie deliciously tired and content. Jake had taken one look at her and hadn't had to ask how the evening had gone; he knew by the expression on her face.

The following Tuesday, as Maggie stirred up a great bowl of batter for biscuits for the noon meal, there was a strange sound behind her; she swiveled and dropped the spoon.

Mr. Murphy had complained when she'd arrived of not

feeling particularly well. It wasn't his rheumatism, but a general discomfort that he hadn't been able to describe with any degree of accuracy; he'd even gone back to the lean-to attached to the rear of the cookhouse to rest for an hour before returning to his kitchen, letting Maggie take over.

Now the old man took a few steps toward her, his eyes wide in fear and pain, emitting a distressed sound like the one that had first drawn her attention. A moment later he pitched forward on his face.

Maggie cried out, too, unaware that she did so, dropping to her knees beside him. "Mr. Murphy! What's the matter? Mr. Murphy?"

There was a strange and terrible noise, deep in his throat; Maggie tried to roll him over, but he was too heavy for her.

Terrified, she rose and ran out the side door of the cookhouse. "Daddy! Angus, somebody! Can anybody hear me?"

There was no reply. She ran toward the nearest sound, that of an ax biting into a tree, stumbling over a root and sprawling headlong before she reached the nearest man of the crew, who happened to be Jim Humphries.

He rested the ax as she plunged through the underbrush, tearing her dress on the blackberry vines. "Maggie? Something wrong?"

"It's Mr. Murphy! He made a terrible sound and keeled over, and oh, Jim, I'm afraid he's dying!"

Jim ran with her back to camp, knelt beside the fallen man, and didn't have to confirm her fears in so many words. There was no urgency in his movements when he stood up. "I'll go get Jake," he said.

Maggie stayed alone with the old cook for the twenty minutes it took to bring her father.

She sat beside Mr. Murphy, tears running down her face unchecked. There was no sign of breathing, nothing at all but the forest silence except for the wind soughing high above in the treetops.

Jake came, squatting beside the old man, then rising and lifting Maggie to her feet. "He's gone. Heart, most likely. Come on, somebody bring the wagon around."

Mr. Murphy had no known family. At least Jake was spared the sad task of revealing another death to somebody's loved ones, she thought.

Maggie was left little time to grieve, although she dripped tears into the bread as she kneaded it and over the vegetables she chopped for stew. Everybody was sorry about Mr. Murphy, but they had to keep on working, and working meant eating.

In a way Maggie was glad there was so much to keep her busy, although since she worked in Mr. Murphy's kitchen everything reminded her of him. It was oddly different to be in charge of the entire meal rather than only taking responsibility for a few things.

The first night she scorched the beans. Nobody said anything. She knew that wouldn't be the case if it happened very often; she'd seen the men dump a kettle of burned stew when a helper had forgotten to stir it, and threaten the helper with dire consequences if it happened again.

For herself, she couldn't eat. Her throat closed at the mere thought of food. She was standing at the table over a pan of hot sudsy water when Angus suddenly appeared at her side.

"Jake's ready to go home, Maggie. He's waiting for you. We'll do the cleanup tonight."

The tears she'd managed to hold back for a while suddenly overflowed. "It was awful, Angus. It happened so fast, and I knew he was dead!"

"He was an old man," Angus said gently, resting his hands on her shoulders. "He hurt a lot of the time. The way his rheumatism was going, he'd likely have been too

crippled up to work before long. He'd rather have gone
this way."

She recognized the truth of what he said, but it didn't
really make her feel any better. She leaned into him,
soaking his shirtfront as she wept. The tears were not even
all for Mr. Murphy. His death made her so much more
aware of the mortality of everybody she loved, of her
parents especially, of little Sarah who did not blossom as
normal children did, and of her grandmother, who was
almost sixty years old, nearly as old as Mr. Murphy had
been.

Angus hugged her and let her cry for a few minutes,
then held her away from him. "Go on, Maggie. Jake's
waiting."

She took off her apron and hung it up, suffering a
momentary paroxysm of renewed grief at the sight of Mr.
Murphy's matching apron on the next nail, and strode off
to where her father waited.


"I'll get another cook as soon as I can find somebody,"
Jake told her. "Do you think you can manage for a few
days?"

"I'll do my best," Maggie promised. In truth, had she
known what her father was going to do, she'd have tried
harder than she did to persuade him that she could take
over the entire job of cooking for the logging crew.

She didn't know, of course. She continued to get up
before dawn, and walk with Jake through the dark woods,
to be there to fix breakfast before the men went to work.
Joe would go with her, frisking around her feet and
keeping her company; he'd been discouraged from accompanying her when Mr. Murphy was alive because the old
man didn't allow animals in his kitchen, but Maggie had
no such compunction.

The men fired up the big black iron stove before she got
there, and after the first morning—which was a virtual

disaster—Maggie made some preparations the night before. She could mix up sourdough pancake batter and have it ready to pour on the griddles as soon as she arrived. The tables could be set ahead of time. At the last minute she would fry ham or bacon or sausages and dozens of eggs. Some of the men ate five or six apiece, along with a similar quantity of pancakes.

She had known that Mr. Murphy began preparing the noon meal as soon as he'd cleared away from breakfast. His day had started earlier than that, when he'd mixed bread and set it to rise before the men in the bunkhouse were stirring.

There was no way she could manage that without sleeping in Mr. Murphy's lean-to, and Jake wouldn't have allowed that even if she'd wanted to do it. So making bread had to be done immediately after the morning meal, and dinner begun, too, and it all took so much more time than she recalled Mr. Murphy needing. There was no time for pies and cakes and cookies; it was all she could manage to get bread and meat and potatoes and beans.

Mr. Murphy had always contrived to sit down for a little while during the afternoon, to put up his aching legs on a wooden box or the flour barrel, and read the latest newspaper brought over after Jake had finished with it.

Maggie had no idea how he'd been able to manage this. She scarcely even sat down to eat her own midday meal; by the time she'd finished serving it and clearing away, she was already late with the supper preparations.

By the time she'd served supper, she was almost tearfully grateful when some of the men offered to clean up so that she could go home. She knew they were tired, too, after handling an ax or end of a saw for twelve hours, but she was near collapse by the time she reached home. She would fall into bed and be unconscious before she could even remember to blow out her lamp.

When Sunday came, she slept until noon. Nobody woke

her up to go to church, and when she came downstairs she found that her mother and grandmother and Celeste had not yet returned from town. Jake was there, though, and he sat down with her when she reheated fried potatoes and a couple of eggs for her own breakfast.

"You won't be alone in the cookhouse from now on," Jake said, lighting a cigar and dropping the match onto a saucer. "The new cook will be there tomorrow. I told the boys to clean out old Murphy's quarters, and put in another couple of bunks."

Maggie paused with a slab of toast, dripping jam over her eggs. "Another couple of bunks? In that little place?" And then, the frown forming even before she'd fully figured it out, "How many cooks are we going to have?"

"You, and Jaisy. That's all. But she'll have to bring the two kids, of course."

Nausea rose in her throat. Maggie put down the toast and watched the jam stain the tablecloth. "Daddy, you can't." Her whisper was barely audible.

"Can't what?" Jake asked, blowing smoke in an obscuring cloud.

"Oh, Daddy, don't! Don't pretend you don't know what I mean! You can't bring Mrs. Pallison into camp!"

"The arrangements are all made. Red took the supply wagon into town Saturday night. He'll bring her and the kids back with their stuff first thing in the morning."

Her appetite was gone. She looked at the food and then away as the sickness spread throughout her system. How could he do this? What would everybody say?

"She's a good cook, Maggie. She's had a lot more experience at it than you have, and while you've done a good job, it's too much for you to handle alone. She's a good person. You'll like her when you get to know her."

For a moment she thought she would throw up, right there at the table. She choked. She wanted to scream at him, *No, I won't! I hate her, and I won't work with her, ever!*

The words didn't come, but he saw how she felt. He reached for one of her hands on the table, covering it with his own. "Honey, give her a chance. She's never done anything to you."

*Only gone to bed with my father, stolen him away from us, taking money from him when we need it here at home,* Maggie thought.

"There's never been a woman cook before," she managed with great effort.

"Well, there's going to be one now. She's a widow, she needs to earn her way, keep her children. And she can cook. On top of that, we can get her a lot cheaper than we'd get another man, even if I knew where to find one in a hurry. She'll work for practically nothing but her keep, hers and the kids'. Be fair, Maggie."

*Fair? What was fair?* Maggie wondered wildly.

The question came out, hard and hostile.

"Have you told Mama?"

"I told the family at breakfast this morning that I'd hired a new cook."

"You didn't tell them who you hired?"

"They've never been interested in my employees before. As long as the job gets done and the bills paid so they can live in this place, they don't care who I hire." There was a hint of bitterness in Jake's voice.

It was echoed in Maggie's words. "I think Mama will care, this time."

"Care about what?" Celeste asked. She came through the doorway, taking the pins out of her hat and swinging the flowered bonnet in one hand.

Maggie hadn't heard them come in. Ann was behind her, carrying the baby swathed in a blanket and wearing an embroidered white dress that came down half a yard below her feet.

"Here, Margaret, hold her, will you, while I get rid of my hat and out of these shoes. They're pinching my toes."

Maggie took her little sister, feeling the emotion that always nearly swamped her when she looked at or touched Sarah. The baby stared up at her with blue eyes from a perfect china-doll face; the little body was warm and fragile against Maggie's breast.

"It's so warm in here," Ann said. "Why don't you open some windows and let the breeze through?" She put the thought into action, drawing back the draperies and the sheer curtains to raise first one window and then a second one. "What were you talking about, Margaret? That I would care to know about?"

Maggie flashed a dismayed glance at her father. Jake ground out his cigar in the saucer and answered for her.

"She thinks you ought to know that I've hired Jaisy Pallison to cook for the crew. She's a good cook, and she needs a way to earn a living."

Ann stood stock-still, one hand immobilized in the act of brushing back a strand of fair hair from her forehead. "I should have thought she'd have better luck plying her trade if she stayed near town," she said finally in a controlled, icy voice.

For a moment there was only silence in the room. Celeste looked from one to the other of them, puzzled, yet knowing that it would be better not to ask, not when the tension fairly crackled in the air between her parents.

Jake was the one who broke the tableau by standing up. "I'm taking on that Wilkie Andreason, too. Half a day a week, to start with. I've decided to try to make it with the crew I have left, instead of replacing Sudds and Harley. If you want to go out and cook at camp, Ann, help yourself. It's too much for Maggie, but there isn't a male cook available at the moment. I'm doing the best I can in a damned difficult time."

He walked out of the room without looking at Maggie

again; she didn't know if he blamed her for the scene or not. It wasn't fair, she thought, eyes stinging.

Mama would have found out sooner or later who was cooking at camp; that would have been worse than learning ahead of time. Not to mention how wrong Jake was to do this.

It had been bad enough when Jaisy lived miles away on the outskirts of Snohomish. What in God's name would it be like now that she was going to live in camp?

## 21

MAGGIE alternated between fury and distress. How her father could do this awful thing, bringing his mistress right into camp where everybody would find out about their relationship—assuming that it was not already common knowledge—and causing total humiliation to his family, surpassed belief.

Jake had never been a pious man, not by Grandma Miles's standards. He smoked cigars, drank whiskey or ale, and knew and used as many profane words as any other logger. He was, however, honest in his dealings with his fellowmen. He was kind, and generous, and fair.

He had always been a *good* man, Maggie thought. She'd never known him to hurt anyone deliberately unnecessarily or to cheat anyone. Why, then, was he now not only unfaithful to his wife, but flaunting the wretched woman almost on Ann's home ground?

Celeste came out onto the front porch where Maggie sat

on the top step, scratching behind Joe's ears. The hound leaned into her, increasing the pressure, and she scratched harder without thinking about it.

Celeste leaned against one of the supporting posts of the verandah. "What did Mama mean about Mrs. Pallison, Margaret? About plying her trade in town? I didn't think she had any trade."

Maggie knew perfectly what the insinuation had meant, but she didn't intend to relay it to Celeste. In many ways, even though she was nearly thirteen years old, Celeste was an innocent, a baby. Even if she weren't, even if she knew about things like adultery and harlots, there was no point in telling her. Why make her feel as upset and distressed as Maggie was feeling?

She moved over to make room for Celeste to sit beside her on the top step if she chose. "I don't know. I guess Mama just doesn't like Mrs. Pallison."

"I've only seen her a few times." Celeste lowered herself after carefully brushing fir needles off the step. "She's rather pretty, don't you think?"

Maggie shrugged. "I never paid much attention."

"Her hair is lovely. I think I'd like to have red hair. Everybody looks at it."

"Everybody looks at yours, too," Maggie pointed out.

"Oh, yes, but blond is more ordinary. There are lots of blondes. The Pallisons are just about the only redheads in Snohomish, aren't they?"

Maggie tugged gently on Joe's ears, earning a lick on the cheek. "Try having plain old dark-brown hair, if you think you aren't attracting enough attention. Celeste, I need to have a hairstyle that's easier to do. I *like* this one, but if I'm going to keep on working as camp cook—or helper—I won't have much time to fuss with my hair. Can you think of anything? I was looking through that new *Harper's Bazaar* Mama had in the parlor, and everything seems to be curls. How do they all make their hair curl without using a curling iron every night and morning?"

"I still think you don't need curls. Your hair is very heavy, Margaret. Maybe we could do something with braids. A pair of very fat braids wound into a knot in the back or something. You could learn to do braids, and they stay in place longer than curls or anything that has to be held with pins. Let's go upstairs where there's a mirror and see what we can do."

Maggie was glad Celeste didn't talk anymore about Jaisy Pallison. But it was impossible for Maggie to stop thinking about the woman.

She dreaded going to camp Monday morning. Joe leaped around her, ready to start the moment she came downstairs. Jake appeared, looking rested and, Maggie decided, eager. Too eager.

Nothing, of course, ever dampened his appetite. "You not eating, Maggie?" He helped himself to oatmeal and toast and boiled eggs. "Or did you already eat?"

"I'm not very hungry," Maggie said. Somehow she could not sit down across from him, could not bear to view his anticipation. For what else could he be anticipating except an easier time carrying on with Jaisy Pallison? "I think I'll go on ahead. I'll see you in camp."

"All right." Jake didn't seem to notice that anything was wrong; his own good humor was enough to suffice for himself and anyone else who happened to be around. "Before you go, see if there's any more of that strawberry jam, will you?"

She left him eating alone. Mrs. Totting and Nancy were in the kitchen; their hours were longer than Maggie's, though Mrs. Totting did rest during the afternoons. Sometimes it seemed foolish to Maggie that they hired a cook and an assistant for her, instead of letting Maggie do the cooking, though she was held back from mentioning it because she couldn't bear the thought of causing the

Tottings to lose their positions. Mrs. Totting had no other way to support the two of them, and there were not many families in Snohomish who could afford hired help. In fact, Maggie thought uneasily, she wasn't sure that the Keatings could afford it.

Maggie'd learned enough to cook quite adequately. Cooking for a logging crew was harder work, but it was better, somehow, than cooking at home. Freer, less confining and restrictive. At least it had been, until she'd learned that Jaisy Pallison was being brought in to take full charge of the cookhouse.

She walked through the predawn chill, hugging a shawl around her, oblivious of the hound trotting beside her. How was she going to greet Jaisy? How could she work beside the woman every day, all day, knowing what she knew about her?

There were still a few stars visible in the sky when she reached camp, but the men were already stirring. She saw the glow of lamplight behind the dirty windows of the bunkhouse, heard someone cough and spit, and registered the slam of the outhouse door.

The supply wagon stood before the cookhouse. Somehow she hadn't anticipated that Red Risku would be there ahead of her with the Pallisons. She'd thought she'd have a little more time to prepare herself.

Joe had run on ahead; now he paused, looking back at her with his tongue hanging out, barely visible in the gray light of dawn.

Maggie moved on reluctant feet toward the open door of the cookhouse. The shutters hadn't been raised as yet, but someone had a fire going. She smelled the woodsmoke and felt the welcome warmth as she stepped inside the building.

A lighted lantern hung from the overhead hook. Red emerged from the door at the back of the dining area, greeting her with a grin. "Morning, Maggie. Just delivered the new cook. The younguns are both asleep so we carried them in. Nobody's done anything yet but put on the coffeepot.''

Had the newcomers been anyone but the Pallisons, Maggie would have tried to do something to put them at ease, to make them comfortable. As it was, she was so upset and resentful that she wasn't sure it was safe to try to speak to them.

Her ears felt hot as she remembered the encounter in the Mercantile. If Jaisy Pallison had ever wanted to be friends with her, it was unlikely she still would after what Maggie had said to her that day.

She tried to blank it all out in her mind, concentrating on the meal that had to be prepared. The tables were set, the pancake batter mixed, the griddles heating.

She heard the sound behind her and froze, unable to turn or utter a greeting.

"Chilly this early in the morning, ain't it?" Jaisy said, and she had to move then.

"It'll be hot enough by midmorning," Maggie replied, feeling choked. She stared at the woman, hating her, hating her father as well, for putting her in this impossible situation. What would Jake do if she told him she didn't want to help in the cookhouse anymore? That she wanted to stay home?

And do what, though? There were plenty of females there already to do what needed to be done. And at home, she wouldn't see Angus.

He came through the doorway then, as if she'd conjured him up by magic. "Morning, everybody. I sliced the bacon, Maggie, to save time. I figured it would be awkward this morning, having a new cook and all."

Maggie thanked him, reached for the bacon, and began to separate the thick strips and arrange them on one of the griddles. She dipped her fingertips into the nearest of the water buckets and flicked the moisture onto the other griddle, where the drops spat and sizzled, evaporating. It was hot enough to begin the pancakes, and she ladled out batter in the large-size cakes the men loved.

"What do you want me to do first?" Jaisy asked.

It was too much, Maggie thought, to expect her to train this woman. Yet she made herself speak. "You can watch the bacon, while I do the pancakes. There are eggs, there, to fry after the bacon's done. They like their bacon crisp. I usually fry about three dozen eggs."

Jaisy looked around. "Is it all right if I use that apron?"

It was Mr. Murphy's, and it was only sensible that she use it, but Maggie again found her throat closing on the resentment she must not set loose.

"Would you rather I didn't? If it was *his*?" Jaisy asked gently. "I've got others in my stuff, only I didn't unpack anything yet."

Wordless, Maggie lifted the apron off the nail and handed it to her, turning away as the woman tied the strings behind her neck.

"I guess Mr. Murphy was a nice old man," Jaisy observed, taking up a long-handled fork to turn the bacon. "Hank liked him. Said he was a good cook. Said you were better with pies, though."

Did the stupid woman really think she could win Maggie over with flattery? Maggie glanced at Angus, who had poured himself a cup of not-quite-boiled coffee and taken a seat at the nearest table.

"Maggie's blackberry and apple pies are the best," Angus said, covering the fact that Maggie hadn't replied. "She's pretty good with biscuits, too. You ought to have seen the ones she made at first, though. Hard enough to break your teeth."

The other men began to filter into the cookhouse, taking their places with the customary racket and banter. Maggie was grateful for it, since it made it less obvious that she was not exactly welcoming the new cook.

The men were not so reticent. They greeted Jaisy matter-of-factly and included her in their conversations, and Jaisy responded in kind.

It was worse after the crew had been fed and were gone, and the two women were left alone in the cookhouse.

It was a relief to Maggie when, about the time breakfast was cleared away and she was starting dinner, Wilkie Andreason appeared.

By that time it was warm enough so that the cookhouse had been fully opened up, and she saw him coming. He stepped through the doorway and reached for one of the cups Maggie had just washed, grinning at her. "Since I'm an employee now, is it all right if I help myself?"

"Of course. Are you starting work today?"

"Well, I'm going to look at the books, anyway. We're going to have to decide where I'm going to work. Do you think your father would be willing to put up an office where we could handle that kind of business?"

Maggie's voice was sharper than it would have been if Jaisy hadn't been listening. "I doubt he'll be willing to do anything that requires an outlay of funds he doesn't have. Things are very difficult in the logging business these days, which you must know, Mr. Andreason, if you're keeping books for them." She hoped that Jaisy would understand that she, too, was a financial burden that Jake Keating could ill afford.

Wilkie sipped at the coffee he'd just poured. "When business is bad is the time when it's necessary to take steps to improve it."

"Not by spending money you don't have, I hope," Maggie protested.

"Sometimes, odd as that may sound, that is exactly what is called for. Becoming more efficient is a way to retain more of the profits. If it wouldn't be a bother, I could work here at one of the tables, to begin with. But eventually Keating Logging should have a proper office.

Not here, but at the landing, probably.'' His gaze now rested appraisingly—approvingly?—on Jaisy. "You'd be Mrs. Pallison, the new cook? I'm Wilkie Andreason.''

They struck up a conversation and Maggie listened to them, seething. Everybody was going to be friendly to Jaisy, that was clear. Well, maybe she'd let them have Jaisy, and find something else to do herself, she thought. Something away from here, where she wouldn't have to be constantly reminded of her father's infidelity, where she wouldn't have to be civil to his mistress.

Maggie didn't know how she'd expected her father to treat Jaisy in public, but she'd taken it for granted that the entire camp would know immediately of their illicit relationship.

However, Jake was no more than cordial, as he'd have been to any cook: he made no undue fuss over her cooking (Jake had long taken good cooking for granted) and spent no more time around the cook shack than he ever had. He came in for meals, and once in a while between times for a cup of coffee and a quick bite of whatever was handy. Outside of the fact that he addressed her as Jaisy rather than Mrs. Pallison, there was no indication that there was anything at all between them.

After the first week, Maggie began to relax her guard a little, to feel less certain that all and sundry knew about her father and the new cook. Not that she wasn't convinced that the adulterous relationship continued (Jake's excuses for being away from home grew more and more careless, and gradually he simply stopped making excuses), but it was a trifle more bearable if she could believe that it was not common knowledge.

In spite of herself, Maggie was drawn to Lucy and Will.

Lucy was nine, now, and Will was nearly seven. Their pale red-gold hair and freckles had amused her at first; after a time, she found them most appealing. Will, especially, had an insatiable appetite, and he was appreciative of anything he was given to eat. It was impossible to see those blue eyes fixed upon her and not hand over the first of the cookies out of the oven, or a thick slice of bread and jam.

Lucy was a solemn child, rather thin like her little brother, though not fragile. It occurred to Maggie that when she'd first become aware of them—right after their father was killed and before *her* father began to overstep the bounds of propriety and good sense—they had looked pallid and undernourished. This was no longer the case, and Maggie was unable to suppress the unwelcome notion that they might well have gone hungry, or even have starved, if Jake hadn't intervened.

Lucy tended to sit where she could watch Maggie, and the admiration was plainly written on her small face. Neither of the Pallison children would ever be beautiful, but they had an engaging way about them, and their growing adoration of Maggie was enough to coax a response from her, no matter how she felt about their mother.

Jaisy was, indeed, competent in a kitchen. Within a few days Maggie was aware that there were many things *she* knew nothing about. Mr. Murphy had been a good plain cook, and so was Jaisy, but she also knew about such things as adding herbs to stews and soups and roasts so that they had exciting new tastes. Her pie crust was the equal of Maggie's and her cakes were superior to Mrs. Totting's.

The men liked her. They were used to Maggie, she'd been around since she was a small child, but Jaisy was a mature woman whose considerable charm began at once to make changes in the men's behavior.

Maggie noted it first, and then even Jake took notice and joked about it.

"What's going on? Everybody's trooping to the river to

take baths every day instead of just on Saturday night. Somebody's washing out socks during the week, and Sol Engstrom has shaved off his beard.''

"So's Tom Dunnigan," Maggie muttered.

"I'm going to have the neatest, best-looking crew in the territory," Jake decided. "Including two of the prettiest cooks anywhere.''

Maggie reserved judgment on how long she would be included in that evaluation. Jaisy was good enough so that, with Lucy's help, she could probably get along fine without Maggie before long, which would be fine with *her*. She would find something else to occupy her time, where she didn't have to watch Jake and Jaisy.

Though there was nothing between them that a casual observer could have objected to, Maggie *knew* they hadn't broken off their affair.

She didn't know where they were getting together; she thought it unlikely that they would make love in that one little lean-to room in the presence of the two young children, even if the children were asleep. And considering the way Lucy chattered away now that she was getting acquainted with Maggie and the rest of the crew, it was even more unlikely that Lucy wouldn't have mentioned it if she'd been aware of any nocturnal activity between Jake and her mother.

Still, the weather was pleasant, there were hundreds of acres of woods, and there was no reason for Jaisy to be afraid to leave Lucy and Will after they'd gone to sleep, to meet Jake somewhere beyond the confines of the camp. Jake looked too contented, when he wasn't contemplating his financial difficulties, to convince Maggie that he was depriving himself of Jaisy's affections.

She didn't think Jake would object if she told him she wanted to stay home from now on. He'd always let her do pretty much as she liked, and he would now, if she said she wanted to do something else.

The problem was that the thought of simply staying at home, doing the kinds of things her sister did, filled her with loathing. Celeste enjoyed playing the piano, sewing, knitting, and painting delicate little pictures to give to family members for gifts. Maggie had no interest or talent in any of those areas.

She had hoped that her new, nearly adult status would make a difference to Angus, and he did dance with her when she attended the lively evenings at the Athenaeum. He didn't single her out for special attention, though; indeed, for a while she worried that he might be getting serious about Deborah McVea, until she overheard the confrontation between them one evening.

It was a warm night, and the dancers spilled out into the darkness between tunes, sipping cider and cooling off. Maggie wanted to speak to Nancy, who was nowhere in sight, though Adam Welker was talking to one of the musicians, so they were not together. It would be safe to seek Nancy out without risking an unwelcome interruption.

Maggie went through the door left open to catch the fleeting breeze and peered around. Several couples strolled in the starlight. She stepped out of the glow from the open doorway and stood to allow her eyes to adjust to the lack of light, and then she heard them, a few yards away.

She couldn't make out their figures, hidden as they were in deep shadow beside the building, but she recognized their voices.

"Deborah, I'm sorry if I gave you any reason to think that. I didn't mean to. We've been friends for a long time, but it's only that . . . friendship."

The voice belonged to Angus, and Maggie froze, unconsciously pressing back against the wall, listening.

Deborah sounded cross, perhaps near tears.

"A friendship between a man and a woman develops into more than . . . than *this*. Naturally I assumed . . . we've been walking out together for nearly *two years*. You can't treat me, now, as if nothing at all has happened, as if nothing matters!''

There was the rustle of garments, as if they'd moved closer together, or would it be farther apart? Maggie strained to pierce the darkness, not even thinking about the fact that she was eavesdropping on something intended to be private.

She recognized the tone: Angus when he was being exaggeratedly reasonable and mildly amused by her own irrationality or childishness. ''Nothing *did* happen, did it? I've never walked out with you exclusively, Deb. I've enjoyed your company, the same as I've enjoyed the company of other girls, but I've made no more commitment to you than to any of the others. I've never talked about love, or marriage, or anything of that sort. We've been friends, that's all.''

Now the hint of tears was plain in Deborah's voice, and so was the anger. ''It's that little snip of a Keating girl, isn't it? She's only a baby, and her father wouldn't let any ordinary logger court her, so you let some other girl think you care about *her*.''

''Maggie has nothing to do with us, Deb.''

By this time Maggie's heart was beating wildly. She pushed the heel of one hand against her chest, willing it to quiet its thunder so that she would not miss anything.

''Is it because the Keatings are rich, and the McVeas aren't?'' Deborah demanded. Again there were sounds that made Maggie think he'd tried to touch the girl, perhaps, and she'd jerked away from him. Her eyes were adjusting, now, and she could make out the two figures, so close together they seemed only one. ''Because if you wait for him to die, or get too old or crippled like Ed Newsome, so he can't run the operation anymore, you can marry that girl and then *you'll* be rich, too?''

''Jake's not rich,'' Angus said with a small laugh. ''He's having the same money problems as every other logger in the territory. And he's a long way from being too old or crippled to run his operation.''

"But he owns a big house, and his own outfit, and he has no sons to take over the business, like my father. A son-in-law would be pretty well off, wouldn't he, married to *her*.''

"Deb, don't be stupid. Maggie's only a kid. I work for her father, and I like my job. I don't intend to lose it, messing around with a girl whose old man would throw me into the deepest part of the Sound if he thought I'd touched her.''

"So what are you going to do?'' Deborah challenged him, anger warring with pain. "Wait until he dies, and then sweep her up? Take over Keating's Landing yourself?''

Angus lost some of his geniality. "What I do about Maggie Keating is really none of your business, Deb.''

"Isn't it?'' Deborah turned shrill, though she kept her voice low. "After you led me on, after I let you—''

"Deb, for God's sake! There are people right over there, and you're making a fool of yourself. I didn't lead you on, and I never made any kind of promises.''

"You touched me,'' Deborah said, her voice breaking. "A man doesn't kiss a decent girl unless he has intentions. . . .''

"That statement only shows how little you know about men. Deb, I'm sorry, but this is pointless. I don't intend to marry you. Not now, not ever. I don't intend to marry anybody for a long, long time. Come on, let's go back inside, or do you want me to send your brother out to take you home?''

"Damn you, Angus McKay,'' Deborah choked. "I pity you when Jake Keating finds out you're sniffing around that girl of his! I hope he beats you to a bloody pulp!''

The smaller of the two figures broke away, crossed the band of light streaming from the doorway, and disappeared on the far side of it, into the night. Maggie thought the girl was crying.

Only then did Maggie realize how compromising her own position was. She pressed harder against the building, into a prickly bush, holding her breath, waiting until Angus had walked past and vanished inside before she dared to move.

She'd forgotten about Nancy. She was disturbed and bewildered by what she'd overheard. She'd listened to enough logger talk to know that Deborah was, indeed, naive about men. They did kiss decent girls, if allowed to, and she had an uncomfortable conviction that they went to bed with them, too, if the women were willing. The way Jaisy allowed Jake Keating to do.

Maggie hesitated about returning to the dance, not sure that she could successfully carry it off without anyone noticing how perturbed she was. Still, her grandmother would miss her and wonder where she'd been, so she had to reappear. Maybe she'd plead a headache, and sit out the rest of the dances until her father came to take them home.

A week later, Deborah unexpectedly announced her betrothal to Sol Engstrom's younger brother John, of all people. That might have been a good sign except that Angus still didn't give Maggie any encouragement. She spent endless hours wondering uneasily if there was any truth to what Deborah had said about *her*, and Angus's interest in her.

In her more rational moments, Maggie knew that the other girl had spoken out of her own misery and disappointment, rather than from any insight or true knowledge. Yet she couldn't quite forget the bitter accusation, or Angus's response.

*I don't intend to marry anybody for a long, long time*.

An ache formed somewhere deep inside of Maggie, and it wouldn't go away.

Angus treated her the same way that he always had. Once when he made one of his thoughtless references to her as a little girl, Maggie flattened her lips and her tone of voice. "I'm nearly fifteen and a half. Plenty of girls are married by that age."

Angus only laughed. "Not you, Maggie. Not Jake's daughter. He'll want you all the way grown-up before he allows anybody to court you."

"You don't think I have anything to say about that, myself?" she demanded, only to evoke more laughter.

"Not very much, I'm afraid. Everybody on the wet side of the mountains knows how Jake Keating protects his daughters. You couldn't ask for a better guarantee for protection against men than having Jake for a father."

She could have struck him.

He was as friendly as he'd always been. When she talked about minor problems, he listened and offered advice if she asked for it. Most of her problems, unfortunately, were major, and she couldn't discuss them even with Angus. He continued to tease her in an affectionate way, he was protective if anybody else teased her too much, or in any way annoyed or offended her; but except for taking her hand a few times when they walked through the woods together—which had an effect on her somewhat similar to what she'd expect from drinking several glasses of wine— Angus was not a romantic.

What could she do to jar him out of this complacent attitude? There was no way of being certain that he still felt about her the way she'd thought he had when he'd indicated he was waiting for her to grow up. She'd *done* that, she was ready to be courted whether her father thought so or not, and now most of the time Angus acted as if he were an older brother.

She didn't want an older brother. She wanted a lover.

Which, in spite of her feelings for Angus, made her susceptible when Wilkie Andreason made his first tentative advances toward her.

## 22

CONSIDERING the fact that he was supposed to work only half a day a week, Wilkie managed to be around quite a bit. He spent a morning sitting at one of the tables in the cookhouse, perusing the ledgers that went back over several years, so that he could get a picture of Jake's overall operation.

Then he took the ledgers home with him (he was boarding with a family in Snohomish) to study further, necessitating bringing them back the following afternoon after he'd been at Jorgeson's camp. This was all preliminary to doing anything with the figures himself.

Naturally, since there was no other place for him to work, he came at once to the cookhouse each time he arrived. He had acquired a horse, which enabled him to travel more quickly from one job to another, and he seemed to find it necessary to consult with Jake frequently about particular entries and practices.

He continued to dress in the fashion in which he had first appeared, though as the days warmed into summer he would often take off his suit jacket and sit in his shirtsleeves as he worked. It did not, to Maggie's eyes, make him any less elegant.

He took care not to be a nuisance to the cooks, but he *was* a distraction, at least to Maggie. She couldn't help being aware of him there, where he could hear what she

said to Jaisy and where she would frequently find his gaze
upon her in what she thought was an interested way. His
presence there tempered what she might otherwise have
said to Jaisy. She strove for polite, impersonal words and
hoped that Wilkie wouldn't think her cold and inhospitable
to the older woman; yet she was unable to pretend to a
civility she didn't feel.

She had gotten the hang of doing her hair in the heavy
braid Celeste had devised, and after a bit of experimenting
on her own had softened the severity of the coiffure by
producing a curling tendril at each temple. It was not so
difficult to tie only two strands of hair into rag curlers each
night when she prepared for bed; as long as it didn't rain
the curl would hold through the day. She liked the effect
when she looked into her mirror, and she thought Wilkie
liked it, too.

When he wasn't engaged in reading the ledgers or
making notes of his own for his next conference with Jake,
Wilkie talked to both Maggie and Jaisy. It was Maggie
who got the significant smiles, however, and the compliments on her appearance, so that she made a constant
effort to stay neat and attractive.

She wished with all her heart that Angus paid as much
attention to her as Wilkie did. And that the two of them
hadn't taken such a dislike to each other.

That antagonism broke into open warfare one evening
when Angus overturned a coffee cup so that its contents
spilled across the notes Wilkie had before him, the result
of hours of work in his neat, legible hand.

Wilkie sprang up with an oath as the hot liquid ran over
the edge of the table onto his lap.

"Sorry," Angus said, in a tone that left no one convinced that it was an apology. "Maggie, could I have a
refill, please?"

Wilkie stared at him as a white line formed around his

mouth, nostrils flaring. "You've ruined my papers. I'll have
to do them all over again."

"I'm sorry," Angus repeated. "This *is* supposed to be a
dining hall, you know. We eat and drink in here."

"And I work in here, when it isn't mealtime," Wilkie
informed him, speaking through his teeth. "I think an
apology would be in order, McKay."

"I said I was sorry," Angus told him, eyes meeting
Wilkie's in a cool manner. "I'll move over there, I won't
bother you again."

Maggie watched them, feeling tense and unhappy. Jaisy
provided a dish towel for Wilkie to wipe off his papers, but
the ink had smeared them impossibly. He'd have to start
over from the beginning.

Wilkie, jaw grimly set, took out fresh paper and applied
himself to the task at hand. The rigidity of his body
revealed how he felt.

Maggie was never sure whether the incident a few
minutes later was truly an accident, or whether it had been
triggered by either Angus or Wilkie. All that was clear was
that as Angus rose to replace his cup where she could wash
it, and headed for the door, he tripped over the foot Wilkie
extended into the aisle. Wilkie often sat that way, because
his legs were long and needed more space than was under
the table, so it *might* have been an accident.

At any rate, Angus, who was so agile on the dance floor
or at the top of a two-hundred-foot tree, went sprawling.

He clipped his chin on the corner of the bench on the
way down, causing him to bite his lip or his tongue; that
wasn't clear, either, only that there was blood on the hand
he wiped across his mouth as he got to his feet.

She had seldom seen Angus lose his temper. Now, with
a muttered curse for which he did not apologize, he
steadied himself for a moment on the edge of the table,
then reached for Wilkie's shirtfront to haul the other man
off the bench.

The next thing she knew, the bench had gone over backward, Wilkie's ink bottle had overturned and spilled out its contents on the table and part of the papers, and several thudding blows were exchanged.

Jaisy yelped and moved backward out of their way. Maggie nearly backed into the stove in a similar effort, feeling its heat only just in time to halt her movement.

It was over as quickly as it had begun. Angus shoved past a pair of avid spectators, striding away toward the bunkhouse. Wilkie, nursing a hand with swelling knuckles, his face first pale and then flushed as his eyes met Maggie's, began a half-hearted effort to clean up the mess.

Maggie found herself wanting to apologize for Angus; the words stuck in her throat. Nobody said anything as Wilkie gathered up the damaged papers and, lifting a lid off the wood stove, consigned them to the flames.

As far as Maggie knew, nobody told Jake about the altercation. But the next day Wilkie pressed, again, for an office, a place where he could work without being disturbed.

"Out of the question," Jake said, tight-lipped.

Wilkie did not give up easily. "It only need be a shack to begin with, if that's all it's possible to do. You have the timber, Mr. Keating. How long would it take your men to put up four walls and a roof?"

"Timber ain't lumber," Jake pointed out, "and I'd have to pay to have the stuff put through the mill. I can't spare a cent for anything I don't have to have."

Maggie, up to her elbows in sudsy water as she washed dishes, was glad they didn't have the office now, or she wouldn't be able to listen in on their conversations. She tried to handle the dishes quietly, so the clatter wouldn't wipe out any of what they said a few yards away from her.

Wilkie contemplated his employer for a moment, and then smiled. "Have you thought of building your own mill, sir?"

Maggie forgot to reach for the next plate, and glanced at the men to see Jake with a sagging jaw.

"Don't you listen to anything I say, Andreason? I just told you I can't afford to build an office, and now you want me to build a goddamn mill! Listen, I hired you to keep my books, not to try to run my business. Which," he added as an afterthought, "is a good thing, from the sound of your ideas."

Wilkie was not in the least disconcerted. "Mr. Keating, you hired me to do more than add up columns of figures in your ledgers. You hired me because I've studied up-to-date business methods, and I can save you money. I can *earn* you money."

"That's a hell of a good trick with today's lumber market," Jake said dryly. "Maggie!" He lifted his cup and she wiped her hands quickly and reached for the coffeepot.

She rather liked Wilkie, certainly she liked the way he treated her, as if she were a young lady rather than one of the boys, the way the crew acted. She hoped he wasn't going to get himself fired by pressing absurd ideas on an already beleaguered employer.

Wilkie didn't look like a man expecting to be fired. He was smiling ever so faintly. "What I like about you, Mr. Keating, is that after you've blown up and said *no* to something, you sit still long enough for me to explain what I'm talking about. And you usually see the sense of it once I've explained it. You're felling timber and floating it downstream to a mill, where it's cut and planed into finished lumber. The mill owner makes a living on that, doesn't he? On cutting up trees into boards? On what the ultimate consumer pays for the product at that stage?"

"At least as good a living as the logger," Jake admitted, sipping cautiously at the fresh cup of coffee. "Only that's not saying a lot, these days, you know. I heard Stover might have to close down because he's *not* making a profit, not enough of one. So it doesn't make any sense for me to build a mill, not when the mills already running are having trouble.''

Wilkie's smile deepened almost imperceptibly. ''If I'm not mistaken, sir, you bought this logging operation when it was in trouble.''

''That's a different matter altogether. It was in trouble because the owner got hurt and couldn't run it anymore, not because of the goddamned economy.''

''But you got it for less than it was worth, really, didn't you? Because the injured owner was in no position to haggle. He needed out, and you wanted in.''

Jake set his cup down with a bit more force than was necessary. ''Make your point, Wilkie. I got to get back to work.''

''My point is that *now* is the cheapest time you're ever going to see to start a mill. Stover is getting out; you could probably buy his machinery lock, stock, and barrel for a fraction of what it'll be worth when things turn around and the price of lumber goes back up to normal. You *do* believe it's going to do that, don't you?''

''Hell, yes. Get somebody different in the White House, in the Congress, somebody cares what happens to—'' Jake broke off and looked at Wilkie in suspicion. ''What are you leading me on to say?''

The smile became an open grin. ''That you believe in the future of your own business, I guess. There have always been ups and down in the national economy. This is a low spot, and nobody knows for sure how long it will last; but everybody is agreed that it *will* improve, things will get back to normal. Land values have dropped a little, and the smart men are buying it up, knowing it's going to be more valuable when this recession eases off. It's the same with a mill. You could cut out the middleman, get your timber made into lumber so you can sell direct to the consumer and pocket the profit from both stages of the

264    WILLO DAVIS ROBERTS

operation instead of only from one. You see the logic in that?''

Jake scrutinized the young man across the table for several seconds. ''All right,'' he said at last. ''Explain to me how, when I'm so damned broke I can barely keep my equipment up and my men paid, I can expand and buy myself a mill.''

At that Wilkie laughed aloud. Though Maggie had finished the dishes, she didn't want to carry the dishwater outside to dump it. Not until she learned where this conversation was going.

She had never heard Wilkie laugh before, though he smiled often. He was a very attractive young man, and she suddenly hoped with some fervency that whatever he was going to say would make sense, although she didn't really see how it could. Jake wasn't exaggerating about his financial status. How could he invest in anything more when he was having such a struggle with what he already had?

To her chagrin and disappointment, Wilkie suddenly stood up. ''I know you're anxious to get back to work. Why don't I walk back with you to the job and tell you what I have in mind?''

''Good idea,'' Jake grunted, and they left her standing there in complete frustration.

Maggie dried her arms and hands and picked up the dishpan to take it outside, turning to find Jaisy's eyes upon her. For some reason Maggie flushed, as if she'd been caught eavesdropping, though the conversation certainly hadn't been all that private or the men would have gone elsewhere to talk. And Jaisy had been there, too, hearing the entire thing.

''Things ain't easy, anyplace,'' Jaisy said.

Maggie swallowed, wanting to cry out that Jaisy wasn't making it any easier, but she bit back the words. It wouldn't do to be in open conflict with this woman, not while her father was so infatuated with her. The insidious idea had been growing within her, that if Jake had to make a choice, he might possibly choose Jaisy over herself.

No, she thought, carrying the pan out and dumping it in the woods behind the cookhouse, it would never come to that. Her father loved her, she was secure in that knowledge. But if he thought he loved Mrs. Pallison, and had to defend her, Maggie might well alienate him by antagonizing the woman.

Wilkie didn't come back to the cookhouse. She saw him from a distance, mounting the retired plow horse he used for transportation, thinking how he ought to be riding a magnificent stallion. He saw her, smiled and lifted a hand in farewell, and trotted off, avoiding the ox team straining to move their load of logs toward the river.

The day grew hot. Maggie opened the remaining shutters on the cookhouse, but it was still uncomfortably warm as they went about the afternoon chores. Lucy came in for a drink, sawdust clinging to her clothes, her damp red hair plastered to her forehead.

Maggie smiled instinctively, remembering how she'd played in the sawdust when she was that age. "Have you been running? It's pretty hot for that."

Lucy nodded, gulping water from the tin dipper. "I wish we could go swimming. Ma used to let us swim in the lake, before." She didn't have to specify before what. "I don't remember it ever getting so hot, do you?"

"A few times. You hungry?" For some reason, although both children now looked perfectly healthy, Maggie felt an urge to feed them.

Lucy wiped her mouth with the back of her hand and considered the question. "I guess," she said.

"You want to take some bread and honey back to Will, too?"

Lucy nodded. "He's always hungry. Maggie, if we was

to walk over to the landing on Sunday, would you take us swimming? In the river?''

Maggie glanced toward the door to the lean-to. Jaisy was back there, resting. Maggie never felt she could talk openly to the children when Jaisy was within hearing range. "I suppose so, if it's all right with your ma."

"Good. I'll tell Will. He sure likes to get wet and cool off."

"Can you both swim?"

"Well," Lucy said, "not exactly. I can sort of paddle and I'm teaching Will. Or I was, last summer, if he hasn't forgot."

She took the two slices of bread, cut very thick, and licked the honey off the edge of one of them. "Thanks, Maggie."

When the little girl had gone, Maggie moistened the end of a dish towel and wiped off her own face and neck and then, after making sure no one was observing, inside her bodice. She was, for a few moments, made aware of her breasts. Surely they had grown a little, which pleased her even though it made her self-conscious about the change being noticed.

Wilkie didn't return the last three days of the week, and when Maggie asked about him, and his idea of buying a mill, Jake was noncommittal. "That fella has some interesting ideas," was all he would say.

The heat held and climbed.

East of the Cascades, intense summer heat was the rule. Maggie had never been on the dry side of the mountains, but Jake had. Plenty of timber, that part was good, but when you descended to the plains it was dry and hot in summer, freezing in winter. Better to stay where they were, on the wet side where the climate was entirely different.

For the most part, wet-side summers were perfect, Maggie thought. Cool enough to sleep under a blanket at night, warm enough for shirt-sleeves and swimming in the daytime. There were frequent rains, which washed everything clean and gave the air a fragrant freshness. Everything stayed green almost year-round. It wasn't often that the temperatures went over ninety degrees, though she could remember a few occasions when it had exceeded one hundred. Those days left everybody gasping and exhausted, though the men never stopped working unless the woods were so dry that it was dangerous. A spark from a saw or an ax could touch off a conflagration that would decimate hundreds of acres of prime timber and take homes and lives.

It wasn't that dry yet, it hadn't been hot long enough, but it was a threat that hovered over them when the heat held for more than a week or two.

Friday noon, as she served a great platter of pork chops and a mounded bowl of mashed potatoes, Angus looked up at her and spoke casually. "Going to be at the Athenaeum tomorrow night?"

"Yes, I think so," Maggie replied, heart suddenly pounding. "Though it may be too hot to dance."

Angus grinned. "Then everybody will wander around outside in the dark. That can be interesting, too."

He forked two chops off the platter and passed it along to Sol Engstrom, the matter dismissed, and Maggie moved away, wondering if that had been simply an offhand observation or a preliminary to an invitation.

On Saturday the thermometer Red Risku had nailed up outside the bunkhouse rose to 102°.

The men worked stripped to the waist, bronzed and muscular torsos gleaming with sweat. God only knew how much hotter it was inside the cookhouse, Maggie thought, wiping perspiration from her face and feeling it form again immediately. Most of the men filled their plates and took them outside, choosing to sit on the ground in the

shade rather than expose themselves to the additional
warmth from the cookstove.

Jaisy wore a brown dress with wet stains forming under
the arms, across the back, and under her full breasts. Her
auburn hair escaped its pins, forming little tendrils around
her face; she didn't look pretty now, Maggie thought.

And then her father came to fill his plate, pausing beside
the hired cook to speak to her—words that didn't carry to
Maggie—and Jaisy laughed. Maggie turned away, not
wanting to see what was between them, not sure whether
the ache she felt was a physical one or an emotional one.
She hated them both, at the moment, for their secret words
and laughter, while at the same time she envied them with
a passionate intensity.

When Jake brought his plate back to be washed, he
paused in the doorway to address them both. "It's too
damned hot to keep that stove going the rest of the day.
Why don't you set out something cold for supper, let the
men help themselves, and take the rest of the day off? Go
on home, Maggie."

He'd never given the cooks time off because of the heat
before. Was he just getting rid of her, Maggie wondered,
so he could be alone with Jaisy?

A look at the older woman made her doubt that, though.
Jaisy looked tired and in need of a bath and a rest. She
smiled at the suggestion. "Sounds good. I'll do it, Maggie,
slice some meat and bread, and some vegetables. If I leave
them standing in water maybe they'll stay fresh that long.
And there's enough pie left to go around."

Maggie was happy to leave. It would cool off toward
evening, and if she left now there'd be plenty of time to
bathe and have Celeste fix her hair in a fancier way, before
the dance. She was glad to have the extra time.

She had saved some scraps for Joe, who came when she
called. He ate them appreciatively, then licked at her
fingers when she didn't draw them away fast enough.

"Now I need to wash again before we go home," she said, only to change her mind at the realization that that would mean returning to where she'd see Jaisy again. She didn't want to see Jaisy.

She walked home through the woods, meeting the team coming back from the landing. Joe barked his customary greeting, and the man handling the bullocks called out a friendly "Leaving already, Maggie?"

"Too hot to work," she called back.

"Ain't that the truth! See you Monday, then."

"Monday," Maggie echoed, and stepped back on the road when the team had passed.

The heat was oppressive. Maybe, she thought, she'd go swimming when she got home. With the hours she was putting in these days at camp, it had been a long time since she'd had a chance to relax that way. She wondered if her sister would go with her.

She discovered Celeste wilting in the porch swing on the front verandah, trying to read, fanning herself with the latest copy of *Harper's Bazaar*.

Maggie climbed the steps and paused. "I'm going swimming. Want to come?"

Celeste brushed back a damp curl that had fallen over her forehead. "Swimming? Oh, that does sound good! What'll we wear?"

"Anything old, I guess." Maggie laughed ruefully. "That describes almost everything I've got."

Celeste flipped the magazine pages and spread them open on the seat beside her. "Look at this, Margaret. A whole page of illustrations of bathing dresses. See, no sleeves, and sort of short trousers beneath, that show one's ankles. Even if Mama would let us wear such an outfit, I don't suppose we could buy anything like that here, do you?"

"Seattle, maybe. Not Snohomish." Maggie shrugged.

"We can't afford anything new, anyway. Maybe we could go in our drawers and camisoles."

Celeste closed the magazine. "What if anyone came along and saw us?"

"Who's going to come on a hot afternoon like this? Mama and Grandma won't stir out of the house; they'd never come downstream even if they did, and the men are all working. We can wear old dresses until we get there, of course."

She was somewhat surprised that Celeste agreed as readily as she did. No doubt it was the heat; it was enough to make one desperate to cool off.

In spite of a week of high temperatures, the river was cold. Fed as it was by melting snows in the Cascades, flowing through stands of firs tall enough to keep it mostly in shade, the water made them gasp when they plunged into it. A few minutes later, however, they were cavorting in delight, reveling in the coolness.

The Pilchuck was not deep enough to actually swim in except in a few places. The one they had chosen was just below the cold deck that awaited a rise in the river level to float the logs to the mill. A bag boom, a few logs encircled by boom sticks to hold them in place, created a sort of dam just below them, giving the water a little extra depth.

Celeste was a poor swimmer and didn't really care. As long as she could sit on the bottom and let the water flow over her, she was perfectly content. It was Maggie who wanted to swim, which she did with contented abandon, wondering why she hadn't found time to swim before this.

"Somebody's coming!"

Celeste's yelp brought Maggie around in a hurry, then sent her into laughter. "It's only Lucy and Will. They asked if I'd take them swimming on Sunday. Apparently they couldn't wait that long!"

Celeste crouched lower in the water, which was so clear

at this time of year that it provided no protection whatever. "How are we going to get our clothes?"

"What difference does it make? Will's only six," Maggie told her, feeling that sounded better than admitting he was nearly seven, "and we're more covered up than if we were wearing one of those fancy bathing dresses." She raised her voice, calling to the two children who had emerged from the woods and were standing irresolutely on the riverbank. "Take off your shoes and clothes and come in in your underwear!"

Will began to shed garments at once. In only a pair of long drawers, his bony arms and torso were revealed as pale and sprinkled with more of the freckles that gave his face its only touch of color.

Lucy approached the bank near where the girls knelt in the river. "We were hoping we'd find you, Maggie. We decided to come today instead of waiting for tomorrow."

"Does your ma know you're here?" Maggie demanded.

"No. She was sleeping, and we didn't want to wake her up to ask her." Lucy pushed back hair soaked with sweat. "It's so hot. I didn't know if Will was going to be able to walk this far. He got pretty tired."

Her little brother was wading out into the water, a grin spreading across his face. "I'm all right. I'll be able to walk back after I swim awhile, Lucy."

Lucy began to unbutton her dress, stepping out of it and dropping it over a rock. "I can't wait to feel how good it is," she said, and stuck a toe into the water to test it.

Then, with a cry of joy that seemed out of character to Maggie, Lucy plunged full-length into the river.

Maggie blamed herself for what happened after that. She took it for granted that Will, who did not actually swim, would play in the shallow water near Celeste. Maggie and Lucy went into the deeper water, and were on the far side of the river when they heard Celeste shout.

"Will, be careful! Come away from the boom!"

Will, however, was already making his way out on one of the floating logs. He'd obviously had some previous experience or he wouldn't have balanced as well as he did, but he was no expert. Maggie had seen the men from her father's crew run all over on floating logs, and log-rolling was a Sunday-afternoon sport. It was not as easy as a novice might suppose, and she didn't like the idea that Will was beyond Celeste's immediate reach.

She had just opened her mouth to add her orders to her sister's when Will stepped off the log onto a piece of drifting bark, and went under.

When it happened to one of the logging crew, it was cause for considerable amusement. As soon as the logger who had mistaken a piece of bark for a solid log came to the surface, spluttering, someone was bound to call out, "What's the matter, didn't you have no place to stood your foots?" Everybody had a good laugh, the inadvertent swimmer headed for the bunkhouse to change to dry clothes, and the work went on.

Only Will didn't swim and Maggie didn't know exactly how deep the water was beneath the floating logs. Besides that, with so many of them held closely together within the boom, the child might be caught beneath all that timber. It would form as deadly a barrier as had the ice that had trapped and killed Ned.

She saw Will's frightened face as he grasped first at the bark, which went under again, and then at a log. He emitted a small, plaintive cry that sent Maggie back across the river as swiftly as she could go.

Celeste was ahead of her, wet underclothes plastered to her body, running toward the boom, then inching her way out onto a log that would enable her to reach the little boy. The trouble was, Celeste had not practiced log-rolling or any other maneuvering around on a bag boom.

The best that could be said was that she tried. To Maggie, dashing out of the water and along the gravel riverbed to the boom downstream, it was as if Celeste ran in slow motion, although in retrospect it all seemed to have happened in seconds.

Celeste had made it halfway out along the three-foot-diameter log when she slipped, or maybe the log rolled beneath her.

She cried out, clutching madly for some handhold, before she vanished completely beneath the bank of logs.

## 23

BEHIND her, Maggie heard Lucy screaming.

She didn't waste time or breath on screaming. Time was of the essence, and there was no one but herself to do whatever could be done.

Maggie had often played on the logs and was fairly adept at jumping from one to the other; she hadn't fallen in since she was about eight years old.

She hadn't done it in several years, however, and never under this kind of pressure, with fear making the blood pound in her ears until she was deafened with it.

She reached the bag boom and began to make her way out onto the treacherous surface until she reached the log from which her sister had fallen. She was glad she was barefoot; in regular shoes, rather than the cleated boots the loggers wore, she wouldn't have had a chance.

Will's small freckled face bobbed above a small expanse of open water; he was white and scared, but he had one arm over a smaller log, and appeared in no immediate danger. It was Celeste she had to find.

The girl had fallen between shore and the spot where Willie clung to the log, so she had to have submerged at about where Maggie stood now. Celeste might try to claw her way under the boom, looking for an opening. If she had the sense to do it, she could probably push logs apart to make an opening to come up in, for the logs were not as tightly packed together as if the boom had been full.

The trouble was that Celeste, unlike Maggie, was not used to swimming with her head underwater. What was perfectly natural for one would be terrifying for the other.

Maggie balanced on one foot and pushed out with the other one against an adjoining log, creating a small space between them. Nothing. No sign of her sister.

Desperate, Maggie shoved at the log on the other side. And there it was, the pale silky hair, floating just beneath her.

She crouched and caught it, bringing up Celeste's head, fighting to keep the log on which she stood from spinning, staring into her sister's wide-open blue eyes.

For a moment she felt a sense of *déjà vu*, although she had not actually seen Ned Pallison's dead face, only imagined it. Water streamed from Celeste's open mouth and her nostrils, and there was no awareness in the staring eyes.

She didn't know whether Celeste was alive or dead; she only knew that she had to get her to shore. It wasn't easy. The log shifted under her, so that she lost her balance and went sprawling. She had time to be grateful that she was wearing drawers, not skirts, for she was able to swing one leg out and over the log as she went down, though she felt skin being peeled from that leg against the rough bark. Miraculously, she'd held on to her sister's hair, though not without dunking her again.

Maggie sucked in air and ignored the pain. How was

she going to do it, lift a weight nearly equal to her own out of the water and carry Celeste to shore, half a dozen yards away?

Celeste made some tiny sound—did she try to speak, or was it only water escaping from her?—and Maggie renewed her efforts, only to give up moments later when it became obvious that she couldn't lift her sister, couldn't haul her to safety while balancing on a log.

There was only one other possible solution that she could see. Maggie, still straddling the log (which was a more stable way to manage than standing, and made it much easier to keep her sister's face above water), threw every effort into getting Celeste over the log, too.

It was impossible, though she did manage to get one limp arm up and over, with Celeste's cheek resting against the bark. Her head was turned away from Maggie, so it was impossible to see if there was life in her face. Maggie heard her own ragged, sobbing breath.

"Celeste, don't die! For the love of God, try to hang on! Hang on to the log!"

Incredibly, the pale fingers twitched, as if seeking purchase on the harsh surface; they encountered a slight protuberance where a branch had been chopped off, and struggled to hold to it.

It was all the encouragement Maggie needed. She kicked out with one foot at the log behind Celeste, pushing it as far away as she could manage, and turned to look at Will several yards farther on.

"Can you hold on, Will?"

The boy nodded. His teeth were chattering, but he seemed unharmed.

"Can you help me push that log back? So I can go into the water without getting crushed?"

Will nodded again, and Maggie slid over the side between the two denuded tree trunks, giving a cry of triumph when her feet touched bottom.

She was in water to her chin, but that was good enough. As long as she could breathe, she could maneuver.

"Will, can you let go of that log and catch this one? So you're on the same one Celeste is on?"

He swallowed spasmodically, opening and closing his mouth several times before he could speak. "I'll try."

"I don't dare let go of her yet. She can't hold on alone. Reach for that bump there, see it? Right behind you. I think you can hang on there."

Will looked, nodded, and stretched out a white, skinny arm. He sent a brief, frightened glance at Maggie, then grabbed out the way she'd instructed.

There wasn't much to grasp, and the log was much too large for him to get an arm around it. Maggie breathed a prayer that he'd be able to hold on, hoisted Celeste a few inches higher, and began to work the log toward shore.

Even though she could stand on the bottom rather than having to swim, it wasn't easy. She was bearing most of her sister's weight, and twice she stepped into holes that brought water lapping into her mouth. More times than that she was struck in the back by another of the floating logs; once she looked down and saw blood oozing from her arm where fir bark had abraded the skin.

Lucy stood at the shore, and as Maggie edged toward her she waded into the water, working her way out, holding the encroaching logs at bay as best she could. When the water reached her waist, Lucy stopped, but she kept fending off other logs until the end of the crucial one bumped against her, guided by Maggie.

"We'll have to turn it around to get them closer to shore," Maggie said. "Help me, like this, shove those that way, so it's not end-on to the bank."

Above her Celeste choked, and began to vomit. Her fingers slipped off the log, but this time Maggie was in shallower water. She let her come, grabbing her around the waist, and dragged her to shore. A moment later, she handed Will over to Lucy, and bent over her sister, who had begun to sob and choke as the spasms wracked her body.

"I never was so glad to hear anybody throw up in my life," Maggie muttered. "Celeste, bend over, and get rid of the water."

Celeste, crouched on her knees, obliged. Then, spent and exhausted, she leaned against Maggie, tears mingling with the river water.

"I thought I was going to die, Margaret. I thought I was trapped under those dreadful logs, and I couldn't find a place to come up. It was just like Ned. . . ."

Maggie turned her head to where Ned's brother and sister were standing on the gravel bank, watching. "You all right, Will? Lucy?"

They both nodded, though there was a bloody smear on Will's arm and he was shivering uncontrollably.

"Celeste, can you sit up?"

For reply, Celeste turned, still on her knees, and buried her face in Maggie's lap.

For nearly ten minutes they remained that way, chilled even further by the rapid evaporation of the water from their clothes and skin, until the sun's heat began to warm them again.

Celeste's hair was soaked and matted, spreading over Maggie's legs. At last she lifted her head to look into Maggie's face.

"You saved my life. Margaret . . ."

Maggie stroked the wet hair back from her forehead.

"I think we'd better see if you can walk, if we can get you home," she said. She glanced beyond her sister to the children, who were no longer shivering. Lucy had gotten dressed, and she handed Will his trousers. "Are you two going to be able to walk all the way back to camp?"

"I reckon," Lucy said soberly. "Maybe we'd oughtn't

to tell Ma what happened. She still cries about Ned, sometimes.''

For some reason that gave Maggie a stab of sensation that might have been compassion. Jaisy might well grieve for a dead son, but that didn't make her a decent woman, did it?

Maggie cleared her throat, looking down at her own bloodied garments, realizing that her scraped leg had been smarting for some time now. Celeste, too, suffered abrasions and contusions, and a massive black-and-blue area had already formed on one exposed shoulder.

"I'm afraid we're going to have to confess. Someone's bound to see all the bruises and scabs, and then they'd be more upset than if we tell them in the first place.''

Lucy looked dubious. "Ma'll be mad.''

Maggie sighed. "Yes. So will ours, probably. But not as mad as if they find out later. Celeste, can you stand up? Can you walk?''

Celeste, not moving, was barely audible. "It was so terrible, not to be able to breathe. Even when I found a place where my feet touched the bottom, there was nowhere to come up between the logs. It was awful, Margaret.''

Tears slid down her cheeks. Maggie knelt beside her and hugged her, saying nothing, letting her cry.


Celeste was put immediately to bed, without protest. Though the distance to the house was not great, the effort of walking there from the swimming spot had further exhausted her.

Millicent and Ann exclaimed over her injuries; Millicent went for a basin of water to make sure the abrasions were cleaned thoroughly before she smeared on her own soothing ointment to promote healing. Through all their ministrations, Celeste lay inert, eyes closed, unresponsive.

Maggie stood for a moment in the doorway, seeing her sister's waxen face, the closed eyes, and knew exactly how close she'd come to dying. She knew with an overwhelming rush of emotion how much Celeste meant to her, how dreadful it would have been to have lost her.

Ann turned away from the bed and followed Maggie into the hallway, closing the door behind her. "Margaret, she looks awful. Did she swallow a great deal of water?"

"Quite a bit came back up, so I suppose so."

"Thank God you were able to get her out of the river." Ann's mouth took on a pinched look. "And all because of those Pallison brats."

"Mama, they're just little kids. *Nice* little kids. Will was playing, the way boys do. He didn't mean to put anybody in danger, rescuing him." She saw by her mother's expression that Ann was unconvinced of any merit on Will's part. "Celeste was very brave, running to him that way. She knew I was too far away to get there fast enough. And she's all right, Mama. She'll be sore, and she was very frightened; but she's all right."

The anger went out of Ann's face and her lips trembled. "She might have died. Celeste might have died. Oh, Margaret, you might *both* have died! I couldn't bear it if I'd lost either of you!"

Spontaneously, Maggie hugged her, and Ann hugged back. It was the closest they had been for a long, long time; they clung together, feeling one another's hearts beat, Ann's tears dampening Maggie's cheek.

Down the hall, Sarah wailed, and Ann drew back, smiling faintly. "Thank God it came out all right," she said, and walked off to the crying baby.

Maggie looked after her for a moment, eyes blurring. She could certainly echo that sentiment.

In the big room that had been intended as the master bedroom of the house, Ann scooped Sarah out of the cradle and held the child against her shoulder, patting her soothingly.

Sarah liked being held upright, and she liked being walked. Ann wondered how many miles she had paced, mostly within this room, comforting the baby. Not that she begrudged Sarah anything, even if it meant pacing by the hour.

She walked now, the infant drooping contentedly against her, and paused beside the window overlooking the river.

The house was built in a pretty spot, on the bank above the water, surrounded by firs, cedars, and a few alders. She had wanted the house so badly. Now she had it, and what good was it to her? Ann's eyes ached with tears she refused to shed. It was a beautiful house, meant for entertaining, but how could she invite people here now? She had dreamed of being a society leader in Snohomish. She'd tried to talk Jake into building in town, not sure people would come this far when she invited them. They had. They probably still would, only the dream was ended, ended by Jake and his animal appetites and that woman.

The only place she saw anyone outside the family these days was at church. Observing the Sabbath with church services was a deeply ingrained habit, one that Millicent urged her to continue. Not even Millicent, however, knew how difficult it was for her to face the people who watched her and speculated and whispered behind her back. None of them had ever said one word to her face about Jake or Jaisy Pallison, yet she knew they knew. She saw it in their eyes, heard it in their words, so carefully chosen not to offend.

The house meant nothing, now. It was her prison; she was locked away here with only her children to give her life any meaning, Margaret and Celeste and precious Sarah. Especially Sarah, who needed her more than the other two ever had.

It was so hot. Perhaps that was why the baby was fussy.

She wondered if it was cooler down by the water, but she knew she wouldn't go there even if that were the case.

She hated the river. It had come so close to depriving her of two more of her children, after she'd already been cruelly deprived of poor Charlie. And her girls had nearly lost their lives because of *her* children.

Ann didn't care what Maggie said, that they were nice children. They were tainted by their relationship to Jaisy Pallison.

Ann knew where her husband went in the evenings. Often as she lay alone in the big bed they had once shared, she heard his quiet steps on the stairs and in the hall, the almost silent closing of the door of the room where he now slept, when he bothered to come home. If it hadn't been for the fact that he and Maggie usually walked out to camp together early in the morning, and some shred of decency compelled him to protect his daughters from the disgusting truth, she suspected he would never have come home at night anymore.

He hadn't been inside her own room in months. She told herself that it didn't matter, that she didn't miss his lovemaking, that the ache that sometimes built within her was a biological fact of life, devised by an incomprehensible and inconsiderate God, that had nothing to do with her own emotions. She didn't miss Jake, she didn't want him back in her bed.

Still, it was disturbing when she dreamed about him, dreamed that he caressed her in the old familiar manner, held her in his strong arms and let her cry, though she never knew why she was crying. When she awoke, she would turn the pillow over to a dry side and try to go back to sleep, feeling only resentment that she could not prevent such dreams.

She convinced herself that she was better off without Jake in her bed. She knew with a bitter resentment that she hated him—and *her*—and could have killed them both for what they were doing. She sometimes tortured herself, lying there in the dark beside the sleeping infant, imagining Jake and Jaisy Pallison, together in the same dark a distance away. And she hated herself, at those times, when her own body betrayed her with cravings she could not subdue.

She knew that if she rose and crossed the hall and opened his door, if she crept quietly into his bed and put out a hand to touch him, Jake would take her back at once. She imagined his mouth on hers, his hands on the curve of breast and thigh, his lean body warm against her flesh. Yet she knew she would never go to him. She could not forgive his infidelity. She would not forgive it, ever.

To begin with he'd shown some sense, some discretion. Now he'd brought the woman right into camp where he could see her every day and easily visit her every night. Ann tried to tell herself it didn't matter, that they were both trash and would eventually have to pay for their sins. Only why did she have to pay for them, too? Here in Snohomish, where it must by now be whispered about, casting a shadow over her and the rest of the family as well as over the culprits?

Sarah whimpered, and Ann began to walk again, patting the small body, cradling the soft, warm head against her cheek. How she loved this child! The child that Jake ignored.

It never occurred to her that she gave him scant opportunity to have anything to do with Sarah, that she could have placed the baby in his arms and he'd have welcomed her, that since Sarah slept much of the day in the room from which he'd been banished, he had little access to her in the few waking hours he was at home.

She thought of Jake and Jaisy Pallison and damned them both to eternal hellfire, and then she thought again of the close call the girls had had today, and hugged Sarah tighter, willing herself not to think about it any further.

\*        \*        \*

Maggie retired to her room to strip off her clothes and examine her own body. The scraped thigh was the worst and had already stuck to her drawers so that the bleeding started again when she had to peel them away. She winced, looking at the mess.

Did she dare try to go to the dance tonight? If it hurt this much now, would it be better or worse by evening?

She'd been so cold, there at the river, and now she was nearly suffocating in the heat again. The breeze stirred the curtains at her windows, with no coolness in it.

She had brought the jar with Millicent's ointment, and she began to spread it gingerly over the afflicted area. Angus had asked if she'd be there, and he'd made that remark about walking outside in the dark. . . .

Maggie made up her mind. She'd go. She wouldn't be any more uncomfortable in town than she was here, she thought. And maybe Angus would finally make some move, some declaration, to show that he felt the same way she did.

## 24

BY the time the buggy reached town, Maggie regretted having come. Her thigh and a place on one elbow smarted unmercifully and the heat left her enervated and dripping. She glanced guiltily at her grandmother, equally uncomfortable in the heat, and stretched out a hand to Millicent's in an impulsive gesture.

"Grandma, are you all right?"

Millicent's hand was surprisingly fragile under hers; Maggie noted for the first time that it was blue-veined, old. It twisted, however, squeezing back, and Millicent managed a smile. "It's terribly warm, isn't it? Makes a person feel half-sick. No doubt it will cool off as soon as the sun goes down." She squirmed on the horsehair seat. "I believe I might have laced my corset more loosely and felt more comfortable."

Maggie, who had no real need of stays, had left her foundation garment off, and felt lucky to have escaped her mother's eagle eye in that regard. "Thank you for coming with me, Grandma. I appreciate it. I do enjoy the dances very much."

Millicent patted at her face and throat with a handkerchief. "You may find it hard to credit, dear, but I remember being your age. Though I wasn't allowed to go to dances, there were church socials. . . . That's where I met your grandfather, you know. I thought he was such a handsome young man." She smiled a little, and Maggie tried to connect the stiff, unyielding man in the daguerreotype on Grandma's dresser, the man Maggie had known, with the suitor Millicent described as a "handsome young man."

"I couldn't come into town if you didn't come with me to the Athenaeum. Thank you," Maggie said, and was glad she'd spoken. Millicent nodded and smiled, sitting up a bit straighter in the seat. It occurred to Maggie that most of what her grandmother did was taken for granted, and she was seldom shown much appreciation for it.

Jake hadn't come with them tonight. He had pleaded business to attend to, and ridden off immediately after supper. Though no one had commented on it, Ann had had that pinched look about her mouth again.

Maggie handled the reins, enjoying being in control. She was glad to pull up with the other conveyances, though, and get into the shade. She felt stiff, getting down, and hoped that the sore places wouldn't get worse overnight, or she might have trouble getting up in the morning.

It was stifling inside the building; the sun was still well above the distant Olympics that would eventually cut off its heat. There was a fruit punch set out for refreshment, cooled by ice from Swanson's ice house, and Maggie took a glass to Millicent before she looked around to see who was present.

"Miss Maggie-Margaret," said a familiar voice, and she turned to see Wilkie Andreason moving toward her. "How pretty you look. Is that a new dress?"

"No, one of Mama's, taken in," Maggie admitted, smiling. "We haven't seen you for a few days."

"I've been busy elsewhere, but I'll see you on Monday." He gave her a speculative look. "Have you talked to your father lately? Has he told you what he thinks about my proposal?"

Maggie shook her head. "No. He didn't seem to want to talk about it."

Wilkie laughed. "Well, maybe that means he's thinking about it, anyway. He didn't tell you I was a crazy fool."

"I overheard a little of what you said. About buying a mill." Maggie couldn't resist. "How could he buy a mill, without money?"

Now the look was approving. "You did listen, didn't you? I suspect you have a good head on your shoulders, Maggie-Margaret. The ice in your punch has melted; would you like another glass?"

She surrendered it to him for a refill, and they stood in line together with the others waiting to quench their thirst. She saw several girls watching her with envy, and she forgot the discomfort in her scraped-up thigh. "Tell me how you think Daddy can do anything about a mill," she urged.

"Well, to begin with, there's one for sale. I've worked on Stover's books, and I can tell you, unequivocally, he *has* to sell it. Sell it, or walk away from it. He can't afford to pay the necessary wages to keep it running for more than another few weeks.''

Maggie felt a thread of uneasiness run through her. ''Isn't that confidential? I mean, whatever you see in someone's books?''

Wilkie's grin was meant to be reassuring. ''Certainly. I haven't quoted you any figures, have I? I promise you, everybody he does business with knows what kind of shape he's in. He has unpaid bills all over the territory. He has, as they say, his back to the wall. He's running out of options. Selling might be a matter of saving face, even if he can't save anything more than that.''

Maggie, who had gone all the way through school with Walt Stover's daughter Alice, bit her lip. What would the Stovers do if they lost their mill?

''How awful for Mr. Stover,'' she said slowly. There was a burst of laughter behind them in the line, and the musicians were tuning up, so their conversation was reasonably private; the necessity to stand very close to Wilkie so that they could converse in low voices made her pulse flutter a little.

Wilkie sobered, looking as sympathetic as his voice now became. ''Yes, it's too bad. It's happening to a lot of people. There's a recession, and there are going to be a lot of changes before the economy recovers. What I'm trying to persuade your father of is that he can benefit from hard times if he has the courage to grab for what's available. Stover doesn't have enough business now to pay him to stay open, but when the demand for lumber rises again— and it will, how can it not, when the country's moving west and everybody will be building?—that mill will be worth a fortune to whoever owns it!''

Maggie frowned. ''But my father can't buy it!''

''Yes, he can. At least,'' Wilkie amended, moving to the head of the line and ladling punch into both their glasses, careful to get a few chips of the precious ice in each of them, "I think he can, if he's willing to take the chance and do what's necessary."

He handed her one of the glasses and they moved away from the table, instinctively edging toward the open doorway where a faint breeze touched their faces. Maggie's frown had grown deeper.

"What chances? What's necessary? It seems so . . . so awful, to take advantage of someone else's misfortune, anyway."

"Is it? Stover's going under, whether your father does anything about the mill or not. It's no different than when Ed Newsome got hurt, and couldn't run his logging show anymore. Your father didn't feel guilty about working out a deal to take it over himself, did he? Newsome was out, no matter what. If he'd just sold his equipment and let the operation die, his men would all have been thrown out of work, and what good would it have done anybody? As it was, your father worked out a payment plan he could afford, borrowed money, hung on by his teeth until he got the debt paid off. Everybody benefited, including the Newsomes. They got something, where otherwise they would have had nothing. It's the same with Stover. He isn't going to survive; but he has valuable assets, and whoever takes them over is going to make money with them, eventually."

More people were arriving, undaunted by the heat. Wilkie touched her elbow to guide her outside, where though it was still a long way from dark it was at least cooler in the shade, and they stood sipping the cold drinks. Now, in midsummer, the daylight would linger until nearly ten. Inside the building, the musicians struck up a lively air, and partners were chosen for the first dance; but Maggie didn't suggest joining the dancers. She wanted to know what this was all about, and if Jake wouldn't talk about it, she'd listen to Wilkie.

Besides, every female who passed by gave her that look, one that said Maggie was a woman lucky to have an attractive man at her side, a woman to be reckoned with.

"All right," Maggie said, returning her attention to her companion. "Say Mr. Stover is going to have to sell his mill, or close it down. How do we take it over without the cash to pay for it?"

Wilkie's voice lowered to a confidential level and he grinned broadly. "I like that *we*, Maggie. You're part of the operation the same as your father is. I've been explaining that part of it to him, how it can be done. So far he just grunts, though he's still listening. A promise of payment to be made in the future, even, to allow Stover to get out without total humiliation. I'm convinced he'll jump at any kind of offer, and everybody knows Jake Keating's a man of his word. People trust him."

The frown seemed permanently etched on Maggie's countenance. "They trust him because he's honest. He won't do anything underhanded. He won't take advantage of Mr. Stover."

"He won't have to take advantage of him. All he has to take advantage of is the situation, and if he doesn't, someone else will. I guarantee you that."

An arriving group of young people called out greetings to her, and she turned to smile at them. "Maybe we'd better go inside," Maggie suggested, "before my grandma wonders what's happened to me."

The evening was a mixed success. Angus arrived late, as was often the case since he didn't usually leave camp until after supper on Saturday night and had a long way to come. Maggie did have the satisfaction of having him seek her out immediately, and it was gratifying that he could tell she hadn't lacked for partners before he showed up.

He had heard about the episode at the river. "Lucy and Will came back to camp looking ready to be laid out with their hands folded on their chests. From the way they told it, it was a pretty close call. How's Celeste?''

"Scraped, and sore. She was terrified," Maggie said. "She was caught under the logs and couldn't find an opening. I guess we were all terrified.''

Angus nodded. "So it was Maggie to the rescue, eh? You know, Maggie, you're a very good person to have around in a crisis. Or even," he amended, looking down at her with the beginning of a smile, "when there is no crisis.''

For Angus, that was a fairly strong statement. She'd heard the term "dour Scot" and though Angus was not exactly *dour*, he wasn't one to lavish praise. Maybe, for Angus, this could even be considered romantic.

It wasn't much past ten when she took another glass of punch over to her grandmother. She was mildly alarmed at Millicent's pallor.

"Grandma, are you all right?" Maggie sank onto the vacant chair beside her, reaching out to touch one of the blue-veined hands. It was reassuring, neither clammy nor overheated, but clearly Millicent was not feeling well.

"I didn't want to put an end to your good time, dear, but no, I'm not feeling as well as I'd like. I think it's the heat. I'm not used to it. It's been several years since we've had a hot spell that's lasted this long, and with all the anxiety this afternoon about Celeste . . . well, I suppose I'm getting old, and things take a toll, these days.''

"I'll ask one of the boys to bring the buggy around, and we'll go home," Maggie said at once. "I'll be back for you in about five minutes, all right?"

She hoped it was no more than the heat and the earlier excitement. Guilt swept over her; she should never have come to town tonight, knowing that the temperature was bothering her grandmother. She was suddenly aware of her own discomfort, held in abeyance by the stimulation of socializing with her friends.

"I'll say good-bye to a few people," Maggie said, and Millicent smiled in gratitude.

"Thank you, Margaret. If you don't mind leaving . . ."

So there was no walking outside in the dark with Angus. She saw Wilkie in apparently amused and amusing conversation with Andrea Clark, and wondered why she should feel a prick of jealousy. She had no claim on Wilkie, she didn't even want to have a claim on him. It was only that she'd enjoyed his company and the glances it had engendered from the other girls, she told herself.

To her relief, Millicent seemed to revive somewhat on' the ride home. While it was still warm, it was no longer the kind of heat that sapped one's strength and made one feel queasy.

The house was silent, a single lamp left burning in the front hallway. Millicent picked up the lamp to light their way upstairs, then hesitated. "I wonder if your father is in yet? Perhaps I should leave the lamp here."

"I'll run upstairs and see," Maggie offered. The house had retained too much of the day's warmth; after the fresh air outside, it felt close and there were cloying food odors from the meal served hours ago.

Only her mother's door was closed. The others stood open to allow for ventilation. A lamp, turned low, sat beside the bed in Celeste's room. She slept under only a sheet, her hair darkened at its roots with perspiration, one arm thrown over her head.

Maggie picked up the lamp and carried it along the corridor to Jake's room, holding it high to show an empty, still made up bed.

She stifled the feelings that evoked, and went back to the head of the stairs. "No, Daddy isn't home yet," she called softly to her waiting grandmother. "Leave the lamp there, and I'll light you up with this one."

When Millicent joined her in the upper hallway, Maggie

replaced the lamp in Celeste's room, leaving her grand-mother there looking down on the sleeping girl.

Maggie didn't bother with a light in her own room. She undressed in the dark, draping her garments over a chair, finding her nightgown by touch, and crawling into bed.

In spite of the open door and windows there was not enough air moving. She thought of taking a blanket and a pillow and going down onto the swing on the verandah, but she was too weary to make the effort.

She did not fall asleep easily. She thought about Angus with regret. Would he have walked out with her in the dark, as he'd halfway suggested earlier? And Wilkie, was he right about Stover's mill? Could Jake acquire it, legitimately, ethically? Wilkie had spoken of having the courage to take a chance. Jake had as much courage as any man. What had Wilkie meant about taking a chance? Her father had too much sense to do anything so risky that it might lose for him what he already had, in a rash bid to gain more. At least she hoped he did.

There had been a time when she'd thought Jake was perfect. Honest, smart, strong. Before he'd met Mrs. Pallison, when he'd seemed to lose a good part of his common sense.

She hadn't seen him in town tonight, and she didn't think that's where he was. He didn't go to the Gem Saloon as much as he had in the past; she knew that because she'd heard the men say to him, on Monday mornings, that they'd missed seeing him on Saturday night.

Maggie flopped over, trying to find a cooler place. It made her want to cry, to think about her father and Jaisy, and there was nothing she could do about them.

She dozed and woke tangled in the sheets, her thin batiste gown sticking damply to her body. She couldn't remember ever being so uncomfortable with the heat at night this way; usually it cooled off so quickly once the sun went down.

She kicked off the sheets and sat up, about to recklessly cast aside the nightdress as well, when she heard the cry.

It was choked, muffled, verging on hysteria.

Without taking time to reach for a wrapper, Maggie ran for her sister's room.

The lamp was still burning, though the oil was running low. Celeste thrashed about on the bed, continuing to make the protesting sounds; her voice was rising to a shriek when Maggie took her by the shoulders and shook her awake. Celeste's eyes were wide and wild; it was not until Maggie spoke to her that she came fully awake and fell back, gasping as if she had been running.

Her fingers dug into her sister's arms as Maggie sank onto the bed beside her. "Oh, Margaret! I dreamed I was there again, caught under the logs, and I couldn't breathe.... Oh, it was awful!"

"It's because it's so hot. It's like trying to breathe something solid," Maggie soothed. "Wait, I'll bring the basin and sponge you off, and you'll feel better."

"Is she all right?"

Millicent spoke from the open doorway, clutching a dressing gown at her waist, an elaborately laced and beribboned garment that must have added to her discomfort from the heat simply because it was so heavily decorated.

"She had a nightmare," Maggie said. "I'm going to get her a fresh gown and stay with her until she goes back to sleep."

Millicent nodded. "All right. Good night, dears."

"It's all over," Maggie assured her sister. "It was just a dream. You'll forget it soon, and you'll feel better in a day or two."

Maggie thought she was speaking the truth. But it didn't happen that way.

Sunday was so sultry and miserable that nobody went to

church. Sarah fussed, and Ann finally stripped her down to a diaper and laid her on a blanket on the floor, though she was somewhat concerned about drafts. The baby seemed more comfortable without clothes and woke up only to eat or be changed.

Celeste was up and around, moving stiffly and wincing when she changed position. She wore a thin summer wrapper and kept a watchful eye out for visitors who might drive her out of the swing and into the house because of her undressed state.

Millicent was fully recovered except for the air of lassitude that infected them all. She gave orders to Mrs. Totting to set out cold foods for the family, and to rest through the afternoon as the others were doing.

Maggie and Nancy didn't need to rest, though they didn't have the energy to do anything strenuous. They considered going swimming, giving the idea up only because they knew their elders would object, after yesterday's near-catastrophe. They sat at the far end of the verandah from everybody else and discussed last night's dance in desultory tones until Nancy finally decided to take a nap, after all.

"I don't feel like moving at all," she confessed, and headed for her room at the back of the house.

Jake emerged a few minutes later and came to sit beside Maggie on the side steps. "Hear you had yourself an adventure yesterday," he said. "All's well that ends well, I guess. Celeste seems all right, doesn't she?"

Maggie felt a small, niggling resentment that he hadn't come home for supper last night so she could have told him about it herself. "I suppose Mrs. Pallison told you."

He didn't deny it. "The kids said you were magnificent. Celeste, too, trying to rescue Will even though she's not used to running around on bag booms. All that tomboy stuff your mother objected to when you were little came in handy, didn't it?"

"We were all lucky," Maggie said. It was one of the few times she could remember being short with him. Why did everything he did and said remind her of his relation- ship with Jaisy? "I looked for you when we came home last night, Daddy."

His dark eyes rested on her with the same love they'd always shown, dimmed a little now with regret, she thought. "Honey, I'd like to be here for you all the time, but I can't be. Any more than I could be there yesterday when Celeste and Will got in trouble. But I've raised you right, haven't I? You're strong and resourceful. You can handle the emergencies when they come up."

Her eyes prickled with unaccustomed tears. "Some- times I don't want to be strong and resourceful. I want to be a little girl again, and have you take care of me." Be the all-powerful, courageous, nonaging father, she meant. Forget Jaisy and be with Mama, make us a family again.

Jake didn't answer that, though she suspected he knew what she meant, that he guessed at the unspoken words. He put an arm around her and hugged her, resting his chin against her head, holding her until they both began to feel too hot, and laughed when they drew apart.

But that evening, after their meal of cold meat and bread and sugared raspberries with cream, Jake went away again and didn't return until two o'clock in the morning.

She knew the time because she'd been awakened again by another of Celeste's nightmares, no less violent than the previous one had been. Maggie went through the same motions as before, sponging her sister off, getting her a fresh nightgown, sitting beside her and holding her hand until Celeste drifted into sleep.

She looked at the clock before she got back into her own bed; it was a few minutes after she'd blown out the lamp that she heard Jake come in, walking quietly to avoid disturbing the household.

It was only because she was so tired, missing her sleep

to be with Celeste, that made her weepy, Maggie thought. She pounded her pillow into a different shape, angrily brushed at her eyes with the back of her hand, and determined to go to sleep and not dream.  •

## 25

IT was near dawn when Maggie woke. She'd slept restlessly, until it finally began to cool off, and then she hadn't awakened at her usual time.

The room was chilly. She groped for the quilt before she realized that she could make out vague shapes of the furniture and the oblongs of the windows across the room.

She sat up, groggy and confused. She'd slept so hard when at last sleep had been possible, and now she was probably too late to leave with Jake.

She had just stood up when she heard the muffled sounds. Sobs? Maggie walked swiftly into the hallway and listened.

The sounds continued, coming from her sister's room.

"Celeste? Are you all right?" It was a stupid question; she knew that as soon as she'd spoken. Nobody cried like that unless there was something wrong. "Shall I light the lamp?"

"No, no." Celeste choked on the words. "Don't."

Maggie padded toward the bed, hit a toe on the leg of a chair that had been moved out of its usual place, and sank down beside the younger girl, rubbing at the injured member. "What's wrong? Another nightmare?"

Celeste was sitting up, hunched over her raised knees.

"Margaret, what am I going to do? Every time I close my eyes, it happens all over again. I'm afraid to go to sleep!"

She began to cough, a spasm so violent that Maggie was becoming alarmed by the time it ended.

"It'll be daylight soon. Nightmares don't last then. Why don't you stay in bed this morning and rest until you really feel better."

"I feel horrible. I feel as if I'm on fire."

Surprised, because she herself was actually chilly, Maggie put out a hand to rest on Celeste's arm, then moved to her forehead. The younger girl was burning up with fever.

Suddenly Celeste began to shake. "What's happening to me? I'm hot and cold at the same time. Maggie, I'm sick."

Maggie pulled up the warm quilt. "Lie down and cover up. I'll call Mama or Grandma. I'll be right back. Do you think you're going to need the basin?"

"No, only I'm frightened. Don't leave me, Margaret!"

She sounded as she had when she was three or four years old. Maggie pulled free of her hands. "Only for a minute. I'll be right back."

Ann came at once when Maggie spoke at her doorway; Millicent was only moments behind. "What is it? What's the matter?"

When the lamp had been lighted, they stood around the bed. Celeste's teeth were chattering, now, and her forehead was clammy.

Ann bit her lip. "See if your father's left for the woods yet, Margaret. I think someone should go for the doctor."

She ran downstairs, her thin gown flapping around her bare ankles. Mrs. Totting was just turning back to her own quarters after having cleared away Jake's dishes.

"Your pa left half an hour ago," Mrs. Totting said. "He told me to let you sleep, you were tuckered out, and it didn't matter if you didn't get to camp today. He said the little girl can help her ma."

"My sister's sick. I'll have to go for the doctor. Would

you ask Nancy if she'll go with me? I'll be down as soon as I've dressed.''

She ran back the way she had come, dread growing within her.

Was Celeste sick because of what had happened on Saturday? Or was it something else altogether?

It was so seldom that they called a doctor; that in itself was frightening. Usually Ann and Millicent took care of things, did whatever had to be done. It was only in the really bad times that they sent for a physician, like when Mama couldn't birth the baby, or when little Charlie died.

Maggie's fingers were clumsy over her buttons as she dressed in semidarkness, shaking so that she couldn't match them with the buttonholes.

Please, God, let Celeste be all right, she begged silently.

The doctor examined Celeste, prescribed bed rest and a cough syrup of brandy and honey, and pursed his lips after listening to her chest. "She may have gotten water into her lungs. Rest, that's the ticket."

It was obvious that she *did* need rest. She dozed off and on, yet found it difficult to get the healing sleep she wanted. As she told Maggie with tears in her eyes, "I'm afraid to go to sleep. It happens to me all over again."

There was no doubting the genuine terror the dreams induced. Or the reality of fevers and chills. Maggie, sitting beside the bed, trying to occupy her mind with reading, watched the moisture come out on her sister's forehead, saw her shivering and shaking, and felt oddly guilty of this, too, as if she'd been responsible for what had happened, though no one uttered a word of blame.

She was relieved that she didn't have to work with Jaisy today, though she'd have to face her eventually. She didn't want the woman's thanks for rescuing her son, or her blame for allowing the children to swim without her own permission, if it came to that. In fact, she'd be happy if she never had to see Jaisy again, she thought dolefully.

Sarah, too, was sick; the fact that she'd always had a weak constitution didn't make it any easier on the family who had to listen to her whimper and struggle to breathe. Ann was kept busy with the infant; Maggie sat with Celeste; and Millicent moved between the two, helping in whatever way she could.

The heat broke more abruptly than it had come.

By midafternoon, Millicent went around closing all windows and even built fires in the sickrooms. She looked down on Maggie and sighed.

"You've been here for such a long time, child. Why don't you go and rest, and I'll stay with her for an hour or two?"

Maggie rose gratefully and stretched. "I don't want to rest, but I'd like some exercise. Maybe I'll take a walk. Thanks, Grandma."

It felt good to be out-of-doors. She called to Joe, who came on the run from the back of the house, and set out at a brisk pace.

Woolrich, the teamster, was adding a load of logs to the cold deck at the landing, the oxen standing patiently while this was accomplished; he called out a greeting and Maggie waved and went on.

She ignored the stiffness in her abraded leg and gradually forgot about it as she loosened up. She was used to exercise; sitting in a chair was a miserable way to spend a day, she decided.

She was deep in her own thoughts, and far into the woods, when the crash of thunder brought her out of her reverie. Maggie looked up to see black clouds boiling out of the southwest, moving at incredible speed. A moment later lightning cut a jagged path through the sky toward a towering dead fir spar no more than half a mile distant. She heard it crack, and saw it fall.

Maggie stopped. "Maybe we'd better head for home," she said to Joe, who perked up his ears questioningly.

She was, however, closer to camp than to the landing. She hesitated for only a few seconds. "It's going to be a good one. Maybe we'd better try for camp and wait it out there."

High in the tops of the firs the wind picked up. There was no movement of air around her at ground level, but several hundred feet above her the slender tops began to bend and sway, whipped by a wind that made a sound like that of the train she'd occasionally heard at Port Gardner, heralding one of the violent storms for which the region was well known.

She'd observed it many times, and it never failed to excite and, a little, to frighten her. As the wind increased, its force would not only bend the trees, it would break them. Branches, from twigs to eight- and ten-foot boughs, were torn loose and scattered on the ground. An ominous creaking sound might be no more than two naked alder trunks rubbing together, but there was always the possibility that it could be the momentary warning before a brittle tree split or toppled, tearing off parts of other trees and crushing anything in its path.

She was used to falling trees, enjoyed seeing them come down as much as the loggers did, but *those* were directed to precisely the spot the faller had chosen. The trees that succumbed to the wind rather than to ax and saw could come down anywhere, on anybody or anything.

The wind was increasing, now, as she hurried along the skid road. Beside her, the lush fern growth was motionless. Above, treetops bent to incredible angles, thrashing as if in their death throes, which for some of them it would be.

And then the wind swooped down into the canyon cut through the forest by the skid road, tugging at her hair and her clothes with a chill she would not have believed possible a few hours earlier. Joe's ears blew back on his head, and he moved so close to her that she nearly stepped on him.

With the wind came rain.

Great pelting, stinging drops of it, a few at first, and then a deluge that left her drenched to the skin, and cold. It was as if the rain had come directly off the snow-covered top of Three Fingers, in drops closer to ice than to water.

She was blinded by it. Maggie tried to run, not an easy thing to manage on the corduroy road, for even after all the logs that had been dragged over it to the river, it was still far from smooth.

She'd lost track of where she was. The trees on either side of her, writhing and twisting, some of them snapping off, all looked alike, and the rain made it impossible to see clearly anyway.

"Maggie? Is that you?"

She staggered forward, trying to see through the curtain of water that made her feel as if she were beneath a waterfall. "Angus?"

"Over here! Give me a hand!"

She followed the direction of his voice and saw to her consternation that Angus had been caught by a falling tree which pinned one leg against a rocky outcropping. There was a gash across his forehead as well, with blood diluted by rain running past his left eye.

"See if you can lift that end while I lift from here," Angus said, and Maggie forgot her own discomfort and fought her way through the thick prickly boughs to grasp the trunk of the tree.

"Is your leg broken?"

Angus fended off Joe's sympathetic tongue. "I don't think so, I think I'm just caught. Wait . . . now, *lift*!"

It took three tries before she was able to raise it. The rough bark tore at her hands; she gritted her teeth, ignored the pain, and heaved upward.

Angus made a grunting gasp and pulled free. For a moment he lay there, breathing heavily. It was not until Maggie disentangled herself from the broken spar and came to kneel at his side that he sat up to examine his leg.

"I don't see any blood, and there's no bone sticking out," he said matter-of-factly. "Let's see if I can walk."

"How far are we from camp?" Maggie asked.

He took a step or two, wincing. "Far enough so I don't know if I want to walk it just yet. I think the line shed is only a little way. If it isn't full we could at least get out of the wind until the storm eases up. Can you see it?"

Maggie shielded her eyes with her hands. "No. Oh, over there! Can you walk that far? Do you want to lean on me?"

Angus took a few more steps. "It isn't bad. Come on. Did you see Woolrich with the team?"

"Back at the landing. He may stay there until the worst of this is over." Maggie put an arm around his waist while Angus rested an arm on her shoulders, though there was no way she could have supported more than a fraction of his weight.

Within a few yards he was walking more easily, with only a slight limp. He squinted through the downpour.

"Bless old Risku for insisting on having a place to leave supplies out here," he said, throwing open the door to the tiny shack. "We all kidded him about being too lazy to walk half a mile, but I'll thank him next time I see him."

He guided Maggie in ahead of him and kicked a coil of rope out of the way. "Wait a minute, let's see if we can clear a place to sit down. No, Joe, stay outside. There's no room."

The shack was no bigger than the three-hole privy at camp, and nearly filled with various bits of equipment. There was no window, so they left the door open a crack for minimal light, and sank onto the dirt floor in the space they'd been able to clear of tools.

Maggie was shivering. "How could it turn so cold so fast?"

"It seems colder because you're wet. Come here, we'll get each other warm." He wrapped an arm around her, drawing her against him.

After a few minutes she did feel warmer, though she wasn't sure how much was due to their combined body heats and how much to the fact that it was Angus's arm around her. Her heart was beating so loudly it was a wonder he didn't hear it, too.

"We missed you at breakfast," Angus said, rubbing a rapidly warming hand up and down her arm in a way that sent wild new sensations running through her, in places far removed from her arm.

*We*, meaning the whole crew. Why couldn't he have said *I*?

Maggie brought out a clean but sodden handkerchief and wiped the cut on his head. It wasn't as bad as it had at first appeared; the bleeding was nearly stopped. "How's your leg?" she asked. A properly brought up young lady probably wouldn't have mentioned a man's leg to him, but under the circumstances that seemed absurd.

The limb in question was resting against her uninjured thigh. Maggie felt a tingling beginning there and spreading in a curious way; she could feel it in her fingertips, too.

"Bruised. That's all, I think. You getting any warmer?"

"Yes. Some. If only we could dry off." She shivered.

Angus twisted sideways. "Here, is this better?"

He put both arms around her, drawing her close to him, and instinctively Maggie encircled his torso with her own arms. It seemed that her heartbeat was louder, or was she now hearing his, as well?

His lips brushed her temple, and then, astonishingly, slid down her cheek and found her mouth.

It was a gentle kiss at first, tentative, as one might kiss a child. And then he groaned, and the kiss deepened as he crushed her against him. Maggie closed her eyes, forgetting how wet she was, and gave herself over to floating, euphoric bliss.

It was Angus who broke away, though she tightened her arms so that he didn't go very far. He swore without apology.

"You aren't supposed to let a man kiss you like that," he told her, a husky note in his voice.

"Why not? I liked it," Maggie said frankly. "Was it . . . did you like kissing me as much as you did . . . Deborah?"

"Deb? Judas, Maggie, what do you know about Deb?"

"Only that you made her think you cared about her. Is it fun, to kiss any girl, even if you don't especially care about her?"

He groaned again, and hugged her hard against him. "Oh, Maggie, what a question! You aren't supposed to ask questions like that, either."

"How else am I going to find out, then?" She knew, suddenly and with a painful certainty, that she could not bear to have Angus toy with her affections, to make her think that he cared if he did not. "I've loved you as long as I can remember, Angus. I've waited and waited for you to say something, and you didn't, and now—I have to know if you're just . . ."

She trailed off, unable to express it further, and though now Angus's arms were so tight they were hurting her, she made no protest.

"Oh, God." The words were expressed as if in anguish, yet that was not what it seemed when he kissed her again.

On the eyelids, the throat, the hollow between her breasts—for a moment she felt shame and regret that her breasts were so small, and then it didn't seem to matter—and back to her mouth.

Her entire body had liquefied. She was drifting in a warm sea of ecstasy, boneless, mindless, giving herself over entirely to sensation. She felt her nipples grow taut as his fingers explored them through the damp material of her bodice, felt a powerful response within her that swept away all inhibition, all fear. This was Angus, and she loved him.

Again it was he who called a halt to things. His arms still held her, but he no longer touched her intimately. Her skirts were still in place, he hadn't carried his invasion *that* far, though she knew she would have allowed it if he had.

His words were unexpected. "I should have known better. We shouldn't have taken shelter here, we should have gone on into camp."

"Why? Are you sorry this happened?" Maggie held her breath, knowing her heart would break if he said yes.

"Oh, God, Maggie! I have no right to touch you this way! Jake would kill me if he knew! You're an innocent, a child, and I've taken advantage of that without even meaning to—"

"I'm not a child," Maggie said, and slid her arms around his neck, drawing his face down to meet hers to prove it.

Was this groaning a part of all lovemaking, she wondered, or unique to Angus? Did it mean he truly did not want to be kissing her this way? Or only that he felt guilty about it?

As his lips bruised hers, Maggie realized with surprising clarity that *she* did not feel guilty at all.

# 26

THE storm increased its fury. It was fully half an hour before the winds dropped and the thunder and lightning ceased. Angus got to his feet and stood at the doorway of the shed to look out.

"It's still raining hard, and by the look of that sky it's going to keep on for a while. We'd better go on into camp and get you into some dry clothes—Jaisy can lend you something—before you're sick, too."

"I don't want anything of Jaisy's," Maggie said stiffly.

He gave her a look she couldn't interpret, but asked no questions. Did that mean he knew about Jaisy and her father? And if that was the case, how many others knew, as well? He reached out a hand to pull her to her feet. "We'd better go, anyway. Here comes Woolrich with the team. We're not going to get any warmer or dry off staying here."

"Can you walk all right?"

Angus laughed. "I forgot all about my leg, kissing you. I forgot everything, even my good sense."

Maggie stared at him. "If you tell me it wasn't good sense to kiss me, if you're sorry you did it, I think I'm going to hit you."

He laughed again, then immediately sobered. "Well, I'm not sorry, because I've been wanting to kiss you for a long time. But it wasn't very good sense, because you're

305

Jake Keating's daughter, and he's made it quite clear that anybody who molested you would find himself minus a few vital parts. I want all the parts I have.''

Astonished, Maggie took a step forward and tripped over an ax handle so that he had to catch her. His eyes were close to hers, clear and steady; his touch made her sway slightly.

"You mean Daddy's threatened anybody who comes near me?"

"Jake has a way with words," Angus said wryly. "He doesn't leave any doubt that he means what he says, and I've never known him to bluff. Why the hell do you think I've held back, kept my hands off you? When you're really old enough to do what you want, when this damned recession is over so I don't have to depend on Jake for a job, we've got some serious planning to do.''

"Are you afraid of my father?" Maggie asked, disappointed.

"Afraid of him? No, not really. But he pays my wages, and I want to go on getting them until jobs start opening up with some other outfit. If I quit, or got fired, I'd be in a hell of a mess right now. Logging crews are being cut back, not hired. But unless he took a gun to me, I don't think he could do me any harm. Jake's a bull of the woods, but he's getting on in years, and he isn't used to fighting anymore. I'd take him on if I had to. Only what good would that do anybody?''

Slightly mollified about Angus having the courage of his convictions, less satisfied with the general picture he painted, Maggie would have pressed the issue further, except that Woolrich and the team had drawn abreast of the shack; Joe had already given away their presence by rushing out to greet the teamster, barking happily in spite of his soggy state.

Angus walked, unflinching, into the rain, lifting a hand in greeting. The men exchanged a few words, and Maggie reluctantly left the small shelter to join them. She felt as if, in her newly awakened state, she must look different, that it must be obvious even to the casual observer that they'd been doing more in that shed than finding shelter from the storm.

Woolrich only nodded in greeting, however, and urged the bulls on, while she and Angus fell into step with him. It wasn't until they dropped behind to stay out of the mud beside the road that she had a chance to speak to Angus, unheard by the teamster, and then she'd no more than opened her mouth when Angus cut her off.

"Maggie, for God's sake, don't give us away. Not to Woolrich, not to anybody. Don't give anyone a chance to gossip about us."

Indignation and consternation rose within her, strong enough to make her forget the rain and the chill. "Do you mean we're going back to the way we were before, that we're going to forget"—she choked, finding the words— "what just happened between us? Or wasn't it important to you?"

"Maggie, if you're old enough to be kissed, you're old enough to learn something about discretion. You know what that is? It's keeping still about things that will stir up a ruckus, make people angry or upset. If Jake decides he doesn't want you to have anything to do with me, he's in a position to stop you."

"He can't stop me," Maggie said at once, glancing ahead to be sure that Woolrich was beyond hearing range. "Besides, he's always let me do anything I really wanted to do, have anything I really wanted to have."

Angus gave her a quelling look, also pitching his voice low. "What I've been trying to tell you is that this is going to be different. Daddy isn't going to like it if you're paid attention by one of his hired hands. He thinks he knows what's best for you, and he's made it very, very clear that that doesn't include any of his crew. And he *can* stop you

seeing me, Maggie. All he has to do is fire me, and I won't be
around anymore. I don't know if I'd even stay in Snohomish,
because nobody's hiring.''

"He won't fire you," Maggie said, though with weakening
conviction. "You're one of his best workers. I've heard him
say so."

"Fine. Very gratifying." There was a grating quality to his
words. "Only good workers are all over the place these days,
a lot of them unemployed. He wouldn't have any trouble
replacing me with somebody just as experienced, and probably married, somebody who wouldn't be a threat to you."

She was silent, then, plodding along beside him through the
rain, concentrating on not getting a foot caught between the
logs that formed the road, the rest of the way to camp.

About half the crew had retired to the bunkhouse to rest or
wash out their socks or sharpen their saws and axes, while the
rest had gathered in the cookhouse. There was the smell of
brewing coffee and fresh bread as the newcomers entered and
were greeted from all directions.

"Got a little wet, did you?" Jim Humphries called cheerfully.
"Lucky you wasn't up a tree when that damn wind started,
McKay. I thought I was going to get killed, gettin' down."

"I was under a tree that blew down," Angus informed
him, heading for the stove and the coffeepot. "If Maggie
hadn't come along and helped haul it off me, I'd have had to
wait for Woolrich. Nobody got hurt, did they?"

Nobody had, though the lean-to where the Pallisons slept
had sprung assorted leaks, as had the bunkhouse.

"Lightning set a fire, over on Bald Knob," Sol Engstrom
offered, "only it didn't last long, once the rain started."

"It's a soaker all right." Angus carried his cup to one of
the tables, where Red Risku and Tom Dunnigan were
playing checkers. He acted as if Maggie were not even with
him, she thought, at first resentful and then uncertain. If he
were right about her father's attitude toward any possible

suitor, she supposed it wouldn't do to expose their new relationship to anyone.

"Jake's a fussin' and a fumin'," Red said, moving a black checker. "No way anybody could work in that wind, but he's mad we ain't gettin' out the last of that stand today. He was countin' on movin' over the other side of the creek by day after tomorrow, at the latest."

"He acts like it's our fault the weather's bad," Tom muttered, contemplating the board to make his next move. "It ain't as if we didn't need the rain, break that damned heat before the woods burn up."

Rich Salter, observing the game, turned his head and spat into the spittoon behind him. "This ain't weather, it's a damned disease. I got mold growing behind my ears already."

This set off a round of ribald remarks concerning Salter's anatomy and his abnormalities, as if the women weren't there.

Jaisy was stirring something that gave off a savory aroma. She put down the big wooden spoon and looked at Maggie.

"You're like to catch your death. I'll get you something of mine to dry off in, if you like. The rain didn't come in where I got my clothes hung up."

Maggie had expected that offer, yet hadn't decided how to deal with it gracefully. She decided there was no graceful way.

"No, thank you. Your things would be too short, and too big around." She knew that wouldn't have mattered, if the offered garments had belonged to anyone else, but the thought of having anything of Jaisy's next to her own skin was repugnant. "I'll dry off in a little while."

Jaisy let that slide, taking up a cleaver to begin chopping vegetables to go into the stew. Behind them, the men were laughing boisterously. "I want to thank you for getting Will out of that fix on Saturday,'' she said. ''I'm glad your sister is all right, too.''

''She's sick,'' Maggie said. ''Mama sent me for the doctor for her this morning.'' Was it only this morning? It seemed eons ago. It was only natural that Jaisy would mention the subject; after all, Will might have been the second of her children to drown if Maggie hadn't been there, and because of him Celeste had nearly lost her life. Why was it so difficult to accept even gratitude from this woman?

''I'm sorry to hear it. I hope she'll be all right. This fool weather, going from hot to cold in a couple of hours, is enough to make anybody sick. If you're going to stay on through supper, you want to make some pies? The kids picked berries this morning before it started to rain, and they're dead ripe. They won't keep.''

Without replying, Maggie set about the necessary steps. The suggestion was a subtle one, but she knew that something had changed. Jaisy had definitely taken over as chief cook. She no longer asked Maggie's advice or deferred to her in the matter of what to cook. She was now giving orders, for all that they were couched in diplomatic language, as requests.

Maggie's clothes didn't dry as quickly as she'd have liked. In spite of the fire that warmed the cookhouse, she felt damp and uncomfortable. There wasn't much she could do about it. It would have been ludicrous to refuse Jaisy's offer of dry clothes and instead put on something belonging to one of the men, as she'd occasionally done before in similar circumstances. She didn't mind taking a slap at Jaisy, but not such an open one as that.

She rolled the crusts, heaped them with berries and sugar and flour to thicken the juice, and put the pies in the oven, then made up her mind. ''I think I'll go on home, if you can manage for the rest of the day. Nobody knew I was leaving the house for more than just a walk. They'll be wondering about me.''

"Sure," Jaisy agreed at once. "Lucy can help me. Don't worry about coming in tomorrow, if they need you at home. We'll manage all right."

Was she suggesting that she'd manage all the time, permanently, without Maggie's assistance? Maggie wondered. Well, maybe she'd get the chance to find out.

The only thing was, if she stayed away from camp, she'd be away from Angus, too, except for the dances in town. The thought of seeing him only on Saturday nights was excruciating. No, she couldn't stay away from camp entirely.

Angus swung around from the letter he was writing to his family back east. "You going home, Maggie? You want a coat or something?"

"If you can spare one," she agreed. Though the rain had slackened to a drizzle, it was still cold.

"Come on, I'll get you one." He anchored his letter with a salt shaker and stood up. "Don't any of you slobs spill anything on that, all right?"

Nobody paid any attention when they left together, other than to say good-bye to Maggie. The two of them trotted across the clearing to the bunkhouse, where several men were sleeping and two others were greasing boots. The latter looked up only momentarily.

Maggie shrugged into the coat, dwarfed by it. Even if it was soaked by the time she got home, it would provide some warmth, because it was wool.

They stood for a moment under the partial shelter of the eaves, shielded from view of the crew in either the cookhouse or the sleeping quarters. Angus pulled the collar of the coat up around her throat and buttoned it, then continued to rest his hands on her shoulders.

"It shouldn't have happened, I shouldn't have let it

happen, but I'm glad it did,'' he told her softly. ''Just keep it quiet for now, all right? Trust me.''

''I do trust you,'' Maggie said readily. ''Only I want to be with you, Angus.''

''It's what I want, too. Let me work on things, will you?''

He bent his head then to kiss her on the forehead. The contact was electrifying; a brotherly kiss was not enough. With another of those groans that disconcerted her, Angus sought her mouth, his arms going around her in a hard embrace.

His grin was rueful. ''Go home. Go home before I do something *really* stupid.''

He swung her around, heading toward the landing, and stalked away, leaving her staring after him in mingled love and frustration. This was not the way she had imagined it happening. She had expected that once Angus decided she was sufficiently grown-up he would court her, openly and joyously. She had expected to feel joyful, too.

She ducked her head against the rain and began to walk, smiling in spite of herself. She *was* filled with joy; no imagined kiss could have equaled those she had experienced today. A delicious tremor of anticipation ran through her. There would be more kisses, more caresses.

And, somehow, she would win over her father, so that whatever was between her and Angus would not have to be kept a secret. She loved them both, and she would make them come to terms with each other, she vowed, striding off through the wet woods with faithful Joe at her heels.

What had happened with Angus buoyed her spirits during the following days when almost everything else conspired to dampen them.

Celeste's fever and chills subsided after four days—days during which Maggie stayed at home and helped care for her—but long after those acute symptoms were gone, the cough and the nightmares persisted.

For the cough, they tried various soothing potions, most of which seemed to help during the day. At night, however, Celeste often woke up, wracked with violent spells that left her aching, exhausted, sometimes ending in episodes of vomiting when flecks of blood could be seen in the basin.

"It's only because she's coughing so hard," the doctor said. "Nothing to worry about, breaking a few blood vessels in her throat. She'll get over it."

She didn't, though. She slept badly, because of the nightmares and the uncontrollable coughing, and she was too tired to leave the house or take part in her customary activities.

Because Ann feared the cough might be contagious, Celeste was kept away from the baby, so it fell to Maggie to spend more time with Sarah.

Sarah was so pretty, with her fair hair and her blue eyes, the picture of Celeste at the same age. Sarah did not learn as Celeste had done. She simply lay in her bed and stared vacantly at whatever moved around her, or at the ceiling. It didn't matter which it was. She fussed only when she was wet, hungry, or ill.

The day that she responded to Maggie's voice, or perhaps to the face suspended above her, was a triumph for the entire family. "Mama, Sarah smiled at me! She did, I swear it! I was talking to her, and she smiled!"

They all stood around, trying to coax another smile from Sarah, until Ann's cajoling entreaties brought forth a second smile—brief, quickly vanished, but something that gave them all hope, that promised Sarah would not be simply an unthinking, unfeeling lump of pathetic flesh as they had feared.

Ann scooped her up and hugged her, waltzing her around the room with crows of enthusiasm. And, after observing the grinning faces around her, Sarah smiled again.

For the most part, however, the days of enforced inactivity— at least by Maggie's normal standards—were difficult. She was used to being out-of-doors much of the day, of taking at least an hour and a half to walk back and forth to camp, of having assorted people to talk to, people who cursed their bad luck, bragged about the good, laughed and joked and cursed at one another.

Because neither Millicent nor Ann was leaving the house now, they had nothing to talk about except what the family members already knew. Much of that concerned housekeeping matters: the pattern for a lace collar, the decision as to how much more jam should be made from the unlimited supply of ever-ripening evergreen and Himalaya berries, the matters of stitching garments for members of the family, a discussion on whether to have a haunch of venison for dinner or a pair of roasted chickens.

The only new thing that came into the house was a copy of *Harper's Bazaar* which Maggie threw down after perusing it for a few minutes. All those illustrations of ladies with perfectly curling hair, wasp waists, well-rounded bosoms, bustles, their garments so adorned with ribbons, braids, bows, ruffles, ruchings, and pleats that it was a miracle they could walk or sit—Maggie sighed in disgust.

The fashions were rather advanced for the ladies of Snohomish, who would perhaps be wearing them some few years hence if they could persuade their husbands to part with the necessary funds, but Maggie knew instinctively that they were not for her.

Celeste said that curls were not right for Maggie, that a more simple coiffure suited her better, and Maggie's own mirror confirmed that. The same was true of her dress; she looked ludicrous in those fancy furbelowed affairs. She didn't have enough bosom, she was too tall and too

angular, and being absurdly overornamented only emphasized her shortcomings.

The pink silk was finished; she would wear it the next
time there was a dance when the temperature was not such
that the dress must be ruined by perspiration its first time
out. She longed to have Angus see her in it, and, oddly,
she pictured Wilkie Andreason's reaction to it, too. Millicent
had made it as Maggie requested, raising her eyebrows
only at the insistence that it be of simple lines with a
minimum of trimming.

Both Ann and Millicent had approved the finished gown
when Maggie had tried it on.

"You look lovely, Margaret," Ann said, smiling, and
Millicent nodded agreement.

"You were right, dear. It suits you this way, although
perhaps just a *touch* of lace, here. . . ."

Maggie shook her head, laughing. "No, Grandma, no
lace!" She had never been more pleased with her own
image in the glass than she was wearing the pink mousseline de soie.

Only now she wasn't sure when she'd have the opportunity to wear it. She couldn't in good conscience go off to a
dance when her sister remained so miserable and her
grandmother was run off her feet seeing to everybody
during the day so that she retired as soon as Sarah had
been settled for the night.

As soon as Celeste is better, she thought. And in the
meantime, even though she didn't see him, there was
Angus to think about.

Saturday evening at supper Jake made his announcement.

"I'm leaving first thing in the morning, going over to
talk to Walt Stover. I probably won't be back until dark,
maybe later than that."

All eyes turned in his direction. Maggie forgot her berry

cobbler and leaned forward eagerly. "Are you going to talk to him about the mill, Daddy?"

He used a toothpick on a stubborn seed caught in his teeth. "I figure the only way to shut Wilkie up is to go talk to Walt, see if Andreason knows what he's talking about. What the hell, at worst I'll only be wasting a Sunday."

Maggie wished she could be there to listen to the conversation. She missed the business talk, the logging crew airing their problems, the association with men instead of only females. Men did interesting things, made the important decisions. She didn't think she'd ever be content to stay at home, like Mama and Grandma, wholly concerned with domestic matters to the exclusion of all else.

Jake was gone before she was up Sunday morning. For the second Sunday nobody went to church, though Millicent gathered the family for a Bible reading after breakfast. Maggie scarcely heard any of it; she was daydreaming about being with Angus again.

She passed the day in desultory activities: leaning over Sarah's crib to wheedle her into smiling, rocking the baby to sleep after Ann had nursed her, sitting beside Celeste's bed while she rested, reading aloud from a rather exciting novel called *Ben Hur* which Ann had borrowed from one of the ladies of the Athenaeum Society.

Celeste fell asleep at last, and Maggie put down the book and silently left the room.

She needed exercise. She called Joe and walked along the river, past the bag boom where the near-tragedy had taken place, indulging in more daydreams, returning to the house shortly before suppertime.

The family was at table, Ann just having said grace, when Jake returned. He took his place, serving up chicken and mashed potatoes and gravy, buttered carrots and boiled cabbage. They ate in silence for several minutes before Maggie, unable to stand it any longer, put her question.

"Daddy? What did Mr. Stover say?"

He raised dark eyebrows dusted with silver. "What? Everything that he said all day long?"

"You know what I mean! Does he want to sell the mill?"

Jake stripped the flesh off a chicken thigh and chewed before he answered. "Well, Wilkie told the truth about *that* all right. Walt doesn't exactly *want* to sell, except that he's in worse trouble if he tries to hang on to it. What he'll settle for, right now, is *out*."

"What will the Stovers do, then, if he can't keep the mill going?"

"He doesn't know yet. He might join his brother, farming down in the Willamette Valley, near Portland. His wife wants him to go to Oregon, she has family down there, too. Or, if it worked out, he'd consider working for the new owner of the mill, for wages." Jake reached for another slice of bread. "That's assuming it would bring in enough money so anybody could pay him."

A crease appeared on Ann's brow, though she said nothing. It was left to Maggie to pry it out of him, word by word. He was going to buy the mill, somehow, she thought with an undercurrent of excitement. It was there in his manner, just under the surface, showing only in his eyes and the way his mouth wanted to quirk at the corners.

"You think you could make it pay," Maggie said, almost an accusation against him for keeping them in suspense this way. "Even the way the economy is now."

The quirk became more definite. "Well, it stands to reason I'd get more of the profits on my timber if I didn't have to pay to have it milled. Enough more, I think, to pay Walt's salary, though I couldn't afford much of a crew to work with him for a while, probably. Evans and Jablonski have already quit; they knew how bad things were, and when they had a chance to work in Seattle, they went, last week. So I'd only have to lay off three men, but if he shuts down, they're out of luck anyway."

Maggie decided to cut through his long-drawn-out story. "Did you tell him you wanted it? Did you reach an agreement with him?"

Jake grinned, but he made her wait until he'd eaten a few more bites. "Can't wait to know, eh? All right. Yes, my little princess, we reached an agreement. He has contracts to deliver another couple of thousand board feet of lumber, and then it's mine."

Millicent and Ann had gone very still. Celeste, not really understanding the ramfications of the recital, watched her father uncertainly. Maggie put the ultimate and crucial question.

"How are we going to pay for it?" She was unaware that she spoke as if she were a partner.

Jake inhaled deeply, then let the air our. "We're going to go into debt, just like Wilkie said. There's a risk—not too bad, at least I don't think so, or I wouldn't be doing it—but this is probably the only chance I'll ever get to buy a mill. I'm sorry Walt's hurting by it, but he's hurt whether I buy it or not. In fact, he's a lot better off with the deal he's making with me than any other way he could have handled it. First of September, you can call it Keating's Mill."

Mrs. Totting had appeared beside him with a tray, and he pushed back his chair. "No pie for me, Mrs. Totting. I have to go out to camp yet tonight. Save me a piece for breakfast, though, all right?"

He stood up, only to pause when Ann addressed him directly for the first time in months.

"Did you mortgage the house? Is that how you did it?"

For a moment Jake's face was devoid of expression, and then he rested a hand on his wife's shoulder and spoke gently. "No, Ann. Your house is in no danger. It's paid for, and it's yours. My security is my timberland." His smile touched them all. "You let me do the worrying and the working; I'll take care of everything."

Maggie had seen her mother flinch when the hand came down on her shoulder, now observed the rigidity fading as Jake turned away. It made her ache, somewhere deep inside, though she was not sure why.

Mrs. Totting served the pie, warm from the oven and oozing deep-purple juice. Maggie inhaled the aroma and cut off a bite which was halfway to her mouth when Ann spoke to her.

"Margaret, can he do it? Can he hold things together, the way the market is now, without losing the timber?"

Maggie gave herself a few seconds to think, using her father's tactic. She put the pie into her mouth and chewed. When she answered, her voice was firm and confident. "Yes. Wilkie thinks so, and so do I. Don't worry, Mama. Daddy won't let anything go wrong."

Ann moistened her lips. "Good," she said. "Good."

Maggie cleaned up her plate, scraping up every bit of juice before she put down her fork. If Jake lost his timber, it would kill him, she thought.

She hoped to God Wilkie was right, and that her father knew what he was doing.

Later that night, a few miles away, in the cook shack where she had carried her mattress because the roof was still leaking over her bunk, Jaisy responded as always to Jake's lovemaking. She knew that Maggie disliked and resented her, and understood why, so she knew as well that what she had with Jake might be temporary. Jaisy didn't think he'd ever patch things up with his wife, not after an estrangement that had lasted as long as this, but it was possible that Mrs. Keating would find a way to put a stop to what was going on, if she chose to.

Jaisy had no idea why Ann Keating hadn't fought for her husband. Jake never talked about his wife, so she didn't know what had caused the rift between them. She didn't really care. All she knew was that she felt safe and loved, and she'd be grateful for that, for as long as it lasted.

He'd told her, with a grin and a slap on the bottom, that she could now address him as *Mister* Keating, since he would soon be a mill owner as well as owner of a logging outfit. He was pleased, and she was pleased for him. Yet she knew him well enough to know that he was not as confident as he sounded.

Going into debt for anything, even something as marvelous as a mill, was not a thing a sensible man did lightly. Using the timberland—the only security of future that he had—was a serious step, and while Jaisy didn't know very much about business, she knew what happened when you put up something for security and couldn't meet your obligations.

Beside her, Jake slept. Jaisy stayed awake, allowing him an hour or so before she would have to rouse him and send him home. She didn't know what would happen to her and the kids if he tired of her, or if that wife or daughter of his found a way to force her out of his life. She only knew that she would enjoy what she had to the fullest, as long as she had anything at all.

It might have amused her had she known that tonight, possibly for the first time, she and Maggie Keating were of one mind. She hoped to God Jake knew what he was doing.

# 27

MAGGIE went with Jake to see the mill in action. She had been tied to the house for days, missing some of the best part of the year to be outside, she thought, except for short walks in the afternoon while Celeste slept.

Though little was said, the family shared a concern over the way that Celeste's cough improved so slowly, if at all. The chills and fever were gone, and the physician pronounced her on the mend, yet his satisfaction was not shared by those who saw her every day.

Celeste had lost weight, so that her clothes hung loosely on her, and there were dark smudges beneath her blue eyes. As Millicent went down with the doctor to let him out, those eyes filled with moisture.

"I don't *feel* better, Margaret. If only I could stop coughing, so I could rest." She didn't mention the nightmares, though Maggie was sure she still had them from time to time. "I'm so *sore*. I feel as if I've been beaten within an inch of my life." She rubbed at the flesh over her rib cage. "And I'm *bored*. Even playing the piano is too much effort to make."

There was nothing Maggie could do to help, except keep her sister company. They had finished reading *Ben Hur* and were now well into a romantic novel that Maggie found exceedingly silly, but their choices were few; any book seemed better than none.

When Jake announced a proposed visit to the mill on a day when it was too windy to work in the woods, Maggie at once put in a bid to accompany him. Even the prospect of getting soaked if the threatening rain developed didn't weigh heavily against the idea of getting out of the house.

She had seen the mill, of course, many times. Yet she'd never been inside it. She would have thought it interesting in any event. Today, knowing that within a few days it would belong to Jake, it was fascinating.

Stover's mill was a small one, operating with a single forty-eight-inch saw to rip the logs lengthwise, after which a pair of cutoff saws would then finish the job by cutting the boards to the desired length. The end product was rough, not planed or sanded as in some of the larger mills, but it looked beautiful to Maggie. The stacked lumber gave off a pungent fragrance like the sawdust she'd played in as a child, and Maggie inhaled it deeply. She was going to like having a mill, she decided.

A few yards away, Jake said something to her. She couldn't make out the words over the buzz of the big saw, but she grinned, and he grinned back.

She stood at one end of the long shed where the milling operation took place, trying not to follow Jake around and listen to what he and Walt Stover were saying. She noticed an old man with a paper carried flat on a shingle, who seemed to be counting or estimating board feet in the stacks of lumber; as soon as Jake had completed his business and they were heading for the buggy, she brought up the subject.

"Somebody has to keep track of how much lumber is cut, don't they? How much stock is on hand, where it goes, who pays for it."

Jake looked into her face, amusement crinkling the skin around his eyes. "You applying for a job, honey?"

"Yes. Let me do it, Daddy. Mrs. Pallison can handle the cooking, especially with Lucy to help, and Wilkie's taken over the bookkeeping. Let me work at the mill, in the office.''

''It's a long way from home.''

''No farther than camp, is it? Let me do it, Daddy.''

He put an arm around her waist and hugged. ''Well, we'll see,'' was his response, but she hugged him back. She knew the answer was *yes*.

Two days later Millicent came to the parlor where Jake was reading the paper while Ann mended a hem, and stood with a letter in her hand, clearing her throat so that they all looked at her.

''A letter from Aunt Lealah?'' Ann asked, biting off a thread. ''Is she all right?''

''She's fine.'' Millicent cleared her throat again, nervously glancing at Jake. He had already gone back to the latest news from Seattle and the other Washington, where Chester Arthur continued his administration in the White House, to the detriment of the country. ''She . . . she'd like me to come and visit her. She's very lonely since Edward died, you know. I suppose it would be terribly expensive. . . . I've been thinking, though. She's always writing about the climate in California. Warm, and dry, even in the winter.'' She hesitated again, then blurted out her idea. ''I wonder if it wouldn't be good for Celeste, to spend the next few months where it's warm and dry, rather than wet and cold, the way it will be here. I've noticed that on wet and windy days she seems to cough more. What do you think?''

Ann put down her mending to consider it, and Jake forgot about President Arthur and his asinine policies that kept the nation submerged in a recession. He scowled.

''You talking about taking Celeste to your sister's? In California?''

Obviously feeling attacked, and compelled to defend herself, Millicent started to crumple the letter, then quickly smoothed it out again. "She's invited me to visit for the winter, and I know she would be delighted if I brought Celeste, too. It's so warm there, and though it rains occasionally it's nothing like the rain here, day after day, and so cold. And there's no snow there at all."

Ann spoke slowly. "It probably would be good for her, though we'd miss her terribly. She might be very home-sick, Mama."

"I know. I've thought of that. But she doesn't really seem to be getting any better, does she, in spite of what Dr. Croyden says. Trouble with the lungs, like that. . . ." She let the words trail off. They all knew how many people died during the winters with respiratory problems. "If everybody wrote to her regularly, it would help. I know"—here she shot a glance at Jake—"we'd have to consider the matter of cost, of course."

Jake ground out his cigar in the receptacle placed at his elbow for that purpose. "I wouldn't send her anywhere she didn't want to go."

"No, no, of course not! I didn't want to mention it to her until I'd consulted with both of you, naturally. Would the cost be within our financial capabilities, do you think? If we went down on one of the steamers to Los Angeles? Lealah would send a buggy for us, for the journey inland; her son would come." She waited hopefully.

Ann, not addressing anyone directly, murmured her opinion. "Perhaps we should think about it."

Maggie waited, breathing suspended, for her father's reaction. When it came, it was anticlimactic. Jake grunted.

"We'll have to see how Celeste feels about such a thing," Ann added. "And perhaps ask Dr. Croyden if he thinks the warmer climate would be beneficial. Providing, of course, that it would be feasible to manage the expense."

Now it was Jake who cleared his throat. "If the doctor thinks it would help her, and she wants to go, I'll come up with the passage money, one way or another."

Millicent nodded, smiled, and left the room. Her parents went back to their mending and reading, and Maggie continued to hold her book in her lap, not seeing the print.

Celeste to go away for the entire winter? Just thinking about it made her throat ache. What if Celeste were horribly homesick and could not return until spring? What if she didn't get better down there in California, more than a thousand miles away? What if they never saw her again?

That prospect, however, didn't seem to enter Celeste's mind when the subject was broached the following day. She perked up, immediately seeing the advantages of a sea voyage down the coast, and of meeting new people in a new place. And when a note came back from Snohomish, in response to the query Ann had written, with Dr. Croyden's opinion that a winter in a warmer climate could indeed be instrumental in clearing Celeste's cough and aiding her return to good health, the planning began in earnest.

The transfer of the mill to Jake's ownership slid into the background as clothes were mended, stitched, and altered. After some consultation it was decided that it was not sensible to fit all garments to Celeste's present measurements, since it was to be hoped that as she regained her health she would fill out once more.

Maggie felt strangely bereft, even before Millicent and Celeste left. She had grown closer to her sister this past month or so, and she knew she'd miss her. Her whole life seemed to be shifting, away from camp, now away from Celeste—though toward what she was not certain. Had it been toward Angus with any clearly discernible pattern, Maggie would have rejoiced, but she hadn't even seen Angus, nor had he sent her any message to lift her spirits. It was as if the episode on the day of the big storm had never taken place.

There wasn't room in the buggy for the entire family to go to Port Gardner to see the travelers off, not if they carried the necessary trunk of clothes to suffice for their stay in California. So Jake drove them, while Maggie and Ann said good-bye at home.

They had no more than reentered the house, Ann with the baby in her arms, than Ann expressed the very feeling that had swept over Maggie. "The house is so empty! However will we bear it, without them both for so long!"

Maggie had no idea, and she did not reply. She felt as hollow as the house, as if someone had died.

September was wetter than usual, which brought the river up so that logs could be floated downstream to the mill, but the rain interfered with normal logging operations. As long as there was no high wind, the men continued to try to work, yet as the mud grew deeper, tempers grew shorter.

Maggie continued to spend some time at camp, pretending not to chafe under Jaisy's now proprietary control of the cookhouse, because it was the only way to see Angus. Even then she saw him only in the presence of the entire crew, which in some ways was worse than not seeing him at all. There were no meaningful glances, no tender words, certainly no caresses.

She saw more of Wilkie than of Angus. Angus worked in the woods except at mealtime, while Wilkie was still compelled to use the cookhouse for his headquarters. While he spent most of his time there with pen and ledgers, he did find time to exchange banter with the cooks, and he made a point of telling Maggie how well she looked, or how becoming her dress was, or complimenting her on her culinary skills. Of course he praised Jaisy's cooking, too, which took a little of the pleasure out of the attention paid to *her*, but Maggie enjoyed his company all the same.

Since the Pallisons would not move back to their cabin by the lake until the operation shut down for the winter, Lucy and Will could not go to school when it opened. So they sat at a different table from Wilkie, when he was there, and did the sums that Maggie wrote out for them; and while she rolled out pie crusts or washed dishes, Lucy read from her reader in halting words.

Jaisy thanked Maggie again. "I don't know much about writing and ciphering," she admitted. "I appreciate you helping the kids, so they won't be so far behind when they get to school later on."

Once more Maggie found it impossible to be gracious, though she tried to be civil. "It's nothing," she said, and turned away.

Her desperation in regard to Angus grew in direct proportion to her loneliness. At home, without either Celeste or Millicent to try to prop up the supper table conversation, the family ate mostly in silence. At first Maggie tried to force some semblance of normality by carrying on all the talk herself, but it was too much to do when Ann did not speak to Jake and Jake did not speak to Ann. She finally gave up and the meals sank to a new low: good food, with no feeling of sharing, no feeling of family. Maggie longed for a letter from her grandmother or her sister, anything that could be read aloud to share, and knew that it might be weeks before any such missive would be delivered to them.

Evenings were pure torture. There was no music, no reading aloud, no laughter and good talk. Jake invariably vanished immediately after supper, if he had bothered to come home at all; he left a standing order to eat without him if he wasn't there on time, since his responsibilities had increased and it was easier to eat at camp with the crew and go on with whatever he could get done while the daylight lasted. Sometimes he rode over to the mill so that the buggy was not even available for their use, though neither of them had anywhere to go, anyway.

If it hadn't been for Nancy, the only other young person in the house, Maggie thought she'd have gone mad.

Nancy's duties were somewhat diminished since there were fewer people in the household, so there was more time to spend with Maggie in her room upstairs, talking, trying on clothes, experimenting with coiffures. Neither of them was as accomplished as Celeste at "doing" hair, but they worked at it and laughed at some of the results. It was the only laughter heard in the house these days, and sometimes Maggie listened to the echoes of it and suddenly felt like crying, instead.

Quite without meaning to, Maggie took on added responsibilities and made more of the decisions about the running of the house. Ann was, for the most part, indifferent to what was cooked or how the place was run. She spent all of Sarah's waking hours trying to teach the child to sit up, or rocking her and singing to her, flooding her with stimuli that might encourage the child to learn. When Sarah slept, Ann withdrew into the novels borrowed from the lending library of the Athenaeum Society, finding in imagination what no longer existed in her own life.

At the end of September, in desperation, Maggie approached her mother. "Mama."

Ann slowly drew herself out of her absorption with the novel in her lap, reluctant to reenter the real world. "Yes? What is it, Margaret?"

"I'd very much like to go to the dance tomorrow night. I can't stay home until Grandma comes back, and I know you can't leave Sarah, but couldn't I go with the Tottings? Mrs. Totting would chaperone us both if we took the buggy."

Ann considered the matter. "Why, yes, I suppose so, if Mrs. Totting doesn't mind."

Relief flooded through her. "Thank you, Mama! I'll go and ask her right now!"

Mrs. Totting was pleased at the thought of having a ride to town rather than having to walk. Nancy, too, was enthusiastic. "What are you going to wear, Maggie?"

"My new pink silk," Maggie said. "Come on, let's go and try things on. Mama mentioned that that blue faille of Celeste's is too short for her now, and it will probably fit you. Then we'll both have new dresses."

For the first time since Millicent and Celeste had left the house, she had something to look forward to.

The evening was off to a good start. The weather was fine, cool and crisp. A spectacular sunset over the Olympics kept them enchanted with its shifting colors as they headed toward town, turning the snowy peaks pink and orange and gold, lifting their spirits with its beauty.

Maggie's eyes searched the crowd as they entered the hall, knowing she looked as well as she'd ever looked in her life. The pink silk clung to her breasts and waist, with a hint of the stylish bustle in Millicent's artful draping at the hips. She wore it unadorned except for a string of crystal beads borrowed from Ann, with tiny matching earrings.

She wanted to see Angus's face when he first glimpsed her, confident that he would be brought to the realization that he had been shamefully neglecting her. And then, as she saw Wilkie across the room, she decided that it wouldn't hurt to be discovered in company with another attractive man.

She didn't have to actively seek Wilkie out. He turned and saw her, expression frozen for a few seconds in a gratifying reaction, then strode to her side.

"Maggie-Margaret! You will stun us all tonight! What a magnificent gown, and how beautiful you look!"

What female could have resisted such a greeting?

She was flushed and happy, the center of the attention of a remarkably handsome young man. After a short time in his company, Maggie realized that Wilkie was in high spirits, too.

He whirled her around the floor to the lively beat of the

music until she needed to catch her breath, when they sat out one number to sip at glasses of cider and talk. Wilkie was grinning, and not entirely because he'd enjoyed being her partner for the dance.

"Are you pleased? At being mill owners?"

"Yes, though"—she felt she could admit it to Wilkie, who certainly understood all the financial aspects of the matter—"it worries me a little that Daddy had to put up timberland for security."

"That's standard procedure. Not only with timberland, but whatever a man has that's of value. It's virtually the only way a man can expand his business, unless he inherits money from a rich relative. Or"—the grin widened—"marries it."

It suddenly occurred to her that Wilkie was uncommonly pleased, himself, for having brought her father and Walt Stover together. She blurted the question without thinking. "What are you getting out of it?"

For a moment she thought his grin faltered, though she might have imagined that; a few seconds later it was still in place, seemingly unchanged. "The satisfaction of seeing your father, my employer, improve his lot. And of seeing another employer, Walt Stover, getting out of a bad situation with minimal damage. Or, rather, the least damage he could have sustained without going under entirely. I'd have lost my job with Stover. I hope this way I'm going to expand the work I do for Jake Keating."

"I've asked to be allowed to work in the office at the mill," Maggie told him. "Someone has to keep track of what's being cut, what's already stacked, where it's going, that kind of thing. So don't count on that being part of your bookkeeping job."

"I won't. I'll be glad to have you doing that part of it; you have a good head for figures, and when I get them from you, I'll know they're right." Wilkie drained his glass and put it down. "Are you ready to dance again?"

She was waltzing with Wilkie half an hour later, feeling like the princess her father sometimes called her, when Angus showed up. To be truthful, she had almost forgotten about the impression she hoped to make on Angus. She was thoroughly enjoying herself, a situation enhanced by the sidelong glances from her friends that acknowledged Wilkie Andreason's attentions to her.

The music ended and Wilkie stopped with a flourish, drawing her momentarily very close to him so that she felt a quickening of pulses; she knew her color was high, and that it would be becoming.

And then Angus touched her shoulder, speaking to Wilkie without looking at him. "I hope you've got another partner for the next dance, Andreason, because I think this one is mine."

For a moment there was such resistance in Wilkie's face that Maggie spoke quickly. "Thank you, Wilkie. Angus, you're bleeding."

He lifted a hand to his jawline, scowling. "Still? It had stopped once. I must have knocked the scab off it. I cut myself shaving." He turned his back to Wilkie and, since the music had not yet resumed, took Maggie's elbow and swung her away toward the refreshment table. "Come on, let's get something to drink."

His touch was electrifying, and she suspected she looked as pleased as she felt, but she couldn't stop herself from saying, "Angus, you were really rather rude to Wilkie."

"I don't like him," Angus said. "Shall we go outdoors for a minute, get a breath of air? We can get some cider when we come back inside."

"Why don't you like him?"

He gave her an unfathomable look and didn't reply, his touch still burning through the sleeve of her dress as they moved toward the doorway. He smiled at her. "You're looking very pretty tonight, Maggie. New dress?"

"Yes." She didn't have to ask if he liked it. That

showed in his face. "Oh, it's chilly out here. Maybe I should get my wrap. . . ."

It was dark, though the half-moon kept the darkness from being absolute. There were several other couples, shadowy forms moving away from the lighted doorway on either side, and Angus drew her at once into a break in the bushes alongside the building.

"I'll warm you up," he promised, and drew her into his arms.

Maggie lifted her face for his kiss, feeling that gelatinous lethargy creeping through her—she had not imagined the sensation, it had actually happened that other time, and was now happening again—and allowed her body to be molded to the lean length of his in an embrace that left them both breathing heavily.

"Oh, Angus, I've missed you." The words were low and intense, as heartfelt as any she'd ever spoken.

"I've missed you, too. God, I've missed you!" He kissed her again, this time holding her face between his hands, and she began to have some idea why those silly females in popular novels swooned at a man's touch. "Maggie, Maggie, how am I going to stand it, if you don't come to camp anymore? Listen, we'll have to meet somewhere else, and I don't mean here at these stupid dances with everybody in town keeping track of how much time you spend outside, and who with."

Maggie hadn't yet considered that; now she remembered that Mrs. Totting was supposedly chaperoning her, and would take her duties seriously, so she dare not stay out here more than a few minutes.

"Where?" she asked breathlessly. This was how she had envisioned romance: secret meetings and stolen kisses. The blood raced within her; she forgot that she'd been cold.

"Tomorrow night," Angus said. "Can you take a walk, just after supper, without making anybody suspicious?

Stroll out toward camp, and we'll meet somewhere in the middle.''

"I can't stay out much past dark or Mama will wonder," Maggie said, though she was not at all certain that Ann would notice, at least not until after she'd settled Sarah in for the night. And it was unlikely that Jake would even be there. "I could say that Nancy and I are going to be doing something in my room, and then caution Nancy to stay out of sight, as she usually does, anyway. Mama almost never checks on me once I've gone to my room."

His chuckle sent prickles along her spine. "You're a natural-born conspirator. All right, tomorrow at dusk, on the skid road. We should meet about at that big dead cedar, the one with the eagle's nest in it." He kissed her once more, long and deep until she was dizzy with sensations that frightened her, a little, though not enough to outweigh the thrill of them. "Come on, we'd better go back in. And try not to look as if you've just been kissed," he suggested, laughing.

There was no way she could control that. She felt the heat in her entire body and knew it was in her face, as well; she needed the cold cider, needed to calm down before she dared get near Mrs. Totting. The cook would see through her at once, Maggie suspected.

Nancy certainly did. They met at the refreshment table, and her friend took one look at Maggie and narrowed her eyes. When Maggie could only smile helplessly, Nancy reached over to squeeze her hand, laughing back, though no words were said.

She danced with Angus, and then with Adam Welker (who talked only of Nancy and whether or not Maggie thought Nancy liked him; Maggie's spirits, already soaring, led her to pretend ignorance on the subject, though urging him to gather his courage and find out), and after that with a series of partners who all found her especially pretty and vivacious.

The only partner who brought her down, a little bit, was Wilkie. "What do you see in that oaf?" he asked.

Maggie feigned innocence. "Who? Sol Engstrom?"

"McKay! He acts as if he owns you."

Even in her near jubilant state, Maggie had sense enough to dissemble. "Angus? He's like an older brother. I've known him since I was a very little girl. The whole crew acts as if they're my keepers, when Daddy isn't around." She wondered if she sounded convincingly disgruntled at that. "They mean well, though. It's because they think I'm still a child."

Wilkie's irritation faded. "One thing you're not, Maggie-Margaret. And that's a child. You're a remarkable young woman, and I'd be very pleased if you'd allow me to call on you tomorrow afternoon. Would I dare to do it without your parents' prior permission?"

She was so astonished that she stepped on his foot, and had to apologize. "Call on me?"

His amusement made her feel that perhaps she *was* rather immature. "That's what a man usually does, when he meets a girl he likes particularly well."

"Do you? Like me particularly well?" Maggie could have bitten her tongue when Wilkie laughed. Her habit of speaking her mind without thinking about it first obviously was one to be curbed, at least when in the company of young men. She felt gauche and stupid, though there was certainly nothing in his manner that indicated he thought any the less of her for her candidness.

On the contrary, he reached for her hand and squeezed it. "Yes, Maggie, I do like you very much. What do you think? If I were to call unannounced, would they turn me away? Or would I be invited in for a cup of tea?"

She was completely taken aback. She had enjoyed his company, had perhaps even more enjoyed the envious glances of the other females when she was with him; it hadn't occurred to her that he might have feelings for her beyond mere friendship.

The idea was disconcerting, flattering, and disturbing. She was not immediately sure which of those was the most overpowering.

And there was Angus, with whom she'd arranged an assignation for tomorrow evening.

If she'd given herself time to think it over, she might possibly have had the good sense to let him down easily and put an end to his hopes before they were fully raised. She could not quite bring herself to do that, however.

A few months ago she'd deplored the fact that she had no suitor; now, it seemed, she had two. How could she fail to be intrigued by that?

"Perhaps," she said, working it out as she spoke, "it would be better to give me time to sound Mama out. If she thinks it's all right, you could come the following Sunday."

Disappointment was clearly written on his countenance. "That's a long time to wait. I've missed seeing you, Maggie-Margaret Keating. It isn't the same at camp without you."

"It isn't the same for me, either," Maggie said, only realizing later that her wording might have led him to misconstrue her meaning as an affirmation of reciprocal feelings toward him.

He spared her having to say any more. "No doubt you're right. Why risk getting off on the wrong foot when by waiting a week we can do it properly? Come on, let's dance."

On the way home Nancy chattered in an animated fashion about what had been her most successful evening yet with Adam Welker. He had recently gone to work for a logging outfit near Lake Stevens as a whistle punk, and while that was the lowliest of the low as jobs went, it *was* a paying position. It meant he could begin to look to the future. While he had made no declaration of any sort,

Nancy was convinced, especially after hearing the things he had asked Maggie about her, that he intended she should be a part of that future.

Maggie heard only about half of what Nancy said. Her own mind drifted back over the evening, remembering everything said and done. Tomorrow evening she would meet Angus, alone, and he would kiss her again; her blood pumped in fiery anticipation.

## 28

MAGGIE stood in the doorway, watching her mother tuck Sarah in for the night, waiting for a reply to her question.

Ann turned sharply, obviously taken off-balance. "To call on you? Mr. Andreason, the bookkeeper?"

"Yes. Next Sunday afternoon, he said. If it's all right. It *is* all right, isn't it?"

Ann moved toward her so that Maggie backed into the hallway and her mother closed the bedroom door before replying. "I know you've been going to the dances for some time, but somehow it didn't occur to me that . . ." She stopped, inexplicable tears forming in her eyes as she looked into her daughter's face. "Oh, Margaret, are you really of an age for *courting?*"

"I'll be sixteen in the spring," Maggie reminded her. "Lots of girls marry at sixteen. You were only eighteen when you married Daddy."

Ann sighed. "Sixteen. Dear heaven, where have the years gone? I'm middle-aged, and my children have grown up, and I didn't even see it happening. Do you already care for Mr. Andreason, Margaret? Or are you simply flattered that a gentleman is showing you attention?''

"Well . . . I *like* Wilkie, of course.'' Maggie didn't know what to say. She wasn't sure she was wise to have asked about having a gentleman caller, except that it was one way to sound out her parents without risking what she had with Angus. She didn't know whether to believe it or not, that Jake had warned his crew away from her in such terms that nobody dared cross him.

She decided to be as honest as she could. "I certainly don't fancy myself *in love* with him.''

Was it relief she read in her mother's face? Yes, it was. Ann's words proved it. "Well, thank heaven for that! I'm afraid, though, that we'll have to consult with your father on a matter such as this one. It isn't a decision I can make by myself, dear.''

The thought of facing Jake with the same request was suddenly enough to make her palms clammy. Her parents ought to be talking together, not existing in this unnatural way in the same household, as strangers after seventeen years of marriage.

"Mama, would you ask him? Would you explain that Wilkie's asked to call, and see what he says?''

Ann hesitated. Maggie read the reluctance, saw that it would cost her mother dearly. Pride, certainly. She felt a deep, poignant ache for the marriage that had gone awry, the love that had been lost. Surely they had loved each other once. What had happened, what *could* happen, to make a couple stop loving each other?

Visibly, Ann pulled herself together. "Yes, of course, Margaret. Give me a day or two. I'd like to choose my time.'' Her smile flickered wanly. "It might make a difference in his answer, if it's the right time.''

Maggie gave her mother a spontaneous hug. "Thank you, Mama. I appreciate it.''

The tears glimmered still in Ann's eyes. "I haven't done much for you in a long while, have I? I've begun to realize that, this past week or so. With Celeste gone, and Mama, the house is so empty. And I know it's just as empty for you, maybe more so, because I have Sarah to fill so much of my time. I see that you and I have drawn apart—so long ago that I don't even know how it happened. You were such a difficult little girl and I got used to thinking of you that way, even when you no longer caused any problems. . . ."

To Maggie's horror, the tears spilled over, running unchecked down her mother's cheeks. "I'm sorry, Margaret. I didn't mean it to happen, believe me. Any more than I intended . . ." Her words trailed off, and then resumed on a firmer note. "What is she like? That Pallison woman?"

Maggie's throat worked for a moment before she could produce audible sounds. "She's . . . cheap. Ignorant. Well meaning, I think, but ignorant."

"Attractive, though, in a rather coarse way, isn't she? I've wondered and wondered, what it is he sees in her." Ann was blinded now by the tears, ashamed of them and of what she had revealed. "And now I've distressed you, too, but you knew about her, didn't you? About Mrs. Pallison and your father?"

The pain in Maggie's throat deepened, spreading through her chest. She hadn't meant to precipitate anything like this. She couldn't reply. She didn't need to; Ann read the answer in her face.

"Sometimes I feel I cannot face anyone, can't go to church, or to the stores to shop, or anywhere, because I'm afraid I'll see it on all the faces, the knowledge that my husband is unfaithful to me." Her face crumpled, and at last she brought up her hands to cover her mouth and her eyes. "I'm sorry," she choked, "I have no right to burden you this way, with a subject not fit for any young girl to know about, but there's no one to talk to anymore.

Sometimes I feel that I'll *die* without someone to talk to! Forgive me, Margaret!''

She spun on her heel, and was gone, back into the bedroom where Sarah lay sleeping, before Maggie could do more than lift a hand to extend after her.

For a moment the hatred rose so fiercely in her, for Jaisy Pallison, for her father, that Maggie felt suffocated with it. How dare he do this to her mother! she thought. How dare he?

There was no answer to that, either. He *did* dare, and he'd made it clear he intended to go on with the illicit relationship, no matter what anyone thought.

Maggie walked to the end of the hall, looking out on her beloved woods behind the house, and wondered why and how such things could happen, and how one was suppposed to cope with the grief of them.

It was a good thing they were used to her going for long walks. Ann had never understood how anybody could spend hours simply wandering around, even in bad weather, looking at thousands of identical trees or staring into burbling little streams with apparent absorption. To Jake, walking was no more than a way to get from one place to another, an interval between jobs when he could think out his problems and come up with solutions to them.

To Maggie, however, the exercise was essential, and most important of all was the fact that when she was alone in the woods, she was free. She could let her mind wander, imagine the most outrageous adventures (in which she always performed rather well), and feel her soul soaring with the eagles that nested in the trees along the riverbank. There was rejuvenating peace in the solitude and tranquillity. Somehow a walk in her favorite places could often help put her problems into perspective, so that even if she couldn't solve them, she would at least be better able to live with them.

She had thought of her mother's words—"You were such a difficult little girl"—long after she was sure her mother had forgotten them. Was I? Maggie wondered. Is it really so terrible to be different from everybody else? To enjoy different activities and interests, how could that be wrong? She was glad Ann had spoken to her so frankly; it was the most honest exchange Maggie could remember between them. She thought it implied trust, and affection, and sorrow that things had not been better between them, all these years. Yet it hurt, too, not so much because Ann had thought her difficult—she'd always been aware of that— but because Ann's own anguish had been laid bare.

It hurt, too, because it put her father in such an incontrovertibly bad light.

Maggie loved them both, but it was Jake she'd always loved best. Everybody knew it, though Maggie hadn't realized that until one day when she and Celeste had wanted something they thought they would be refused. Maggie no longer remembered what the something had been, but she'd never forgotten what her sister had said.

"I'll ask Mama, and you ask Papa," Celeste proposed, and Maggie, considering this to be overkill, demanded to know why they should go to such lengths when permission from one parent would be sufficient.

At the age of eight, Celeste had proved her wisdom. "Because," Celeste said, "you're Papa's favorite, and he's more likely to say yes to *you*, and I'm Mama's favorite, and she's more likely to say yes to *me*."

Each of them had won an affirmative response from her favorite parent, and Maggie was convinced within her heart that had they each approached the *other* parent, the results would have been quite the opposite. It was a system they had used to good advantage several times since then: without conscious thought Maggie had always taken it for granted that if she wanted something very much, the one to ask was her father.

Only in this matter of giving permission to a suitor to call, she did not want to be the one to face Jake. Not even if it meant that her mother must speak to him, when she otherwise would not have done so, for Maggie suddenly lacked the courage to broach the subject to him.

It was only that Angus had made her feel peculiar, she thought, about an open courtship on his part. He insisted that Jake would not take kindly to any suitor, at least not one from among his logging crew, and that insistence had intimidated her. Her father could not reasonably keep all men away from her forever, she thought. Especially when she'd grown up running unfettered in a logging camp.

She saw no indication that Ann had yet made any move to approach Jake on the subject. Jake spent Sunday morning at the mill, came home to eat, and immediately vanished again, without saying where he was going, though it didn't take much intuition to guess, Maggie thought bitterly.

At any rate, there was only Ann to consider when it came time to leave the house. Maggie had been almost too nervous to eat supper, though she'd managed enough to avoid comment from her mother.

For the most part they ate in silence. Once Ann smiled at her across the too large table and said, "You know, I think Sarah is getting stronger. She sat up for a few seconds by herself, with only a little help from me."

"That's wonderful," Maggie said, her face nearly cracking with the attempt at a natural smile. She was acutely aware of the empty places, and for a moment imagined that the ghosts of the others sat on either side of her, then wondered what was the matter with her.

It was an unnatural household, that was all, she told herself. Other families shared their activities and their thoughts around the supper table, as the Keatings had once done. She had hated her parents' squabbling, but the silence was far worse, and this—having nobody here except Ann and herself—was terrible.

"I'm going for a long walk," she said as soon as they rose from the meal. "I feel like walking for hours and hours."

"Not near the river," Ann said, anxiety touching her face.

"No, just as far down as the skid road. Don't worry, Mama, I won't fall in. The water's down again, anyway. Don't worry about me if I don't come right back; I want to walk until I'm really tired."

Ann paused, one hand on the back of a chair. "Haven't you been sleeping well, dear?"

"Not particularly well," Maggie said, a gross exaggeration, yet a convenient one. "I'm used to much more exercise. When Daddy lets me start going down to the mill on a regular basis, I'll feel better."

"I hate to see you taking on a job like that. I never liked your being in the cookhouse, and this will be just as bad."

"I'd much rather do those things than sit around home, sewing or knitting. I'm no good at those things, Mama. Lots of women work in their family businesses. I like dealing with figures and getting out of the house."

Ann's smile was rueful. "I know. I don't understand, but I know. You've always been different, Margaret, and I haven't always understood you. But I do love you, you know."

The declaration was so unexpected that Maggie felt tears in her eyes. "I love you, too, Mama. I wish your life were happier," she blurted, and saw her mother's mouth twist in an effort to keep her lips steady.

"My life is what I've made it, I suppose," Ann said. "Or what God wanted it to be. I don't know quite why He's chosen this path for me, but it's the one I have, and I'll make the best of it. Have a good walk, dear, and take Joe with you. I feel better, knowing he's there, too."

"I can't get away without Joe," Maggie told her. "I'll be back in an hour or two."

She let herself out of the house into the evening chill, not feeling it. Already the blood sang through her veins, warming her, at the thought of meeting Angus.

Joe came at her call, and they set off at a brisk pace. It would not be dark for another hour, and in any case she was not nervous about darkness in the woods, which were as familiar to her as her own home. On the way back, Angus would be with her, and she knew that with Angus she would fear nothing, nobody.

Except, she thought, perhaps her father. If Angus was right about him. She'd have liked to ask someone else— Red Risku, or Tom Dunnigan, perhaps—if Jake had actually warned the crew away from her in such terms that no sane man would have overstepped the boundaries so drawn. She dared not. It would be a clue to the fact that she and Angus shared something forbidden, and she couldn't risk it.

Joe saw him before she did. The hound yelped a greeting and ran on ahead, and Maggie felt the enveloping joy that was, oddly, tinged with shyness as well.

He had kissed her on two occasions, yet she was suddenly hesitant, stopping first so that it was he who strode the last dozen yards between them.

He didn't kiss her this time. He was smiling, and he looked down into her face with such happiness that her momentary uncertainty was washed away.

"Come on, let's walk back to the river," he said, reaching for her hand, and she was comfortable again, with her old friend, Angus.

Afterward she couldn't remember much of what they'd talked about. It had been ordinary conversation such as they'd always shared, about camp, the cooking, the rest of the crew, the weather, the prospects for working late into the fall.

None of it romantic, except for the fact that they walked

hand in hand. Until Angus abruptly asked, as they sat on a huge boulder beside the Pilchuck, "What in hell are we going to do when the weather turns cold? The fuzzy caterpillars are more black than brown; the Indians say that means a hard winter, or an early one. We can't meet in the woods in the rain or the snow. And seeing you at a public dance a few times a month isn't going to satisfy me."

"Or me," Maggie agreed, smiling. "If Daddy would give his permission, would you come calling at the house?"

His eyebrows went up. "You thinking of asking him?"

"Well, not exactly. Not yet." She put down the twinge of guilt at the knowledge that she was asking permission for Wilkie, not for Angus; she didn't think this was a good time to reveal that. "But I'll be sixteen in the spring, and he's going to have to agree to let me see young men sometime."

Absently, he lifted her hand to his mouth and kissed the back of it, sending marvelous tremors through her, then turned the hand over to brush her fingertips with his lips. "I wish I had something to offer you, Maggie. Something that didn't depend on me working for your father. Enough pay to save something out of. The last of my sisters just got married, so I don't have to keep sending money home anymore, the way I've been doing for the past ten years. My mother's going to live with them. I have my full pay now, but it still comes from Jake Keating."

All this time she'd known him, and she'd never realized he was helping his widowed mother to support his younger sisters. She had not, in truth, given much thought to finances, assuming that any man who had a job could support a wife. It sent a jolt of uneasiness through her.

He had done with kissing her fingers and now allowed their joined hands to rest on his knee, another contact that distracted her from what he was saying. "Maybe this winter I'll start building a place of my own. Not in town, I don't want to have to buy a lot, but there's land for the taking upstream. And plenty of timber to build from, if I use logs instead of milled lumber. Nothing fancy, just something that will belong to me. It would give me an excuse to pass by Keating's Landing, on the way from town.''

She was silent, heart beating audibly, waiting for him to come up with a perfect solution to their problem. She had taken it for granted that when the time came Angus would know all the answers, be able to sidestep any difficulties, and sweep her away in a romantic frenzy of mutual ecstasy.

It was only now becoming clear that this would not be the case. She, as well as Angus, would have to consider the practicalities.

Yet she had faith in Angus and in the love she felt for him. She leaned toward him, sparking an immediate response as his hand tightened around hers.

''We'll find a way. Won't we?''

''We'll find a way,'' Angus promised, and drew her into his arms, as she had been waiting for him to do.

It wasn't until the darkness had settled in earnest, and the rock seat grew uncomfortably hard and cold beneath them, that they drew reluctantly apart.

Maggie was at once aware of the dropping temperature. ''I suppose I'd better go. When will I see you again?''

''Tell you what. You take walks all the time, don't you? So if you head out along the skid road every evening after supper, walk as far as that dead cedar, I'll try to do the same. I won't always be able to make it. Jake's working us hard, long hours. He wants to get as much timber out as he can before it gets too wet to work anymore, and we're spending more time repairing equipment than we should be. Some of what we're using is damned near past fixing. It should be replaced, only he says there's no money to replace it yet, not until he gets paid for this year's timber.

If it's a choice between walking out to see you and sharpening my saw, it'll have to be the saw.''

He laughed softly. ''I'd rather choose you, but I'd play hell bringing down trees with a dull saw, and Jake won't stand for us doing the sharpening during daylight hours when we could be in the woods. It's the best I can do right now. And I'll be at the dance Saturday night, of course.''

She didn't have to consider the matter. ''All right. I'll be at the dead cedar every evening, if I can get away. I'll be disappointed when you don't come, but if I don't see you within a quarter of an hour, I'll just go on back home.''

''Good.'' He reached for her once more, kissing her lightly on the lips. ''God, you're lovely, Maggie. You were such a skinny little girl, with eyes too big for your face and bones sticking out all over. Remember, when you thought you were ugly, and you'd never be beautiful like your sister?''

''I'm still not beautiful like Celeste,'' Maggie said honestly. ''I never will be.''

''I told you then, you'd be more stunning someday. All those bones were too big for you, and you didn't have enough meat over them.'' The back of his hand brushed the front of her dress, causing a quickening of sensation throughout every part of her. ''Now you're filling out in all the proper places, and you've become a beauty, Maggie. You really have. Just don't let anybody else tell you that, will you?''

The guilt returned, sharp, accusatory. She laughed and hoped it didn't sound as false to him as it did to her. ''I don't exactly have suitors lining up to pay me compliments,'' she said, which was only a *small* lie. One other man didn't constitute a line, did he?

''They will,'' Angus said with conviction. ''Until I have a brand on you, they will. There're at least four men on the crew who would have, already, if they weren't afraid Jake would break their necks.''

''Really? Who?'' she demanded, intrigued.

Her quick question made him laugh aloud. "I'm not going to tell you that, sweetheart. You think I'm crazy? You might decide one of them would be a better catch than I am." His amusement faded. "Maybe they are. God knows I'm no great catch, but I'll tell you this. I don't intend to work for somebody else all my life, and I don't intend to keep my wife and family in a log cabin forever, either. It may take a while, but I'll provide for you the same as Jake has, as soon as I can."

He wrapped her in a hug that was intended to be a quick farewell gesture, but that went on until Maggie felt she was being drawn into his very soul, and he to hers. The flesh seemed to melt on her bones as their mouths fused, bodies straining together in an urgency born of their mutual need.

With a shuddering breath, Angus at last broke free, setting her firmly away from him.

"Oh, girl, what you do to me! Go home. Go home now, before I do something I'll be sorry for. I'm not even going to walk you to the house, I don't trust myself that far, even if there's no danger of anybody seeing us." He laughed a little. "I may have to be careful going back to camp, make sure I don't meet Jake coming home. He'd want to know what was making me so damned happy, and I sure couldn't tell him. Good night, Maggie."

It was all she could do to summon her own voice. "Good night, Angus. I'll see you tomorrow, I hope."

He didn't reply to that, taking off in quick strides into the deeper darkness of the woods, leaving her to make her own way up the embankment and along the path with Joe at her side.

Her father *was* at camp, then, which could mean only one thing. He wasn't doing business there at this time of night. There was no legitimate task that could be done in the dark. If he was there with Jaisy, Angus knew it, and no doubt so did everyone else. Why did anger at her father have to spoil what she felt?

She was still shaken, tremulous, breathing rapidly. She had covered half the distance from the landing to the house when she stopped, struck by a totally new idea.

Was this, what she was feeling, what her father felt with Jaisy Pallison?

She had pictured the two of them many times, together on Jaisy's mattress in the blackness, doing wicked things. She was vague about the exact nature of that sin, the breaking of the commandment about adultery, though because of her conversations with Nancy Totting she was not in total ignorance.

It had never occurred to her, however, until this very moment, that Jake might be drawn to Jaisy in the same irresistible way that Maggie herself was drawn to Angus.

Was this why Jake constantly sought out the other woman? Denied his wife's affections—and there was no question that Ann had refused him her bed, or he wouldn't have been sleeping across the hall all these months— did he feel he must find that shatteringly overwhelming passion from some other source? Could anyone, once aware of the true nature of such rapture, willingly give it up?

The idea shocked her as nothing else in her life ever had. She, who had not yet fully experienced what was possible between a man and a woman, was so transformed by Angus's kisses, his caresses, that she felt a totally different person.

Her entire outlook on everything in life had changed; colors took on more depth, her awareness of everything from the beat of her heart to the slightest change in vocal intonation from her beloved had increased a hundredfold, and there was more to come.

In the cool darkness, she felt heat in her face—no, throughout her body—and knew that she looked forward to surrendering totally to Angus as she had never looked forward to anything else in her life.

Was that, she wondered, forcing herself to move again along the invisible path, what it was like for her father? He had told her, sadly but firmly, that she did not know what she asked of him, when she'd begged him to break off the relationship.

Now she knew.

<br>

# 29

THE heightened awareness stayed with her. Maggie found herself studying each of her parents—indeed, everyone around her—with a new perceptiveness that was as disturbing as it was revealing.

How did Jake really feel about Ann? Maggie wondered. She had blamed him, strongly and bitterly, for the rift between them, and she still didn't know, of course, what had caused it. Now she was faced with at least a hint of understanding of what it would be like for a man whose wife had ejected him from her bed, from her affection, even denying him her conversation.

What would *she* feel like if Angus, having loved her, withdrew that love? Now that she knew what it was like to drown in an embrace, a kiss? Would she, like Jake, seek that passion elsewhere?

Could anyone, once having known such enchantment, simply give it up without regrets? Resign oneself to the lack of something as vital as life itself?

She knew the answer to that. Her resentment of Jaisy had not yet faded, but she had begun to empathize a bit more with her father.

She didn't know if she understood anything about her mother, except that she, too, obviously suffered from the estrangement, though perhaps not in the same ways. It was true that Sarah was not a normal child; her development was very slow, and she required more time than Ann had given to either of her older daughters. Still, even Sarah did not demand *all* of her mother's attention; there should still have been some time to devote to a husband had Ann cared to do so.

Though it appeared that the choice was Ann's, it was impossible to know for certain. Maggie did know that it was Ann who had asked Jake to move out of the bedroom they had shared, using Sarah and her needs as an excuse. That excuse was no longer valid, for Sarah now slept through most nights the same as any other child of ten months; there was no real reason why she could not have been given a room of her own.

Maggie had tended to see the world around her, the people and their behavior, in shades of black and white. Black was bad, white was good. Now, as she turned introspective, she realized that a great many things could legitimately be viewed in varying shades of gray.

The animosity she had felt toward Jake in regard to Jaisy softened. How could she look at him, see how he was aging, see how the pressures of life drained him of his former vitality, without concern? And, on the few occasions when she went to camp, how could she watch him in Jaisy's presence, and not have at least a reluctant flicker of compassion?

Not that there was anything open between them, not to the casual observer. Jaisy was no more likely to allow her hand to brush Jake's when she served his coffee than to do so with anyone else. They exchanged no personal remarks.

Their voices, in speaking of mundane matters, were kept carefully under control. If there were speaking looks, it would take a sharper observer than Maggie to intercept them.

Yet there *was* something. Some spark between them, that could not be entirely hidden.

After a while Maggie thought she knew what it was. Jake seemed more relaxed, more his old familiar self, when in Jaisy's presence. He laughed more easily. He was less irritable, less unreasonable when one of the crew reported some new crisis, large or small, of running the operation. The lines, so deep in his face at times that he was almost a caricature of the man she remembered from a few years ago, seemed to smooth out, to make some of the years drop away, at least briefly.

Maggie watched Jaisy, too, though that was harder to do because Jaisy had a perceptiveness of her own. She was likely to meet Maggie's eyes almost at once, and while Maggie read no hostility there—only a guarded neutrality—she would flush and feel forced to turn away.

Still, she had looked enough to be convinced that Jaisy returned whatever it was that Jake offered her. She didn't sleep with him like the whore Ann had inferred she was. Perhaps she had been desperate, after Hank's death, for Jake's help, and had repaid him in the only way she could; but now there was no doubting the liking, the affection, between them. And if there was passion on Jake's part, why was it not equally possible that what he felt was love, and that Jaisy felt the same way?

Maggie could not refrain from thinking about the two of them, imagining them together, and her thoughts caused both embarrassment and excitement, because they made her remember how she had felt when she was with Angus. She'd always thought of what her father and Jaisy did with disgust. Now, though she could not condone it, it was impossible not to have some sympathy for them, and perhaps even a touch of envy.

It was more difficult to read her mother. Ann, after her unexpected confidences, was restored to calmness and the cool detachment she had displayed as far back as Maggie could remember. In repose, her mother showed lines, too, though less pronounced than Jake's. Her mouth had taken on a seemingly permanent droop of sadness, except when she was with Sarah. Yet she did not allow any further openings for Maggie to confide in her, or offer any confidences of her own.

It was Friday evening, and Maggie still had no word on the subject about which she had asked Ann to intercede for her. She had mixed feelings, by this time, about even going through with it. She knew she didn't want Wilkie to court her; she wanted Angus. She could simply tell Wilkie that her parents had decided she was too young for courting. He'd never know the difference, and the burden would be lifted from her conscience.

On the other hand, if they gave permission for Wilkie to call, she could justifiably argue that Angus be allowed to call, too, and solve the problem of how to meet him through the bad weather without the misery of assignations in rain or snow. If they said no to Wilkie, she might at least get an idea whether their objections were personal, or general—if not Wilkie, then anyone else? And if she asked permission for Angus, and they said no, it could well make it far more difficult, even impossible, for her to see him at all, since they would then be on guard.

She was still in a quandary, having actually rehearsed the words to retract her request, when she came down after supper in the evening to learn that Jake had come home. They had eaten without him, and now her mother was confronting him over the meal Mrs. Totting had brought into the dining room.

The housekeeper had gone back to the kitchen. The only

lighted lamp was on the table between her parents; Maggie herself stood in the darkness of the hall, having come to an abrupt halt when she heard her mother's opening words.

"Jake, I need to talk to you."

"Well, that's a novelty." Jake picked up his fork and speared a slice of side pork, biting off the end of it as Maggie eased into the deeper shadows at the base of the stairs. She could see her father plainly; all that was visible of Ann was her hands, gripping the back of the chair behind which she stood facing him. Even in the lamplight, Maggie thought she could make out white knuckles. Had it really taken that much courage for her mother to speak to her own husband on a family matter?

Jake paused in his chewing. "What's the matter? Something wrong with Sarah?"

"No. No, nothing's wrong with anyone. There's a decision to be made, and I told Margaret I could not make it by myself." The pale fingers curled even more tightly around the chair back.

"Maggie? I've already told her she can work in the office at the mill, but she'll have to wait to start until I can go with her so we can work out just what she'll have to do. Old Smythe said he'll show us. Maybe the next rainy day."

"It's not about the mill. It's about having a gentleman caller."

Jake forgot about eating. "It's about *what?*"

"I said it's about Margaret having—"

"I heard what you said. A caller? *Courting?* Maggie?"

"She's nearly sixteen—"

"She's not near old enough!"

"—and that's only a little younger than many girls marry."

Jake made one of those grunting sounds that so often passed for his opinion these days. "And see how we turned out. Hardly a persuasive argument for early marriage."

"She isn't asking to get married, only to have a caller. And if she were, it would hardly be an early marriage, Jake. Many girls are mothers by the time they're fifteen or sixteen."

"Not my daughters." Maggie watched the scowl form on his face. "If one of those louts from my crew has dared to make advances—I warned them all from the time she was twelve to stay away from her. I told them I'd fire a man first, and break his neck afterward, if anybody touched her."

The seemingly disembodied hands released the chair back, stretching as if they had cramped, then reattaching themselves to the polished wood. "I'm just as concerned about her as you are, and she *is* growing up. She can't be kept away from all men, forever. And it's the men in your logging crew that she knows. What do you have against loggers? You were one when *we* married."

"One with ambition, not content to drink away my pay and let his family go hungry." Was that an oblique reference to Hank Pallison? "Who is it? Who is the nervy son of a bitch?"

"How can I talk to you when you take this attitude?"

"What attitude? You don't expect me to be concerned about my daughter?" He had lost interest in his supper, pushing the plate back. "Just tell me, Ann. Who is the gentleman she wants to call?"

"Wilkie Andreason. Did you warn him away from her, too? He's an educated man, isn't he? Refined, polite?"

"Wilkie!" Jake swore, and for once Ann didn't remonstrate over the blasphemy. "Why, he's no man at all. More interested in keeping his boots clean than doing a job."

"Is having dirty boots a prerequisite for keeping books?" Ann asked. She moved, now, around the table, so that Maggie could see her, too. If she had looked straight ahead, she might have caught the blue of Maggie's gown in the dimness.

She didn't look in Maggie's direction, however, but at Jake, as she sank onto the chair nearest him. There was distress in her manner, and there was anger, too. "He's well thought of, Mama said. She's observed him at the dances in town, and she says half the girls in Snohomish are making eyes at him."

"And he's making eyes at Maggie." Jake swore again. "How can she think she's in love with the likes of him?"

"She doesn't think she's in love with him, she merely likes him, and he's asked to call on Sunday afternoon. How can you expect her to have the wisdom to choose a husband if you don't allow her to get acquainted with a number of young men?"

"It's too early to think about a husband, and besides, how many young men did *you* know? Dozens, as I recall. They all came to services to look at you. And your choice didn't turn out so well, did it?"

His face, and his voice, suddenly changed. He stared at his wife, in profile to Maggie now so that she couldn't read his eyes. "What happened to us, Ann? We were in love once, weren't we?"

Ann's throat worked convulsively for several seconds before she could speak. "That woman—"

Jake shook his head. "No. Don't blame it on Jaisy. Everything went sour between you and me before I ever laid eyes on Jaisy. Even before you got in the family way with Sarah, things weren't good between us anymore. And when you kicked me out of my rightful bed— Well, Ann, there are some things you can't do to a man and expect him to roll over and play dead."

Maggie wondered if her mother were going to faint. Ann's lips trembled, one hand curling into a fist on the edge of the table. Maggie felt a tremor of her own, only now fully aware of what this was costing her mother. A part of her wanted to reach out and touch them both, yet she could not move; she had to remain hidden in the shadows. She didn't think of herself as an eavesdropper; she was simply here, and it was beyond her ability to retreat.

"You make it sound so . . . so clearly my fault," Ann said, voice lowered so that it barely carried to the hallway, and surely would not be heard in the kitchen. "I used to think you were a fair man, Jake, but you haven't been fair to me."

He sighed heavily. "I gave you what I thought you wanted. This house—hell, I never wanted it for myself. You've had a good living."

Ann visibly pulled herself together. "Is that what you think was important? The house? Yes, I wanted a decent house instead of that little cabin! I wanted to be able to entertain my friends, and have enough rooms for privacy. But I also needed a husband, and when I needed you the most, you weren't there, Jake Keating! You were never there!"

His response was low but forceful. "That's not true, and you know it. Oh, I'll admit I wasn't at home every time one of the kids stubbed a toe or needed discipline, but what man is? I had a living to make, for crissake, and you'll have to admit I've done that, I've provided for all of you, including your mother."

Ann had to compress her lips for a moment before she could reply to that. "I don't think there's any point in going on with this conversation. Except that Margaret asked me to intercede for her in the matter of allowing Wilkie Andreason to call. It seems to me a reasonable enough request for a girl who is nearly a young woman, but I suppose you'll decide however you like. You always have." She swallowed audibly. "Do you want to give her your decision, or do you care to tell me what it is?"

He stared at her, then exhaled noisily and ran a hand through his hair. "All right. Let him come, but you'd better hope to God she doesn't take him seriously. I doubt if he earns as much as a grease dauber. That bookkeeping of his isn't going to make him a rich man. If you think *I* did a poor job, wait and see what you can expect from a *bookkeeper.*"

Ann had her answer, but Maggie had to admire her spirit (even as she herself chafed at Jake's evaluation of Wilkie) in staying long enough for a parting shot as she rose from the chair. "As I understand it, Mr. Andreason is only in his early twenties. He's educated beyond most of the men in Snohomish, and at least ten years younger than you were when I married you. You didn't achieve any sort of success until you were considerably older than that, and then you gained the logging outfit only because Ed Newsome got hurt and couldn't run it himself anymore. And now you've acquired the mill the same way, off someone else's misfortune. I don't quite understand where all this pride comes from, that makes you think you're so much better than anyone else."

A nerve jumped in Jake's cheek. "I never noticed you were reluctant to spend the money I made, no matter how I got it."

Ann forced a brittle smile, already moving toward the door. "I never asked, but I've been curious. Did you tell *her* she had to watch expenses, too? Or only us, your own family?"

She gave him no chance to reply, unless he'd flung the answer after her retreating back. He simply sat there, until she'd left the room, then savagely attacked the cold food on his plate.

There was no time for Maggie to go anywhere. Instinctively she pressed backward against the wall, and Ann rushed past her, hands covering her face, blinded by tears.

Maggie swiveled, staring after her, remorse a dreadful ache. She ought never to have asked her mother to speak for her, ought instead to have recognized how deep the chasm was between her parents, to have known that in her own selfishness she had created something even worse. Neither of them would ever forget the hateful words that had been spoken tonight, nor would she.

She wanted to go after her mother, and could not. She listened to Ann's running feet on the stairs and along the upper corridor, heard the muffled closing of the bedroom door behind her.

Wilkie could call. And Angus had not .exaggerated Jake's opposition to any of his crew making advances toward his daughter. There was no satisfaction in the knowledge, any of it. Maggie wondered if there would be any solace in crying, and knew that her hot, dry, aching eyes would give her no such relief.

After a moment, she turned away from the vision of her father's head, bowed over his solitary meal, and made her own way up the stairs to her room.

Wilkie arrived, damp but immaculate, smiling, at two on Sunday afternoon.

Ann let him in. She was dressed as if for church, though she had not attended, and only an extremely keen observer would have noted the slight swelling of her eyelids. Her greeting was cordial as she led him to the front parlor—the one reserved for company, though Maggie had pleaded to use the family one, which was less formal and more comfortable—and sat with them for a few minutes. The meaningless ritual of chitchat was maddening to Maggie; she wished her mother would go away and leave her alone with Wilkie, because she couldn't think of a thing to say, and even replying to his remarks was difficult, with Ann listening in.

She had danced with him the previous night, as well as with Angus and half the rest of the men in town, but there had been no romantic interludes. Even Angus's enthusiasm for an outdoor excursion had been reduced by a cold, pelting rain.

It had, for a time, been touch and go as to whether or not Mrs. Totting and the girls would take the buggy to town, because of the bad weather; Maggie and Nancy had won out with the argument that the top would keep off the worst of the weather and they'd bundle themselves well against whatever would blow in from the sides.

The rain was a fact of life in the Pacific Northwest; in a territory where the economy depended largely upon the timber industry, there were few who begrudged the precipitation that made such harvests possible.

"We can't stay home every time it rains, Mama," Maggie had pointed out in some desperation, for such a decision might set the pattern for the entire winter to come. "Nobody else does."

"I know." Ann had continued to look concerned. "It's only that I'd hate for you to take a chill. . . ."

She didn't mention Celeste, but Maggie knew she was thinking of the younger girl's cough, and of the fact that because of it Celeste was far away in California.

"I never take chills," Maggie reminded her quietly, and it was true. She was almost never sick.

They had won Ann over, and they'd attended the dance, where everyone had enjoyed themselves, for all that there were no truly private conversations. Angus's touch, the way he smiled at her, were enough to make Maggie happy.

She was glad that Wilkie kept his voice low when he bade her good night. "I'll see you tomorrow," he promised, and Maggie nodded nervously.

By the time he actually arrived on Sunday, she was in a state bordering on panic.

Why had she allowed him to come, thinking that she was receptive to his attentions? She'd known from the beginning that it wasn't fair to him, and now she knew it wasn't fair to herself, either. What would she do if he tried to kiss her?

What nonsense, he wouldn't try to kiss her without some encouragement from her, not on his first visit, not with the door open and her mother in the back parlor right next door.

She expected to feel more at ease when Ann had withdrawn, but she didn't. Wilkie at the cookhouse or the Athenaeum was one thing; Wilkie in her own parlor was another.

He had already said the conventional things. "Rather an unpleasant day, isn't it? This is a charming room. I see that the Keatings are readers. Is that Mr. Hawthorne's *House of Seven Gables*?"

In point of fact, nobody ever read in this room. Except for Mrs. Totting, who came in once a week to dust, Maggie didn't think anyone had been in it in months. In an attempt to make it seem homey, Ann had left the book lying on a table, as if someone were reading it.

When Ann had gone, Wilkie looked at her and smiled. "You're looking lovely today, Maggie-Margaret."

She was, she knew, looking hag-ridden. She'd slept badly, something that seldom happened, anticipating this meeting. She'd been mad to allow it to happen, and now she didn't know what to do next.

"You aren't nervous about my coming, are you?" he asked gently, reaching for her hand.

She jerked it away as if it had been scorched, then felt idiotic. The hand continued to tingle. "Yes," she said frankly, "I am. I've never had a gentleman caller before."

Wilkie laughed. "Don't think of me as a gentleman caller. Think of me as your friend from camp, who sits around in his shirt-sleeves and scribbles columns of figures, who likes your pie and your coffee."

It *was* absurd, of course. It wasn't as if he were a stranger. Yet he was a stranger in this setting—*she* was a stranger in this setting, she thought wildly—and she was as tense as if she'd just become betrothed to a man she'd never met.

Wilkie settled back in his chair, seemingly at ease. "It's customary, when a lady has a caller, to entertain him in some mutually agreeable way. Sometimes she plays the piano—"

"I can't play a note," Maggie interjected.

"—or displays her drawings—"

"I can't draw, either."

"—or reads poetry."

Maggie pounced upon that. "Would you like me to recite Longfellow's *Song of Hiawatha?*" She stood and struck a pose, hands clasped at her breast.

"Should you ask me, whence these stories?
Whence these legends and traditions,
With the odors of the forest,
With the dew and damp of meadows,
With the curling smoke of wigwams,
With the rushing of great rivers,
With their frequent repetitions,
And their wild reverberations,
As of thunder in the mountains?
I should answer, I should tell you—"

Wilkie held up a hand, laughing. "Good grief, you're not going to recite the entire thing, are you? Do you actually know it all?"

"Not all," Maggie admitted. "But a lot of it. It's my favorite reading. I have the book, I got it for Christmas when I was ten. My favorite part—"

Wilkie came out of the chair, still laughing, and reached for her hands. "I'm sorry I suggested reciting poetry. I've read it, too, and I agree, it's marvelous. But I didn't come here to listen to Longfellow, I came here to get better acquainted with a very charming young lady!''

This time she didn't pull away from him, though the contact was disturbing. She was not sure why that should be, why she should be feeling some of the same sensations she felt when Angus touched her when she didn't really care for Wilkie at all.

''It's too bad the weather is so vile,'' Wilkie said. ''I think you'd be more comfortable outside. If we were walking through the woods, you'd be able to relax and talk to me the way we've talked before. Wouldn't you?''

''I don't know.'' She was sure that even Celeste, baby that she was, would have handled things better than this. Celeste had an instinct for things that escaped Maggie altogether. Wilkie's reference to walking in the woods didn't exactly help, since it only reminded her that she did that with Angus. ''I think maybe it was a mistake, Wilkie, for you to come—''

The amusement went out of his face as if snuffed like a candle.

''Maggie, don't say that! I'm sorry, I've taken things too fast, and though you seem so mature and I thought I could come to the point, I see that's not the case. Look, you don't have to be a performing bear or anything like that. We're friends, aren't we? For now let's just keep it that way, let's get better acquainted. Sit down. You there, me here, and I won't get you flustered by trying to make things move too fast. How would it be if I told you the story of my life?''

She did feel better when he was no longer touching her. Within a few minutes he even had her laughing aloud at an obviously embellished tale of his early years.

Ann stood in the doorway for several minutes, smiling, before they noticed her. Wilkie sprang to his feet to take the tray she carried, to lower it onto the small polished table between their two chairs.

"I've been telling her my life story," he explained to Ann. "Perhaps next week she'll tell me hers."

Maggie was still smiling, and she was no longer tense or apprehensive. But she'd made up her mind that Wilkie would not be coming back next week. Not if she could help it.

## 30

THE rain continued for twenty-two days.

The crew worked through the first week. When the earth became too saturated to handle any more moisture, so that boots sank to their tops in mud, when the rivers were swollen over their banks and the oxen mired down attempting to move their heavy burdens, when every garment in camp was sodden and there was no way to get them dry, Jake finally shut down operations.

The smells of wet wool and tobacco and sweat made both bunkhouse and cookhouse unpleasant. Tempers flared during the enforced inactivity; fights broke out like lightning fires in summer. Someone brought a jug back to camp, and the alcohol fueled an already explosive environment. After Sol Engstrom lost two teeth in a fistfight, and the teamster, Woolrich, grew so enraged with one of his stubborn beasts that he struck it with a sledgehammer, Jake made an angry search of the bunkhouse and threatened to fire the next man who brought a bottle into camp.

"Go into town if you have to drink," he snarled, which had the effect of emptying the camp.

The bull had to be butchered at once. The meat would be tough as shoe leather, and Jaisy would be expected to do her best to make it palatable, cooking it slowly for hours until the worst of the fibers broke down to a chewable consistency. The ox wouldn't be replaced this fall but was added to the list of necessities that Jake knew he'd have to deal with in the spring.

He cursed, and did the butchering himself with a repentant Woolrich's nearly tearful assistance.

At home, Maggie stared through the windows at the slashing rain and gritted her teeth.

Any day spent entirely within the house tested her reserve of patience. When day was added to day, and the rain cascaded from the sky like the great falls of the Snoqualmie, as icy as those waters formed of snow-melt, there was no way to meet Angus, or to send him a message, although Maggie composed several notes in the privacy of her room, throwing them into the fire to be sure that no one discovered them.

Sarah developed a cough and a runny nose, which distracted Ann's attention and demanded more of Maggie's time entertaining the baby. The child was able to sit unaided now, and would reach for bright-colored objects dangled before her, things she should have done months earlier; they took what satisfaction they could in her doing them at all. Ann, at least, had harbored the secret fear that her youngest child would never do anything more than lie in a cot and gaze at the ceiling.

Jake went to camp every day but seldom stayed long. When he was home he was in a poor humor. He spent some time hunched over his books, now neatly kept in Wilkie's legible hand, as if trying to squeeze something more out of them than they could be made to produce.

The mill continued to operate with the logs Jake had managed to get downstream before everything mired down to the point where it was impossible even to get the logs to the river. Jake found little gratification in that, as he knew that by the time he'd paid wages, he'd be lucky to break even.

Although the exchange between them had hardly been cordial, Maggie had foolishly hoped that her parents might have reestablished lines of communication, that they might continue to speak to one another. This was not the case. The only voices heard in the house were Maggie's own, and those of the Tottings, in the kitchen. Even the servants seemed hushed by the oppressive heaviness of the atmosphere.

Maggie had spent a sleepless night after Wilkie's visit. It hadn't been so bad, once she'd broken through her own reserve and responded to his repartee, though she'd been glad when he had taken his leave. She had not, however, made it clear to him that she didn't want him to call again the following Sunday, and the conviction had built within her that if Angus learned of the call—no, *when* Angus learned of the call—he would be furious. Not only with Wilkie, but with her.

Men talked. Why in God's name hadn't she considered that, when she'd agreed to ask permission for Wilkie to call? She'd heard the men in camp often enough, exchanging confidences, bragging of their prowess among the girls of the town in much the same way that they bragged of their fighting ability or the knack for bringing down a tree precisely where they wanted it. Wilkie would mention to someone that he'd called upon her, and they'd all know about it within hours. Especially after Jake had made his stupid threats against the crew, it was bound to be a matter of general interest when someone broke through that barrier to call on Maggie.

The only bright spot that first week was a letter Jake brought back from town, to toss onto the table before his wife. Ann pounced on it with a cry of joy. "It's from Mama and Céleste!"

She read it aloud to them, jiggling Sarah on her lap.

Maggie listened with stinging eyes. She missed them both, especially her sister, and would have given anything to have had Celeste at home with her now.

" 'We had a good trip,' " Ann read, " 'though it was quite tiring for both of us. Lealah has a comfortable home and has given over a bedroom for our use; she is somewhat troubled by a leg that was broken a year ago, so I am able to make myself useful. Celeste spent several days in bed, resting, when we first arrived; the damp air at sea seemed to make the cough worse, but since our arrival here, well away from the Pacific, there has been notable improvement. She is eating better and has, I think, regained a little of her lost weight. She will write herself when she is feeling a bit more energetic. Right now she is in the chicken yard, feeding the hens. There are plenty of eggs and she is having two each day, which I'm sure is good for her.' "

It was a newsy, chatty letter, though briefer than they would have liked. There was no suggestion of when they would be returning home, of course. It had taken the letter three weeks to reach Snohomish.

"I'll write to them this afternoon," Ann decided when she'd finished reading. "Why don't you write, too, Margaret, and your father can send our letters off the next time he's in town?"

Maggie wrote the letter, filled with descriptions of Sarah's accomplishments, news of the logging crew and the mill, town gossip picked up at the Athenaeum. She did not write of the things that really pressed upon her, did not mention Angus at all.

Her longing for him grew to the point where, after on two successive days she had suggested a walk and been forbidden by a scandalized mother to venture outside in such wretched weather for fear of catching her death, Maggie gave in to temptation and deception.

"I think I'll read this afternoon," she announced carelessly after Mrs. Totting had served soup and hot bread for the noon meal. "It's so dreary I have to take my mind off it for a while."

"I'm going to read, too, while Sarah naps," Ann agreed.

In her room, Maggie threw down the novel she had carried upstairs and began getting into the proper clothes for her excursion: her oldest shoes over heavy wool socks, a drab gown that wouldn't be missed if she ruined it and had to throw it away, and the warmest outer garments she could find.

She stared at herself in the mirror. Well, she wouldn't win any competition for well-dressed young ladies, but anticipation had put some color into her face. She'd walk all the way to camp, if she had to; she was determined to see Angus and find a way to arrange for future meetings. The weather was only going to get worse for months yet, and she could not bear another day—not another hour—in this house that resembled nothing so much as a tomb.

Even the cold slashing rain was an improvement, she thought, letting herself out of the front door a few minutes later. It felt clean and fresh, untainted by undercurrents of animosity such as swirled through the big house that was to have made all of them so happy.

She strode briskly along the path above the Pilchuck—much closer to the water than was customary—noting with rising enthusiasm the swiftness of the current that carried with it odds and ends of debris and an occasional log from some operation upstream. She tried to read the brand on the end of a bucking log and could not; she doubted that it was Jake's. The crew hadn't been cutting close to the river upstream lately.

It felt strange to be without Joe. She had deliberately not called him because she didn't want him to give her away if she tried to move surreptitiously. Mud squelched over her shoes and the cold chilled her feet before she'd reached the

skid road, but she ignored the discomfort. Seeing Angus
had become all-important.

No wonder they'd shut down, she thought, for even the
road was nearly impassable. The logs laid crossways to
form its bed had sunk into the muck the loggers called
"tiger crap" so that the best she could hope for was that
there would be a solid level somewhere beneath the surface that would keep her from going in over the tops of her
shoes.

She slogged along until she caught sight of the great
spar that marked their former trysting place. She felt a
wrench of disappointment that she knew was absurd. What
did she think, that after days of this impossible weather
Angus was going to be waiting out here for her, at a
different time of day from when she'd come before?

She kept going, hoping Angus wouldn't already have
fled the boredom of camp for the saloons in town. She
wished she'd thought up some credible excuse for arriving
in camp, and then decided that it didn't matter. They all
knew she liked being outside, and the truth—or part of
it—would suffice. They'd understand that it had been
imperative to escape the house after days of confinement,
even if they didn't know quite how bad it was there, with
nobody talking to anybody else.

Camp looked to be totally deserted, except for the
smoke rising from the cookhouse. There was none from
the bunkhouse a short distance away, a bad sign. As cold
as it was, if anybody was there, he'd have a fire going.

There were no sounds of voices. The oxen stood with
their backsides to the wind, stolidly enduring until their
services should again be needed. They did not look up at
her approach.

Maggie tugged at the cookhouse door, opening it upon
the odors of wet wool, cigar smoke, and simmering
birdseye tenderloin, as the men called the ox meat that
bore the marks of the bullwhacker's goad stick.

Jaisy turned from her seat at one of the tables, where she and Lucy and Will were sitting with a book open before the little girl. "Well, didn't expect company in such dirty weather," Jaisy said easily, though there was a wariness in her eyes.

Maggie tried to remember if she'd ever before seen the woman sitting at a leisure activity this way, and couldn't. The only men in the place were Woolrich and Rich Salter, hunched over the checkerboard, who greeted her casually.

"Lookin' for Jake, he went to town," Salter offered. "Along with everybody else. Had any place to stay, so's we wouldn't have to walk back through mud up to our *be*hinds in the dark tonight, we'd of gone, too. Give Jaisy a complete day off, 'stid of havin' to cook for the two of us."

"Don't matter," Jaisy said. "Had to cook for me and the kids, anyway. And there's all that meat'll spoil if it ain't cooked soon. There's oatmeal cookies, if you're hungry, Maggie."

It was one of the few times Jaisy had addressed her by name. Maggie hadn't realized it until this moment, that both of them had avoided any such familiarity.

She wasn't actually hungry, but for some reason she accepted one of the cookies, still warm and full of plump, sweet raisins. "Thank you," she said.

"I'm reading Ma and Will a story," Lucy told her. "Only I forget some of the words. Like this one." She turned the book so that Maggie could read from the page.

" 'Undaunted,' " Maggie supplied. "It means . . ." She hesitated, searching for a definition that would be clear to the children. "Not discouraged, or not giving way to your fears."

Lucy nodded her thanks, keeping her finger on the place. "I wish we had some more books, or some paper to draw on, or something. It's so boring when it keeps on raining."

It hadn't occurred to Maggie that the Pallisons had far more reason for boredom than she did, though the people surrounding them were at least on speaking terms with one another. They were confined to a very small space, had no privacy except that of the cramped lean-to at the rear of the building, and no amenities such as comfortable chairs, books to read, and decent lamps to read by. They were warmed by the cookstove, which didn't affect the temperature in the lean-to, and Jaisy had to launder one garment at a time in the dishpan; she had draped the dripping clothes from a line hung across the rear of the main room, where it would probably take them days to dry. Since nobody had more than a few changes, the disadvantages were myriad.

"Next time I come, I'll bring you a few books," Maggie promised. "We still have some that my sister and I had when we were your age."

"Oh, good! Thank you," Lucy said, grinning at her. She wriggled on the hard seat and helped herself to one of the cookies.

Maggie wondered if Lucy knew what she was missing, and then amended the thought. Maybe Lucy and Will weren't actually missing anything. Their mother was fond of them, openly if casually affectionate; they had a roof over their heads, adequate food, and enough clothes to keep from going naked.

She was amazed at the pang of envy she felt, for the closeness of the Pallisons. For that instant, she would have traded everything the Keatings owned for a loving, supportive family that enjoyed doing ordinary things together.

She finished the cookie and licked the last crumbs from her fingers. "Well, I guess I'll head on back."

"We'll be waiting for the books," Lucy said. "Don't forget."

"I won't," Maggie told her, and was rewarded by Jaisy's smile.

"It's kind of you to think of the kids," she said.

Maggie felt embarrassed; she didn't know quite why it was so difficult for her to accept a compliment in a graceful way, when it was so easy for most other people. "It's all right. We don't read them anymore and Sarah probably won't ever—"

She stopped. She didn't want to say it aloud, especially to people who didn't love Sarah, that her little sister would never be able to read the books.

She walked back through the wet woods. The rain had diminished to a heavy drizzle which soaked through her borrowed coat. She was as weighed down by depression over not seeing Angus as by the wet; she hoped to be able to gain her room and get out of the sopping clothes without being seen, or she'd have something else to be downcast about.

As she approached the midpoint in her walk, the old spar marking the spot as it was etched against the glowering sky, she wasn't thinking about meeting Angus anymore. He'd gone to Snohomish, he'd be drinking with the rest of the men, and since he could go to McAllmer's to sleep, he might just stay in town until the weather cleared. Which meant that she was out of luck until the next dance that she was allowed to attend.

"Maggie? Is that you?"

She turned and saw the tall figure on the path emerging from the forest, a foot trail the men sometimes took as a shortcut when they were going to town instead of to the landing. She wouldn't have expected anyone to choose it under these conditions, however, for the mud would be deep.

"Angus!" There was no maidenly concealment of her joy as she ran toward him, to be enveloped in a wet embrace. Their lips met, cold noses touching, setting them laughing.

"I'll bet this is what it feels like to kiss an Eskimo,"

Angus said, holding her away from him so that he could look into her face. "You been at camp?"

"I had to get out of the house. They said you'd all gone to town. Why are you coming back through the woods?"

"Because I was sitting across the table from your old man, drinking a glass of ale, and he made a remark about the barn. *Your* barn. Where he keeps that nag and the buggy, said he'd fixed a leak in the roof and had run out of things to do, and he was going crazy waiting for things to dry up, same as the rest of us. And I had an idea. So I came back instead of spending the night in town. Figured the woods couldn't be much worse than the regular road; mud's deep everywhere. I didn't expect to be lucky enough to run into you out here, though."

"The barn?" Maggie echoed. "The barn! Of course! Nobody ever goes in there except to get out the buggy or to haul hay! And it's close to the landing—it could be a meeting place, and we could leave messages there, too. I know where there's a loose board, and there's a space under it—"

He bent to kiss her, shutting off the flow of words, and not even the iciness of their lips kept it from being a satisfying kiss.

"I'll meet you in the barn whenever you say," he told her. "We can sit where it's dry, and, with the hay around us, it shouldn't even be too cold. Just to talk, you understand. We have to be able to talk."

Maggie considered quickly. It would be easiest after everyone else had gone to bed so that there was little likelihood of being caught out. "At ten?"

"Ten it is." He lifted one booted foot to show her the great clods of clinging mud. "I'm lucky I made it through the woods. I've made better progress through Snohomish swamp, and I'm wet through. I've got one change of clothes left if somebody hasn't swiped it while I wasn't watching, and it looks like the clouds are lifting a bit. If it doesn't do worse than this drizzle, I should be able to get there in fairly good condition. I'll see you then.''

He kissed her once more, swiftly, and was gone, and Maggie hurried on toward home.

She had set herself a dangerous course, and she knew it. But she had no intention of backing out.

She would be in the barn at ten.

## 31

MAGGIE had always taken pride in the fact that she said what she thought, with little evasion and almost no deliberate untruthfulness.

Now she was faced with the necessity for deception, and she was not sure she was equipped to deceive successfully. She felt as if her face must surely reveal every lie she told, no matter how small.

She bolstered her conviction of the justification of this course with the belief that she was being unfairly treated in not being allowed to accept Angus as a suitor. Most of the girls she knew were free, within rather loose limits, to be courted by whomever they liked. As long as the man wasn't an out-and-out rotter, parents eager to see someone else supporting their daughter would often overlook minor faults, such as the amount the young man drank, for instance. After all, most young fellows drank a bit, and most reformed suitably after they were married. If he had a job, if he was willing to work at it, if he and their daughter professed to love each other, what more could a parent reasonably ask?

It wasn't fair that Jake was so fussy. She was *not* too young, and she knew what she wanted. If Jake would not be reasonable, then she would have to take matters into her own hands.

Deciding that, and putting it into action, however, were two different things.

She had to appear normal when around anyone else in the household, to avoid suspicion. It would no more do to give herself away to the housekeeper than to her parents. She thought Nancy would cover for her, even act as co-conspirator, but unless that became absolutely necessary, Maggie preferred keeping her devious plans to herself.

For the first time she saw an advantage in having parents who didn't speak to each other. There would be no piecing together of small bits of evidence to incriminate her. She had only to offer a logical explanation to escape their presence, and she wanted to do it with a minimum of deception.

Jake was not there that first evening. Presumably he was still in Snohomish, drinking and talking with his crew. Unfortunately, he'd ridden to town, which meant that if he came home and put the horse back in the barn, she wouldn't want to be there with Angus.

Ann talked more than usual during that meal; she was encouraged by Sarah's learning to sit up, and by her newfound ability to grasp the objects Ann held out to her. "I really think she's going to be able to learn," Ann said earnestly, "and though she's rather slow, I believe she'll be able to creep and walk, like any child."

Maggie hoped so, too, though she was less optimistic than her mother. She felt pity for them both, the mother and the child. Yet overlying those feelings was the need to escape her life in this house, the life that had become close to intolerable since Celeste and her grandmother had gone from it.

"I'm going upstairs, Margaret, for the evening," Ann said as they rose from the supper table. "Sarah is so restless with this stuffed-up nose that I think it would be better if I did my reading where I can hear her. I hate to leave you on your own, but there's a fire in the back parlor. . . ."

"It doesn't matter. If you've finished with that novel, I may take it up to my room and read for a while, too." Maggie had come down for supper with her hair still damp; she had washed it as soon as she'd come in that afternoon, so she wouldn't have to lie about why her hair was wet, and then Ann hadn't even noticed.

She did try to read, almost an impossibility. The drizzle continued, too light to make any sound on the roof. The wind had risen. She'd always liked to listen to the wind whipping the treetops, making that roaring sound high in the firs; tonight it was an irritant, covering any smaller sounds that might have reached her. Her father arriving home, for instance, or Angus opening the barn door.

Poor Angus, coming all that way through wet and muddy darkness, for a brief rendezvous with her. She wished he didn't have to do it, yet was warmed by the knowledge that he wanted to, in order to be with her.

The minutes ticked away so slowly. She looked at the dying fire on her bedroom hearth, debating whether to replenish the wood or not. In the end she decided to let it die down to coals, and rolled a blanket to put into the bed beneath the quilts; that way, if anyone looked in, they would assume that she was asleep.

Excitement, mingled with fear of discovery, coursed through her as she let herself out into the upper corridor. The door to her father's room was open; he had not yet returned. There was no band of light under Ann's door, and no sounds from within. Ann was presumably asleep, though she couldn't count on that. She carried her shoes in her hand and padded quietly past her mother's room and down the stairs without benefit of light.

Maggie continued through the familiar rooms toward the back of the house. Mrs. Totting and Nancy were long since asleep in their room on the ground floor; she heard the housekeeper's rhythmic snoring.

One of the Tottings had taken pity on Joe because of the weather and allowed him inside; he rose from his sleeping place near the black iron stove, which still exuded a comforting warmth, and joined her.

The latch made a faint clicking sound as she opened the outer door, another as she closed it behind her. She stood on the back porch, awkwardly balancing to get her shoes on; then wrapped herself in the cape she'd taken down from the nail just inside the door. It was early, but anything seemed better than sitting up there in her room, waiting, she thought.

She ran across the yard toward the barn, wondering why she hadn't thought of it herself as a meeting place. The small door, which squeaked on rusty hinges as she opened it, led directly to the lower mow where they heaped loose hay when it was tossed down from above to feed the horses. There were three of them, and one whickered a greeting as she entered.

She had no more than closed the door behind her when Angus spoke out of the darkness.

"Maggie? That you?"

Laughter, love, exhilaration bubbled up in her throat. "It had better be, or someone is going to be asking what you're doing in the barn!"

"I heard Joe. I knew it was you. Besides, I can smell you."

"Smell me!" Indignation rose, dissolving the moment he touched her.

"Soap, woman smell. Ummmm." He buried his face in

her hair, holding her against him. "Maggie, I love you. I think I knew, even when you were that scrawny little girl, that I was going to love you someday. I've waited a long time for you to grow up."

She felt breathless. "So have I. Angus, Daddy's still out. We'll have to listen for him to come back; he rode Sandy, and he'll have to put him in his stall."

"I met him on the way here. He's in camp, he won't be home for hours."

Maggie felt the withering sensation that had become familiar, though she'd never gotten used to it, whenever she thought about her father and Jaisy being together. "What if he realized you were coming here?" she asked in alarm.

"He didn't see me. He was whistling, and I heard him coming. I stepped off the road until he'd gone by. He doesn't know anything." He kissed her again, drawing her with him toward the mounded hay. "Come on, I've hollowed out a place for us, so we won't freeze. It's damned cold out here."

She sank onto her knees with him, smelling the sweet alfalfa hay, feeling the prick of it through her garments. "You're sure it was Daddy? You couldn't have seen him."

"Couldn't see a thing, but I'd recognize that whistle anywhere." Angus chuckled. "He couldn't carry a tune in a basket. He whistles off-key. It was Jake all right. Who else would have a horse? Here, look, swing around this way, and we can sit close together; I'll pull some hay up over us to keep us warm."

He had unbuttoned his jacket; he drew her hands beneath it, around him so that the heat of his body would warm them, while his arms held her close. "Comfortable?"

"Lovely," Maggie murmured. "Oh, Angus, how long are we going to have to do this?"

His lips were at her temple, then touching her ear and

moving down her throat. "I hope to keep on doing it for the rest of my life."

"I mean meeting here, in secret, as if . . . as if there were something *wrong* with being together! There isn't, is there?"

His answer was a kiss that left her shaken, carried away on a tide of bliss that made her forget everything except Angus and the sensations he was able to arouse with no more than his mouth on hers.

That evening set the pattern for the following nights.

The need to see him, to hear his voice and his low laughter, to feel his arms around her and his lean body pressed to hers so that she could detect his heartbeat, quickened like her own, was overwhelming, blotting out everything else.

She moved in a dream the rest of the time, often preoccupied, finally grateful for the fact that nobody seemed to notice her moods, except for Nancy. Nancy was engrossed in a romance of her own, carried on mostly by notes posted when either she or her mother went to town for supplies, and at the dances when the weather permitted them to go. Mrs. Totting balked at walking in the rain, and agreed to chaperone only when Maggie was allowed to go, too, so they could use the buggy.

Maggie knew the dangers of dancing with Angus on those evenings. She was so happy that it must surely be apparent to any observer, shining from her face, reflected in her eyes. Yet it was only Nancy who seemed to see, and Nancy was so preoccupied with Adam Welker that she simply wished her friend happiness without becoming involved in the matter.

Mrs. Totting might have been more observant than her daughter had she not grown increasingly nearsighted. Maggie made it a point to try to keep well away from the older woman when she was with Angus.

Maggie dealt with Wilkie Andreason as best she could. She might have gathered enough courage to tell him bluntly that she did not have strong feelings for him and never would, which should have put an end to his attentions. He provided some cover, however, for her relationship with Angus; as long as she danced with him and he came to call, why should anyone suspect that her love was entirely for Angus?

As far as she could learn, Wilkie had not mentioned to anyone that he had called upon her. Of course, the loggers were not particularly friendly to him; while there was little open hostility, they didn't engage him in friendly conversation or invite him to join their drinking bouts. Maggie prayed that Angus would not learn of Wilkie's attentions; he tended to glower from the sidelines when she danced with Wilkie, but Angus had agreed that it would be wise if she went on dancing with everyone, though it went against the grain.

She settled for whatever excuse she could think of, to keep Wilkie away. Sarah, her mother, the weather, even, on one or two occasions, her own indisposition; the latter was mildly embarrassing, since she left her symptoms vague in the assumption that he would accept this as normal monthly female distress. In truth, she never suffered any.

"Until we get through this winter, anyway," Angus said, though with regret that any other man should claim her, even for a dance. "Until we're through with this business of moving the mill, so I'll get paid for that, and in the spring, who knows? Maybe the price of lumber will be up, and I can go elsewhere for a job if Jake takes a dislike to the idea of me courting his daughter. That's as long as I'm going to wait to bring it out in the open."

The job of which he spoke provided some distraction from other considerations. Jake had decided that, once the logging operation had shut down for the winter, the mill would be dismantled and reassembled at Keating's Landing. It would make both operations more efficient, and give his crew an extra month or two of employment. Granted, bad weather would interfere with that transfer, too, but while more difficult in heavy rain or snow, it would not be impossible, as the logging was.

His decision was based partly on the fact that two more logging operations were operating upstream, and both owners had agreed to continue milling at what had been Stover's mill. There was even talk of running a spur from the railroad the additional distance upriver as soon as the economy improved, which everybody hoped would be during 1884.

This was exciting for several reasons. Maggie would be working there, and Ann's objections would be diminished if the office was right near the landing. Also, the office could be used for both mill and logging operations, satisfying Wilkie's desire for a proper place to work.

The Pallisons moved back to their cabin on the lake in late November. Lucy had been overjoyed with the books Maggie took to her. Maggie had spent some time in camp helping her with her reading, and the child proudly reported her improving skill when Maggie encountered her at the Mercantile shortly before Christmas.

Jake spent long hours doing hard physical labor along with his men, taking down the mill walls and roof in sections, transporting both buildings and machinery on crude rafts pulled upstream by the stolid oxen, then reassembling everything at the landing.

Ann grew used to Maggie spending hours on the site. Few questions were raised at home when the opportunity arose to meet Angus during the day. Angus put in the same hours as the others, and after a few days of plodding through mud to the bunkhouse at camp, the crew persuaded Jake to allow them to throw up sleeping quarters nearer at hand. With a new shack only a ten-minute walk from the landing, it became much easier for Angus and Maggie to meet. Even when those encounters were brief, they were exciting and satisfying, as satisfying as anything short of open courting could have been.

First snow fell the day before Christmas, a light covering that touched the landscape with magic. Maggie had knitted a pair of mittens for him. Angus brought her a new copy of *Hiawatha;* she had lamented the damage to her original one when Joe chewed it in a puppyish demonstration of frustration after he'd been inadvertently locked in her bedroom one afternoon. They exchanged gifts in a snowy clearing, well out of sight of the house or the landing, clasping hands and exchanging kisses as well before they parted.

It was the first Christmas the Keatings had not all been together. There were small, handmade gifts from Celeste and Millicent in California, and similar presents among themselves. Ann had allowed Maggie to persuade her to include the Tottings in their Christmas-morning gift opening, on the theory that the lack of two of their family members would be less noticeable if the room held more people.

A pretense was made that they were a loving family, yet it fell so flat that Maggie wanted to cry. If her parents could thank one another for the brightly wrapped gifts, why couldn't they speak the rest of the time? She'd have traded every gift she received for the pleasure of hearing her mother and father simply talk about normal, everyday things.

Jake had brought in a beautiful twelve-foot blue spruce, and Maggie and Nancy had decorated the tree with popcorn, cranberries, and paper chains saved from previous years. The tiny candles were carefully lighted, and they shared for a few moments a pleasure in watching Sarah's face at the spectacle. The baby was beginning to try to crawl, which they all encouraged. When Sarah squirmed toward him, Jake caught her up and tossed her in the air, eliciting a crow of laughter even as Ann began a protest.

"She likes it," Jake asserted, and Ann's objection died.

Yet not even Sarah and the addition of the servants to swell their meager ranks could have made the day a success. There should have been laughing and loving, open affection; except for what was lavished on Sarah, there was none.

That first snow was gone within two days, but by mid-January, another storm brought snow aplenty, and something new had to be considered. Maggie went out to the barn to feed the horses one morning and saw the footprints in the snow, Angus's and her own.

She stopped in alarm. She glanced around to see that no one watched from the house, then scuffed over the marks close to the door, wondering how they could have been so foolish. The marks were still there, leading off toward the house and the path to the landing, telling a story that her father would certainly read in an instant if he returned before dark.

He hadn't ridden off on a horse, since he'd only gone to the landing a short distance below the house. That was no guarantee that he wouldn't enter the barn later on, however. Maggie looked hopelessly at the remaining tracks, then stalked to the nearest cedar and broke off a bough to use for a broom. She was thankful that the snow had been no deeper, for she could not have brushed over deep indentations without leaving traces.

As it was, she could only blot out the tracks nearest the barn, and hope to providence that Jake would not notice the telltale markings from the cedar bough. If only it would begin to snow again soon, that would erase the evidence.

She would have to talk to Angus and warn him against coming again until it could be done more safely.

She didn't really feel guilty about the meetings with

Angus in the barn, after the household was asleep. She told herself that she'd much rather have entertained him in the parlor, if she'd been allowed to do so, and that nothing illicit actually took place when they were together. Any courting couple held hands and kissed and hugged. It hadn't gone beyond the bounds of propriety, except for the fact that they were alone together in the barn.

Not that either of her parents could be expected to condone what she did; therefore, she would keep it a secret until such time as circumstances changed and made it feasible to tell them.

She fed the horses and then headed along the path toward the landing. She could hear the ring of hammers and axes from as far away as the house, and found the crew hard at work reassembling the walls of the mill. Jake was in the midst of the activity, lifting a hand in greeting without interrupting his task; she waved back and kept going toward the office.

Since it was only about ten feet square and had been moved in two sections, it was the first thing to be finished on the new site. The iron stove had been stoked up at once, so that the men could go inside for hot coffee and to warm their hands occasionally. Wilkie was there, perched on a stool behind the counter; he looked up with a smiled greeting.

"Good morning. Puts the roses in your cheeks, doesn't it?"

She returned his greeting, pulling off her mittens and holding her hands toward the stove. "I didn't see Red and Angus. Aren't they working today?"

"I think they've gone to town for nails or something," Wilkie said carelessly. "Would you mind pouring me a cup of coffee, if it's done?"

She poured two cups and stood sipping her own after leaving his at his elbow. It was too strong, but the heat of it felt good. "How long ago did they leave?"

"I don't know. Maybe they haven't even gone yet, they were just talking about it. Maggie, I'd like very much to call on Sunday. It's been three weeks."

"I know. It seems foolish to come out so far in horrible weather." She was suddenly glad he didn't get along well enough with the logging crew to be invited to sleep in the bunkhouse. "I don't know, Wilkie. Sarah's so fussy, and Mama needs me. . . ."

She let it trail off, hoping he'd be discouraged enough to forget the matter.

"She's sick a great deal, isn't she?" His dark gaze was fixed upon her and for a moment she felt sure he saw through these subterfuges to keep him away from the house. "More than most infants?"

"Yes, she's always been sickly. She's so sweet, though, when she smiles. She's good-natured, never cries unless she's hurt or sick."

"Must be extremely tiring for your mother."

Maggie tried to read anything extra behind the words and could not be sure. "Yes. It helps if I take over part of every day, keep Sarah entertained." She didn't mention that if her little sister were not entertained, she seemed content to sit in the middle of her blanket on the floor and stare at her plump fingers. Ann was convinced that if they worked with her constantly, the child *would* learn, so it was true that Maggie did spend considerable time with her.

She took a final swallow of the bitter coffee and opened the door to throw the rest of it onto the trampled snow outside. "I'll be glad when my sister comes home. She was very good with Sarah."

"Will she be coming soon? I'm eager to meet her," Wilkie said, resting his pen for a moment. "I've heard she's very pretty."

"Yes, she is. Nothing like me at all," Maggie said, sounding more clipped than she'd intended. "Well, I'll see you later, Wilkie. Mrs. Totting is making cookies; I'll bring some down later this afternoon.''

"Maggie, about Sunday—''

She tried to produce both tone and facial expression of regret. "I think we'd better wait, until Sarah is over this latest cold. Mama's worn out, I'm afraid she's getting it, too. I want to give her the chance to rest as much as she needs to.''

She slipped out and closed the door behind her before Wilkie could say anything further.

She missed the cookhouse where the men had always gathered and wondered how they were making out shifting for themselves. Angus had mentioned, with disgust, the pot of beans left soaking overnight, then simmering all day so there would be a meal at night, with only a few chunks of salt pork to add flavor.

"Once in a while isn't bad,'' he'd said, "but this is the fifth day in a row, and last night they weren't completely cooked. The fire went out during the afternoon.''

They were buying bread in town, she knew, a dozen loaves at a time, and keeping the cooking to a minimum since none of them really knew anything about it, and their facilities were so limited. They groused about the matter continuously.

Maggie skirted the area where piles of lumber littered the ground, and the mill equipment stood exposed to the weather until the building to house it could be completed. Wilkie was mistaken about Angus's having gone to town; she caught a glimpse of his red knitted hat, canted at a rakish angle that left his ears uncovered and pink. She had to talk to him, and in such a way as not to attract undue attention.

She spoke to several of the workers, pausing to watch a section of wall go up, before she approached Angus. He was working with Rich Salter, however, and private speech was impossible.

He grinned, waving a hand mittened in her Christmas gift to him. "Good morning."

She echoed the greeting, including Salter, then said, "I hope it snows some more today. I like it when the snow is clean and unbroken. Now it's all tracked up and muddy, and it's ugly."

Salter, who was not looking at her but at the section of wall they were raising into place, snorted. "More snow won't help us much. Wish for some dry weather for a few days."

Angus, however, had been watching her face. His eyes narrowed, and Maggie nodded, deliberately making a footprint in a relatively clean area, then stepping aside. He nodded, and reached for his hammer. "Anything you want from town? We're going in later, have a decent meal instead of more of those damned beans. Probably stay overnight and come back in the morning."

She gave him a little smile. "No, nothing, thanks. See you later."

Angus would not come that night, and he knew what she meant about the tracks.

She did not meet him secretly again for four days, days filled with a longing for his touch, for the words that buoyed her spirits, for the kiss that sent them soaring.

While the men were in Snohomish, they had picked up the mail. After the first letter had arrived, Celeste and Millicent wrote once a week, and the letters came regularly. Both were homesick, but Celeste was feeling better in the warm, dry air, and Aunt Lealah needed them. It was small comfort to those who missed them more than they admitted even to one another.

The winter was a comparatively mild one in Washington Territory, with more rain than snow, the temperatures seldom dropping below freezing. The mill was reassembled, and then the men could work inside, though Angus swore it was colder within the unheated building than outside of it. At least it was dry. There was as yet no work for Maggie to do in the office, and except for taking cakes or pies or cookies down to the appreciative men, she had little excuse for hanging around the landing.

Had it not been for the nights when she and Angus were able to meet in the barn, practically burying themselves in hay to keep from freezing, she didn't know how she would have survived those long, bitter months.

They were bundled heavily against the low temperatures. Only hands and mouths provided skin contact, but it was enough, though there were times when Maggie felt the oddly frightening, yet exciting, sensations that kept her aware of the dangers of these meetings.

Angus kept her aware of the risk, too. Once, when they had simply sat close together in companionable silence for a time, a long sigh escaped him.

"What's the matter? Are you tired?"

"Physically tired, yes, but when I'm with you, it all sort of melts away. I forget sore muscles and being worn out. You're good for me, Maggie. The trouble is, I'm not sure I'm good for you."

"Oh, yes, you are," Maggie said quickly, but he didn't laugh.

"I know I'm a fool for meeting you this way. Jake would kill me—maybe literally—if he knew about it. And it's not fair to you, asking you to take such chances. You're such a baby, you don't even know what the risk is."

Maggie bristled at once. "A baby! How can you say that?"

"Because you're an innocent. You like being hugged and kissed, but you don't know what that's eventually going to lead to. You don't know what it's doing to me, every time I kiss you, and how hard it's getting for me to keep it at this level, without going any further."

There was something about his tone that convinced her he was dead serious. Something that almost frightened her.

She pressed closer to his side, against the welcome and now familiar warmth of him. "Tell me, then," she said.

He strangled on the laughter that sounded closer to anguish, though she didn't see how that could be.

"Maggie, darling, I love you. I want to marry you, when the time comes. I don't want to seduce you, but it's getting harder and harder not to do what comes naturally. Hard enough so that sometimes I swear I won't come back here, won't see you this way anymore, in order to protect you. Only I need you so"—he buried his face in her hair, nuzzling her cheek—"that I can't summon that much willpower. Maggie, do you know what it means, to seduce somebody?"

She felt her cheeks grow hot and was glad he couldn't see them. He'd only be convinced he was right about her innocence. "Well, sort of," she admitted.

He groaned. "Sort of! That's what I mean! *I* know what all this can lead to, and you don't, not really. You read those fool novels, and it's all romanticized and glossed over, and you don't *know* a thing."

"I know there must be something wonderful, between two people who love each other. Something beautiful. And I love you, Angus, and trust you."

He groaned again. "If you think you're making this easier, you're mistaken. Don't trust me, Maggie. Don't trust any man. The feelings of a man are stronger than a female's, and after a certain point a man may not be responsible, even though he wants to be."

It struck Maggie as highly unlikely that his feelings were any stronger than hers. She felt as if she might fly into a million fragments, right now. How much stronger could emotion be?

"Of course I trust you," she said, and reached up a hand to turn his face so that their lips met. The kiss, on her part, was gentle and chaste, and it started out that way with Angus; and then, quite suddenly, he swore and thrust her away from him.

"I'd better go. It's late, and I have to be on the job as soon as it's daylight in the morning." He hauled her to her feet and brushed blindly at the hay he knew was clinging to her clothes. "Good night, Maggie."

She expected him to kiss her one last time, as he usually did when they parted at the barn door. Tonight he didn't touch her again at all. The hinges creaked as he opened the door, and he was gone, vanishing into the darkness.

Maggie stood for a moment until the sounds of his footfalls had died away, then headed for the back door. She was bewildered and a little hurt, though the latter had pretty much faded by the time she reached her room. It was because he loved her that he was concerned for her, and she supposed she ought to be grateful he didn't intend to seduce her. She laughed suddenly, peeling off garments and throwing them over the chair beside her bed.

She suspected she'd be very easily seduced, if Angus put his mind to it.

# 32

THERE was an air of suppressed excitement in Angus's manner as he settled into the hay beside her. He didn't even bother to scoop up any of it as a blanket over them, as he usually did, although the barn was cold enough so that Maggie was sure they'd see their breath vapors before them had there been enough light.

"What is it?" she demanded. "What's happened?"

"Remember Tom Berquist and Jim Ballantine?"

"Yes, of course. Tom got his arm broken about the time I met you, and I went to school with Jim's younger sister Sally. They both left town a year or two ago. What do they have to do with anything?" Whatever she'd expected, it wasn't mention of two men who had once been part of Jake's logging crew.

"They went to Oregon. Up in the Blue Mountains, a couple of hundred miles east of Portland, beyond The Dalles, then south of the Columbia River."

Her voice was tart. "I don't need a geography lesson, Angus. What about them?"

"They went down there to see if there wasn't an easier way to make a living than logging. They're home for the winter, and I talked to them last night. They've made me an offer, and it may be a way out for us."

He hugged her, but for once Maggie wasn't interested. She didn't like the way the conversation was going, and she didn't feel comfortable with that undercurrent of anticipation, or whatever it was. Not if it had to do with two former loggers who'd gone to Oregon. Oregon was hundreds of miles away, and had nothing to do with her or Angus.

"What are you talking about?" It struck her then, and she pulled back from him. "Gold? Angus, you're not talking about hunting for gold?"

He laughed. "You bet I am. You know how much gold they've taken out of those mountains in the past twenty years?"

"Oh, Angus, you can't be serious!" She felt as if she'd suddenly been subjected to the effects of an avalanche. "You can't mean to go off to some isolated place on the chance that you'll find gold nuggets lying on top of the ground! I've listened to the talk, too, and most of those prospectors don't find enough to keep them in cheap whiskey. Jim and Tom didn't come back rich, did they?''

He laughed again, drawing her close in spite of her effort to hold him off. Most of the time she enjoyed the fact that he was so much stronger than she was; at the moment, it was extremely irritating, especially since he didn't even seem to realize that she didn't share his exuberance.

"They came back so broke they didn't eat the last three days on the road, except when a kindly farmer's wife gave them supper for chopping wood for her.''

"Then what are you talking about?" She didn't know whether to feel relieved or apprehensive.

"I'm talking about gold in Oregon. Maggie, they've taken millions out of those mountains. There's every reason to think there are millions more, still buried in the ground. Tom and Jim staked a claim, and it's true they haven't gotten much out of it so far, just enough to keep them going. But on the next claim over, the land adjoining theirs, the guy just made a big strike. They're convinced the vein runs right on through their land. They got snowed out, or maybe they'd know by this time. It'll be a month or two yet before they can get back in there, maybe more than that. Their claim is between Granite and Sumpter, and it's six, seven thousand feet, up there. The snow probably lasts until April or May, anyway. They'll go back and stay in town, hike up to their claim as soon as they can get through.''

"So?" Her tone ought to have warned him, but he was like all men in that respect. She'd noted the same flaw in her father. When he was keyed-up about something, he didn't hear the nuances in a woman's voice, or even note her words.

"So they're broke, but they're convinced the gold is there, and they expect to find it in the spring. They need a grubstake, enough money for supplies, grub and tools, and they need to build a flume. They're willing to make the mine a three-way partnership, with anybody who can come up with enough cash to keep them going.''

"But you don't have any money," Maggie protested, "only your wages."

"I've been putting some aside ever since Rosa got married. I told you, my mother doesn't need my help anymore. And I've got extra wages for moving the mill, I've managed to stash practically all of it. Maybe you've noticed I haven't been spending many evenings in town, so I haven't wasted much on drinking." He nuzzled her neck, which ordinarily sent prickles of delight through her; at the moment, it had no more effect than when Joe licked at her hand. "This is cheaper, and a lot more fun," he said, breathing into her ear.

Exasperation exploded through her. "Angus, for heaven's sake, just tell me and be done with it! Have you taken all your savings, everything you were putting aside for''— she choked over the words—"for *us*, and handed it over to two idiots who are convinced there's a fortune in a hole in the ground, if they can just find it?''

"Honey, they aren't idiots. The Blue Mountains have produced a lot of rich men. If they find the gold, I'll have a share of it without having to do anything but put up a comparatively small sum of money."

"And if they don't find it, your savings will be gone. It's such a gamble, with so little chance of success!''

"Darling, everything's a gamble. You think logging isn't a gamble? Every time a man climbs one of those trees, he risks his life, and the damned logs are just as dangerous to handle once they're on the ground. A rope or a chain breaks, a saw binds up, a man's foot slips, and he's caught under a few tons of Douglas fir. Hell, Maggie, this is no risk at all! Just a little money.''

Money he'd been setting aside for them to get married on, she thought, unable to subdue her resentment.

"I thought you'd be as excited as I am about it."

"Why should I be excited about your giving away money you already have on the remote chance that you might eventually get it back? I don't understand you, Angus."

"I thought you'd be pleased, that you'd be as adventurous as I am. It's a very small investment, with the possibility of a very large return. If it pays off, we won't be under your pa's thumb anymore. We can do what we please. Like get married."

He pulled her over backward in the loose hay, leaning above her with his face close enough so that she felt his breath. "Maggie, I want to marry you so bad I sometimes think I'd kill for you. I love you. I want you for my wife, and regardless of how things go with the mine, we'll get married within the year. You'll be seventeen in April, and if I save all my pay through the summer, it'll be enough to get us started. Love me, Maggie. Love me."

*Married within the year.* The words were balm to her soul, and his touch scorched her skin. Her lips parted beneath his; the miracle of wondrous sensation deprived her of resistance. Angus cajoled her and won her over in the way of men throughout the centuries, with hands and mouth and body.

She had waited for this moment, dreamed of it, was ready for it.

Maggie drifted in euphoria, aware of nothing beyond the moment, having no memory of garments disarranged or divested, or of the chill within the barn. There was only Angus, the lean, firm length of him, the smell and taste of him, the depth of emotion she had imagined so surpassed by the reality that even the sudden thrust of pain—unexpected, quickly fading—did nothing to diminish the exultation.

They lay together, spent at last, limbs tangled, breathing

slowing. Maggie was aware of a mild discomfort, yet it was nothing to compare with her joy, her sated senses.

Beside her, Angus groaned.

She turned her head, feeling the roughness of the hay on her cheek, beginning to be aware of the chill, though Angus had thrown his coat over her and her own skirts had been rearranged to cover her lower limbs.

"Why are you making that sound? Didn't you like it?"

Quite suddenly, she was drenched with the fear that she had been inadequate, that she was not worthy of becoming Angus's wife. The breath caught painfully in her chest.

"Like it?" The words were a moan that ended in rueful laughter as he rolled toward her, his mouth seeking hers again. "Oh, my God, Maggie, you were wonderful! Only I'm a damned fool for letting it happen—just the way I told you it would if you didn't fend me off. I knew it was too much to expect of you, to have the willpower I didn't have, but I kept coming here, kept seeing you. . . ."

He sat up, drawing away from her, though one hand still rested on the soft curve of her breast, where she clasped it with her own. "And now it's going to be worse than ever. Now we both know what it's like, so how are we going to be able to stop?"

"Will we have to stop?" Her voice was a whisper.

"Maggie, for the love of heaven, think what you're saying! I told you not to trust me, not to trust any man, and I shouldn't have let us get into a situation where neither of us could be trusted. I'm the one who's guilty, I'm the one who knew what I was doing, and it's no excuse that I wanted you so. . . . Listen, Maggie, we can't go on this way. It's too dangerous. We'll have to stop meeting here, see each other only in circumstances when this can't happen again, until we can be married."

Not meet again this way? Maggie sat up with a stifled cry. Deprive themselves of bliss when they had only just discovered it?

"We don't want any trouble," Angus told her, reaching for both her hands. "And that's all this can lead to. That would spoil any chance we'd ever have of getting your parents' blessings. Come on, it's time to go in. God knows what time it is, I completely lost track. I'm the one who's going to have to take the responsibility for what happens, and this isn't going to happen again. Not until we can get married."

Maggie sat frozen in dismay. "For a year? Angus . . ."

"Well, maybe we can work something out sooner than that." He gave a strangled laugh. "We'll have to. We'll never live through a whole year, keeping our hands off each other."

Maggie allowed herself to be lifted to her feet, leaning against him for a final moment of contact.

She wasn't sure she could live through a day without him, let alone a year.

## 33

In the days that followed Maggie was first astonished, then chagrined, and finally angered to learn that Angus meant just what he had said. There would be no more meetings anywhere it was possible to repeat that soul-altering episode in the barn.

Remembering was sheer bliss, though in the cold light of day there was also a thread of rationality. What they had done was wrong, by all moral standards of her family and the community, though guilt was by no means uppermost in her mind. While a part of her deplored her departure from everything she had been taught was right, Maggie's newly awakened body gave her no peace from her desires.

In dreams she lived it again—his kiss, his caress, the muscular strength of his body against hers. Yet, waking, she had to fight her conscience and recognize the validity of what Angus insisted upon.

"If you love me as much as I love you," she had said passionately to him during their next meeting, in plain view of various men working on the mill, "how can you insist that we can't see each other?"

Angus kept his words as low as hers had been, and there was no less fervency than she had displayed. "It's because I love you, you silly little twit, and I mean to protect you, even from yourself. I don't insist that we not see each other—God Almighty, I think I'd die if I didn't go on seeing you—but not *that way.* Not in places where we can lose our heads. If Jake wasn't in such a foul humor all the time these days, I'd talk to him, tell him we're in love and we want to get married, but he's impossible. He snarls at everything. Talking to him would only make things worse. Trust me, Maggie, to work something out as soon as I can, won't you?"

She recognized the sense of what he said, yet it was difficult to accept it. They could not even say what they wanted to say, in the presence of others, let alone touch. And the way she felt, like those idiotic heroines in the popular novels, she feared she would expire without these things.

It was only in her mind and her emotions that Maggie experienced emptiness. Her days were filled, for Mrs. Totting had taken ill with some malady the doctor had not yet diagnosed.

Nancy was kept running, tending to her mother. The housekeeper suffered abdominal pain and fever. She was able to do nothing beyond lie in her bed, often crying out despite the laudanum Dr. Croyden had left for her.

Maggie was drafted to take over the chores normally done by the Tottings. Housekeeping was not particularly a problem; with so few people in the house, it didn't get very dirty. This time of year there was not even dust filtering in from outside. Maggie quickly decided to ignore everything but the matter of keeping people fed and the laundry done, enough in themselves to leave her little leisure.

Nancy, always thin, grew positively scrawny. Even Ann, not the most perceptive observer, took note of it. "Is she eating, Margaret? She looks almost ill herself."

"She's eating a little. Mostly she says she's too tired. I don't think she's getting enough sleep at night, her mother's so restless."

Ann sighed. "Well, take care that you don't succumb to exhaustion, too. We can eat very simply, and if the house is not cleaned, why, it will simply have to wait until we can do it."

Accustomed for some weeks to sneaking out of the house after the other inhabitants were asleep, Maggie was finding it difficult to rest. She would retire at the customary time, only to lie awake, staring up into darkness, aching for the forbidden, then stagger out of bed at dawn, long before she felt refreshed.

Jake was, indeed, in a foul humor. It seemed to his men that he flew off the handle at every small obstruction to their progress with the mill, though delays were common enough in any job they might have set themselves to do. The warm winter, bringing rain rather than snow, complicated everything. It was impossible to accomplish very much in a sea of mud that sucked their boots into its depths and bogged down the oxen struggling to move supplies.

Not even Maggie connected his ill temper to the fact that Jaisy had removed herself to the edge of town. The press of work on the mill kept Jake on the job such long hours that it was not feasible to make nightly trips to visit her when he would arrive soaking wet and chilled, only to have to make the return trip within a matter of hours to be at the landing at daylight.

Lack of Jaisy's companionship was not his only pressure, of course. He hadn't expected that reassembling the mill would take as long as it was turning out to take; his funds were limited, and anything that made it necessary to pay out additional wages made him more apprehensive about the final outcome of this speculative venture.

The men were short-fused, as well. There were more than the usual number of fights, many of them set off by no more than a few ill-considered words. And as each fight invariably decreased the productivity of the crew, Jake yelled and swore at an unprecedented level. None of this behavior did anything to expedite their tasks.

Maggie tried to walk to the landing once a day, choosing a time when she didn't have to neglect too many of her own chores, unable to resist the compulsion to see Angus for a few minutes even if they couldn't talk at all, as was sometimes the case.

Any activity of a social nature was out of the question, though Maggie tried to pave the way for improvement. "Mama, when it's spring, can't we entertain again? We haven't had a party for ages, and it isn't because of Sarah, now. She'd be fine."

Ann looked at the child sitting on the floor. Sarah looked normal. She was a pretty baby, as Celeste had been pretty. It was only that she didn't *do* anything. No doubt everybody in the territory knew the Keatings had a mentally deficient child, but it was a difficult matter to put her on display.

"Celeste will be fifteen soon," Maggie urged, "and both of us need to have social contacts. By the time she comes home, she'll want to see her friends and meet young men, the same as I do. We could have small,

private dances here, couldn't we? Or a musical evening—
Celeste could entertain at the piano, or sing—and the
house wouldn't seem so empty." With no deliberate attempt to sway her mother by it, Maggie shivered. "Sometimes I feel as if we're living in a mausoleum, not a home.
It's so quiet, so empty."

To her surprise, Ann nodded slowly. "I know what you
mean. I feel it, too. Perhaps you're right. It isn't fair to
either you or Celeste to shun all social activity; it's only
reasonable to want to entertain young people, meet young
men. We'll think about it, Margaret."

Though it was better than she'd expected, Maggie couldn't
help pushing a little further. "Soon? Could we do something soon? We don't have to wait until Celeste comes
home, do we?"

"We'll see," Ann promised, and with that Maggie had
to be content for the moment.

A tentative date for Millicent and Celeste's homecoming
had been set, in mid-May. Their letters revealed an increasing homesickness, compounded by each one they
received in return from Maggie or Ann. Aunt Lealah's
health was not good, and she begged them to stay on. This
pulled Millicent in opposing directions, for she was by
now nominally in charge in her sister's house, while she
had always felt something of an unwelcome guest in her
son-in-law's more pretentious home with those she considered her immediate family.

If anyone truly appreciated the house at Keating's Landing, it wasn't Maggie. She couldn't wait to get out of it.

One afternoon when a watery sun offered a tepid hope
of coming spring, Maggie set off for the landing with a
cake for the men. She walked carefully, for the footing
was slippery, looking up and ahead only as she approached
her goal.

She realized then that the sounds of tools, of hammering
and sawing, had ceased. So had the voices.

The men stood in a rough circle around two of their number, the taller one identifiable by the red cap Maggie had knitted so long ago, worn at its customary rakish angle. She knew at once that the crew's stances spelled trouble.

She forgot the cake and started forward too rapidly, nearly going down with it before she reached a firmer footing and a pile of lumber that would serve as a place to set the cake.

She reached the edge of the circle of observers and stopped, appalled. The other man in the center of the ring was Wilkie Andreason.

Nobody paid any attention to Maggie. She looked around anxiously for her father; Jake was not in sight. Of all times for him to be absent, when Angus and Wilkie were going to do something stupid, she thought.

Both men were peeling off their winter jackets.

Maggie's throat tightened. She wanted to scream at them to stop, and did not dare.

"I have no desire to fight with you, McKay," Wilkie said, in a tone belying the words.

Angus's lips drew back in a feral grin. "I'll bet you don't," he agreed, tossing aside the jacket without looking to see where it fell. "But I've had about enough of your remarks, and I think it's about time somebody taught you a lesson."

"Perhaps you have a lesson coming to you, as well," Wilkie said, and his jacket, too, was flung away from him.

Maggie's throat ached. It wouldn't be a fair fight, it couldn't be. Wilkie spent his days writing figures in ledgers, while Angus had been swinging axes and pulling crosscut saws for years. They were not at all well matched.

Maggie saw the muscles bulge within their shirt-sleeves, watched as hands were formed into fists held high and ready. Beside her, Maggie heard someone mutter under his breath, "Get him, McKay."

She'd watched men fight before. It was always unsettling, but it had never before affected her like this. Why had they squared off to begin with? Please, God, that it didn't have anything to do with her. If anything would make Jake furious, it would be two of his employees trading blows because of his daughter. He'd probably hold her as much to blame as the men.

Angus jabbed out at the other man, catching Wilkie on the chin and rocking his head back; Maggie felt as if the shock waves traveled through her own body. Wilkie staggered back a step, rallied, and threw a respectable punch of his own that left a trickle of blood on his opponent's lip.

The watching circle of men was mostly silent now, except for an occasional grunt or sigh, as blows were delivered and absorbed. Blood gushed from Wilkie's nose, ignored, to drip onto his white shirtfront. The sound of flesh thudding into flesh was a sickening one, and it was with mingled relief and apprehension that Maggie heard the voice that put a stop to it.

"What in hell's going on? Stop it! Damn it, I said stop it!"

Jake's bellow finally penetrated the consciousness of the culprits. The men stepped reluctantly apart to allow him through; both fighters were still on their feet, breathing heavily.

"Get back to work! The whole damned lot of you! What do you think I pay you for? The next man of my crew gets into a fistfight and leaves a mark on anybody else in the crew is fired! You hear me? Fired!"

It was hardly a reasonable threat. Maggie read resentment on their faces. Loggers—hell, men in general—had always settled their differences with their fists.

"If everybody took a poke at anybody got fired, wouldn't be a man working in the whole of the territory," Tom

Dunnigan muttered, a sentiment echoed through the group in defiance of the edict.

Still, the fight had come to an end. Angus, nursing split knuckles, put up a hand to wipe his mouth. Wilkie, his breath rasping audibly, stared for a moment into his opponent's face, then turned away toward the office. The handkerchief he held to his nose immediately turned a bright, wet scarlet.

"Get back to work," Jake snapped again, and the men began to move, scattering.

Maggie turned to the man nearest her, catching his sleeve before he had taken more than a step. "Red, what were they fighting about?"

Red Risku shrugged. "That Andreason, he ain't got much of a sense of humor. Don't know how he's lasted this long in a logging camp, without somebody knocking his block off."

He turned away, not seeing Maggie's indignation.

Angus had bent to pick up his discarded coat. He shrugged into it and was buttoning it when he saw her. "Well, sorry you had to witness that."

"Why did you provoke him into a fight?" Maggie demanded in a low voice. "You know he's not a fighter."

"He did pretty well, for a bookkeeper," Angus said without animosity. "I hope I didn't break his nose. And to be perfectly accurate, it was Andreason who did the provoking."

"Why did you have to do it? Was it about me?"

She knew the moment the words escaped her lips that they were poorly chosen. Angus gave her a briefly searching look.

"No, why should we fight about you? If he'd said anything out of the wrong side of his mouth in that regard, I'd have broken more than his nose. You bring that cake over there for us?"

She didn't care about the cake. She had decided they

didn't deserve it; she'd leave it where it was and it didn't matter if the chipmunks came out of hibernation and ate it, or a bear, or if it fell in the mud.

"Why, then?"

"He's got no sense of humor," Angus said, and was spared further explanation at that time by Jake's angry summons.

Maggie stared at his retreating back in exasperation. What did Wilkie's sense of humor have to do with it? She didn't have much of that commodity herself, at this point.

She walked toward the office, where she could see Wilkie now pressing a towel or something to his face, since he'd drenched the handkerchief.

Sol Engstrom, grinning, met her with a hammer in his hand. "Quite a little tussle," he said, highly entertained.

"What was it all about? Everybody keeps talking about Wilkie's sense of humor, or lack of it. Was Angus playing pranks, and they backfired?"

Since Jake had vanished inside the partially completed mill, Sol felt safe in pausing. "Oh, wasn't only Angus. Everybody's been doing little things, off and on for weeks. That damned Andreason and his polished boots and his white shirts, sets everybody's teeth on edge. So he's been finding pins stuck in his sleeves when he puts on his coat, sawdust in his coffee, water bucket spilled on his lunch, that kind of thing. Nothing to get upset about. Only like the fellows said, he ain't got any sense of humor."

"And what did Angus do today, to test his sense of humor?"

Sol chuckled, missing the acidity of her words. "Well, I don't rightly think he *intended* to do anything, this time. Andreason was comin' out of the office, between that machinery there and that stack of lumber, and McKay was comin' from over that way, toward him. McKay got about to here"—he gestured with the hammer—"and saw there was a great big spiderweb wove in that opening. With the spider hisself sitting in the middle of it, just about eye level. McKay done what anybody woulda done; he batted down the web. Threw that fat old spider right onto Andreason's forehead." He laughed aloud. "One of the funniest things I ever seen."

"And Wilkie took offense," Maggie supplied. She could imagine the spider on her own face. If they'd already been tormenting him, she could understand how Wilkie would have taken it as one more assault upon his person.

"Did he ever! Called McKay a name I won't say in front of a lady, and McKay told him to watch his mouth, and one thing led to another." Sol laughed again, and waved the hammer at her. "I reckon old Jake'll fire me for standing around gabbin' as fast as for fightin', mood he's in today. See you later, Maggie."

Had Angus deliberately flung the spider into Wilkie's face? Or had it simply been instinctive, to knock it down and out of his way, without thought of the consequences? At least it hadn't concerned *her;* she supposed she should be grateful for that much.

Wilkie turned toward her as she entered the office. He lowered the towel from his face and tentatively wiggled his nose with a finger, wincing as he did so. "Hello, Maggie. I suppose you were a witness to my humiliation? I didn't make much of a showing, did I?"

She decided the most prudent course was to ignore that aspect of the matter. "Is your nose broken?"

"I don't think so, but it hurts like hell. I beg your pardon."

"I've heard all the words. I think it's stopping, the bleeding, I mean."

He regarded the towel in his hand. "I wonder if there's enough of an unbloodied end on this to clean myself off?"

He scooped a dipper from the water bucket and dampened the towel, then began to make tentative patting motions at his face.

Maggie reached for her own clean handkerchief. "Here, let me do that. Sit down, so I can reach you. You'll never get it all without a mirror."

He sank onto his stool, allowing her to take over. His left eye was beginning to swell and discolor; the gush of blood had slowed to a faint trickle. Maggie cleaned up his face as best she could, handing him the square of linen as a precautionary measure.

"Your shirt's a mess. Maybe you should take it off and rinse it out; if you hang it by the stove it'll dry in a few hours."

When she stepped back, Wilkie stood up and stripped off his shirt. He wore nothing under it, and though his skin was untanned, his torso was well built and muscular. He reached for his jacket to wear in place of the shirt, and pulled the stool back to the counter where he worked. "I'm sorry you had to see that, Maggie."

"I'm sorry it happened," she said. "I'm really sorry, Wilkie."

He managed a grin, then. "I'm going to look like the devil, aren't I?"

"For a day or two, probably," she admitted. "Is there anything I can do here to help you?"

"No. No, I'll be fine." Unexpectedly, he reached out for her hand and pressed it. "Thank you, Maggie."

She felt peculiar as she let herself out and headed for home. There had been an odd sort of sensation at his touch, almost the way she'd felt when Angus first held her hand, and it left her bewildered and mildly upset, because she didn't understand it. She was angry with Angus and the others for instigating an unpleasant situation, and she sympathized with Wilkie; but that hardly seemed reason enough to react to him with palpitations.

She walked on toward home, leaving the cake sitting on the stack of lumber, forgotten.

# 34

I'M in love, Maggie thought. It should be the happiest time of my life, yet I'm miserable. Why is everything going so wrong?

Mrs. Totting succumbed to her suffering, Nancy and Dr. Croyden at her side, a week after she had taken ill. Maggie came downstairs as the doctor was taking his leave, to find Nancy weeping in quiet despair.

"A pity," he said. "If there'd been a surgeon available, he might have done something for her, but I'm not trained for anything like that." His gaze flickered to Maggie. "A ruptured appendix, I suspect. It poisons the system, causes the pain and the fever, you see." He cleared his throat. "I'll send Mr. Shadpole out, if you like."

Nancy nodded, not speaking, though after the door had closed behind the physician, when Maggie had embraced her friend in a futile attempt to comfort her, she tried to pull herself together.

"What's to become of me? By the time I've paid the undertaker there won't be a penny to spare." She stared at Maggie, her face mottled, lips unsteady.

"You'll stay on here with us, of course. You and I have run the house since your mother was taken ill. We'll go on doing it."

A pair of tears coursed down Nancy's cheeks, and then

she collapsed in Maggie's arms and cried until exhaustion put an end to the tears.

Ann tried to rally the household, but while it was true that Sarah no longer required constant attention—indeed, it was perfectly safe to leave her on her blanket on the floor, for she simply sat there until they returned for her, unless someone got down on her level and coaxed her to crawl— Ann was obsessed by the conviction that if she worked with the child constantly, Sarah could be made to develop and learn. She did not want to give up that task to reassume household chores, which were therefore turned over to Maggie and Nancy.

Spring came early, warm and wet. Maggie attributed her growing malaise to having to stay indoors so much, to having almost no chance to speak to Angus privately, to the deterioration of the companionship she'd always enjoyed with her father.

With the completion of the reassembly of the mill, Jake had turned his attentions elsewhere. It was still too wet to resume logging operations, but it wasn't too early to talk about it. And when he made his daily trips to Snohomish to join the other men at the saloons to discuss lumber prices and methods of moving timber, it was only natural that he would head for home by way of Blackman Lake, and Jaisy Pallison's cabin.

His staying away from home almost all his waking hours—and some of his nonwaking ones—should have made it easier for Maggie to rendezvous with Angus. It didn't, because Angus didn't allow it to.

When they met on the edge of the woods at dusk, the rain didn't dampen the ardor of the kisses they exchanged. But not even the most impassioned of lovers could have gotten further carried away with rain trickling down necks and chilling any exposed skin.

"Angus, please, let's go into the barn, out of this

horrible wet,'' Maggie would plead, only to meet Angus's determined, tight-jawed resistance.

"We're not safe in there. No, Maggie. It isn't going to happen again. Listen, we can't go on this way.'' That was one point on which they concurred, Maggie thought. "As soon as you're seventeen, the end of April, I'm going to talk to Jake. Tell him we love each other, and we want to get married. He can't do any worse than fire me.''

"He won't fire you. Not when I tell him how much I love you,'' Maggie said, though with less confidence than she would once have made such a statement. Jake was less predictable these days.

The prospect of Angus approaching Jake for his permission to marry did not cheer her as much as it might have. Not after she'd heard what he said to her mother about Maggie being courted by any of the loggers. Still, she thought she'd eventually win him over. And if she didn't, if she and Angus together could not do it, why, they'd simply have to run away to be married; she was determined that there *would* be a wedding soon, one way or another.

There ought to have been more comfort in that than Maggie was able to summon. She was overly tired, and she hated keeping house. And most of all, she felt deprived of even the simplest of joys to which Angus had introduced her.

She was surprised when Jake announced the reopening of camp, for it was still far too wet to work.

"We've got to move camp,''he said, "so we might as well get at it. Be ready when we can start cutting trees again. We're going upstream. I want to get into that big stand of fir on top of North Ridge. Be an easy chute down to the river from there; we shouldn't even have to build a skid road except for the last mile or so.''

It meant the men—and Angus—would be farther away. Besides that, it meant that Jaisy would return to camp, because the men wouldn't stand for doing their own so-called cooking any longer. If they were going to work twelve-hour days, they expected well-prepared meals with no additional effort.

"Lucy and Will will have to withdraw from school. Maybe I'll plan on going to camp a day or two a week, to tutor them so they don't get behind," Maggie suggested.

Jake agreed with a grunt. "Fine. Oh, Maggie, Wilkie asked if he could call on Sunday. He'll be here about two."

Her heart lurched. She'd put Wilkie off in so many ways that she'd run out of believable excuses. Still, maybe entertaining anyone was better than sitting around feeling sorry for herself, though it was high time she put an end to this. She would have to tell him that her affections were engaged elsewhere, even if it meant unwelcome speculation about the object of those affections.

When she learned that Adam Welker was coming on Sunday to call on Nancy, too, Maggie's spirits rose a little. "Let's entertain them together, to begin with, anyway," she suggested.

Nancy's eyes widened. "Together? What would your ma say?"

"Chances are she'll be upstairs with Sarah and won't know the difference. You can't entertain Adam in your bedroom, so you'll have to see him in the parlor, won't you? Nancy, you're not a servant, you're a part of the family. Let's make some little iced cakes, and we'll serve them with tea, and then I'll take Wilkie somewhere else— to look at the stereoscope in the family parlor, maybe— and leave you and Adam alone. Then we can each have a private talk."

Though Nancy was dubious about Ann considering her part of the family, she allowed herself to be won over. She harbored the hope that Adam was about to propose marriage. She was grateful for Maggie's friendship and the fact that she'd been given refuge at Keating's Landing, but it wasn't what she longed for. A home of her own, with a loving husband, would do a great deal to restore her to good spirits.

The planned Sunday afternoon activities never took place, however. Catastrophe struck on two fronts, in ways neither of the girls had anticipated.

Maggie rose on Saturday feeling decidedly unwell. She heard her mother talking animatedly with Sarah as she carried the child down to breakfast; when Maggie opened her own door, the odor of frying bacon rose through the house, sending her on a sudden urgent quest for a basin.

She felt somewhat better after she'd emptied her stomach of its meager contents, though the episode left her feeling clammy and trembling. What on earth was the matter with her?

She wiped her mouth, rinsed it, and emptied the basin into the slop jar. The thought of breakfast was repellent, but she supposed she'd have to go downstairs and get busy making the cakes for tomorrow. She was better at that than Nancy.

To her astonishment, she heard Jake's voice as she approached the dining room. Jake was never home this time of day except on Sunday, and for months had not even been here then. She swallowed against the lingering nausea and entered the room where the others had been gathered around the table.

She was in time to hear the small, pitiful sound that issued from Nancy's bloodless lips as a platter of bacon and eggs slid from her hands onto the polished oak floor.

Jake grabbed for the girl herself, who was so pale that Maggie thought she'd had some sort of seizure. "Here, sit down," Jake said, easing the girl onto a chair. "Put your head down on your knees." He glanced around and saw Maggie. "Clean up that mess, will you, honey?"

Maggie forgot her queasiness. "What's wrong?" She used a napkin to push the spilled food back onto the platter and set it aside to be given to Joe later. "What's happened?"

Ann, the baby on her lap where the child was crumbling toast over both herself and her mother, looked stricken. "Oh, my, how dreadful! Nancy, I'm so sorry, dear."

"What?" Maggie demanded. She took several quick steps and knelt beside Nancy's chair, reaching for one of the knotted hands. It was ice cold. Maggie looked up at her father, who still stood with one hand on her friend's shoulder.

"I brought the news from town," Jake said heavily. "Adam Welker was killed last night."

For a moment Maggie was so dizzy she thought she'd fall the rest of the way to the floor. "Adam? What happened?"

He wasn't working in the woods yet, nobody was, not when the rains fell every day as if there were no end to them. "What happened?" she asked again, this time in a whisper.

Jake told the story in a flat, dispassionate voice. "He signed on with Rohner to make some repairs on a flume before they open the mill for the season. He slipped and fell onto the rocks. His neck was broken."

His hand tightened on Nancy's shoulder in the only gesture he could make to show his sympathy, then released her as Maggie's arm crept around the girl's waist.

"It's been a hell of a day, all the way around. I fired two men this morning."

That jerked Maggie out of her horror over Adam Welker's death. "What? Who?"

"Woolrich, damn it. He was so drunk he didn't know what he was doing. He was trying to get a team to move a load of lumber the men tore apart yesterday, the rest of the cookhouse, and he put too much on the sledge, and then tried to take it through the woods, right into that little swamp east of camp. The sledge sank out of sight, naturally, as he'd have expected if he'd been sober. And the damned oxen—'' He inhaled, then sighed. "They got mired to their bellies, one of 'em fell down, and damned if the old fool didn't kill that bull and its mate before anybody could stop him. Then they had the devil's own time getting the other bulls out of the muck; they were all in a panic by then, with the smell of the blood and the bellowing.''

He wiped a hand over the lower part of his face. "I should have fired him the other time, when he hit that ox with a sledgehammer. Now I got three of the goddamned things to replace.''

Within the circle of her arm, Nancy shook uncontrollably. Maggie tightened her embrace and had to swallow before she could ask, "Who else?''

He turned away and therefore did not see her face.

"McKay. We got in a yelling match, and I told him to pick up his bedroll and walk with it. Damn it, it's my outfit. I've got to be the one to make the decisions, and I don't aim to argue every one of 'em.'' He had chosen a cigar from the humidor on the buffet, and busied himself lighting it. "I told them before, I don't intend to put up with this fighting and I can't have a bullwhacker that gets drunk and kills his own bulls, either.''

Maggie felt the vertigo return; she was hanging on to Nancy now to keep from falling, afraid that she was going to faint.

"Daddy, you can't have fired Angus.'' The words did not emerge with the force she'd intended; they were barely audible. "He's a good worker, you know he is, and whatever your quarrel was, it'll blow over, the same as it always has with any of the men.''

"Not this time. I told Wilkie to pay him off, and he's gone. I heard he grubstaked Berquist and Ballantine in some diggings in Oregon; he'll probably go work with them. Nobody hiring loggers in this part of the country that I know of.''

The blood roared in her ears, and there were black spots before her eyes. "He's already gone?'' He couldn't be. Angus wouldn't go without seeing her, no matter what had passed between him and her father.

Jake inhaled cigar smoke and exhaled it, looking at her through the haze. "Had some damned fool notion of coming up here to the house first. Had to talk to Maggie, he said. Well, I let him know he wasn't welcome here, and it wouldn't change anything to upset my womenfolks. I knew you'd argue about me firing him, honey, but a man's got to draw the line somewhere. I can't run an outfit unless I'm the boss of it. Set an example with McKay, and maybe the rest of them'll see I mean what I say. He's a good worker when he's doing his job, I'll admit it, but he's a damned agitator. Says what he thinks and gets everybody else thinking the same way, like that business with Wilkie. The whole damned crew was getting crossways of Wilkie, trying to stir up trouble, just for the hell of it. I depend on Wilkie, I respect his advice, and there's no way he can do a good job with all that schoolboy stuff going on. I don't know who the hell put the dead squirrel in his coat, but the coat still stinks, and the man's going to have to buy a new one or hang that one outside for the next six months. That kind of thing may seem funny, but it's costing me money, and I've had enough of it.''

She hadn't heard about the dead squirrel. It didn't seem the kind of thing Angus would have thought up. She made a bleat of protest. "Daddy, you can't have fired Angus because of things everybody was in on! That's not fair!''

"I don't know who did all that crap, but I know Angus McKay talked to me this morning in a way I don't have to take from anybody. With him gone, the rest ought to settle down. I told him plain out, when he insisted he had to talk to you, that he might as well forget it. I told him Wilkie was courting you, we'd given him permission to call, and Wilkie backed me up, said he'd been calling for months. Between us, I think we pretty well convinced McKay he was wasting his time."

Maggie forced herself to her feet. "You couldn't have. Angus wouldn't accept anybody's word for that but mine!"

"Why the hell not? There's nothing between you, is there? And you *did* ask permission for Wilkie to call. If you have to take one of them, Wilkie's probably the best bet. At least I don't have to argue with him every time I open my mouth."

He turned away, pausing only to chuck Sarah under the chin with one bronzed finger. "I have to go back to town. I'll have to find another pair of bulls, and a bullwhacker, too, I guess. Don't expect me for supper."

Nobody ever expected him for supper these days. Maggie fought the impulse to run after him, to pound on his chest and make him understand the enormity of what he'd done.

But there was Nancy. Nancy, deprived first of her mother, and now of her lover. The man who might have proposed marriage, had he come to call tomorrow. How could she abandon Nancy at such a time?

Nancy was lifting her head, making an attempt to pull herself together. "Maggie—go, if you want to. I'll be all right."

It was patently untrue, yet her own need was great, too. "You sure?" Maggie asked. "Nancy, I can't tell you—" It was literally true; the words stuck in her throat.

Nancy swallowed convulsively. "Nothing's going to bring Adam back, is it? But you might still . . ."

Ann was frowning slightly. "What are you going to do, Margaret? Where are you going?"

"I have to find Angus and talk to him, before he really leaves town. I'm going to take the buggy, Mama."

She didn't wait to hear Ann's puzzled protest. She

snatched a cape off the hook beside the door and was gone before her mother could move to stop her.

She caught up with him on the edge of town, walking in long strides with his coat slung over one shoulder. He didn't turn at the sound of the horse and buggy; it was not until she'd passed him and stopped in the middle of the road that he acknowledged her presence.

His face frightened her as badly as she'd ever been frightened in her life. It was cold and hard.

"Angus, wait. I have to talk to you!"

"Not a hell of a lot to talk about, is there?" He kept on walking.

Maggie dropped the reins and jumped down, running after him. She grabbed his sleeve, which did succeed in bringing him to a halt. She released her hold immediately and looked up into that savagely angry countenance.

"Daddy just told me he'd fired you, but oh, Angus, you can't go!"

His mouth was flat and tight. "I can't very well stay. Jake didn't mince any words. About me being fired, or about you. You and Wilkie Andreason."

"I can explain about Wilkie—"

"He's been calling for months?" Angus asked. "Wilkie's been courting you, with family approval, for months? And you never saw fit to mention it? Did you sleep with *him*, too?"

The terrible words rocked her back as if he'd struck her. Indeed, it would have been less painful if he had.

"No! Angus, no! My God, listen to me—"

"I see now why you thought we might have been fighting about you. And why your handkerchief was in his pocket; it fell out when he was putting his coat on, the afternoon of the fight. I see a lot of things, Maggie Keating, and I don't like any of them."

"He asked if he could call, and I thought if they said

yes to him, eventually they'd have to say yes to you! I was afraid to ask about you calling, first, for fear if they said no they'd find a way to keep you and me apart, and I couldn't have stood that! Angus, please, talk to me! Let me explain!'' She knew she sounded incoherent, yet she felt so hysterical the words wouldn't come calmly, rationally.

There was no softening of the granite features. ''What is there to explain, Maggie? You were leading me on—God!'' He gave a short, barking laugh with no amusement in it. ''I felt so damned guilty because I thought I'd seduced you, and all the time you and Wilkie—''

''No!'' She screamed it at him, clutching desperately at his arms. ''Angus, don't do this! It's not true, Wilkie's nothing to me, nothing ever happened between us! There's never been anyone but you, ever since I was a little girl, I swear it!''

''And that's why you asked if we were fighting about you? Did you think we'd never find out, either one of us, that you were seeing the other one? Just because we didn't like each other, didn't talk to each other? It won't wash, Maggie. I feel like you cheated on me, and you sure as hell cheated on *him*. Well, maybe if you're lucky he doesn't know that yet; maybe you can land him before he finds out, because I don't intend to be around to tell anybody. Good-bye, Maggie.''

He pulled loose from her hands, tossing her aside as he would have brushed at a fly. He strode away, his long legs outdistancing her at once when she took a few steps after him. She would have had to run to keep up, and she couldn't physically hold him still long enough to get through to him. In fact, at the moment she wasn't sure there was anything that *could* get through.

Maggie stared after him through the blur of tears. She felt as if something shattered and tore in her chest, something that could never be mended.

# 35

Mrs. Totting's death had come first, then Adam Welker's. The third one, Maggie reflected darkly, ought to be her own.

It had finally dawned on her why she felt so terrible. Not anguish over losing the man she loved, at all, though he'd certainly played his part in what was wrong with her.

She was carrying Angus's child.

Nancy's jaw sagged when Maggie told her. "Oh, mercy! Are you sure?"

"As sure as I can be, without having Dr. Croyden verify it. Which I don't intend to do. I couldn't bear to have him examine me. Besides that, he's such an old foof, and I'm not sure he'd keep still about it."

Nancy pressed a hand over her heart. "Dear heaven. What are you going to do?"

"I don't know," Maggie said slowly. "Nothing shows yet, does it?" She remembered so vividly how the women had been able to tell, when Ann was pregnant.

"No, no. Your dresses aren't tight yet, are they?"

"No. But I suppose it won't be long. I don't know why I didn't realize what was happening before, when I felt so dreadful there for a few weeks. I've never paid any attention to when I have my monthly show. It's never caused any discomfort, like so many women have, and it's never stopped me from doing whatever I felt like doing.

417

So I didn't notice when it didn't happen, at least at first. And then when I began to wonder why . . . I'd been upset about so many things"—there was no need to enumerate them for Nancy's benefit—"and sometimes that makes a difference, I've heard. Only now I've missed three of them. And I *did* feel sickish, for a short time."

Nancy was staring at her in complete dismay. "You must have thought of something, by this time," she said. "Something to do."

Maggie's face felt as if it were cracking with the strain. "I suppose the only sensible thing to do," she said, "is tell my father."

Nancy didn't look as if she thought that prospect a helpful one, but she had no other suggestion to make.

"This afternoon," Maggie said, rather firmly considering that her insides were quaking jelly. "I'm going to leave a note for him at the mill, and ask him to meet me at the old cabin in town, when he can get loose. I don't want to talk to him anywhere we're likely to be interrupted."

Nancy's only reply was a soft sigh.

It was late when Jake finally came. Maggie saw him through the unwashed window and her heart set up a staccato beat that felt as if it should be visible through the white silk of her shirtwaist.

The tears had dried. She wouldn't meet him in tears; she was moderately proud of that. Her clasped hands knotted below her breasts, and she forced herself to breathe deeply.

Jake had to duck his head to come through the doorway. The drizzle that had lasted for days had finally cleared, and a watery sun outlined him for a moment, there in the opening, before he stepped across the threshold.

"Maggie? You here?"

She moved toward him, wishing with all her soul that she did not have to do this to him. Maybe she *should* have killed herself. No, that was stupid, that would have hurt him even more, hurt everybody who cared about her. It would be the cowardly way out, creating more pain for everyone but herself. She'd never considered herself a coward.

"Daddy . . ."

She had rehearsed the words all the way here—she had walked to town, so there would be no telltale horse or buggy to give away her hiding place, or to arouse unwelcome speculation—but now that the moment had come, her throat had closed. She was unable to speak at all.

He came toward her in the dimness, reaching out a hand to rest it on her shoulder. "Maggie? What's wrong?"

Without knowing she was going to do it, she flung her arms around his neck and buried her face against him, as she had done when she was a little girl.

He held her for a moment, then put her away from him, his big gentle hands on her upper arms. "What is it, honey? What's the matter?"

Somewhere a bird sang. She ought to know what kind of bird it was, but she couldn't remember.

"Maggie? It can't be so bad we can't talk about it. We've always been able to talk about things, haven't we?"

Had they? They certainly hadn't been able to talk about Angus, the most important thing in her life, though maybe if she'd tried a little harder, if she'd explained fully to him before Angus left town . . . Who knew?

She drew another breath and willed the words to be spoken, no matter how badly they hurt. "Daddy, I'm going to have a baby."

For a few seconds she thought he didn't hear her, or understand her. Then the fingers gripped her arms until they surely made bruises on her flesh.

"A baby?"

"I can't tell Mama," she said.

A shudder ran through him, much like what happened to a mighty fir when the ax and the saw had bitten through it and it finally began its fall. He was like those trees, strong, yet vulnerable when the force of man or nature was brought into play.

"A baby." That was said gently enough, and then his voice deepened, growing harsh. "Wilkie? And he hasn't asked you to marry him?"

"Not Wilkie."

His breath rasped and his hands fell away from her.

"Not . . ?" Comprehension came, then. "McKay? Jesus, honey, not McKay?"

She did not know she put all the longing and heartbreak of her seventeen years into the words. "I've loved Angus all my life, Daddy."

"And he took advantage of you. . . ." His big hands clenched into fists. "I'll kill him."

"No. No, he didn't take advantage of me. I was more to blame than he was, because I stupidly insisted on meeting him in such a way that it was bound to happen. He warned me, he tried to keep it from happening, but I wanted him so much. So much, Daddy." Her voice broke.

"And he didn't want you." He sounded like a man who has just taken a powerful blow to the midsection.

"He did, once. Until he thought I'd . . . I'd deceived him, with Wilkie. Wilkie is just . . . a friend. You'd made it so clear you wouldn't allow any of the crew to have anything to do with me, and we were afraid of you. It was stupid to be afraid of you, wasn't it, Daddy?"

She did not shed any more tears, but they were there, in her voice.

"Oh, God, Maggie. I'm sorry. I'm sorry, I wish I'd known."

"I haven't been able to think what to do. I can't hurt Mama."

"No," he agreed at once. "We can't hurt your mama."

She knew, when he said *we*, that he would take care of everything. That he would, as he had always done, make it all right, somehow.

It wasn't easy. When Jake announced that Maggie had decided to go away for six months to a school for young ladies, Ann was astonished.

"To school! But you've finished with school! And you absolutely refused to think about going away for an education!"

"There are things I didn't learn," Maggie said, keeping her tone steady. "Things they don't teach in Snohomish."

Ann cast a bewildered glance at her husband, then returned her attention to Maggie. "What sort of things?"

"There's a school in Portland that prepares people for business," Jake said. "Wilkie Andreason went to something like that, to learn accounting. Maggie really wants to help run the mill and the logging operation, and this could help."

"Business?" Ann's face plainly showed how foreign the concept was to her. "Margaret, dear, are you sure? To leave us for six whole months, to go to a strange place? To learn to do . . . whatever it is?"

"Yes," Maggie said firmly. "I want to go. Celeste will take over here at home, Mama. It's not what I want, the things I've been doing these past months. I want to be part of what Daddy does."

Ann nibbled on her lower lip. "I thought we were very pressed for cash. This would be expensive, surely."

"Well, prices seem to be holding even, and I should get top dollar for what we're going to be cutting the next month. It's prime timber. And she's right, she could help me a lot with a little book knowledge to go along with her own common sense."

She held the lip between her teeth. "Portland. Isn't that three or four hundred miles away?"

"It's a lot closer than California," Maggie reminded her. She even managed a smile. "And you'll have Grandma and Celeste home soon."

"Six months," Ann said faintly. Jake and Maggie exchanged glances. They had won the first skirmish. Now there remained the real battle.

Nancy went with her. A woman from the village, a Mrs. Appling, was hired to assist in the house. Clothes were prepared, packed into trunks, and good-byes were said. "So quickly, without giving me time to think," Ann complained.

Neither of the girls had ever traveled so far. They took a steamer from Port Gardner and sailed north, up Puget Sound, out through the San Juan Islands and the Strait of Juan de Fuca, and then down the coast of Washington Territory to the mouth of the great Columbia.

They might have thoroughly enjoyed the voyage had it not been for the necessity of it. The scenery was wildly beautiful, and neither of them so much as thought of being seasick. They spent hours staring across sparkling blue water at the mysterious islands thick with virgin timber, at picturesque rocks and isolated, tempting beaches. Someday, Maggie thought, she would travel this way again, under happier circumstances.

They had discussed making the sojourn only into Seattle, which would have been much less expensive, and much quicker to reach and to return from. But in those very things lay its hazard. For there were those who traveled from Snohomish—not very often, but occasionally—into Seattle. To be encountered there by an acquaintance, with her belly unmistakably distended in pregnancy, would have undone all their efforts.

It was most unlikely that they'd see anyone in Portland they'd ever met before or would see again. Maggie found herself, alone at night and unable to sleep, imagining that

Angus might be found there—after all, he had to pass through or by the city in order to reach the Blue Mountains in eastern Oregon—but she knew it was no more likely than that she'd meet her sister there, on the way home from California.

At Cape Disappointment the steamer headed east, up the broad Columbia, through a land lush and green with spring. Maggie swallowed hard, realizing that the vine maples would be scarlet and the maples turning gold, before she passed this way again.

Jake had not told her how he made the arrangements for them in Portland, or through whom. There *was* a school, and Maggie would attend, for as long as it would be possible for her to go. All she knew was that she had been enrolled under the name of *Mrs*. Miller.

The rooms had been arranged for, also; two of them, in a shabbily respectable house within walking distance of the school. Maggie applied herself diligently, determined that Jake should have some return for all this beyond a grandchild he would never see.

Nancy passed a week in exploring the city, then announced her decision to seek employment. It was pointless to sit and do nothing while Maggie went to school. The position she obtained as maid to a wealthy family would provide funds to ease Jake's burden in keeping them here.

The house in which she worked was built high on a ridge overlooking Portland; from the gardens it was possible to see five snow-capped peaks rising majestically against the sky, a poignant reminder of home.

One Sunday she took Maggie there to show her the view. "There's Mount Adams," she said, gesturing, "and Mount Saint Helens, and Mount Hood." She swung around, facing farther to the south. "And Mount Jefferson, and the Three Sisters. Isn't it beautiful, Maggie?"

With a lump in her throat for her own beloved mountains, Maggie had to agree.

A Mrs. Framer came to visit them. She was a pleasant-faced, middle-aged woman, with an exceptionally soft voice. "You have only to call upon me when the time comes, Mrs. Miller," she said, and something in the way she spoke the name told Maggie plainly that Mrs. Framer was in no way deceived. "I assure you that I have assisted in the births of over a hundred infants, all of them safely accomplished. I understand that since you are widowed, and will have to work for a living, you do not wish to keep the child. There are always those willing to take a good, healthy little one. By the time you take to your bed, I'm sure I will have arranged for suitable adoptive parents. That is what you wish, I believe?"

Maggie's mouth was dry, her heart pounding, but she replied calmly enough. "Yes, thank you. That is what I wish."

She did not really like Mrs. Framer, though she knew her dislike was irrational. She walked to the school every day and applied herself to the lessons, finding them interesting enough to make her forget, for a few hours at a time, what had necessitated this experience.

It was at night, sleeping beside Nancy, that grief and homesickness overwhelmed her. Grief for the loss of Angus—how many letters did she pen, trying to make him understand, to believe, only to burn them, for there was nowhere to send them?—and longing for her family.

Though she did not often speak of Angus, he was seldom out of her thoughts for long. During the evenings she read aloud from the book he had given her, and the familiar words both provided solace and increased her melancholy yearning for home.

"Ye who love the haunts of Nature,
Love the sunshine of the meadow,
Love the shadow of the forest,
Love the wind among the branches,

And the rain-shower and the snow-storm,
And the rushing of great rivers
Through their palisades of pine-trees,
And the thunder in the mountains,
Whose innumerable echoes
Flap like eagles in their eyries—''

She had to pause in her reading because of the tears that blurred her vision; when she had wiped her eyes, she saw that Nancy, too, had need of a handkerchief.

Celeste and Millicent did not return home as scheduled, in June. Aunt Lealah had taken a turn for the worse, and they could not in good conscience leave her. And then, after her sister died in late July, Millicent herself suffered a stroke. There was no question of her traveling. Celeste wrote that she was managing fairly well, with the assistance of Aunt Lealah's son, and that they would travel north as soon as Millicent's health permitted.

Maggie awoke one muggy night in mid-August, feeling uncomfortable and restless. Half an hour later, wandering about the small rooms quietly so as not to disturb Nancy, she realized that she was in labor.

Nancy was roused to go for Mrs. Framer. Maggie was alone, only a little nervous, not really afraid. She was in excellent health, and walking to and from school had kept her agile and strong. She welcomed the pain that meant it would soon be all over.

"Very good, dear," Mrs. Framer said, beaming. "Now, push!" The woman was beside her bed, and after a time Maggie forgot who she was, concentrating only on expelling the infant that was tearing her apart. Soaked in sweat, gasping, welcoming the cool washcloth that Nancy used to bathe her face from time to time, Maggie knew why they called it *labor*.

Four hours from the time Mrs. Framer had arrived, she

smilingly laid the infant in the crook of Maggie's arm. "Beautiful little boy," she said. "Now, see if he'll nurse, and then you can rest."

Maggie twisted her head to look down at him, this tiny bit of humanity with the red face and the fuzz of dark hair, and felt as if the earth shifted beneath her.

The tiny mouth, at first coaxed, then seeking, fastened on her engorged nipple, and Maggie knew, beyond any doubt.

She could never give up this child. Never.

"Please, Nancy," Maggie begged. "Please. I'll do anything you ask, for the rest of my life. Only claim this baby as your own, and come home with me."

She knew the enormity of the favor she asked. It was to Nancy's credit that she hesitated, instead of refusing at once.

"Your ma's gone, there's no family to disgrace. Your cousins aren't even still in Snohomish, and they'll never hear anything about you from Idaho. I can't take him home, it would be such a scandal my mother would never survive it, not to mention Celeste and Grandma Miles. Celeste still has to find a husband and marry, and an illegitimate nephew might ruin her whole life. I swear, if it were only my own reputation, I'd let them ostracize me forever, but I can't do it to *them*. Only I can't give him over to strangers, either, I can't!"

Nancy put out a tentative finger and felt the baby's hand curl around it. A smile teased the corners of her mouth. "He really is a darling, isn't he?"

"I've never loved anyone so passionately in my life," Maggie said, exaggerating only slightly. "Please, Nancy, at least think about it."

On the following day, when Mrs. Framer came to collect the baby, bringing with her the couple to whom she had promised the child, Nancy and Maggie faced her together.

"I'm sorry. I've changed my mind," Maggie told her

huskily, with a certainty that made the woman's color heighten. "I'm going to keep him."

"Oh, I say, now, you can't do that!" the gentleman protested. Maggie looked at him more closely, then, and saw a man who reminded her of Grandpa Miles, as he'd looked in the picture his widow kept on her night table. His wife was a thin, nervous woman in a stylish mauve gown, dripping ruffles and lace and a handsome bustle. She, too, made a squawking sound.

"I'm sorry," Maggie said, though she wasn't. She didn't want these people ever to touch her precious son. "I didn't mean to cause anyone any inconvenience, but—"

"Inconvenience!" Mrs. Framer's eyes snapped. "My dear *Mrs. Miller,* may I remind you that I have looked after you all these months, helped the little one into the world, with the understanding that—"

Maggie drew on her recollection of Jake at his most authoritative. "I'm very sorry. I've signed nothing to that effect. You'll be paid for your efforts—unless, as I believe to be the case, you've already been paid—but you cannot have my son. Nancy, please show our visitors out."

"Yes, ma'am," Nancy said, and moved with an authority of her own to open the door, allowing them no choice except to leave.

The trio filed out, still blustering, disgruntled and disappointed, and showing it. Nancy closed the door behind them.

"You're right, Maggie. We couldn't let them take our baby."

They clung to one another, laughing and crying at the same time, until the baby's wail sent them running for the bedroom, eager to attend to his needs.

# 36

"For the first time in my life, I have a bosom," Maggie said, "and I don't dare go home and show it. We may convince everyone that he's your child, but not if I'm the one who has to feed him."

"How long will we wait?" Nancy asked, and Maggie read the longing in her friend's words. Though she had no family to return to, she, too, was homesick.

"Until he's at least three months old, I think. Then maybe I can bear to feed him from a bottle. I love feeding him, Nancy."

Nancy smiled. "You love everything about him, even changing diapers. When are we going to stop calling him *him* and give him a name?"

Maggie bit her lip. "He's going to be your son. Maybe you should be the one to name him."

Nancy shook her head. "No. You're his real mother. That should be your right, to give him a name."

Maggie felt as if she were seeing most of the world these days through a mist. "I daren't name him after Angus. My second choice to that would be to call him Jacob, but that wouldn't do, either."

Nancy had to laugh, though there was a thread of fear in it. "I can imagine the reaction in Snohomish. The old biddies would think I'd gotten pregnant by my employer, and he'd sent me away to have the baby and I'd been too stupid to get rid of it.''

Maggie's gaze locked with Nancy's. ''Do you think I've been foolish? To try to keep him by pretending to the world that he's yours?''

''No, no,'' Nancy said quickly; she shifted her weight from one foot to the other and bent over the bed they'd improvised out of a wooden cracker box. ''I know why you can't bear to give him up. I don't think I could do it, either. Only it isn't going to be easy, fooling everybody.''

She didn't mention how difficult it would be for *her,* allowing everyone to believe she was an immoral woman.

''It'll be hard for him, too,'' Nancy pointed out. ''Being illegitimate. Children can be crueler than their elders, and their elders will make sure they know about him. They're going to think he's Adam's child, you know. I've only just realized that. If Adam had—had lived—and we'd married, there would have been only a spell of gossip about him being born a bit too soon. People let that sort of thing die down. It happens to enough of them so they can't make a big thing of a seven months' baby. But this little one—''

''I know,'' Maggie whispered. ''But I have to keep him near me, somehow. And we haven't solved the problem of his name, have we? I'll have to think about it.''

Nancy continued in her position as maid. Maggie was content to stay at home and care for the infant. She held him, rocked him, sang to him, and read to him. One day she cuddled him against her breast, reading as if he understood every word.

''In the kingdom of Wabasso,
In the land of the White Rabbit,
He it was whose hand in Autumn,
Painted all the leaves with scarlet,
Stained the leaves with red and yellow;
He it was who sent the snow-flakes,

Sifting, hissing through the forest,
Froze the ponds, the lakes, the rivers,
Drove the loon and sea-gull southward—''

She broke off suddenly, struck by the idea.

"That's what I'll call you! Henry Wadsworth Longfellow Totting!" The book slid, unheeded, from her knees as she jiggled the baby, staring into his unfocused eyes. "Oh, Lord, no, I can't put all that on you! Henry, though, if Nancy likes it. Henry Longfellow Totting. How does that sound to you?"

A bubble formed, grew, and broke on the rosebud mouth, and Maggie's crow of laughter dissolved in tears. "Oh, how am I ever going to bear it, not being able to have you for my own?"

By the time Nancy returned, however, Maggie met her with a smile. "I've found his name," she said, and Henry it was.

They sailed for home on the twelfth of November.

Maggie had given no hint in her letters home of impending or actual birth. She and Nancy had discussed it endlessly, and as Maggie had summed it up, "There's no point in giving Mama any ammunition to fight until we've reached the battleground."

Nancy admitted to extreme apprehension. "What if your ma refuses to have me and the baby in the house? She well might, and no one would blame her."

"Daddy and I will gang up on her, as we've had to do in the past when something was important. Nancy, I can't tell you how much this means to me, your willingness to do this. I'll love you forever."

Nancy's mouth quirked. "You loved me before I'd done anything for you," she said. "Now you're the only family I have, and it's not likely there'll be another Adam come along. The life I thought to have is ended, anyway."

It didn't ease Maggie's conscience very much, but she

wanted Henry so desperately that any other consideration was secondary, even Nancy's life, or her own.

Celeste and Millicent were still in California. Though Millicent had recovered to a large extent, the local doctor had advised against an extensive journey before spring.

Maggie thought of her sister, who mentioned nothing in her letters of any social life, and wondered how she was bearing up under playing nurse to an elderly lady. Poor Celeste, she thought. Well, at least Maggie hadn't ruined her chances of making a good marriage by damaging the family reputation. Not if they could get away with this. She refused to think of the consequences if they were unsuccessful.

Jake met them in Port Gardner. He gathered Maggie into his arms for a quick hug, then stared in consternation at the baby in Nancy's arms.

"What in hell? . . . Maggie, you've brought him . . . is it a boy?".

"His name's Henry," Maggie said, and watched the play of emotion on her father's face. "We're going to tell everybody that he's Nancy's. I couldn't give him over to those people, Daddy. I couldn't."

Jake reached for the bundled infant and folded back the covering so that he could see the baby's face. Maggie had never heard him speak so gently. "No, of course you couldn't. Good God, what are we going to do with your mother?"

"Persuade her, since Nancy is alone in the world except for relatives who have all left the territory, and she is my best and dearest friend, that we must keep her with us."

Again she had rehearsed the words so that she could say them with confidence. They exchanged glances, and the baby was handed back to Nancy; they headed for the buggy. They all knew it would not be easy.

\*　　\*　　\*

Ann was aghast.

"Margaret, did you know when you left here that Nancy was expecting?"

"No. She didn't know it, either," Maggie said, which was the absolute truth. "Mama, I know this is upsetting to you, but it's happened. Henry is a darling, good baby, and Nancy needs a home. I've promised her she may live here with us."

For an instant anger sparked in Ann's face. "You promised? Without consulting me or your father?"

"Daddy's given his permission. Mama, there's no reflection on you; more than likely you'll be regarded as a Good Samaritan, that you've taken in an unfortunate girl and her baby. You'll come to love Henry as much as I have, I know you will."

Ann gave no such indication. She had scarcely glanced at the infant, or at Nancy, though she had not stopped the girl from taking the baby upstairs. She glared upward, however.

"What are you planning? To settle them into the best bedroom?"

"There are plenty of bedrooms, Mama. And Mrs. Appling has Nancy's old room, doesn't she? Please, be nice to her. She needs someone to be nice to her."

Maggie kissed her mother and left her in the lower hallway, to join Nancy and Henry on the second floor. Nancy stood just inside the guest room, the baby in her arms. Maggie closed the door behind her, taking Henry to hold him against her heart.

"Oh, my darling, from now on I cannot be your mama! But I will love you forever," she whispered passionately against the small, soft head. Then, eyes glimmering with unshed tears, she managed a smile as she handed him back to Nancy. "From now on, he's yours. Take good care of him."

\*     \*     \*

There were times when Maggie questioned her judgment in keeping her child.

Not that she could allow herself to think about losing Henry, but the obstacles rose around her from anthill to mountainous size.

She had known that Ann would not be easily won over to the idea of having a live-in servant with a baby. She had been prepared for hostility toward Nancy; it was something she and Nancy had talked about, and both had felt that Henry himself would eventually win her over, and that Nancy would manage to cope with being tolerated instead of wanted by the woman of the house.

Neither of them had expected the hostility to be as strong as it was. Ann had at first resisted vigorously, only to retreat from her entrenched position when Jake joined Maggie in insisting that Nancy be allowed to stay.

Indeed, Ann felt a flicker of suspicion at Jake's inexplicable championship of the girl, although he had never seemed to pay the slightest attention to her during the years Nancy and Mrs. Totting had lived at Keating's Landing. Had it not been for the fact of Adam Welker's death, and Nancy's obvious shock and grief over it, Ann might well have let her imagination run riot. After all, a man who is unfaithful to his wife might not stop at one such illicit relationship.

In the end, however, Ann accepted as truth the tacit assertion that Nancy had given birth to Adam Welker's child.

In the village, Adam's family heard the rumors and did not discount them. They held their heads high and ignored them, the only solution open to them, for they knew Adam had intended to ask the girl to marry him. As his father remarked, "There's more as jumps the gun than don't, seems like. And he had his heart set on that girl."

Ann did not succumb to the charms of a chubby, gurgling little boy. She continued to work with Sarah, who had at last learned to stand hanging on to a hand or a chair, and for the most part ignored the second child in the household as best she could.

She did not, however, fail to mention the inconvenience of having him. "I heard him crying half the night," she would say at the breakfast table, looking weary from lack of sleep. Or, "Really, Margaret, how do you expect to get any work out of a maid who spends so much of her time tending to an infant? It's an absurd situation!"

For the most part, Maggie remained either mildly defensive of Nancy and the baby, or glossed over her mother's complaints without full response to them. It created a strain, however, for there was no way to have a baby in the household who did not in any way interfere with or at least influence the normal routines.

What Maggie had underestimated was her own maternal pull toward the baby. She had thought that, pretending he was Nancy's child, she could still show him some open affection. Since it was quite acceptable for a female to be captivated by infants, why should she not be allowed to hold him, to talk to him, to rock him?

Except that her love was so full, so overwhelming, that both Nancy and Jake cautioned her about expressing it so openly in Ann's company.

"She's not blind, honey," Jake said gently. "She's going to see something out of line in such a strong attachment. You'd better save it for when she's not around."

That was easier said than done. Henry was a handsome, happy, healthy child. He did not suffer from having been put on a bottle at an early age. He grew, and developed, and learned. Maggie loved him more with every passing day.

Jake, too, had his difficulties regarding Henry. Since Sarah had learned to get around a little on her own, in an odd, crablike, sideways crawling action, Ann no longer kept her isolated in their room upstairs. He had seen more of her, and he'd become very fond of her, and demonstrative in his affection.

He knew it was a source of wounded pride with Ann that Sarah often sought him out, holding up her arms to be picked up and tossed in the air, for he had had almost nothing to do with her for the first year of her life. It would perhaps have been more fair to Ann if Sarah's total allegiance had been to her, yet Sarah instinctively sought Jake as a giver of pleasure. He felt the child's need was as important as his wife's, and he thought as well that a retarded child needed love in a greater measure than a normal one, since so many of the other avenues of satisfaction would be unavailable to her.

He, too, found it difficult to keep from showing that same affection to Henry. His grandson, whom he could never acknowledge. Since Henry was supposedly the child of a servant, he knew it would be cause for comment if he paid any attention to the boy at all. Yet it was impossible not to be as drawn to him as Maggie was.

They all hoped that Ann would come around, eventually. She didn't. In fact, the older Henry got, the more annoying Ann found him to be. When he was past the age of sleeping most of the day and had to be brought downstairs where Nancy could see to him while she worked, Ann's irritation increased. Particularly when Sarah took a liking to him.

She would stand beside his basket, staring at him, delighted with his every movement. If they did not restrain her, she poked a small finger into his eyes or mouth, and once she tried to feed him a bit of her toast.

When Nancy sat in the rocker in the kitchen to give him a bottle, Sarah would stand at her knee, absorbed, fascinated. She had never shown this much interest in anything.

"Mama, I think she needs a doll," Maggie said. "A soft baby doll of her own."

A doll was obtained, the right size for Sarah's small

arms, and she did, indeed, become most attached to it. She would rock it and make crooning noises to it. But it was the real, live baby who drew her back, time after time.

Sarah's first steps were a triumph in a household that had not really held out much hope for the child's development. It also added to the problems, for once Sarah could walk, she went everywhere. And where she most wanted to be was near the baby.

Her first word, spoken so softly at first that none of them realized it was not simply another of her meaningless sounds, was "baby."

"Ma'am!" Nancy said, startled when the word was repeated. "I believe Sarah is talking! She said 'baby'!"

"What?" Ann paused on her way through the room, looking sharply at the domestic tableau of her own small daughter at the maid's knee, touching one tiny foot of the baby in Nancy's lap.

Sarah looked into the little face only inches from her own and smiled. "Baby," she said.

And so, even in the rush of joy Ann felt over the proof that Sarah could, indeed, be taught to speak, there was pain that the first word had not been "Mama." Especially when Ann had worked so hard to teach it to her.

Sarah's enchantment with Henry might have won Ann over to similar sentiments. It did not. Ann spoke sharply to Maggie about the matter on the following day.

"Margaret, you and your father have forced me into accepting what is essentially an unacceptable situation. You knew how I felt about out-of-wedlock babies, yet you brought Nancy and that child back here, to shame our household as well as themselves. Nancy is being paid her old wages, yet she's not available to do a quarter of the work, since so much of her attention is focused on her baby. He's beginning to creep, and he's going to require even more attention if he isn't to demolish the house. We can neither afford to hire another maid to do Nancy's tasks nor do without the chores she ought to be doing."

Maggie didn't realize how much she was becoming like her father, even to the tone of voice Jake utilized when he intended to brook no opposition.

"All right. Since I'm determined that Nancy is to be kept on, and we can't expect her to leave Henry on a refuse heap, we'll have to find some other solution. Maybe the one Daddy used with me, when you found me impossible." She smiled to take any sting out of the words, and to cover her sudden inner agitation. "I'll take the baby to work with me for part of the day. That way he'll be out of your way, and Nancy can get on with the house cleaning."

She could tell by her mother's expression that Ann thought she'd lost her mind, but she didn't mean to back down. The plan would solve some of her own problems about Henry, too.

"I'll have the men build a walled-off area in one corner of the office, and after he's had his breakfast Nancy can bring him there, to stay until he's ready for his nap. He'll be out of your way entirely."

Ann was unable to refrain from putting her thoughts into words. "You don't know the first thing about babies, you won't get anything at all done in the office with a child there!"

"Well, let's try it and see, shall we? Daddy took me off to the woods; I'll take Henry to the office. I loved the woods. Maybe Henry will learn to love the mill."

Since she'd spoken without thinking it out ahead of time, Maggie had only now begun to see the danger in what she proposed. Would her mother suspect that she had too strong an interest in someone else's child, to take on so much?

"You speak of how busy you are, at the office, yet you contemplate having a small child there! Margaret, it won't work!"

"Well," Maggie said again, "let's try it. If it doesn't work, we'll think of something else. Only Nancy and Henry are not going to be turned out in the cold."

Maggie turned away, putting an end to the subject, at least for the moment.

To the astonishment of almost everyone, it worked out very well indeed.

The men, at first skeptical, warmed to the idea once they got started. They created a penned-off area, with bars instead of solid walls ("So's you can see him when he falls down, and he can see out," Red Risku said. "Don't you think he'll be happier if he can see out?"), the dowels carefully sanded so as not to leave any splinters in tiny hands. They made a pad so that Henry could crawl on a soft surface. Tom Dunnigan carved a boat small enough for the child to hold in his hand. Sol Engstrom went that one better and made a jointed clown that could be made to dance on a string.

It was true that Maggie was very busy. During the season she'd been gone, the mill had been in full operation, and while it didn't make much money—with the price of lumber so low, Jake said, how could anybody make any money?—it had at least held its own.

Walt Stover had stuck around long enough to make sure Jake knew how the mill was run; several of his employees were retained to keep it going when the Stovers packed up and moved to Oregon.

The operations, both mill and logging, had shut down for the winter shortly after Maggie's return home; by spring things were moving again. When the Pilchuck rose enough to make floating logs possible, the two camps upstream sent down timber to be milled, and there was almost more work than Maggie could keep up with.

She was glad she'd actually attended the school; she'd learned things that were very helpful. One of the things she had decided, almost at once, was that the office needed to be larger; an addition to serve as an office for the bookkeeper had been constructed during the winter, so that Wilkie didn't interfere with her own duties on the full day he was spending there each week now.

Kurt Jorgeson had closed down his logging operation the past fall in shaky financial condition. He didn't reopen in the spring, and Rich Salter voiced the common thought with a sigh.

"Well, too bad. That means that much more for the rest of us, though, I guess."

Two Snohomish-area mills closed down; Jake was able to keep his going on the business that was left. Money was tight; Maggie was paid no wage for what she did, and she didn't mention it. When there was money for a salary, she knew she'd get it.

She was busy, and having Henry there for a good part of the day turned out to be much more demanding than she'd thought it would—Ann had known more than she had about taking care of babies—but Maggie didn't mind.

She was young and strong; she could put in long hours. The joy of having Henry beside her was enough to enable her to overcome enormous obstacles.

At first he was only there for a few hours a day. And then, as he grew older and demonstrated his ability to take a nap in one corner of the pen, undisturbed by the whine of saws, the shouting of the bullwhacker, the clatter of logs being yarded only a few hundred feet away, Nancy stopped coming for him for his afternoon rest. Maggie had him virtually all day.

The workload increased for everyone when Wilkie came up with another idea that Jake eventually implemented in the mill. Someone had invented a device to make shingles by machine rather than by hand, and it was one more area that might show a profit if a man dared take a little risk in getting started.

Jake had not managed to save any money and he was

still being very frugal, but he was paying his bills. He decided to make shingles, as well.

The shingles had to be dried, so a kiln was added to the operation at the landing. It was one more thing that Maggie got to oversee when Jake was busy in the woods.

She had worried about displaying too much affection for Henry in front of the men. She need not have. Henry was shortly the object of everyone's affection.

Those of the men who had families responded to a sturdy, laughing little boy. Those who did not were lonely, with no recipient for their stored-up emotions. Whenever one of them dropped in at the office, he took a moment or two to play with the child, who never showed fear of even the fiercest bearded giant.

One of those benefiting the most from the new arrangement, aside from Henry himself, was Jake.

With all the men fussing over the child, there was no reason why he couldn't do the same, especially since Ann was not around to observe.

Henry adored him. While he may not have understood that Jake was his grandfather, he knew when he was loved. He responded in kind.

One day Maggie saw Jake dangle his watch over the low railing for Henry to play with, then drop it into the child's lap.

"You know," she said softly, for there was no one else in the office, "one of the things I worried about, when I was trying to think how to manage to keep him near me, was what it would be like for a little boy to grow up without a father." She smiled, watching her father and her son, laughing into each other's faces. "That was one worry I could have spared myself. He has dozens of fathers."

Jake straightened, sobering. "Have you thought about his real father? Letting him know he has a son?"

Maggie shook her head. "No. That's a chapter in my

life that is closed. Angus made it very clear he wants no part of me; he thinks I lied to him and cheated him. Henry is Nancy's son, now, not mine, as far as the world is concerned.''

They were close again now, Maggie and Jake. His schedule remained such that he was seldom at home; she knew he was spending whatever free time he had with Jaisy Pallison. Yet there was always business to bring him to the landing, necessary discussions between them, and, whenever he was nearby, he stopped to visit with Henry.

There was no such closeness with her mother. Maggie had begun to fear that there never would be. Even the fact that Sarah had begun to speak their names, and make known simple wants, did not release Ann from her dedication to stimulating the little girl by constant attention.

Maggie loved Sarah, too. She would never be bright, like Henry, but she was sweet and good, and she sought affection, too. Maggie would hug her, tickle her, and read to her; and all the while she wished that she dared to do the same, openly, with her own son.

The other situation she had to contend with was manifested as soon as they reopened the office. Wilkie was there more often than ever, and he quickly made it known that he liked and admired her.

A year ago, she reflected, she'd have been too innocent, or ignorant, to realize that she was being courted. Now there was no doubt in her mind at all.

She had mixed feelings about this. She didn't love Wilkie. She suspected she'd never love anyone, ever again, in the same way and with the same intensity that she'd loved Angus.

Yet Angus was gone. There had been word of him, through the Berquist family, so she knew he'd joined Tom and Jim Ballantine at the mine somewhere in the Blue Mountains in eastern Oregon. The chances were that he'd never return to Snohomish, no matter what happened at the mine.

She was not yet nineteen years old. Did she intend to stay alone and single for the rest of her life?

It was a subject Maggie gave considerable thought. At times she was convinced that anything less than what she'd had with Angus would be nothing at all. At other times, alone in bed at night with the mere thought of Angus arousing now unwanted physical yearnings, she knew that she could not go on for years and years with only memories.

The evening that they had both worked late—Nancy had come to take the baby home an hour earlier—Wilkie emerged from his lean-to office with a sigh, stretching. "Come on, I'm quitting, it's time you did, too."

"I know. I'm putting things aside until morning." Maggie rubbed at her neck and shoulders. "How do you sit hunched over books day after day without being in constant discomfort?"

"I try to sit straight, for one thing. And take an occasional break. Here, let me see if I can't knead out some of the soreness."

He didn't wait for permission, but turned her around and stood behind her, strong fingers pressing firmly on tight muscles, working them loose. It was painful at first. She stood patiently, trying to ignore the slight tingle set up at his touch and relax under the massage.

"That does feel better," she said after a few minutes. "Thank you, Wilkie."

He stopped and turned her to face him, staring down at her with a faint smile. "Is that the best you can do? 'Thank you, Wilkie'?"

Uncertain, she stood there, and he bent to kiss her.

It was a nondemanding type of kiss. There was not the thrill that she had felt when Angus had kissed her. Yet there was . . . something.

"I've wanted to do that for a very long time," Wilkie told her. "I'd like to do it again."

This time his embrace was more firm, the pressure on her lips more insistent; she felt sensations, long suppressed, flood through her, and her lips parted involuntarily beneath his.

It wasn't the same as with Angus. She knew she didn't love him, and she was bewildered and alarmed at her physical response; her breathing was too rapid, and the sensations were slow to subside when Wilkie released her.

"Come on," he said, "I'll walk you home. It's going to be dark before you get there."

Maggie swallowed. "No. No, I'll walk alone, the way I always do. I need to . . . think."

His smile broadened. "Think about me, will you, Maggie-Margaret? You're a grown-up young lady now. It's time you gave some serious consideration to a serious courtship. Not calling on Sunday afternoons when nobody in the family has a pain or the rain has stopped, but on a regular basis. With a serious end in mind."

Was he proposing to her? Or suggesting that he intended to propose, if the idea wasn't displeasing to her?

"Good night, Wilkie," she said hastily, reaching for the wrap she had needed in the chill of the morning. "I'll see you later."

"You'll think about it?" he asked, not quite as gently as before.

"I'll think about it," she promised.

She strode off through the twilight toward the house, emotions churning. She was disturbed by the feelings he had roused within her—feelings that lingered—and she didn't know yet whether she wanted to feel them or not.

"Angus, Angus!" The name was a groan, an ache that threatened to tear her chest wide open. Yet Angus was gone, and she needed something to live for, besides a son she could not claim.

The pain in her chest grew worse. She stopped when she had reached the house, where lamplight showed in the dining room. It was a long time before she could make herself walk up the steps and into the house, before she trusted her control in front of the family.

## 37

SHE was glad that Wilkie wasn't due back at the mill until the following week. She had a lot of thinking to do. Thinking, and feeling.

Quite deliberately Maggie tried imagining Wilkie making love to her. Even in the privacy of her own bedroom, it made her face hot. She'd liked being made love to, and she'd thought it was because her lover was Angus. Now she was no longer certain how much difference that made.

Oh, there was no question in her mind that she could never find satisfaction in the arms of someone she didn't care about. She'd proved that readily enough by turning her fantasies to some of the other males she knew—including some she liked very much, as friends—and decided at once that even deep friendship was not enough.

Her father had loved her mother, once. She didn't know all that had gone into the destruction of that relationship, only that the love between them no longer existed. And when her father had ended one love, he'd sought and found another.

If that was the case, wasn't it possible that she, too, might find someone else? Someone she might not love with the same passion she had had for Angus, but a man who could fill her life with genuine liking, respect, and affection? A lover who could stir her physically?

The matter was on her mind so much of the time that she often discovered she'd been reading without comprehension, or adding figures that blurred together and had to be added again.

The last day of the working week found her no nearer a conclusion regarding Wilkie. It had been a frustrating day. Henry was apparently cutting teeth; he ran a slight fever and whined at her disconsolately whenever she tried to do anything that didn't directly involve him, so that she'd had to break off her own work and take him up to the house, to be handed over to Nancy.

Nancy cast a meaningful glance toward the parlor, where Ann was stitching a new dress for Sarah. "I suppose he needs to be held, poor little tyke. He needs the comfort of his mama when he don't feel good. The trouble is, your ma's expecting me to finish up washing the ground-floor windows yet today. I can't hardly do it, rocking a baby."

Maggie jiggled him against her shoulder, where he clung to her neck with a tenacious grip. "I know. Damn it, I'll admit there were things I didn't think about, Nancy, when I asked you to do this. For once I wish something would work out the way I'd planned for it."

Nancy reached out to take the little boy, who had no objection, as long as someone held him. "Maybe I could give him a few drops of laudanum, so he'll sleep through the afternoon, until I get done with the windows."

"I guess so," Maggie agreed. "He hurts, or he wouldn't be so fussy."

She left him with Nancy and hurried back to the landing. To her surprise, old Woolrich was there, helping himself to a cup of coffee.

"Hello, there, Maggie." He grinned at her through

stained teeth and emitted a cloud of alcoholic vapor that made her step backward. "Just havin' some coffee. Hope you don't mind if an old man has a cup o' coffee."

"Sounds like just what you need," Maggie said. Except for a time or two around town, from a distance, she hadn't seen him since Jake had fired him. It bothered her that he was here inside the office with no one else around, though she didn't see any sign that he'd touched anything. She took her place behind the counter that served as her desk much of the time, startled to find the old man at her elbow almost as soon as she'd taken her seat. "Yes? What is it you want, Mr. Woolrich?"

He had the rich, ripe odor, one not entirely unfamiliar, of a man who seldom bathes. "Thought as how I'd see Jake," he said, resting his cup on the edge of the papers before her.

Maggie pointedly moved the papers and picked up her pencil. "I'm sorry. My father's in the woods today. They're working about four miles upriver."

Woolrich rubbed his mouth with the back of one hand. "You know, girl, I ain't never found no job since Jake fired me. 'Cept an odd job here and there, no more'n enough to keep me in grub and a bottle, once in a while. Nothin' steady. I'm a bullwhacker, but there don't seem to be nobody needs a bullwhacker. Too many outfits done shut down."

"I'm sorry to hear it," Maggie said, though she remembered clearly why Woolrich had been fired. "If you're wanting to talk to my father about a job, I'm afraid it's no use. He's not hiring."

"Can't run a loggin' outfit without a bullwhacker," Woolrich stated.

"He has one. Name of Patterson." Maggie didn't know the new man very well, only that Jake was pleased with his performance, and he wasn't likely to take a sledgehammer to his team if they got stuck in the mud. "Excuse me, Mr. Woolrich, I have work to do."

"I thought as how Jake might think about it. Givin' me back my job," Woolrich said.

Maggie stared into his face, knowing he'd been drinking, feeling sorry for him and unable to do anything to help him, uncomfortable because she didn't want him hanging around.

"I'm sorry. He can't do that. He's hired someone else," she said, hoping that she was getting through to him and that he'd go away without creating any trouble.

He wiped his mouth on the back of his hand again. "Don't have to be handlin' a team, missy. Just any job. You got the mill now, too. I can move lumber, sweep out the place. Anything."

"I'm sorry," Maggie repeated. Through the window she saw the approaching team, straining with their load of cedars for the shingle mill. "Excuse me, I have to speak to the teamster."

She brushed past him, glad for the fresh air, not sure what she was going to say to the new bullwhacker but knowing she wanted help in getting the old man out of her working quarters.

The bullwhacker was a young man, no more than twenty-five, with a short, square, muscular build. His name was Merle Patterson. Nobody who wasn't looking for a fight ever addressed him as anything but Pat. His looks were quite ordinary, except for bright, intelligent blue eyes.

He drew up the team and left them, flanks shining and soaked with sweat, to walk to meet her.

"Brung you some shingles, ma'am," he said, smiling a little.

Her glance slid over his load. "Several hundreds of thousands of them, I guess. I don't suppose you've seen any of the old-timers around, have you? Or my father?"

"Ain't seen nobody since I left South Camp. Jake's with the other crew." His blue eyes swiveled toward the unpainted building that housed the office, seeing old Woolrich standing there in the doorway. "You ain't having any trouble, are you?"

"Well, not trouble, exactly. The old man wants Daddy to give him his job back. It isn't going to happen. He's been drinking, and except for the crew in the mill, there's nobody else around."

"You want him out of here? Easy enough," Patterson said, and stalked toward the old man, Maggie following in time to hear Woolrich's protest.

"I don't have to take nobody else's say-so. Jake Keating's the one does the hiring."

"Not for no bullwhacker, he don't," Patterson said flatly. "He hired me for that, and I'm no drunk, mister. I take good care of my teams."

"I got a right to see the boss," Woolrich insisted.

"Miss Maggie's the boss o' this part of the operation, and she already told you, didn't she? There's no jobs. Tell you what, though. You want to talk to Jake and make sure, you sit over there by the river and wait for him, till he comes in from the woods. All right? Don't bother Miss Maggie. She's got lots of work to do, and we don't allow anybody in the office, during working hours, that don't work for Keating."

He wasn't obnoxious about it, or overly tough; it was plain enough to look at him that Patterson *was* tough. Though he was stocky, there wasn't an ounce of superfluous flesh on him; his bared arms looked as powerful as one of his bulls.

Woolrich cast her a reproachful look. He nodded reluctantly. "All right. I'll wait for Jake."

"Over by the river," Patterson repeated, to make sure the old man understood. "Not in the office, and not in the mill, neither. It's dangerous in there. It's off limits, 'less you work there.''

"I'd work anyplace," Woolrich said, and headed in the direction Patterson had indicated, his shoulders sagging, the ripe aroma lingering after him.

"Thank you," Maggie said with a wry smile. "I don't suppose he means any harm, but I wasn't having any luck getting him out of there.''

Patterson shrugged. "No trouble. Any time you want anybody throwed out, you let me know." He glanced inside the building, where the only activity was a fly crawling across her desk. "The little fella's not here today?''

"Henry? No. He's teething, running a fever. I took him over to . . . his mother.''

"Cute little fella, ain't he?''

"Yes, he is.''

"That Nancy, his mother—she ain't married, they told me.''

Maggie's throat hurt. "No, Nancy isn't married.''

"Nice girl," Patterson observed. "She ain't stepping out with anybody?''

The ache deepened. "No, she isn't.''

Patterson hesitated, shifting from one foot to the other. "You think she'd maybe consider going to a dance in town? She like to dance?''

"She used to dance. She might like to go," Maggie said.

Patterson moistened his lips and tugged at his dark mustache. "You reckon anybody'd mind, if I walked over to the big house, after supper, talked to her? Asked her?''

"I don't see any reason why anyone should mind," Maggie said, her mouth so dry that the words came with an effort.

He nodded. "Good. Thank you, ma'am.''

She stared after him as he walked to the open door of

the mill, yelling to make himself heard over the sound of the saws. "Hey, anybody want a load of shingle-makings? Let's get unloaded!"

He knew Nancy wasn't married, that she presumably had a child, yet he wanted to take her to the dance. A part of her was glad for Nancy. He was an attractive man, perhaps not well educated but intelligent, hardworking, strong. The kind of man Nancy needed, and had convinced herself she would never again find.

He didn't mind about Henry. Unless, of course, he thought Nancy would be easy because she'd had a baby out of wedlock. She had looked into his eyes, though, and she didn't think that was it.

What would she do if Nancy married? If Nancy had to take Henry away from Keating's Landing?

It was some time before she could concentrate on what she was trying to do at her desk.


Jake showed up about the time Maggie was closing the office. She saw old Woolrich hail him, saw them standing talking, though not for long. The bullwhacker should have waited long enough to have completely sobered up, she thought, and wondered if her father had always had a knack for handling people, taking responsibilities, or if he'd had to grow into it. She wanted to be just like him.

He'd apparently convinced Woolrich that he wouldn't hire him back, for the old man had disappeared the next time she looked, and Jake was striding toward her when she left the office.

"Good news," he called, and waved a letter. "Red picked up the mail. Celeste and your grandma are coming home; we're to meet the steamer next week."

"Oh, Daddy, that's wonderful! It's been so long!" They hugged each other spontaneously, and she knew how much she'd missed those hugs that had once been a daily occurrence.

"Let's go tell your mama," Jake said, and they walked toward home in the twilight, happy, talking about how wonderful it would be to have the family complete once more.

She walked with him to the back of the house, where he wanted to check on the horses grazing along the riverbank, and then they went inside. The kitchen smelled of roasting pork, and Maggie, who had not previously thought of hunger, was suddenly ravenous. There was no better-smelling food than roasting pork, she decided.

Mrs. Appling, a plump, cheerful woman, greeted them with a smile. "Just in time! We're about to put it on the table!"

"I'll wash up, be with you in five minutes," Jake said. In passing he put a hand on little Henry's head, where the boy sat on Nancy's lap to have his bib tied on for his own meal, and ruffled the child's hair before he walked out of the room.

For a moment Maggie stood there, looking at her son on the other girl's lap, saw Nancy laughing down at him and Henry giggling in return as the bib strings tickled the back of his neck.

Dear God, what she'd give to be able to hold him that way, in front of everybody, to let them know he belonged to her! For a few seconds she wondered if it were possible to die of wanting anything so badly.

"Something wrong, miss?" the cook asked, and Maggie started.

"No, no. I'm just tired. I'll wash up down here, I guess. Is Henry feeling better, Nancy?"

"He slept all afternoon after the laudanum," Nancy told her. "He's still a bit warm, but not so much. I think he'll have another tooth soon."

Maggie crossed to the stand with the washbasin and washed her face and hands, hardly considering what she was doing. If anything happened between Nancy and Pat

Patterson—or anyone else—Nancy would have to take Henry away with her.

If Maggie married Wilkie, there would be other children.

The thought hit her with the impact of a physical blow.

Other children. None of them would be Henry, of course, and no matter how many children she had, he would always be the first, the dearest.

Could she ever love another child the way she loved Henry?

She reached for the towel to wipe her face, forcing the thoughts out of her mind, and turned toward Nancy with a smile. "There's good news, Nance. Celeste and Grandma are coming home next week."


The seed had been planted. Wilkie, and children. It colored her thinking from that point on. Would Wilkie make a good father? Would he want to have a large family?

They'd be handsome, if they took after him. What else would they be?

She was nervous about Wilkie's arrival on Monday. There were several of the mill hands around when he came in, and they greeted each other as usual before Wilkie retired to his cubicle with the books.

It wasn't until hours later, when the saws were shrieking in the mill and a load of logs was being decked beyond the windows, that Wilkie came to stand beside her, looking out on the activity.

"You like this, don't you?" he asked. "Being in the middle of men's work."

She glanced at him self-consciously. "Yes, I do." If she married him, would he expect her to give it all up? That hadn't occurred to her until now, and the idea was an unwelcome one. "I'm no good at women's work, except for cooking. I'd rather do this."

He lifted a hand and rested it casually on the back of her

neck, which affected the rhythm of her breathing. "You need another neck rub? You feel tense."

"I'll be all right. I'm going to walk out to South Camp this afternoon; the exercise will take out all the kinks I've made sitting here. Nancy's going to take Henry back to the house for his nap then."

He glanced at the pen where Henry was amusing himself with a pile of stones one of the men had brought up for him from the riverbed, trying to place them one atop the other without much success.

"Doesn't it bother you to have him here all the time?"

"No. I enjoy it. Don't you like children?" The rigidity in her intensified.

"I never was around them much. They seem awfully . . . messy."

Maggie had to laugh. "Well, yes, they are. But they're worth it."

His hand squeezed her shoulder, relaxed, squeezed again. "As much devotion as you give to somebody else's kid, it'll be interesting to see what you're like with your own, when you have them."

She couldn't resist looking at him. "Don't you want children?"

"Certainly. What man doesn't want sons to carry on his name? His business. His traditions. I suppose you get attached to them, when they're your own."

She laughed again, and stepped away from the unsettling kneading fingers. "Oh, yes, I'm sure that's the case. Did you hear that my sister's coming home, and Grandma? Daddy's to meet the steamer on Thursday."

"Wonderful. You've all missed them. Maggie, I want to come on Sunday and meet them, if that isn't too soon. I want to know all your family. I don't really even know your mother, I've only seen her a few times."

"Well, yes, of course. I'll tell Mama you're coming," she agreed, and wondered if she'd taken the first step

454 Willo Davis Roberts

toward a commitment, and if she had, whether it was the right or the wrong thing to do.

# 38

CELESTE swept through the house like fresh air, sunshine, and spring flowers.

She was more beautiful than ever. She had grown an inch, her bosom had filled out while her waist had slimmed, and her eyelashes had a way of fluttering that made Maggie groan with envy. She could imagine the effect her little sister was going to have on the boys.

"Oh, I'm so glad to be home! I've missed you all, terribly!" She hugged Maggie, drew back, and exclaimed, "You are so different, Margaret! So mature, and self-confident, and . . . stunning! You really are stunning!" She leaned forward and added in a whisper, "Your bosom is *magnificent*!"

Maggie laughed, though the reason for the bosom wasn't exactly amusing. She had not written to Celeste about Henry, because she could not bring herself to tell the lie that he was Nancy's child. Obviously Ann had reported on the situation as she saw it, for a month or so after they'd brought Henry to the landing, Celeste had written to ask Maggie about him.

"Is he cute? Mama doesn't say."

After that, Maggie had had to be very careful to curb the urge to write reams about Henry; when she described the baby and his antics and achievements, she had dutifully balanced the adulation with reports on Sarah, as well, and hoped that she didn't sound too enraptured with Henry.

Now Celeste turned to a smiling Nancy and held out her arms. "Will he come to me? I've heard so much about him. Ah, he is a darling, isn't he?"

Millicent, overtired from the journey, kissed them all around, admired both Sarah and Henry, and begged their forgiveness for having to retire to her room to rest. Celeste, however, was overflowing with energy, keyed-up in her delight at being home. She talked and talked, asked question after question, petted Joe, greeted Mrs. Appling, and ran up and down the stairs so many times that Ann declared the girl made her giddy.

Everybody laughed and smiled, and Celeste was still hugging people several hours after their arrival. "I *missed* you so," she said to each of them, over and over.

Maggie watched her, smiling, though the smile had an underlying sadness. Celeste made her feel so *old*.

Under Ann's eyes—misting over in gratitude that her mother and daughter were again under her own roof—Maggie knew she had to be more careful than ever about reacting to Henry.

When Celeste hugged him and swung him in the air, and kissed his fat neck, Maggie kept still. When Celeste looked over at her, laughing, and said, "Babies are wonderful, aren't they?" Maggie was content with a smile.

Sarah came in for her share of attention, too, of course. She gave no sign of remembering this big sister, but anyone who fed her sweets and cuddled her won Sarah's immediate friendship.

"She's walking, and talking, too! I know you wrote about it, Mama, but it was so hard to believe. She only sat and did nothing when we left, and now look at her. You like the baby, Sarah? Do you want to play with him?"

"Baby," Sarah echoed, and patted Henry's cheek, carefully, as she had been taught.

It was a gala homecoming. The house had been waxed, polished, and dusted. There were wild flowers in most of the rooms, a paper streamer in the front hall that read WEL-COME HOME, and the best china and silver had been brought out. Mrs. Appling had outdone herself in an attempt to cook or bake every food either Millicent or Celeste had ever expressed a liking for, with the result that everybody overate.

This was what a family should be like all the time, Maggie thought, listening to the laughter, the chatter. For a few hours, there was no evidence of the estrangement between Jake and Ann. In their common pleasure, they had made a momentary truce.

Why couldn't it stay this way? she wondered, and knew that it was too much to hope for.

Ann was nervous about her first entertainment in such a long time. She fussed about everything, making sure the table and the food were just right. Mrs. Appling, the jolliest and most easygoing of women, rolled her eyes at Nancy behind Ann's back.

"It's only a few old friends, coming for a buffet," Ann had said when they'd planned the Sunday open house. "Probably about fifty, if they all come. It's awful, I've forgotten what to do!"

"You leave it all to Nancy and me, missus," Mrs. Appling had said, and wished heartily that Ann would actually do that.

Maggie joined in the preparations, putting down the nagging reminder that her own pleas to entertain had come to nothing; it was not until Celeste returned to Keating's Landing that guests were invited again. "I've asked Wilkie for Sunday afternoon," Maggie had said, and Ann only nodded.

"Of course, dear. Whomever you like."

Wilkie was one of the latecomers, arriving only after the

yard was full of horses, buggies, and wagons. Ann's fear that the stigma of having a live-in maid with an out-of-wedlock child would cause many to shun them had proved groundless, or perhaps, Maggie thought cynically, some of them came simply to view the sinner.

Nancy did not look guilty or repentant. Indeed, Maggie had never seen her looking better. There was unaccustomed color in her face—whether from the heat of the kitchen or from an inner excitement was impossible to judge—and she had taken on a vivacity that was new, too. Did it spring from having walked out with Pat Patterson, going to the dance in Snohomish with him on Saturday night?

Nancy let Wilkie in, took his hat, and directed him to the dining room. "There's punch on the sideboard, sir. I'll tell Maggie you're here."

Maggie, fetched from the kitchen where she had been helping Mrs. Appling deal with a minor crisis when the top layer of a cake had been discovered to be sliding sideways, came at once, delaying only to say over her shoulder, "Stick some toothpicks in it, and it should hold until it's time to cut it."

She made her way between two fat women she couldn't remember having met, and touched Wilkie on the shoulder. "Welcome. I thought perhaps you'd changed your mind about coming."

"I'd never do that. You're looking lovely, Maggie-Margaret. That color suits you."

She was wearing the pink silk, which had had to be taken out all around to accommodate fuller hips and bosom; fortunately the original seams had been deep enough to allow for this. It was the first time she'd been dressed up in nearly a year and a half, and while she was mildly self-conscious, she was feeling good about herself, too.

Wilkie accepted a cup of punch and stared around the

room. "Where did all these people come from? I don't think I know very many of them."

"I'll introduce you to them. To most of them, anyway. A few are strangers to me, too."

"I don't see any of Jake's crew."

Maggie wrinkled her nose. "No. Mama wanted this to be a purely social affair, to welcome Grandma and Celeste back, and for once Daddy didn't say"—she made her voice go deep in imitation of her father's—" 'Either my crew comes or we don't have the party,' the way he used to do."

Wilkie raised an eyebrow. "Then I'm flattered to be included." He was staring over her shoulder, and his tone changed abruptly. "Who is that? The stunning blonde?"

Maggie spun around, then laughed. "That's my sister, Celeste. Come and meet her."

She led him across the crowded room and introduced them. And felt a sensation as if a cold wind blew over the hair on her arms, making it rise off her skin.

For Celeste stared up at the handsome young man with wide, startled blue eyes, eyes that made no attempt to conceal her interest. And Wilkie was looking at her in a way that left no doubt the interest was mutual.

"They told me you were beautiful," he said softly, taking her hand. "They didn't say you were a goddess. Look, do you really have to stay here with all these people, or could we go out on the verandah where it's possible to talk?"

Celeste's dimples surfaced. "I think that would be very nice, Mr. Andreason."

"Wilkie," he corrected. "And I'm going to call you Celeste, if I may."

Maggie watched them go, stunned. He hadn't even remembered she was there, she thought. He'd come close to asking her to marry him, and the moment he met Celeste, he'd forgotten that Maggie existed.

He *hadn't* proposed, and Maggie had known all along that she wasn't in love with him. Yet it hurt, just the same, to be left standing there by herself while the two of them walked away.

She supposed the party had been a success. Celeste was flushed with excitement, much of it centering on Wilkie. "You never told me how good-looking he is," she accused, and didn't wait for a response before she announced that Wilkie would be calling for her to attend the play being held the following Friday night at the Athenaeum.

Maggie tried to tell herself that if Wilkie had not really been in love with her, either, it was better they'd learned it early on, before anything became complicated. She went back to work, where there was plenty to keep her mind occupied.

Three weeks after Celeste returned home, she and Wilkie Andreason announced their engagement.

It was a strange interlude for Maggie. Wilkie came as usual to do his work, then appeared at the house virtually every evening, where he and Celeste were given the privacy of the front parlor. During the time he was there, Maggie contrived not to meet him except once or twice by accident.

Whether at the house or the office, Wilkie treated her the same as he had for ages, in a friendly manner with no suggestion that he'd ever hinted at more than that. Maggie managed a surface calm that masked humiliation, hurt, and anger.

Why had he acted as if he'd intended to propose? There was only one explanation she could think of. He'd thought it to his own financial advantage to form an alliance with Jake Keating's daughter. When he saw Celeste, *she* was the obvious choice between the two of them.

Maggie's self-esteem, having been somewhat on the mend, took a nose dive. She did not allow it to show, however. She poured out her love upon Henry, even to the point of some risk if it occurred to the men that she was excessively affectionate over someone else's baby.

Ann was delighted with the wedding news. Nobody, to Maggie's knowledge, pointed out how young Celeste was. Nobody curtailed her plans. Jake seemed happy about whatever made Celeste happy, though he did seek Maggie out to probe gently into her feelings about the matter.

"I had the idea there, for a while, that Wilkie was getting a little sweet on you."

Maggie shook her head and made her lips form a smile. "No. Wilkie and I are just friends."

If he saw the falseness of her smile, Jake didn't mention it. He hugged her. "Good. You deserve somebody better, anyway."

It wasn't until later, when she was alone, that it occurred to her that Jake had, quite unthinkingly, revealed that she was still his favorite. Wilkie wasn't good enough for Maggie, but it was all right if he married Celeste.

She loved him for it, but it made her want to cry, too.

The wedding took place at Keating's Landing on the tenth of September.

Henry had passed his first birthday. He was walking and trying to talk, though none of it was intelligible as yet. His dark hair was as straight as Maggie's, his eyes gray. His good humor was boundless, as why should it not be? Millicent asked, amused.

"He's such a charmer, everyone does what he wants them to do," she said, and Maggie's heart warmed with the praise she could not openly accept as partly her own, loving her grandmother for seeing what her mother refused to see in the child.

It had become harder for Ann either to ignore or to criticize Henry, however. With Millicent and Celeste now added to his admirers, crowing about each new achievement, Ann would have been churlish indeed to continue to resent him. And when he showed so clearly his love for Sarah, Ann began to soften.

It was Celeste who revealed that the newlyweds would be living at Keating's Landing.

"It's only sensible," Celeste said, "don't you think, Margaret? Wilkie lives in rented rooms in town, and I've been away from home so long I don't really want to move out again, not yet." Her smile flashed. "I want to have my cake and eat it, too. I want to have Wilkie and all my family, at the same time."

The engagement had been a blow; learning that Wilkie would be moving into her own home was another. He treated the entire matter as nothing out of the ordinary, and Maggie was unable to put down the underlying resentment she felt toward him, even as she worried about her sister. She hoped that he genuinely loved Celeste, as Celeste so openly displayed her affection for him.

From being almost a hermit, Ann had succumbed to the persuasion to host a series of entertainments, from an engagement party to a lavish reception after the wedding. When she asked Jake what they could afford to do, he told her to plan whatever she liked on Celeste's behalf, that he would manage to pay for it. Ann took him at his word.

"Isn't it wonderful how Mama's coming out of her shell? I hope she'll continue to do it, to let us have guests and parties, don't you?" Celeste asked, and Maggie tried to sound enthusiastic when she agreed.

If there were any unkind remarks passed about Sarah, none of the Keatings were aware of them. She was a pretty little girl, and seldom caused any difficulties; she smiled when people were good to her, and after her initial introduction to society brought no adverse reaction, Ann gained courage. Ann, too, began to bloom again.

Everybody was blooming, Maggie thought morosely, except herself.

Certainly the bride and groom made a strikingly hand-some couple; Wilkie moved into Celeste's big room up-stairs after they had returned from a three-day honeymoon at Snoqualmie Falls.

No late-night sounds issued from the room. Maggie remembered how she had heard her mother and father, through the walls, all those years ago, without understand-ing what was happening between them. This house was better built; unless doors were open, if people were rea-sonably quiet, sounds did not carry as easily.

The first night they were home, Celeste, cheeks pink and eyes glowing, faced the family in the parlor. "I hope you'll all excuse us if we retire early. I got rather tired on the trip back today. Good night, everybody."

Maggie stayed up as late as she could, hoping the exhausted couple would be long asleep before she went to her own room. From the look of Wilkie, she suspected that Celeste had more to be tired from than a trip downriver from the falls; and though Maggie herself was very weary, it was a long while before she slept.

It was Wilkie who casually dropped the bombshell a few weeks later.

He continued to work for other companies, so he rode back and forth to Snohomish frequently, though he now spent two full days a week at Keating's Landing. Maggie wished he would not; his presence was inhibiting when she felt like picking up Henry and squeezing him, kissing him. He was trying hard to repeat the words they said to him; on the day that he'd tried to say "Maggie" and it had come out more like "Mama" she had felt something close to panic when Wilkie spoke behind her a moment later.

"Did he say what it sounded like he said?"

She tried to school her face into blandness. "I'm trying to get him to say my name. He can do the *M* sound, can't he? I guess the rest of it is still too difficult for him."

"You're going to teach him to call you Maggie?"

She felt a muscle twitch in her cheek. "What do you suggest I teach him to call me? Miss Margaret, or Miss Keating, would be quite a mouthful for a toddler."

"He's a servant's child," Wilkie said. "Isn't he?"

Her breath caught in her chest, and she glanced quickly at him. Did he suspect? Did he know?

There was nothing in his expression to confirm that, however. He lit a cigar—odd, she thought, how Jake's cigars had never bothered her, but she hated it when Wilkie lit up one in the office—and took a puff on it.

"It may strike your mother as inappropriate to have a servant's child addressing adult family members as equals, by their first names."

Anger sparked within her, and Maggie reminded herself to be careful, not to overreact. Wilkie might see more than the others with his outsider's eyes.

"Nancy's been my best friend since we were about ten years old," she said with outward calm. "I don't regard her as a servant so much as a companion and a friend. If the rest of you want Henry to address you formally, by all means say what you want and we'll teach him to say it, when he's able. For myself, I hope Henry will be as much a friend as Nancy is, and *Maggie* seems perfectly appropriate to me. Excuse me, I have to check that order of shingles for tomorrow's shipment."

She felt as if she'd had a close call. After he'd gone back into his own cubicle, she realized she was shaking, which wouldn't do. Sooner or later, he'd notice that sort of thing. And there were going to be so many more moments like this, as Henry grew older. She swallowed despair and told herself that Wilkie and Celeste would eventually decide they wanted a house of their own, and move out; please God, it would be soon!

"Oh, Maggie, I almost forgot." Wilkie had reappeared in the doorway between his work area and hers. "Heard something interesting in town yesterday."

She tried to sound pleasant. "That's the nice thing about you going back and forth more often than the rest of us, Wilkie. You can relate the gossip."

He laughed. "Well, as a matter of fact, both Celeste and your mother seem to enjoy hearing who's doing what with whom. This isn't their kind of news, but I thought it might be of interest to you. Angus McKay is back in Snohomish."

She stopped breathing.

She covered her shock by knocking a pencil off the counter onto the floor and bending over to pick it up. Control, she told herself, maintain control, and was afraid to speak for fear it would all be there in her voice.

"I . . . hadn't heard," she managed, reaching for a sheet of paper.

"I didn't think you had. Nobody mentioned it at home, and I thought Jake might have, if he'd known. They're all back, the three of them—McKay, Berquist, and Ballantine. Mine ran out, I understand."

"That's too bad." She sounded better that time, off-hand, uncaring.

"Oh, from what I heard they took a fair amount of gold out of it before that happened. They didn't come home poor."

"Really? Well, that's lucky for them, isn't it."

"Berquist was spending money like it was water, they said. Not McKay. Those Scots, they know how to pinch a penny, don't they?"

He left it at that and returned to his desk.

Maggie sat with her back to him, pretending to work, mind racing yet going nowhere, only one coherent thought spinning around and around, making her dizzy.

Angus was back.

Angus, Angus, Angus. It was a litany in her brain, engulfing her in a sea of emotion she had thought long dead.

Angus was back.

# 39

MAGGIE seldom went to town. She'd had no reason to go. Now she felt cold, stark terror at the prospect.

Angus was in Snohomish. It was not a large town. Sooner or later she would meet him, face-to-face. It was only a matter of time.

She imagined it, over and over and over. What would he say to her? "Hello, Maggie," probably, and walk on by as if she were a barmaid he'd tumbled in the hay in his youth.

She grew clammy when she thought about it; perspiration soaked her garments; she felt sick to her stomach.

"Margaret, we're going to the play tomorrow night. Do come with us," Celeste would say, and it got harder and harder to come up with convincing excuses not to go.

Once, when she'd turned down an invitation to attend a dance, Celeste had paused to look down on her with sudden concern. "Margaret? You . . . you weren't in love with Wilkie, were you? When I met him?"

"No, no! Good God, whatever gave you that idea? Wilkie and I are only friends." Even that was a lie now, she thought, voiced only to reassure her sister.

The furrow across Celeste's forehead vanished. "Oh, good. I didn't *think* so, because you mentioned him in your letters, and you didn't sound as if you were in love with him. I would feel dreadful, if I'd stolen him away from you, Margaret."

"You didn't. Don't worry about it. I suppose I just don't have much energy left after I've finished down at the landing every day, to go out and dance or whatever."

"Papa would let you off early anytime, you know that. Just tell him you want to rest during the afternoon."

"No, no, there's too much to do. Besides, I'm more interested in what I do at the landing than in dancing, anyway. Go on and have a good time, Celeste."

Celeste's endurance was apparently unlimited; though of course, since she could sleep until noon if she liked, it was not surprising that it didn't tire her too much to dance past midnight. On the few occasions that Maggie was there when she came downstairs in the morning, she had a sleepy, happy, satisfied look.

Maggie remembered the feeling, and wondered if she'd ever experience it again, the satiation of love and the ensuing delicious lethargy.

Nancy was walking out regularly now with Pat Patterson. The first time she asked Maggie if she'd mind keeping an eye on Henry, she was hesitant about it. "I've put him down, and he's sleeping. He shouldn't wake till morning. We're only going to walk down to the landing and talk, is all, but I wouldn't leave him unless it was all right with you."

"Yes, of course," Maggie told her. She felt as if she spent a great deal of time forcing her lips into a stiff smile, and she was amazed that those she smiled at didn't seem to see how false it was. "I'll be glad to watch him anytime, Nancy."

It gave her an excuse to go into Nancy's room and look down at the sleeping child, to say a prayer over him, and if she subsequently retreated to her own room to shed a few tears, why, nobody saw them.

All through that fall, when the vine maples took on their crimson foliage, when the oaks were splashy golden beacons in the dark-greens of fir and cedar, when the smell of woodsmoke hinted of the winter to come, Maggie stayed away from town, and thought about Angus.

Jake wondered if he was getting old. It was harder to get going in the mornings, these days, and he was more tired when the day's work was done. Things were more pleasant at home since Celeste was back. She was a delight to watch, so pretty, so happy. Sometimes he thought Maggie was happy, especially when she was with little Henry, but he worried about her. She ought to be finding herself someone else, though he was glad it hadn't been Wilkie Andreason.

Ann was even speaking to him occasionally. Oh, not about anything personal or important, only about things concerning the children and everyday matters. He felt a little better about Ann. He thought she was taking a long-overdue interest in life, and would be the better for it, as would everybody else.

He hoped to God the damned timber prices would start to rise again soon. He wasn't going to go under, as so many others had, at least he didn't think he would, unless things took a turn for the worse. It was stretching him pretty thin, though, running a big household at the landing and keeping Jaisy's bunch going, too.

Not that he begrudged Jaisy anything. She more than repaid him for whatever time and money he spent on her. Without Jaisy, Jake admitted, his life would have been sheer hell these past few years.

He might have harbored far more rancor toward his wife had it not been for Jaisy. It wasn't easy for a man to be denied his wife's bed and her body, and even after Jaisy had come into his life, he'd continued to resent Ann's rejection of him. He didn't think she'd made herself any happier than she'd made him, either. Well, if having Celeste living at home helped, so much the better. And it was about time Ann stopped worrying about what people were going to think if they saw Sarah. Sarah was as she was, and no amount of wishful thinking was going to change that; the rest of them could only get on with living and provide a loving home for the little girl.

He sighed when he thought about Henry. God, what he'd give to be able to carry the boy around on his shoulder, the way he used to carry Maggie, and brag about his grandson. He thought it would have been easier on them all, the boy and Maggie included, if she'd let those people—or someone— adopt him, but he understood why she couldn't have done it. And part of him was glad the boy was here, too. Now if there were only something to be done about Maggie herself.

He made it a point to come by the landing every night on the way home, even if he'd been working upriver, just to make sure everything was going all right. What he wanted tonight was to stop long enough to have a cup of coffee with Maggie—after sitting on the stove all day, it would be so strong and bitter it would hardly be drinkable, and he'd throw out the last half of it—and walk on up to the house with Maggie, if she hadn't already gone.

She was still there now; he saw her head bent over a ledger or something, through the side window of the office. He had never been a churchgoing man, but if there was a God—and he supposed there was, the world was too marvelously constructed and populated for it to be accidental—then he thanked God for Maggie. How empty his life would have been without her!

There was somebody waiting for him in the shadow at the end of the mill. At first he thought it was one of the crew, and then he recognized the tall figure and stiffened. He glanced quickly toward the office; he didn't think Maggie was aware of the visitor.

"Hello, Jake."

Angus McKay came toward him, looking the same as ever. No, Jake amended, not quite the same. He looked a little older, still heavily tanned and muscular, with something added. There was a maturity, an air of self-confidence, that surpassed what had been there the last time Jake had seen him.

He thought of what this man had done to Maggie—and whatever she said about it, McKay *had* seduced her, he'd been the one who knew what it was all about—and Jake felt his animosity rising. "Sorry, we're not hiring," he said shortly.

Angus was unruffled. "I'm not looking for a job. Maybe you heard, we hit a rich vein. Even split three ways, it paid off pretty well."

"I got nothing to say to you," Jake told him.

"You're the one fired *me*," Angus said mildly. "Seems like the anger ought to be running the other way. I don't hold any grudges."

"Well, *I do*," Jake informed him. "A man hurts my daughter the way you hurt Maggie, I'm supposed to be grateful?"

Something flickered in the gray eyes, though Jake couldn't exactly read it. "I knew you always had a temper, Jake, but I never thought you were a hypocrite."

Jake felt his hackles rising. "What the hell's that supposed to mean?"

"I mean, like the Bible says, let him who is without sin cast the first stone. I never threw any stones at you, Jake, and I'm not sure you have any right to throw any at me. If you think you have, go ahead. Only listen to me afterward, all right?"

"You got nothing to say I want to hear," Jake assured him. "Maybe you just better not come out to our part of the country. We don't need you."

"That's not the way I hear it. The way I hear it, you've slid a little bit behind in your bills, and you're stretched about as thin as you can get without something giving."

Heat climbed from Jake's neck into his face. "I don't

need you telling me what my business is, or how to run it. Get the hell out of here, McKay!''

He turned and stomped off toward the office, and then was sorry when Maggie looked up. Saw him, and beyond him.

Her face went white, even to her lips.

She was stricken, glancing from Angus to her father.

''I told him to get the hell out. Close up shop, girl, let's go get some supper.''

He tried to be offhand about it, but he could see that she was badly shaken. When he turned around, however, McKay was gone, and that was for the best, he thought. Whatever McKay had been after, it didn't matter to the Keatings.

''What did he want?'' Maggie demanded as they walked home.

''Said he didn't need a job, he had money from that mine. Said he heard we weren't doing so well, that we were in bad shape financially.''

Maggie hesitated. ''We are, sort of. I mean, we're paying our bills, barely, and the men's wages. There isn't much profit.''

''True enough. But who the hell is talking about my business, all over the county? And whatever's happening to us, it's none of McKay's affair.'' He reached up to massage his left chest and shoulder. ''God, I'm tired tonight.''

''Your shoulder hurt?''

''Oh, a little. It's been doing that, off and on, for a few weeks now.'' He gave her a rueful grin. ''Your old man's getting old, honey. Wearing out.''

She put an arm around his waist, hugging him. ''You've got lots of wear left in you yet. Maybe you ought to slow down, though. Let somebody else climb the tallest trees. You know.''

He laughed. "You know me, girl. The tallest trees are the most fun. The only challenge."

They entered the house arm in arm.

Angus had been observed at the landing. Several of the men asked about him. "Heard McKay was around yesterday. He ain't looking for a job, is he?"

Maggie fielded their questions with surface calm. "No. Just wanted to talk to my father."

"Good man, McKay. Wouldn't mind working with him again," Red Risku said. "I reckon he don't need to buck no timber anymore, though. Heard he struck it rich."

She hoped they'd stop talking about him. She didn't want to think about Angus.

Jake woke up feeling the now familiar ache in his chest and arm. He lay looking up into blackness for a while, hoping it would go away. It didn't. After a time, he got up and pulled on his pants and his shirt and shoes. Sometimes he felt better if he moved around a bit.

It was a warm night for early November. Maybe, he thought, he'd take a walk outside, smoke a cigar. He hadn't been sleeping very well lately. He'd resented Angus's evaluation of his business affairs, though they'd been accurate enough. Keating's mill and logging operation were marginal, at best. If only the goddamned prices would start going back up!

He let himself out of the house, the cigar forgotten. Joe came running to lick at his ankles, and he spoke to the dog. "Come on, fella, let's get some fresh air, eh?"

Except for the sounds of the river, gurgling over its rocky bottom, it was silent. The house behind him was dark. No breeze stirred the tops of the trees. There was a sprinkle of stars overhead, and a full moon just edging up over the mountains. It couldn't be very late if the moon wasn't up yet.

Below him, on the landing, something cracked.

Jake paused, listening, and Joe pricked up his floppy ears.

"You hear it, too, fella? Let's go take a look, what do you say?"

Joe trotted ahead of him along the path. The moon eased higher, touching the landscape with a cool, pale light. At the landing the buildings were black, shadowy, vacant.

Or were they?

Where there should have been only darkness, there was a spark.

A spark? What the hell?

Jake quickened his steps, and the hound, running ahead, barked a warning. Jake broke into a run. "Hey! Somebody down there?"

He had nearly reached the toolshed when it exploded, sending flame and debris and reverberating sound in every direction. The pain shot through his chest and along his arm, and then it was all-encompassing. He stumbled and went down; he heard the dog's pathetic whimper, and then there was nothing.

The explosion was heard in Snohomish.

It rattled the windows of the house above the landing, and without remembering how they came to be there, the family poured into the hallway. Only Wilkie had thought to light a lamp, and they stared at one another, bewildered, frightened, only half-awake.

Ann clutched a wrapper around her, dazed and alarmed. "What was it?"

"Sounded like dynamite to me," Wilkie said, handing the lamp to his wife. "I'll get dressed and go down to the landing. Is there a lantern handy?"

"I'll get it," Nancy offered, and ran downstairs without considering the immodesty of running about in her nightgown.

"I'm going with you," Maggie said, and had turned

toward her room when she realized that Jake was not among them. "Where's Daddy?"

He had been home that evening and had gone to bed at the same time as the rest of them. It wasn't likely he'd have gotten back up again to go to Jaisy's, Maggie thought. She pushed open his door, saw the rumpled bed, and noted that his shoes were gone.

For a moment she felt as if all the blood had drained from her head, leaving her unable to think.

Wilkie had vanished, presumably to dress; Maggie hurried to do the same, and reached the foot of the stairs, still buttoning her shirtwaist, at the same time Nancy handed the lighted lantern to him.

They could see it now, through the intervening trees: fire, the leaping orangy flames. The rest of the family followed them out onto the porch in various stages of undress; as she ran along behind her brother-in-law, Maggie heard her sister cry, "I'm going, too! Papa's down there!"

By the time they reached the landing proper, the fire had already begun to die down.

"The toolshed," Wilkie said, panting. "Was there dynamite in the toolshed?"

"Not that I know of. It won't spread now, will it? To the office or the mill? Or the shingles?" The shingles stood ready for shipment, hundreds of dollars' worth of them. Maggie stared wildly around for some answer. "Daddy! Daddy, are you here?"

Over the diminishing sounds of the fire, Wilkie spoke.

"He's here," he said, in a tone that told her the worst.

Jake's death left them in a state of shock, a ship with neither rudder nor helmsman.

The news spread rapidly. Loggers from all over the area came to the funeral. Maggie listened to the awkward words of sympathy as if from a great distance, murmuring replies, accepting the pats on the shoulder, the offers of help, from within a cocoon of numbness, not really feeling much.

She'd imagined Jake's death many times. Working in the woods was a hazardous job. She'd expected that eventually he would fall from one of his beloved trees and die as she'd seen others die.

She'd never pictured anything like this.

He hadn't been burned to death. She was grateful for that. Dr. Croyden said that it appeared his heart had given out in a moment of great stress; in his opinion, Jake had suffered very little.

Maggie buried Joe herself, in the woods behind the house. She moved as if in a nightmare from which she could not free herself.

Until the family gathered after the funeral and Ann put the primary question into words.

"What are we going to do about the logging operation, and the mill?"

She was drawn and chalky, with deep smudges under her eyes. Whatever she had thought of Jake over the past few years, she had needed his financial support, and now that was gone forever. She was frightened, and she showed it.

Wilkie reached out to press her hand. "Don't worry, Mother Keating: I'll take over the business."

"No!"

Maggie hadn't known she was going to speak until it was done, and even she was startled by the strength of her voice, the vehemence of the single word.

Every face turned in her direction.

"No," Maggie said again, more quietly but with conviction. "*I* will run the business."

Wilkie straightened and laughed uncertainly. "Maggie, you're only a girl! You can't run everything by yourself!"

"Not by myself, maybe, but I can run it. I've been in the woods since I was three years old. I know more about logging than you'll learn in a lifetime of keeping books." Visibly, she drew herself together, established control. "I'll talk to Red Risku about taking over as foreman on the timber crew. And I'll keep on running things at the landing the same as I've been doing."

Wilkie's face was a mask. Celeste, beside him, rested a hand on his arm, watching his face, her own expression troubled.

Ann, too, looked at Wilkie, and then at her older daughter. "I think he's right, dear. You're much too young, and a woman, besides."

"What has that to do with anything? I don't expect to buck logs myself, any more than Wilkie would. I expect to pay one man a little bit more for being foreman, and Red's perfectly capable. Daddy used to put him in charge when he couldn't supervise the job himself. As for the mill, there's a good crew. They know their jobs. They'll continue to do them."

"It seems so . . . inappropriate, for a young woman. I'll never understand you, Margaret, why you want to do a man's job."

"No, I don't suppose you will, Mama. But it's *our* business, it was Daddy's and mine. If I were a son, everybody would take it for granted that I'd take over. Well, I'm the nearest thing he had to a son, and it's my responsibility, and my privilege to run it now."

Ann twisted her hands in her lap. "We know it's a family business, dear. But we have a son-in-law, now. A man, to do a man's job."

"It's only reasonable for Wilkie to do it," Celeste put in.

"Is it? Why? Wilkie knows the bookkeeping, and that's all he knows. There's a hell of a lot more to it than the bookkeeping, I'll tell you that." She heard her grandmother's indrawn breath at the profanity. "It's what I *know* that's important, and I know a lot more than Wilkie does about both the woods operations and the mill. My sex or my physical strength doesn't matter at all. It's what's up *here*." She touched the side of her head. "You all like living here, in this house. Well, if you want to keep on living here, leave the business in my hands. They're the most capable you're likely to find, and it's my right, as Daddy's trained hand, to do it."

Millicent cleared her throat. "I think perhaps Margaret's right, Ann. She *is* trained. She went to that school to learn about running a business, and she's worked with Jake since she was a little girl. Surely Wilkie couldn't do it all, bookkeeping and all the rest of it, by himself, anyway. Why don't you let her try it?"

Maggie was astonished and grateful for her grandmother's championship. It wasn't the end of the matter, by any means, for Celeste and Ann both brought various arguments into play over the following weeks; Maggie let them slide over and around her, and kept on with what she was doing.

The mystery of what had caused the explosion that had killed Jake and Joe remained. All employees, when questioned, insisted that there had been no dynamite or any other explosive at the landing.

"What about that McKay?" Wilkie asked thoughtfully. "I understand he was out here, just before it happened. Had a fight with Jake. Maybe he came back and got even. They use explosives in those mines, don't they?"

Maggie's response was immediate and angry. "You have no right to insinuate a thing like that! Yes, Angus was here, and Daddy told him to leave, but there was no fight. Not even a real argument. I watched them the entire time, so I can attest to that. And," she added, "if Angus wanted to destroy the landing, he'd have done a more competent job of it. All we lost in supplies was what was in the toolshed. If anybody wanted to wipe us out, they'd have fired the mill and the office.''

Wilkie looked at her with raised eyebrows, but he dropped the subject.

If he was frustrated by her refusal to allow him control, he didn't flaunt it. He was at his desk when he was supposed to be, he kept his ledgers neatly and legibly, and he deferred to her on various matters with a courtesy as impeccable as it was cool.

It was Celeste who could not let the matter rest.

She sought out her sister in Maggie's room one evening, skirting the issue with vague talk about clothes and parties until Maggie finally said, "Celeste, what is it? You didn't come here to talk about parties you know I didn't attend and won't attend. What's the matter?''

Celeste moistened her lips with the tip of her tongue. "Well, I hope you won't take this the wrong way, Margaret, but I can't forget it. I don't think it's fair, what you're doing to Wilkie.''

"Oh? What is it I'm doing to Wilkie?'' Maggie put down her hairbrush and waited.

"Not letting him take over. Don't you see what that does to a man, to relegate him to second place?''

Maggie took a moment to calm her instinctive spurt of anger. "Is that what you think is important? Wilkie's tender feelings? Celeste, a good man will rise to the top, eventually, if he works toward it. Wilkie is not qualified to run either the logging or the mill operation. He simply doesn't know enough. I don't know it all, either, but I know a lot more than *he* does. And the important thing right now is to stay in business. We're all dependent on the income from the businesses that Daddy set up, and if we can ride it out a little longer, things will improve. They're starting to already. Right now, it's too much of a risk to turn anything over to someone who can't handle it. Don't you think, if Daddy had thought Wilkie was the one to do it, that he'd have handed over part of the responsibility to Wilkie when you got married?''

"Papa wasn't one to delegate authority," Celeste reminded her, with some truth.

"He delegated quite a bit to *me*. I'm sorry, Celeste. I know you love your husband, but it's too soon to talk about letting him run things just because he's a *man*. That isn't a good enough reason."

She knew she'd hurt her sister's feelings. She didn't know what she could do about that. What she said was true.

Still, running the whole shebang wasn't easy. Red Risku readily agreed to become foreman, and the woods operation went on almost as usual. There were plenty of other problems for which Maggie saw no simple solutions, things on which she longed to consult Jake. Other than in that regard, she couldn't allow herself to think about him. She had never dreamed anything could hurt as badly as losing her father; and if the rest of the family thought her stoical and unfeeling, well, it was the best she could do, keeping this tight rein on emotion that might otherwise have swamped her completely.

Much to her own surprise, Maggie found she could make some decisions with no difficulty at all.

"One thing we can do now," Ann said during a family gathering, "is get rid of that woman."

Nobody asked *what woman*. Not even Millicent. They all know, Maggie thought, heart lurching. They've all known for a long time.

"There are plenty of men available without jobs. We don't have to have her on the payroll any longer."

"If you're talking about Jaisy Pallison," Maggie said, and once again was amazed at how much she sounded like her father, "you can forget about it. She's a good cook. The men like her."

A spasm twisted Ann's face. "Oh, I'm sure the men like her, Margaret. That isn't the point."

"What is the point?" She tried to temper the defiance in her voice and couldn't. It was there, and it was strong. "She cooks very well, better than Mr. Murphy ever did. You know how long we'd keep a crew if we didn't feed them well? And if you're thinking about appearances, Mama, firing Mrs. Pallison would do just the opposite of what you want."

Ann stared at her. "What do you mean?"

"I mean that if she continues to work, nobody's going to think anything of it. But if we fire her, there's going to be talk. Why was she fired? Because she was sleeping with Jake Keating, and now his widow's getting even? You think that's going to put you, or any of the rest of us, in a saintly light?"

Ann put a hand to her mouth, her bosom suddenly heaving, her cheeks flaming. "I can't help thinking this is a mistake, Margaret. Allowing you to do a man's job. You're becoming coarse."

"Coarse? To say what you've all been thinking for years?" It didn't occur to her that she'd left herself out. "That's why you hate her, isn't it? Because Daddy slept with her. It's none of my business why he didn't have a wife to sleep with here at home, but running the camp *is* my business, and I say the wisest thing is to leave Mrs. Pallison alone. Let her cook. Don't give anyone any reason to gossip any further."

Ann went white, then flushed again, speechless.

Wilkie's support was unexpected. "Maggie's right. If Jaisy's fired, she has no means of support, and she has two children. No matter what she's done, there are people who'd sympathize with her. After all, she's a widow, too. And firing her's bound to create talk."

Outgunned, Ann subsided, though it was clear she felt that getting even with Jaisy was something that deserved to happen. She simply didn't want to bring any criticism on her own head by doing it.

If Ann had known how the problems piled up, how Maggie struggled with large difficulties and dozens of small ones, she would have pressed harder for turning things over to Wilkie.

It was one of the small things that precipitated the biggest crisis yet.

It was a cold, wet day, and they all knew they'd have to suspend logging operations soon. Maggie had slogged through mud over her shoetops to walk to camp and back, to talk to Red. He was of the belief that when they'd finished cutting the stand on which they now worked, they'd better pack it in for the winter.

"Winds are getting high. Had some bad gusts yesterday, when Rich was rigging a tree; he damn near fell. We get this last stand, we'll meet all the contracts, won't we?"

She'd been chilled and damp, and stopped at the cookhouse for a bowl of soup before she headed back to the landing. Nobody she knew made better soup than Jaisy.

There was no one else around, except Lucy and Will, doing lessons at the far table.

Jaisy brought her the soup, then stood facing her until Maggie paused and looked up.

"Did you want to say something?"

Jaisy met her eyes squarely. "Yes, I do. I want to know if I'm going to be hired on again in the spring, or if I'm out of a job now."

It hadn't until that moment occurred to Maggie that even if the woman were not fired, Jaisy had no means to keep her family through the winter. She supposed her father had seen to that, before, ever since Hank Pallison was killed. She knew what Jaisy was paid, and knew as well that probably not very much of it could have been saved to get her through the winter.

"You'll be hired on in the spring, with the rest of the

crew." She saw the relief that Jaisy couldn't mask, deep in the green eyes. "How will you manage until then?"

Jaisy considered, then shrugged. "The kids kept up a garden. We got a few things laid by. Maybe I can get myself a buck, for meat." Her lips twisted. "I'm not a very good shot, but necessity is said to be a good incentive, ain't it?"

"One of the men should be able to get you some venison. Ask Red. He's a good shot."

Jaisy nodded. "I'll do that, then." She cleared her throat. "I didn't want to upset your ma, so I didn't go to the funeral. But it wasn't because I didn't have respect, you know. It wasn't that I didn't care."

Maggie had forgotten her soup. "I know that." She felt awkward, embarrassed, yet she knew that something else was called for, something only she could offer this woman. "I think you gave my father the only happiness he knew for a great many years. I didn't always understand that, but I do now. I think he loved you. And you loved him, didn't you?"

Jaisy's mouth trembled, then firmed. "Yes," she said. "I loved him."

Maggie's eyes misted so that Jaisy took on a softened look. "I guess that's one thing we had in common, then, isn't it?"

"I guess it is," Jaisy said softly.

Maggie ate her soup, and headed back along the skid road to the landing.

She missed Joe. Sometimes she thought she ought to get another dog. There wasn't time to look for one, though, and besides, there were enough complications in her life at the moment. Maybe in the spring somebody's dog would have pups, and she'd get one. It would be nice for Henry to have a dog.

If Henry was still here.

It was no secret that Pat Patterson was courting Nancy.

One had only to look at her face to realize what her answer was going to be when he proposed.

In good conscience, Maggie could only wish Nancy well. Losing Henry, though, if Nancy moved away from Keating's Landing, was one more worry she could not put out of her mind.

In the way of worries, when she thought she already had more than she could handle, Maggie stumbled over yet another one, this one a genuine crisis, and all because she needed a pencil.

## 40

THE pencil rolled off her desk and, unseen, wedged between a leg of her stool and the wood box. When Maggie stepped backward, she heard the pencil crack as her weight came down on it. She picked up the pieces and disgustedly dropped them into the trash to be burned in the stove.

There were always plenty of pens and pencils on Wilkie's desk. She'd simply get one from there, since he'd stepped outside for a smoke. Otherwise, she avoided his work area. She could see him through the window, talking to one of the mill hands.

Maggie put down a small twinge of curiosity about why, since Jake's death, Wilkie was suddenly spending so much time talking to the hired help. He hadn't shown any interest in them before. More than likely he pictured himself running the outfit one day, she thought with grim humor; well, it wasn't going to happen, no matter how many people he talked to.

Wilkie's desk, like the man himself, was tidy and businesslike. The ledger he was working on lay open exactly in the center of the desk, and there were pencils aplenty. She had picked up one of them, not consciously looking at the ledger at all, when one line of the neat writing leaped out at her.

She stared down at it, pencil forgotten. Wilkie was meticulous about his work; he always checked and rechecked his figures before they were entered in the ledger. So why did he list their most recent shingle sale at a fraction of what it had actually been?

She put out a hand to turn the ledger to a more comfortable angle to read it again. There was no mistake. Well, there *was* a mistake, the figures were in error, but they were what Wilkie had entered. Her gaze moved across the page, to the price they'd been paid for the shingles, and again the figure was not what it should have been.

For a moment Maggie was motionless, profoundly disturbed and not yet fully aware of the reasons for this.

"Maggie? You looking for something?"

She hadn't heard Wilkie come in; he lounged in the doorway behind her, smiling a little.

"I needed a pencil. Wilkie, why does the ledger say that we shipped two hundred bundles of shingles to Constantine last week?"

The faint smile seemed to congeal. "Didn't we?" Wilkie asked.

"If memory serves me, the figure was two hundred and eighty-five. That's a difference in price of . . ."

He stepped into the cubicle that served as his office. "Don't give me an arithmetic lesson, Maggie."

Was there an air of insolence about him? She stared into his dark eyes, instinctively challenging him.

"It seems someone must give you a lesson of some kind. Either you made an error in your accounting, or you're deliberately recording what you know to be false figures."

The words were said before she thought, before comprehension, like a sudden plunge into an icy river, swept over her.

The smile was back, oddly altered. The dark eyes held hers, compelling, almost mesmerizing.

She was totally unprepared for what he did next.

Another step brought him to her. He reached for her, bringing his mouth down on hers in a hard, demanding way that set up a violent reaction within her. Revulsion, dismay. And fury. Blinding, incoherent fury.

Maggie jerked her face aside, pushing against him with both hands, gasping for breath. She felt as if she wanted to scrub off her mouth, cleanse herself of the moisture he'd left there. She felt as if she were going to throw up.

He didn't seem to read any of that in her face; he was still smiling.

"You know, I think I married the wrong sister. A tactical error. Celeste is very pretty, but that's all there is. You're the one with the brains. The drive, the push. Jake's daughter all the way."

Incredibly, he would have reached for her again if she hadn't raised a knee as well as put out her hands to ward him off. She was hampered by her skirts—damn the confining garments they made for women, anyway!—and she didn't do him any damage, but he got the message.

The smile slid away, though he'd lost none of his composure.

"You're a very attractive woman, Maggie-Margaret." Did he think that old pet name would bring her around? she wondered wildly. The man was insane. "You know I've always been drawn to you. You work too hard—you don't do anything to relax. Don't be afraid of me—"

"I'm not afraid of you!" She practically spat the words at him. "I despise you! How long have you been making false entries in the books? Did you do it while my father was alive? Or did you only get brave enough after I took over? How much have you cheated us out of?"

"Cheated? That's an ugly word, Maggie. It's a family business, after all, and I'm family, aren't I?" The smile was back, tentative, testing the waters. "Listen, we can talk things out. We can do things for each other."

She thought if she'd been a man she would have hit him. Hard. Hard enough to kill him.

"We're not going to do anything for each other, Wilkie. So there won't be any possible misunderstanding, I'll spell it all out for you right now. This is *my* business. I will run it my way. I'm going to take the books and go over them, page by page, and see how much damage you've done to us. After that we'll talk again. But I don't need to go over the books to make everything perfectly clear."

Anger drove her on, ignoring the narrowing of his eyes, the tightening of his mouth.

"You may have married the wrong sister—I take it which one of us it was didn't matter, since your primary purpose was to steal from the company, or cover up what you'd already stolen; and, of course, you thought with Daddy gone you'd be able to take charge of everything. But I'll tell you this, Wilkie. You married Celeste, and you'll not only stay married to her, but you'll treat her like the loving innocent she is. You'll be a good husband, make her happy, and from this point on you'll keep honest books—with my assistance and supervision, of course—or brother-in-law or not, you'll go to jail."

The look he gave her was enough to send tremors down her spine. She could read much of his speculation, and it frightened her. He still thought he could win her over, still thought he was going to weasel out of this, probably was convinced that he could charm Maggie into some sort of illicit relationship that would calm her down, keep her under control, and, in his viewpoint, provide the favor of sexual release to his poor spinster sister-in-law. And failing that, he was capable of getting nasty.

She swallowed against rising nausea. "There's one more thing. Did you have anything to do with the explosion that killed Daddy?"

That jerked him out of his unwarranted complacency. "For crissake, Maggie! You can't mean that! No, God, no! I never would have done anything like that, never! You can't be serious!"

"I'm serious enough that if I ever find out the truth, and you had any connection with it whatever, I'll see you hanged," Maggie said, and read recognition of the truth of her intent in his face.

He swore again, with feeling. There was a beading of moisture on his forehead. "Maggie, I swear to God, I don't know anything about that explosion. I had nothing against Jake, I *liked* Jake, and I wouldn't have done anything to cause financial harm to the company, either."

Thinking about it later, she was inclined to believe that part of what he said. The dynamite, or whatever it was, had been detonated at night, at a time when there should not have been anyone around. Certainly the perpetrator could not have anticipated that Jake would be there, be caught in the blast and killed. And Wilkie, already in the family, would have had no reason to damage company assets.

Still, it was gratifying to see that she'd finally managed to shake him.

Maggie picked up the ledger and held it against her breast. "I'm going to take this with me. I don't know how long it will take me to go through the entire thing; you'll just have to start another ledger, anyway, since from now on you're going to do a duplicate set of books and I'm going to compare them and check every entry. Provided that you continue as bookkeeper, of course, and as an attentive and faithful husband to my sister.''

Wilkie's eyes were cold and furious. "I always knew you were a bitch, Maggie.''

"You'll find I'm worse than that if you stray the slightest little bit.'' Though she was shaking, she met his gaze squarely, unwavering. "Of course, I'll take precautions so that if anything happens to me, the truth about you will be made known. It won't do any good to arrange an accident for me, or anything like that.''

His jaw went slack. "For God's sake, do you think me capable of anything like that? I'm no murderer!''

"You'd better not be," Maggie said, and walked past him and out into the main part of the office, praying that her legs would get her out and away from him before they allowed her to collapse.


It took her over a week to go through just what was in this one ledger, and what she found made her ill.

Wilkie had been systematically stealing from the company for as far back as this record went. She had no doubt that earlier ledgers would reveal previous treachery as well.

No wonder they'd all worked so hard and for so little profit. There had actually *been* profit, only Wilkie, the trusted bookkeeper, had siphoned it off for his own use.

She found enough to convince her that what had begun as pilferage, when Jake was still in charge, had advanced to substantial embezzlement after she took over.

What was she to do?

She'd already put a stop to the ongoing theft, at least as long as she double-checked everything Wilkie did. That would increase her own work load considerably, at a time when that was the last thing she needed. The only alternative, however, was to fire him completely and hire another bookkeeper, and how could she do that without explaining to the family *why?*

She found it almost impossible to look at Celeste, to see her happy face, the aura of contentment that radiated from her. Millicent and Ann both liked Wilkie, too, and depended heavily upon him as the sole male in the family.

How could she destroy all that? Destroy her sister? Would Celeste ever forgive her, even when confronted with the evidence?

No. She had to go on this way, protecting herself as best she could, and protecting the rest of them as well.

There was one minor consolation. If the embezzlement ceased, there should be a little more cash to work with. Which was academic, at this point, since they were shortly to close down for the winter, and there would be no more business conducted before spring.

Maggie felt as if she'd survived a devastating conflagration, singed on all sides, clinging to life and sanity by bloodied fingernails, waiting for the flames to be renewed and devour her.

She knew nothing to do but continue to hang on.


"Maggie."

She looked up to see Nancy at her bedroom door, carrying Henry, who had grown so much that he was more of a load than she could manage without resting him on an outthrust hip.

"Could I talk to you?"

"Certainly. Come on in, and shut the door." Maggie closed the old ledger she had been going over, a depressing business at best, and smiled at the squirming little boy. "Let him run. He can't hurt anything in here."

Nancy let the child slide to the floor. "I wish that were true of the whole place. He broke a vase this afternoon. Your ma was quite put out, though when Sarah does it, it's not so upsetting.'' She flushed. ''I'm sorry. I've no right to speak that way, have I?''

''To me you do. Sit down. What's the matter, Nance? Besides the fact that our boy is normal and breaks things sometimes?''

Color unexpectedly flooded Nancy's face. ''Pat's asked me to marry him, Maggie.''

Maggie stifled the clutch of fear that made a tightness in her chest. ''That's wonderful, Nancy. You love him, don't you?''

''Yes. I never thought I'd find anybody, after Adam was killed, but Pat is . . .'' She couldn't find the words, laughing a little. ''He wants us to get married next week.''

''Next week!'' Maggie couldn't keep the shock out of her voice. She'd been anticipating such news, but next week? It took her breath away, leaving her hollow and apprehensive.

''He wants to head north. He has a friend who's going to start logging along the Skagit, in the Sedro-Woolley area. The man needs a bullwhacker.''

Maggie's throat closed convulsively. Nancy reached over to put a hand over hers, squeezing it. ''There's something else, Maggie. I know you swore me to secrecy about Henry, but I had to do it. Please understand.''

The words were a whisper. ''You told Pat.''

''Yes. It wasn't that he wouldn't take me, thinking I'd had a babe out of wedlock, you know. He thought Henry was mine, and he wanted me anyway. It's not all men as would have done that.''

Maggie nodded. ''I know.''

''The thing was, it didn't seem fair to him to let him think I was *that* kind of girl. He didn't, I mean he never tried anything, you know, like he believed I was an easy woman. And I wanted him to know the truth. But what really decided me was when he asked me to marry him. On our wedding night''—her face flamed again, the color

climbing her neck and turning even her ears bright-pink—
"how would I explain I was a virgin? He'd know that,
wouldn't he? That I couldn't have had a baby, and still be
so . . . ignorant."

Maggie's breath escaped in a small sigh. "Yes. Yes, of
course, you had to tell him. How—how does he feel,
knowing Henry is *my* son?"

"He's a good man, Pat is. He was prepared to take the
boy before he knew, and he'll still take him, now. Only
he's had an idea, said to tell you, see if you think it would
work."

Hope, extinguished, was rekindled. "What?"

Nancy hesitated. "It ain't that we won't take him, you
know. God knows I love him like he *was* my own, and the
thought of leaving him behind about tears me up—and
maybe it wouldn't work, anyway; but Pat says he don't
care what people think of *him*, if they want to think he's
un-Christian, why, there's many another man's felt the
same way—and besides, Sedro-Woolley is far enough
away, we probably won't even meet anybody from
Snohomish, unless we come back for a visit—"

"Nancy, you're babbling! What are you talking about,
for the love of God? If you don't take Henry with you,
what will happen to him?"

"Oh!" Nancy dissolved in combined laughter and tears,
wiping at her eyes with the corner of her apron. "I know,
I'm not making sense. I'll try, I really will." She took a
deep breath and spoke more slowly.

"Pat says, we can tell it around that he don't take to the
idea of marrying and taking on somebody else's son. That
he wants *me*, but don't really want a boy with no last name
but his ma's. There's been others have felt that way."

"Yes." They were clasping hands, holding on as if to
save each other from drowning. "Yes, go on."

"Pat says, we can say the condition for our getting
married is to find somebody else to take the boy. And

maybe, because everybody already knows you're attached to him—everybody here is, except maybe your ma, and even she's nicer to him than she used to be—maybe you could say because we been friends for so long, and you want me to be happy and get married—maybe you could say you want to raise him. I know it ain't usual, for an unmarried woman, but everybody already knows how unusual you are. Nobody thinks any the less of you for it, running everything the way you do. There's plenty as admires you, the way you took over after your pa died. They'd think it . . . different . . . for you to take the boy, but they might not be suspicious, that he was yours. Nobody seemed to question he was *mine*."

Maggie released the pent-up air she'd been holding. "Dear God, would it work? I wouldn't care for myself, Nancy, you know I wouldn't, if everybody knew he was mine, I could bear the shame of it." She thought, fleetingly, of Jaisy, and how she'd loved Jake enough to give up her own reputation for his need. "It's Mama and Celeste I worry about. If *they* didn't get suspicious—Oh, Nancy, maybe it would work! Maybe it would!"

They cried together, blew their noses simultaneously, then hugged; Henry drew their attention back to him by pulling a runner off a table, so that a lamp crashed to the floor.

"Oh! Another item for Mama to be upset about," Maggie said, getting down to clean up the spilled oil and the shards of glass chimney. "Only I won't tell her."

Kneeling there on the floor, she looked up at her friend.

"God bless you, Nancy. And God bless Pat, too, if this works."

It had to, she thought. It was the only way she could avoid losing Henry. She was determined to become the most experienced liar in the world, if that was what it took to make it work.

\* \* \*

By the following evening, she still hadn't made any attempt to break the news to the family that she was considering taking on Nancy's child to rear. Of them all, she thought Wilkie the most likely to guess the truth, and she wasn't afraid of Wilkie telling.

He'd stared at her insolently when she'd demanded, and taken, the ledgers from him. "What you're doing is blackmail, you know," he told her gratingly. "That's a crime, too, Maggie."

"Not as big a crime as embezzling. If it weren't that my sister thinks she loves you, I'd let them lock you up forever. And if the time comes when she is dissatisfied, you'll answer for it."

Hatred glittered in his dark eyes, but he'd said nothing more. If he got ideas about Maggie and Henry, he wouldn't say anything about that, either. He knew she wasn't bluffing.

She stepped out of the office and hesitated to lock the door before she went home. They'd never locked doors before, but since the explosion, and her discovery of Wilkie's treachery, she'd kept it locked except when she was there.

A shadow moved at the end of the mill. She turned swiftly, then recognized the figure.

"Oh, Jaisy, you startled me."

"I'm sorry. Didn't mean to." Jaisy moved toward her, pulling her old coat high at the throat against the chill of dusk. "I hope this isn't a bad time to talk to you, Maggie."

Jaisy had never kowtowed to her, either before Jake's death or after it. She'd never called her "Miss Keating" or "Miss Maggie," though many others would have, under the circumstances. Maggie had felt a grudging admiration for her father's mistress; now she didn't even begrudge it very much.

"It's as good a time as any. It's cold out here, though.

There's still a little heat in the stove. Would you like to go inside?''

Jaisy shook her head. "No. What I got to say won't take long. First off, I want to thank you for the extra money in my pay envelope. I appreciate it.''

Sometimes it seemed to Maggie that she had a perpetual ache in her throat. "It's what Daddy would have wanted.''

Jaisy smiled. "He thought you were the best thing that ever happened to him, do you know that? I sure got tired of hearing how wonderful Maggie was.''

They both laughed a little, not comfortable with each other, no longer hostile, either.

"Anyway, I thank you. And for keeping me on again, come spring. I got me a job through the winter, waiting on tables at the Penobscot Hotel. It'll keep us going.''

"I'm glad,'' Maggie said sincerely.

Jaisy licked her lips. "I heard something there last night, I thought you ought to know about. You remember that old Woolrich, Jake fired after he killed them bulls?''

"Yes, of course.''

"Well, he came in for dinner. Got himself a job cleaning out the livery stable, he was celebrating his first pay, eating at a decent place, you know. Had a bit to drink with it. They don't take kindly to drunks in the dining room, hurts the trade, so they asked him to leave.''

Maggie waited, the late November wind turning up her skirts, a promise of winter soon to come. Yet she wouldn't have cut this short for anything. She slid her hands into her coat pockets to warm them.

"I got off work about two hours later and headed out for home,'' Jaisy related. "I met him again, only by then he was really drunk. Falling-down drunk, in fact. He was sitting on the edge of the sidewalk, crying.''

The scene was vivid in Maggie's mind. She waited, almost smelling the stench of the old man.

"I stopped and tried to get him to get up and go home. He didn't want to go home. He wanted to talk."

Maggie was tense by this time. This was something important; Jaisy hadn't come all the way out from town for anything trivial.

"So I stayed there and listened to him. He's the one done it, Maggie. Set off that dynamite here at the landing. He was mad because Jake fired him and wouldn't take him back on. He wanted to get even. He didn't know Jake would be here, didn't think anybody would, that time of night. He intended to fire the mill, too, burn the whole thing to the ground, he was so drunk and so mad. He didn't think anybody'd know till it was all over with. He heard Jake and the dog coming, scared him off, and he nearly killed himself, running away back to town."

Not Angus or Wilkie, Maggie thought. A little of the tension eased out of her.

"He didn't know until the next day that Jake was killed. It's on his conscience bad, Maggie. If you report it to the constable, I reckon they'll lock him up, but I think he's going to kill himself with drink, anyway. The guilt's eating at him like poison."

Maggie sighed. "I guess it would be. He worked for Daddy for a long time." She was silent a moment, then spoke from the depths of her heart. "Thank you, Jaisy. I needed to know."

Jaisy nodded. Her auburn hair was blowing in the wind, whipping across her face so that she held up both hands to pin it back. "I figured that." She hesitated, about to go, and Maggie had actually taken a step when Jaisy's words stopped her.

"There's another thing. None of my business, and maybe it don't matter to you, anyway. But it might."

"Yes? What is it?"

"It's about Angus McKay."

There was no denying the jolt that gave her. She'd tried

to tell herself she'd forgotten Angus, that what he did had nothing to do with her anymore. Her mouth was dry. "What about Angus?"

"He's back. You musta heard that. He tried to talk to Jake, but Jake wouldn't listen to him. He wants something, and maybe you should see him." This time the hesitation was even more pronounced. "Maybe you ought to tell him about that baby, Maggie. Maybe he's got a right to know about Henry."

Maggie sucked in a breath and held it. "Daddy told you about Henry?"

"It hurt him, bad, what happened to you. He had to tell somebody or die of it," Jaisy said softly. "Nobody else knows. I figured out for myself that when he told McKay there was something between you and Wilkie, he made a bad mistake. McKay was already gone off to Oregon by the time I knew, so there wasn't nothing to do about it then. But I used to watch you, and I had it figured, it was Angus you was after, not Wilkie. When I heard about the baby, I knew it. That boy loved you, Maggie. Maybe still does."

"It's not likely," Maggie said over the sudden pounding of her heart. "I went after him, talked to him, or tried to. He wouldn't listen."

"He was hurt. Angry. Men don't always listen when they're hurting. Thing is, I just happened to be there at the Mercantile the day somebody mentioned Wilkie was marrying Celeste. They'd been talking about the wedding, and Angus stood there in that stone-faced way he has when he don't want anybody to know what he's thinking. And then somebody said, anybody'd be lucky to get that Celeste, she was such a beauty, and it was like somebody took a pick to the granite, right in front of my eyes. He tried to hide it, but he couldn't. Not to somebody knew him the way I do, was looking right at him. He said, 'Celeste? I thought he was marrying Maggie!' And by the time anybody else looked at him, he was all closed up again. But I saw it."

She felt faint, weak in the knees. Could it be true? Could Jaisy be right?

Jaisy's voice was soft, barely audible above the sound of the rising wind. "I got no right to give you any advice, Maggie, but it don't seem to me your ma's ever been real good in that department. Besides, she don't even know about you and Angus, does she? Anyway, I'm going to tell you. If I was you, I'd make the first move. See Angus, talk to him. He's a man with a lot of pride, and he's got no reason to think the Keatings got any love for him. He's been kicked out a couple of times, now, and he won't risk having it happen again. If you want him, girl, go after him."

If she wanted him? Did she?

She was suddenly swept with a wild, sweet joy, a hope—no, an exultant determination.

"Yes," she said softly into Jaisy's waiting face, "yes, I want him. Will you wait a minute? Will you take a note back to town?" It occurred to her then that Jaisy had that long walk in the dark still to accomplish. "I'll get out the buggy, ask Wilkie to drive you back."

Jaisy shook her head. "No need. I'm used to walking. I'll just wait for your note."

There wasn't time to compose a masterpiece. In fact, the way she was feeling, it was a wonder she could think to write anything at all.

*Angus: I understand you tried to talk to Daddy, and he wouldn't listen. I'd like to know what you had in mind.* She hesitated over the ending, then signed it, ambiguously, *As ever, Maggie.*

She didn't bother to seal it. Let Jaisy read it, if she liked.

Her heart was soaring as she headed home a few minutes later, and at the same time she was afraid. Afraid of what it would do to her if this came to nothing.

# 41

Two days passed. From ecstatic anticipation, Maggie's spirits dropped into her shabby boots. Angus had read her note, had thrown it away. He no longer cared.

And then, on the morning of the third day, when she'd just put Henry back in his pen and was leaning over the railing talking to him, the door opened behind her.

She knew before she turned that it was Angus.

He stood in the doorway, filling it. Wider through the shoulders, gray eyes a bit flinty, fair hair towsled by the wind, the red cap she'd made protruding from one pocket of his jacket.

"Hello, Maggie."

She couldn't tell anything from his voice.

"Hello, Angus. Come in and shut the door; you'll give Henry pneumonia."

He glanced at the child, then back at her. "That's Nancy's baby? Good looking kid, isn't he?"

The pain, the pain. How could she think? How could emotion cause such physical agony?

"Yes, isn't he?" she made herself say.

"I heard she's getting married soon, to that Patterson fellow."

"Yes, that's right." She heard her voice, sounding perfectly normal, at least to her own ears. "Unfortunately,

Pat doesn't want someone else's child. Nancy's talking about . . . leaving him with me."

Did his eyes narrow a trifle? She couldn't be sure. He advanced toward the stove and extended his hands. "Jaisy gave me your note last night. It was too late to come then. I don't suppose you could spare a cup of that coffee?"

"Yes, of course." She filled the cup and handed it over, proud that her hand was steady. "You still drink it with sugar, don't you?"

"My tastes haven't changed much," he said, accepting the cup. He sipped, then looked her full in the face. She wondered if he tried to read her emotion as she did his. "I spent a year and a half in that damned mine. It was plenty long enough to convince me I'm not a miner. Tom and Jim are going back in the spring, stake out another claim. I'm out of the partnership. Maybe mining in California, on top of the ground, wouldn't be so bad. But I don't like working in a black hole. I need blue sky, wind and rain in my face, tall trees. I'm a logger, not a miner."

"So you came back to Snohomish."

His reply was an oblique one. "I thought you'd be married by this time."

She didn't know where the courage came from to reply the way she did. "I only met one man in my life I wanted to marry, and it wasn't Wilkie Andreason. There was nothing between us, Angus, between Wilkie and me. I was stupid in the way I tried to fool my parents, but that's the only thing I have to feel guilty about."

He didn't comment on that; she didn't know if that was good or bad. He slipped again at the coffee. "I brought back money from that mine, you know. I want to use it to get back to what I know—logging. I maybe got enough to start up my own outfit, but that wasn't quite what I had in mind. I thought maybe . . . Jake would be interested in a partnership. I heard he was having a hard time, but the recession's easing. Prices are going to be up for sure in the spring, and the shingles ought to be paying their way, aren't they?"

The Scots burr was strong in his words, the only sign that this wasn't as casual a conversation as it might have appeared to an outsider. Angus had always slipped back into that burr when emotion—fear, anger, tenderness—became strong in him.

"Yes," Maggie said, waiting.

"He wouldn't even hear my proposition."

Still she waited.

"They tell me you're running things now. Doing a pretty good job of it, they say."

She didn't wait any longer. It was now or never. "Yes, I'm running it. We've had some financial problems. I've learned what the worse one was and have taken steps to correct it. We're on a sound footing. We don't have to borrow to stay afloat. But I'm interested in your proposition."

There. She'd done it. She'd taken the plunge. From here on, it was up to Angus.

"An inventory of your assets," Angus said at once, "to determine the value of what you already have against what I have to invest. We'd split control fifty-fifty, with equal assets."

He paused, then added deliberately, "I wouldn't take orders from Wilkie Andreason."

Her mouth flattened. "Neither of us would take orders from Wilkie. He's the bookkeeper, nothing more."

For long seconds he scrutinized her face, then broke into a grin and extended his hand. "Done?"

"Done," Maggie conceded and felt her hand engulfed, tingling, a tingling that raced through her bloodstream and sang in her ears.

Behind her, Henry fell and let out a shriek of pain and rage. She turned to scoop him up, crooning, reaching for a handkerchief to blot the drop of blood on his lip.

Angus watched, amused. "Has a good pair of lungs on

him, doesn't he? Looks like the two of you are good friends. You're going to miss him if Nancy gets married and takes him away. You weren't serious, were you, about her leaving him with you?"

No sooner over one hump, she thought numbly, than on to the next one. She couldn't look at him when she returned Henry to his padded pen. "Yes, I was. We haven't told anybody, but it's pretty well decided. Nancy's not taking him."

A frown carved itself into his forehead. "Why the hell would she marry somebody that wants her to give up her kid?"

She braced herself for the lie. "Pat doesn't want another man's child. He wants Nancy, though. I'm sure he really loves her, and she doesn't want to lose him. I've agreed to take Henry. I love him almost as much as she does."

The scowl deepened. "You mean she's willing to give him up for some damned bullwhacker? Her own kid?"

She kept her face turned from him, pretending to do something with Henry. "It's a choice between them, and she loves Pat, too. She might never have another chance to marry somebody she loves."

"What the hell kind of man is he to ask that of her? Or Nancy to buckle under to such an unreasonable demand? For God's sake!"

She felt such a pain in her throat, spreading through her chest. She tried to speak, failed, and tried again. "It's up to Nancy and Pat. And Henry's attached to everyone here, the whole family—" That wasn't entirely a lie, even her mother had begun to smile at Henry's antics, at his attempts to walk and talk. Change the subject, she thought wildly, hurry!

She forced herself to straighten, to turn toward him, though she wasn't able to meet his eyes. She moved toward the desk where she kept paper and pencil. "I suppose we'd ought to have a lawyer draw up a legal agreement, hadn't we? A partnership? And someone impartial to do the inventory—"

"Why not do the inventory together?" Angus said, and it registered, just barely, that she'd successfully turned him away from the matter of Nancy and Henry. "Who knows the business better than you do, and I? Besides, it'll save money."

She managed to look at him, then, and saw his mouth twitch. His mouth—for a few seconds she was mesmerized. She ought not to have looked at his mouth. It was too easy to remember the taste of it, the feel of it, and the longing that swept through her was so strong that she actually swayed toward him, catching herself only with overwhelming effort.

"Daddy always said you were thrifty."

Angus laughed. "*Everybody* always said I was thrifty. When do you want to begin?"

She suddenly felt reckless, exuberant, although the thread of fear was still there underlying the emotions swirling through her. "Tomorrow morning? At seven?"

"All right. I'll be here," Angus said. "I'll talk to Tom Jesson tonight, have him draw up a tentative partnership agreement. Then we'll go over it together and make whatever adjustments need to be made."

"Fine," Maggie agreed. She was smiling. There was no way she could contain all that joy without a little of it spilling over in a smile.

Yet when he was gone, the joy didn't last, at least not entirely. It was a beginning, but that's all it was. The fact that Angus wanted to be her partner didn't mean he wanted to be anything else. It didn't prove he still loved her.

She knew one thing, though. She still loved him. Her body physically ached for him, in a way her mother would have found shameless and disgusting, she thought. Jaisy would understand, though.

She scarcely knew how she got through the day; she

went back time after time to the ledgers, realizing she did not know what she had just read, having to read it again and again and still not making sense of it.

People spoke to her and she responded, only to wonder a few minutes later what they'd said, how she had replied.

She didn't care. Angus had returned, she had a second chance, and she intended to make the most of it. On the way home she indulged in some outrageous day-dreaming, imagining throwing herself into his arms, rekindling the flame that had never completely been extinguished for all that she'd tried so hard to do it.

Dinner was a gala meal, for Celeste made an announcement, blushing and laughing, reaching for Wilkie's hand for moral support, she told them that she was expecting a baby.

"I suppose it's indelicate to mention it so soon." Her color deepened becomingly. "It must have happened on our honeymoon, at Snoqualmie Falls. That's such a lovely spot, and this is such a lovely thing for me, for us! I can't bear to keep it a secret, I want you all to be as happy as I am!"

Maggie, only partially insulated by her own burgeoning happiness, watched the two of them. Celeste was so beautiful, so young, so innocent. Wilkie played the proud expectant father to the hilt, conveying with subtle hints that not only would he be head of his own family, but could be counted on to take a larger part in all Keating affairs, including his willingness to assume additional responsibilities down at the mill.

Ann and Millicent were eating it up, Maggie observed. She supposed she couldn't blame them. Both had depended upon a man, a husband, for support and protection, and now each experienced having to rely upon a son-in-law. They trusted a man more than they trusted her.

Wilkie gave her a smile, open, broad, across the table

graced by fine china and crystal and silver. *See?* the look said. *They think I'm wonderful.*

Maggie hoped that her returning gaze carried as clear a message: *Well, I don't think you're wonderful, so watch your step.*

Something shifted, almost imperceptibly, in Wilkie's face. Ah, he'd gotten the message she thought, but almost immediately he was his customary bland self. "I think this first time, we'll have a boy," he said. "An heir to the mill and the logging operation. A boy to grow up and follow in my footsteps."

It was a challenge, Maggie recognized, thrown directly in her face. She did not reply, and after the first flash of resentment—clearly not shared by anyone else at the table—Maggie hugged her own news to herself. Even alone, she'd be a match for Wilkie, she decided. And with Angus sharing the authority, there was no way that Wilkie could hope to gain the upper hand in any phase of the business.

She wouldn't spoil Celeste's evening by breaking the news now. That there would be outrage and opposition was a foregone conclusion. Wilkie would be furious; Celeste could be expected to follow his lead, with some justification that could only be refuted by breaking her heart, and Ann was completely won over by Wilkie's charm and assurance. Millicent might be on Maggie's side, but her opinion had never carried much weight and probably would not now, though she had as much to lose as anyone if the mill and the logging operation failed. Or as much to gain if both succeeded.

No, she wouldn't tell them anything tonight. She supposed she'd have to tell them tomorrow; the minute Angus appeared on the landing in the morning, everybody would be speculating as to the reason for an inventory, and she'd have to tell them. Maggie wondered if she could manage to break the news to Wilkie while Angus was present, and then thought guiltily that it was a cowardly idea. She wasn't afraid of Wilkie, was she?

She watched him bend toward his wife, planting a husbandly kiss on Celeste's cheek, and admitted the truth. Yes, she was afraid of Wilkie. She was afraid of what his anger could do to this family, united since Jake's death in a way they had never been while he was alive.

She wasn't apprehensive about what Wilkie could do in regard to the Keating business, though. She knew she was right about that, and Angus would back her up in that regard. It made the warmth creep through her to think about Angus, being at her side.

The shocking thought slashed through her, and she was glad nobody could read her mind. She didn't want Angus only at her side; she wanted him in her bed. And somehow she'd get him there.

## 42

THE following morning, after a night made restless by tormenting dreams that she supposed no decent woman would have dreamed, reality was regained. What had seemed not only possible but certain, in the dark privacy of her own room, now seemed most unlikely.

Though she reached the landing early, Angus was there before her. It was a gray day with a drizzle that would have quenched enthusiasm in any but the most ardent outdoorsman. Maggie was used to it, but she wished it had been clear and sunny; it would have seemed a better omen.

She'd neglected to lock the office door the previous evening, and Angus had let himself in and started the fire. She could smell the coffee, just beginning to perk.

He turned with a half smile that made her remember the dreams and Maggie hoped he'd think the pink in her cheeks was from the cold.

"Morning. Hope you don't mind that I've made myself at home."

"It's only a little premature after all," Maggie said, aware that her own smile was crooked. "Is that ready to drink?"

"Not quite. I just tried it." He gestured toward a cup that he'd put down on her desk. "All you can say for it is that it's hot, so far. Give it another minute or so."

The cup was one that had been Jake's. No one else had used it since his death. Maggie reached for it, compelled to do something other than stand there, realizing only as she tilted the steaming liquid to her mouth that Angus's lips had touched the rim only moments earlier.

It was almost as if those lips now brushed hers. Maggie swallowed, strangled, sputtered, and coughed, and he took the cup from her and patted her on the back.

"I didn't think it was that bad," he told her, grinning, and strode to the door to throw out the underperked coffee before refilling the mug with a darker brew.

Oh, God, Maggie thought, I love him so much. I want and need him so much. What if Jaisy is wrong? What if all he really wants at Keating's Landing is a share of the mill and the logging operation? What if he doesn't care for me at all anymore?

She knew the answer to that. If he didn't care, she would die. Inside, the love that had reblossomed so fully would wither, and when it died she would die with it.

It was a melodramatic thought, yet she knew it was true. She had managed to convince herself that she was over Angus, that she could survive by herself if she had to, and now she knew she couldn't. Oh, she'd survive physically, no doubt, but the price she'd pay, emotionally, would be too high. She'd find little in life worth living for; even having Henry couldn't entirely make up for not having his father.

The men were arriving at the mill and she saw curious faces turned toward the office. The word would run through the crews like wildfire that Angus McKay was on the landing. She'd have to make an explanation before long, or they'd be demanding one. And she had to tell everyone at home first that Angus was buying a full partnership in the family operations.

When Wilkie came, she'd tell him right away, Maggie decided. Maybe it would be a tactical error, not to make an announcement to the family as a unit, but Wilkie's reaction might be uncontrolled, even violent. To provoke that, before Celeste, could only make matters worse. Somehow she must protect Celeste.

Wilkie, however, did not come. After a time Maggie remembered that this was his day to spend on the other side of town; no doubt he'd left before she even came down to breakfast, and would not return until dinnertime.

She was both relieved and disappointed. It would have been better to get it over with. Now it would hang over her until evening, and she might have to tell Wilkie and the others at the same time after all.

She carried her board with paper and pencil to make up the list. Angus called out the items for it, frequently asking for verification of the value of the equipment. He provided his own figures for shingles and timber, figures Maggie knew to be fair and accurate. He hadn't forgotten how to estimate, and he knew the going prices.

It was a strain, to walk beside him, to respond in an unemotional way. She had told Nancy that she would have to be outside of the office for most of the day, so she did not even have Henry there to ease some of the tension. No doubt it was a good thing; Angus was too perceptive, and it would only be a matter of time before it dawned on him that her love for the child was too strong to be explained by the supposed circumstances. And then what?

Somehow she got through the day. Red Risku, stopping in with a report, put the question she knew everyone wanted to ask. "What's McKay doing here?"

"Making an inventory," Maggie said, and then, knowing it was no answer and that Red deserved more, added, "I'll explain it all to you tomorrow, Red. And you can tell everybody else, all right?"

He gave her a look that suggested he was making some accurate guesses, but he only nodded. "All right, Maggie."

By midafternoon it was obvious that they couldn't complete their job in one day. They had taken shelter in the office because the drizzle suddenly turned into a brief squall, and they stood together waiting for wind and rain to subside, sipping at the coffee that had become too strong but not quite bad enough to throw out.

"You're about ready to shut down for the winter," Angus said, shoving a chunk of wood into the stove and stirring the fire with the poker. "So I don't need to think about living quarters until spring. For a few days, though, until we get it all ironed out, would you mind if I stayed here?"

Maggie, hung up on the unwelcome realization that if he stayed in Snohomish she wouldn't see him at all, didn't immediately answer. Now that she was in the family way, Celeste wouldn't be running to dances and entertainments as she would otherwise have done, so Maggie couldn't count on accompanying her and Wilkie. Not that she thought she could bear to join them, anyway. Her antipathy for Wilkie was beginning to show in spite of her best efforts not to let that happen.

"If you don't mind, I could bring over a cot from the old bunkhouse," Angus said. "Stick it in the corner there behind the stove, maybe, just for a few nights, until we're all squared away." He gave her one of those grins that had the power to liquefy her bones, her whole insides. "That way, it'll be warm when you get here in the morning and the coffee will be ready. I could ask Jaisy to send over enough grub to keep me going for a day or two. If you trust your not-quite-partner in here with your books and records, that is. I promise not to tamper with them."

"I have a duplicate set of the books at home," Maggie said without thinking, and saw at once that she'd been right about his perceptiveness.

"You have? Why?"

Why, indeed? How to explain without saying more than she really wanted to say at this time. And then she didn't have to say it.

"You having trouble with the bookkeeping? Andreason?" His eyes narrowed, his mouth flattened. "Is that it? That son of a bitch has been diddling the books?"

"Not any longer," Maggie said.

Angus swore. "That why things have been so tight? Some of your cash being siphoned off for his private use?" He swore again, without apology. "Does he know?"

Bitter amusement twisted her mouth. "Oh, yes. We've discussed it. If he weren't my sister's husband, I'd have charged him with embezzlement. As it is, I've taken steps to make sure it won't happen again."

Another man, in these circumstances, might have assured her that now that he was here, *he'd* take care of the larcenous bookkeeper. Instead, Angus looked down on her with an expression that quickened her breathing, making her aware of the rise and fall of her bosom under her best-tailored white shirtwaist.

"You're quite a woman, Maggie. Jake couldn't have had a better successor than you. No crying, no collapsing, no running to the nearest male for help. You just do it yourself, whatever needs to be done. You're one tough lady."

Tough? It was laughable, considering the way she felt, just being in the same room with him.

"I do what I have to do," she said. "Whether I want to or not." And don't do what I want to, she thought, even when I want it desperately.

"Is it all right? If I bring a bedroll in here for a couple of nights?"

"Yes, of course," Maggie said, and the moment passed. The wind had died down, the rain reduced to the drizzle they were both quite used to, and they went back outside.

There were numerous occasions during the day when they might easily have made physical contact, a brushing of hands when they both reached for the same item, of shoulders when they went through a narrow aisle between stacks of shingles. After a while Maggie began to wonder if Angus was making a determined effort *not* to touch her.

Was it possible to love someone completely, more than life itself, and then to lose that love, to have it die so that it could never be resurrected? Yes, of course it was. Her parents had been in love, hadn't they, when they married? She'd never known exactly what had driven them apart; she was certain now that Ann had rejected Jake long before he'd begun his affair with Jaisy.

If it hadn't been for Jaisy's appraisal of Angus's reaction to the news that it was Celeste, and not Maggie, that Wilkie was marrying, she would have been convinced that she no longer meant anything to him. And there was always the possibility that Jaisy was mistaken, she thought miserably.

She didn't give in to the misery, however. Would Angus want to own part of Keating holdings, to be working closely with her, if he didn't care about her at all? Well, maybe it wouldn't matter to him, especially since he must believe that *she* no longer cared for *him*.

As long as he was here, there was hope, Maggie

decided, and was sorry when Angus called a halt to the activity for the day.

"I'll bring over a bedroll, then, and see you in the morning," he said as they headed for the office.

"I'd invite you up to the house for supper," she told him, "if I thought it would be a comfortable evening for anyone. I haven't told them yet that you're becoming a partner, and I'll have to do it tonight."

He held the door for her, looking down from the height that had always made her feel petite even when she knew she wasn't. "That going to be difficult to do?"

Maggie laughed ruefully. "Yes. I'll be honest with you, Angus, I think it's likely to be equivalent to tossing a hornet's nest onto the middle of the table. I fully expect to be stung. But don't worry, I've made it clear I'm running things; and it won't matter how much they object, we'll sign the partnership papers as we've agreed."

"Sure you don't want reinforcements?"

She shook her head. "No. It wouldn't make the battle any less ferocious, and it will be less embarrassing to me if you don't overhear any of it."

He laughed. "All right. You're the boss. Until the papers are signed, anyway."

She gave him a coolly appraising look. "Maybe we'd better write some safeguards into that contract. About who's to make decisions when we don't agree."

His amusement might have been offensive in any other man, but she knew Angus was not being condescending. "We'll do that. You think about what you want the provisions to be, and we'll talk about them. Good night, Maggie."

She walked up to the house, feeling the inner tension build as she approached the rest of the family. Her convictions were strong, she knew she was right, but to say that the evening ahead of her would be difficult was the understatement of a lifetime, she thought.

## 43

THEIR faces would remain indelibly imprinted on her mind.

It was Wilkie from whom she had expected the most immediate opposition, and it was he she watched when she dropped the news into a lull in the conversation around the table.

Wilkie went stark-white, then flaming-red as anger supplanted shock. To his credit, though, he controlled his temper. It was Celeste who cried out.

"Angus McKay? When you won't let Wilkie have the slightest thing to say about anything?"

"When he invests a considerable sum, he'll naturally be entitled to have something to say about how the business is run," Maggie told her sister. She wished there had been some way to do this without hurting Celeste, and knew that eventually her sister was going to be hurt, one way or another, simply because she was married to Wilkie Andreason. Yet would she be hurt any less if Maggie allowed her husband to take control? In the long run—or maybe not so long—Wilkie would ruin them all.

Ann was upset and confused; Millicent, at least, was willing to listen to Maggie's reasoning. Celeste listened but did not hear; she wept in frustration, so that Wilkie finally led her upstairs.

Ann looked at her bewildering older daughter in consternation. "Is this really necessary, Margaret? Can't we manage without Mr. McKay's involvement?"

"Yes, probably we could. We're in no danger of going under, not if the economy continues to improve. But with Angus's investment we'll do a lot better. We'll be able to grow, which we can't do on our own for a long time. Angus is a woodsman; he knows the business inside and out. It will give us a security we don't have now. And while I feel competent to run things, I'll have to admit that a lot of our customers would be more confident dealing with a man, even if he isn't any more knowledgeable than I am, simply because they're not used to females who give orders. Trust me, Mama, as Daddy trusted me. I'm doing the right thing."

She hoped to God she was right about that.

She had scarcely eaten any of the excellent supper Nancy had prepared. It was not until nearly nine o'clock that hunger drove her downstairs for some of the leftover roast and bread and butter.

In the lower hall, balancing the tray, Maggie met Nancy, who carried a whimpering Henry.

"What's the matter? Is he sick?" Maggie put out a hand to brush back the soft hair from the child's forehead. "He's hot."

"Just teeth, I think. Maggie, could you possibly take him in with you for half an hour or so? He may go to sleep if you rock him. Pat's on the front porch, but I didn't want to keep Henry outside."

"Of course I'll take him. Let me get rid of this tray." She lowered her burden to a nearby table and reached for the baby, who was quite content to burrow into her shoulder; he had, she realized, become more used to her than to Nancy, spending as much time as he did down at the landing.

"Pat says there's a light on at the office," Nancy told her. "Is there supposed to be?"

"It's Angus McKay. He'll be sleeping there for a few nights, until we get this business sorted out." She tried to sound offhand, and knew she hadn't succeeded.

"Maggie? Is . . . is it going to work out between you, after all?"

She was unprepared for the sting of tears. "I don't know. Nancy, do you really think it'd be bad for Henry to take him outside? It isn't raining now, is it? He's so hot, I'd think it would feel good to him to have the fresh air."

Nancy sounded dubious. "Well, maybe. But I'd wrap him up good, so all the coolness he gets is on his face."

"I don't think Angus had any supper. I was afraid to ask him up here because I didn't want him to witness the scene when I broke the news to the family. I'm going to put some more food in a basket, and take little Henry with me down to the landing. I'll put him to bed when he's fallen asleep, so you won't have to worry about him anymore tonight. Go along with Pat."

It seemed like a good idea. She'd have an excuse for looking in on Angus, at a time when they weren't distracted by columns of figures. It would be better than going to bed and lying there in the dark thinking about him, so near and yet so impossibly far away.

She wrapped Henry in a quilt, hung the basket over one arm, and let herself out of the house. It was a soft darkness, with no moon or stars, yet she could make out the shapes of the great trees beside the path. She didn't need light; she could have walked the trail in her sleep, or with her eyes shut.

The tiny beacon from the lamp led her across the landing to the office door. She could see Angus through the window, sprawled on the cot he'd set up, reading something by the light from the kerosene lamp.

He sprang to his feet when she tapped awkwardly on the window, and came to open the door, relieving her of the basket. "What's the matter? Something wrong with the kid?"

"Nancy thinks it's only teeth. I didn't know if you got anything to eat from the cookhouse, so when I fixed something for myself I decided to share it with you." She put Henry into the penned-off area where he'd spent so many hours, and dropped her shawl over the railing of it. "I couldn't eat at suppertime, but now I'm ravenous."

Angus lifted the towel that covered the basket. "Umm, looks good. Thanks for thinking of me." He helped himself to one of the hefty sandwiches. "Did they give you a bad time?"

Maggie shrugged. "I made it clear we were taking you on as a partner. Don't be surprised if Wilkie tries something underhanded, but if I hold firm, there's nothing he can do about it."

She, too, took a sandwich and sat down beside Angus on the cot. The "something" he'd been reading was one of the ledgers that Wilkie had manipulated, but she didn't want to get into that. Not now.

It had been difficult spending the day with him, pretending that there had never been anything personal between them. Now, at night, she felt the pressures even more strongly. He smelled of damp wool and woodsmoke; his plaid shirt was open at the throat to reveal a strong neck and chest. Maggie's heartbeat quickened as she lifted a wrapped slice of cake out of the basket and extended it toward him. "Dessert and everything."

"Now all we need is something to drink," Angus said, putting the cake aside in favor of another sandwich.

"Oh, I'm sorry! I didn't think about it. There's water in the bucket, I guess." She gestured toward the pail on the stand beside the door. "Or—there's some of Daddy's whiskey left. He kept it under the counter, there."

Angus gave her a measured look. "I don't think we'd

better drink any of Jake's whiskey. Not here, at night, by ourselves. While sitting on my bed.''

Maggie's face flamed, and she rose abruptly, having lost her appetite all over again. Was that intended to be a rebuff, of any possible advances on her part as well as of the whiskey? Or could it have been a warning, for her own good?

She didn't know, and she was both excited and confused. In his pen, Henry was trying to pull the fuzz off the blanket; when he succeeded, he put the resulting mess into his mouth, and she moved quickly to retrieve it.

When Henry let out a wail of protest, she scooped him up, pressing the hot little cheek against her own. For a moment a reply trembled on her lips, an offer to drink the whiskey with him here or any other place he chose, and to hell with the consequences.

The impulse died before it was fully formed. No, though she longed for Angus as desperately as she had ever done in the dark days after he'd abandoned her, she knew that she couldn't settle for a few moments of bliss now and again. She couldn't risk another pregnancy. She had to be able to live with herself, and she couldn't be like Jaisy, who had had her own peculiar sort of courage.

Angus spoke behind her, voice suddenly gone thick, the words reluctant, as if he couldn't help himself. ''You're still the most beautiful woman I've ever known, Maggie Keating.''

Maggie swung slowly around to face him, the breath catching painfully in her chest.

He was staring at her in the lamplight, then at Henry, and back at her. There was no way she could control the warmth in her face.

He swore again, very softly. ''He isn't Nancy's child at all, is he?'' Angus demanded.

She couldn't reply. She couldn't tell the lie, simply could not do it.

"He's your child," Angus said slowly. "Yours . . . and mine. Maggie, why didn't you tell me?"

She drew an unsteady breath. "I didn't know, the day Daddy fired you. By the time I did know, you'd left town. I didn't know anywhere to write to you, and besides, I had a little pride, too. You'd made it clear you thought I'd cheated on you."

For a few seconds the only sounds were those of the fire roaring in the stove and the sudden patter of rain on the roof. Henry tugged at her hair and she reached up to disengage the small hand.

Angus's shoulders sagged. "I didn't really think so, not after I got away and calmed down and thought about you. My God, Maggie, how I thought about you! All day, down in that damned black hole, and at night, lying there looking at the stars, remembering how we'd looked at them together—no, I didn't really believe you'd been with anyone else. I didn't understand, but I didn't think you were . . . anything but the Maggie I'd loved since I was a kid."

Henry began to whimper. For once Maggie ignored him.

"And now?" she asked huskily. "Where do we stand now?"

For an agonizing moment he hesitated. Then he started to grin. "It sounds foolish for the parents of a kid who's over a year old to start courting all over again, doesn't it? Maybe we should just try a kiss, and see what it does to us."

She moved into his arms, lifted her mouth to his, felt as if she sank into him, became part of him, as if he'd never been away.

"I think," she said, sounding strangled when he had finally released her, "that it does everything a kiss is supposed to do."

"Maybe we'd better do it again, just to make sure," Angus suggested. "Put the baby down, Maggie."

She didn't even remember replacing Henry in his pen. She was only dimly aware that he whimpered again before folding forward onto her shawl and putting his thumb into his mouth.

Angus's calloused fingers brushed the hair at her temples, traced an ear and her jaw, and held her chin. "Maggie, I love you. I've loved you forever. I was going to give you plenty of time—"

She choked on a cry that was mingled laughter and tears. "Plenty of time! Angus—"

"I know. I know." He bent his head to brush her lips gently with his own. "It's been too long already. I should have married you then, the hell with what Jake thought, the hell with the job I thought I needed. I thought I had to wait until you were older. . . ."

"I'm old enough now," Maggie said unsteadily. "I've always been old enough to know I loved you. Oh, Angus!"

They clung together, mouths locked in a kiss that deepened until Maggie felt it to her very soul. How had she lived for so long without this, without the touch and the taste and the strength of him, without his body pressed to hers, without this singing in her blood and her senses?

When he finally spoke, he sounded as shaken as she felt. "Did you know how much I needed you to come to me? Oh, Maggie, I don't know how to tell you how much I love you!"

The lamp beside them flickered, and Angus glanced at it. "The lamp needs more oil."

He had scarcely begun the slightest of movements away from her when Maggie slid her arms upward, around his neck. "Never mind it. Let it go out."

A moment later, in the darkness, Angus swept her off her feet and held her close against him. "Maggie, love, are you sure? . . . I don't want to do anything ever again to spoil things between us."

In the faint glow from the door of the stove, she could

barely make out his face, the dear, beloved face of her childhood friend, her youthful lover, and now . . .

Her mouth fastened on his, giving him her answer with her kiss.